Dear Readers,

Many years ago, when I was a kid, my father said to me, "Bill, it doesn't really matter what you do in life. What's important is to be the *best* William Johnstone you can be."

I've never forgotten those words. And now, many years and almost 200 books later, I like to think that I am still trying to be the best William Johnstone I can be. Whether it's Ben Raines in the Ashes series, or Frank Morgan, the last gunfighter, or Smoke Jensen, our intrepid mountain man, or John Barrone and his hardworking crew keeping America safe from terrorist lowlifes in the Code Name series, I want to make each new book better than the last and deliver powerful storytelling.

Equally important, I try to create the kinds of believable characters that we can all identify with, real people who face tough challenges. When one of my creations blasts an enemy into the middle of next week, you can be damn sure he had a good reason.

As a storyteller, my job is to entertain you, my readers, and to make sure that you get plenty of enjoyment from my books for your hard-earned money. This is not a job I take lightly. And I greatly appreciate your feedback—you are my gold, and your opinions *do* count. So please keep the letters and e-mails coming.

Respectfully yours,

WILLIAM W. JOHNSTONE

PRIDE OF THE MOUNTAIN MAN

CODE OF THE MOUNTAIN MAN

PINNACLE BOOKS
Kensington Publishing Corp.
http://www.kensingtonbooks.com

PINNACLE BOOKS are published by

Kensington Publishing Corp.
850 Third Avenue
New York, NY 10022

Copyright © 2007 by Kensington Publishing Corp.
Pride of the Mountain Man copyright © 1998 by William W. Johnstone
Code of the Mountain Man copyright © 1991 by William W. Johnstone

All Kensington Titles, Imprints, and Distributed Lines are available at special quantity discounts for bulk purchases for sales promotions, premiums, fund-raising, and educational or institutional use. Special book excerpts or customized printings can also be created to fit specific needs. For details, write or phone the office of the Kensington special sales manager: Kensington Publishing Corp., 850 Third Avenue, New York, NY 10022, attn: Special Sales Department, Phone: 1-800-221-2647.

Pinnacle and the P logo Reg. U.S. Pat. & TM Off.

ISBN-13: 978-0-7860-1903-8
ISBN-10: 0-7860-1903-4

First Pinnacle Books Printing: September 2007

10 9 8 7 6 5 4 3 2 1

Printed in the United States of America

PRIDE OF THE
MOUNTAIN MAN

1

Bill Anderson picked a piece of stringy beef from between his yellowed, broken teeth with the tip of a bowie knife. He sat by a fire on the Kansas Territory prairie, surrounded by his men. These were not ordinary men: travelers, cowhands, or drummers in search of a buyer for their wares. In flickering firelight from a shallow pit dug into flinty soil between endless miles of rolling hills, twenty-nine hard faces watched Anderson as he laid out his plans for a forthcoming raid. These same men had been with him since the end of the war, trusted members of a gang he selected with care, with a purpose. After the collapse of the Confederacy and Lee's surrender at Gettysburg, remnants of a band known across the middle of America as Quantrill's Raiders were left without a cause, without an excuse or a reason for their black deeds, other than simple greed and bloodlust. Bill Anderson had become widely known as "Bloody Bill" for his penchant to draw blood from victims, even those who were utterly defenseless. A trail of bodies marked Bloody Bill Anderson's passage across the states of Missouri and southern Illinois, and territories such as Kansas and Nebraska. Looting, robbing, and taking a terrible toll in human lives, the remaining members of Quantrill's Raiders roamed free as they had during the war, taking whatever they wanted by violence long after the Confederate States of America had ceased to exist, running from the law now and then, a small force of United States Marshals charged with policing vast, empty stretches of the western frontier.

"There's two banks in Dodge City," Bill said, his thick voice commanding the full attention of those around him. "Both're full of cattlemen's money, accordin' to what I've heard. We hit 'em both, hard an' fast, right after they open. Divide up in two parties. Kill every sumbitch we see ridin' in, so folks don't get no crazy ideas 'bout shootin' back if they's got guns. They've got 'em a young City Marshal. Last name's Earp. He's got two or three part-time deputies, mostly farm boys who won't know which end of a gun shoots lead. We strike fast an' hard. Make examples out of them that tries to fight back. Gun 'em down like ducks comin' off a pond . . . turn them dirt streets red an' we won't have no trouble to speak of."

"I hear Dodge can be a tough town, Bill," a voice said from a dark spot beyond the circle of firelight. "Maybe you hadn't oughta figure it'll be that easy."

Bill's pale gray eyes searched for the owner of the voice among the faces he could see. "There ain't no room in this here outfit fer a man who ain't got backbone." Anderson stood up slowly, his gaunt, six-foot frame outlined by what was left of his Confederate uniform, a pair of low-slung pistols tied around his slender waist. "Was that you, Curly? You the one who said that?"

Men backed out of the way until Bill could see Curly Boyd standing by himself at the rear of the group. Curly was from Missouri, a seasoned veteran of dozens of raids despite his youth and poor eyesight requiring spectacles.

"All I said was, it might not be so easy," Curly replied to

Bill's question, sensing the danger he'd put himself in with a casual remark.

Bill's lips drew back across his teeth, a twisted grin with no mirth behind it. "You done turned yellow-dog on us, Curly. I got no use for a damn coward . . ." As he spoke, Bill drew one Colt .44 with characteristic speed, a quickness that put fear in the hearts of brave men. "You ain't left me no choice, Curly. I gotta make an example outa you." He aimed for Boyd's head, and for a brief moment some members of the gang wondered if this were only a ploy. Would Bloody Bill actually shoot a member of his own gang?

"You ain't . . . gonna . . . shoot me, Bill?" Curly stammered as the click of a pistol hammer ended a few seconds of silence. "We been together since the war . . ."

The explosion of a .44 slug ripped through the night quiet, Bloody Bill's only answer to Curly Boyd's question.

Curly's head snapped back. The right lens in his wire-rimmed spectacles shattered. His hat flew off, swirling into the night as the force of impact made him stagger backward. Those who were standing close to Curly saw a plug of his curly black hair erupt from the rear of his skull, spiraling like a child's top toward the ground. A spray of dark crimson blood followed the twist of hair and bone fragments away from the back of his head, squirting across his sagging shoulders, running down the back of his shirt, falling like red rain on flinty soil behind him.

"Jesus, Bill," someone muttered softly.

Curly's knees buckled. He sank to the ground as though he meant to pray, blood pumping from the back of his skull, pieces of glass still clinging to the wire loop in front of his right eye socket. Curly remained on his knees a moment, staring up at Bill with his one remaining eyeball.

"How come you got to shoot Curly like that, Bill?" another voice asked from across the fire. "All he said was, Dodge had a real bad reputation as a tough town . . ."

Bill ignored Curly to glance across at the speaker, a tall, whipcord-thin gunman named Tom Hicks, a former artilleryman from Boonesboro, Tennessee.

Bill fired point-blank into Tom's open mouth. The crack of lead striking teeth sounded like snapping green kindling wood in the fleeting aftermath of Anderson's blasting pistol shot.

Hicks fell over on his back, feet kicking, reaching for his mouth with both hands.

"Son of a bitch!" a husky voice said. "Lookee there! Tom's front teeth come plumb out the back of his neck. Two of 'em's layin' there underneath his skullbone. Look, Shorty! Them's two of Tom's busted teeth, sure as snuff makes spit."

"I see 'em," a stocky gunman replied, standing a few feet from Hicks. "I reckon he shoulda kept his mouth shut."

The acrid scent of gunsmoke swept across the firepit, a blue cloud carried away by the wind.

"Any more of you sons of bitches got anythin' to say?" Bill asked, sweeping the assembled men with an icy stare. "We's gonna rob them Dodge City banks just like I said. Any man in this here bunch who wants out can saddle his horse an' ride, or he can say what's on his mind an' wind up like Curly an' Tom."

Curly Boyd fell over on his face, groaning once. His boots began to shake with death throes. Everyone could see a large hole in the rear of his head where a tiny fountain of blood was spurting forth in regular bursts, keeping time with the slowing beat of his heart.

Across the fire, Tom Hicks made soft choking sounds as blood filled his neck and lungs. The rest of the gang stood silently, looking from one dying man to the other.

"I ain't heard nobody else complainin'," Bill said, with a final glare passing across faces illuminated by the fire's yellow glow. "Dodge City," he said again, almost a challenge.

"We're gonna empty them vaults. Kill a bunch of folks, so everybody'll remember not to tangle with Bill Anderson an' his boys. We'll show 'em."

"We could hang that City Marshal. String him up by his neck to a tree some place so people in these parts'll know we ain't just foolin' around," said a gunman with heavy black beard stubble hitching his thumbs in his gun belt.

Bill nodded. "We'll put folks in this Territory on notice we mean business. I like your idea, Roy. We'll hang that Earp feller right on Main Street."

"Sounds good to me," a kid by the name of Carruthers said as Tom Hicks began whimpering softly.

"We could burn down some of the town," another said from a spot near Curly Boyd.

"It'd make a pretty fire," a gunslick from Missouri by the name of Sammy McCoy announced, his smile easy to see since he stood close to the fire. "Light up half the damn sky in Kansas Territory."

"A fire sounds good to me," Bill replied, holstering his Colt when it became clear that no one else would challenge him. "It would be a reminder to them Kansas farmers an' cattlemen who come up from Texas that we ain't just foolin' around."

"I like fires," Sammy said, grinning. He had eyes that were badly crossed, so it appeared he was continuously staring at the end of his nose. "We could burn the whole damn place plumb to the ground."

"Shut up, Sammy," his brother Claude said. "Every man in this outfit knows you ain't right in the head. Shut up so's we can listen to Bill."

"Them banks are gonna be stuffed plumb full of money this time of year," Bill said. "Cattle buyers are havin' money sent so they can buy herds early in the spring. This one's gonna make us rich, boys."

Tom Hicks called out for his mother in a blood-and phlegm-choked voice. "Help me, Momma! Please help me! It hurts so bad, Momma!"

Heads turned toward the dying man's prone form.

"Somebody shut him up," Bill snapped. "I'm tired of hearin' him complain."

"How we gonna do that?" Sammy asked. "How we gonna shut him up when he's damn near dead anyways?"

"Smother him with your saddle blanket," Claude replied in a dry, emotionless voice, "or find a big rock an' put it in his mouth so he can't say nothin'."

"But he ain't got no teeth in front, Claudie," Sammy said. "How the hell's a rock gonna stay there?"

"Why don't both of you shut up?" a booming voice said from the shadows beyond the fire.

Faces turned toward the speaker . . . everyone knew the sound of Jack Starr's voice. Starr was a remorseless killer, a man who took pride in the number of victims he had claimed over a lifetime.

Starr ambled over to Tom Hicks. "I'll take care of it," he said, pulling a Dance Colt conversion from a cross-pull holster tied to his waist.

He cocked his pistol, aiming down for Tom's forehead. "He never did have no gumption," Starr said. "Now he's layin' here cryin' for his mama like a sugar-tit baby." Starr fired, and the explosion echoed from the silent prairie around them.

Tom's body stiffened. Bill Anderson grinned when he saw Tom's muscles contract, then relax. A final, bubbling breath of air escaped Tom's bloody mouth, then he went still.

"Nice shootin', Jack," Bill said, still smiling, "only it ain't gonna win you no prize money on account of you was standin' so close."

"Got tired of listenin' to him," Starr replied, glancing

across the fire at Curly Boyd. "If Curly makes one more noise I'm gonna do the same to him."

"Curly wasn't no bad feller," Sammy offered. "He just had trouble seein' things on account of them spectacles."

"He turned yellow on us," Bill snarled, reading the faces he could see in the firelight. "Any sumbitch who turns yellow on me is gonna die just like these two."

Boyd had the misfortune to groan right then, putting a deep scowl on Jack Starr's face. Starr walked around the firepit with his pistol dangling from his fist.

"Are you gonna shoot Curly, too?" Sammy asked, like he couldn't quite believe it.

Starr looked over his shoulder. "I'm gonna shoot him, an' you besides, if you don't shut up, Sammy," he said, cocking his Dance again. "How the hell are we gonna sleep tonight with them two makin' all that noise?"

Sammy fell silent. Starr aimed down at the back of Boyd's head and calmly pulled the trigger.

As the noise from the gunshot faded, Bill Anderson addressed his men. "Get some sleep, boys. Come the next week or so we're gonna rob us a couple of banks an' spill a little blood. I want everybody rested. Let's turn in . . ."

2

Smoke Jensen took his wife in his arms. "I love you, Sally. We won't be gone long, maybe four or five weeks. These Hereford crosses don't trail as well as a longhorn. It's those short legs that slow 'em down. Dodge City ain't all that far, and it's the closest place to sell these crossbreeds to eastern cattle buyers. Let's just hope short legs won't keep us from makin' it that far."

Sally smiled up at his rugged face in the glow of an early morning sunrise peeking across the mountains. "Those short legs carry more beef," she said, an undeniable fact. Crossing their longhorn cows with Hereford bulls had been her idea. "I told you so."

"Can't remember a time when you didn't claim to be right," he said, grinning into her beautiful eyes, seeing his reflection in them as if they were liquid pools.

"I *am* always right," she said, widening her smile.

He cast a glance down at the meadow where more than three hundred long-yearling steers, fattened and ready for market, grazed peacefully under Pearlie's watchful eye while

Cal saddled a young horse at the barn. An early fall had painted the grasses with frost, and as the sun rose, a silvery mist lifted from the meadow. "Right pretty sight, ain't it?" he asked, reluctant to let go of the woman he loved, the woman who had changed his life so dramatically from a gunfighter to a peaceful rancher high in the Rockies, helping him build a ranch they had named Sugarloaf.

"It is a pretty sight," she told him quietly. "Just make sure you get back here in one piece to see it with me for the rest of our lives."

"Can't hardly see how there'd be any trouble. Nothin' much between the Dodge City railheads and here besides open country and a few hills."

"You seem to have a knack for findin' trouble almost any place," Sally reminded him, her smile fading, worry replacing it in her face.

"That was before, when my past wouldn't leave us alone. I figure all that's over now."

Doubt lingered in Sally's eyes. "Promise me you'll avoid it, Smoke. I worry every time you're away."

"Then stop worryin' this time, woman," he said, a mock note of reproach in his voice. "This is gonna be the most peaceful cattle drive in history. That's why I'm only takin' Pearlie and Cal along, 'cause we've only got three hundred steers to worry about, and it's empty country. I'm leavin' Johnny to help you keep an eye on the place while we're gone, an' to lend a hand with chores."

"Just promise me you'll swing wide of trouble," she said again.

He gazed down at her lovingly. "You've got my word on it, Sally."

A ruckus at the barn distracted them. Cal, too young to fully understand the nature of a green horse on a chilly morning by noticing a hump in its back, swung his leg over the saddle cinched to the back of a bay three-year-old colt.

The bay gave a snort and downed its head, beginning to buck as hard as it knew how away from the barns and corrals.

Cal wasn't ready for the suddenness of it, his reins held too loosely to pull the colt's head up. All he could do was hold on to the saddle horn for all he was worth while letting out a yelp like a scalded puppy, trying to fit his right boot in a free-swinging stirrup to help him keep his balance.

Rocking back and forth, losing his hat, his face as white as winter snow, Cal tried desperately to hang on as the bay sunfished and crow-hopped, lunging several feet into the air to rid its back of an unwanted load.

A roar of laughter echoed from the meadow when Pearlie saw Cal's dilemma. "Ride 'em, cowboy!" Pearlie cried between spasms of laughter, suddenly gripping his sides.

Cal managed to survive eight or nine jumps aboard the colt's back before he went sailing over the bay's head, his arms outstretched to break his fall in the frost-laden grass.

"Lookee yonder!" Pearlie exclaimed, pointing to Cal's quick departure from the saddle. "I'd nearly swear that boy's done gone an' sprouted hisself a pair of wings!" He broke into another fit of heehaws.

Cal landed on his chest with a grunt, skidding along on the slippery grass, looking about as helpless as a newborn lamb until he slid to a stop, sprawled flat on his face.

Sally stifled a giggle. "I hope he's okay, Smoke."

"He's fine. That grass is near 'bout as soft as a feather mattress. It'll teach him a thing or two."

Cal raised his head, noticing that Smoke and Sally were watching from the porch of the ranch house. And he couldn't help but hear Pearlie's endless laughing from a spot near the edge of the herd.

Cal spat out a mouthful of frosted grass. His face was red with embarrassment. He spoke to Smoke. "Sorry, boss. I reckon I pulled that cinch too tight first thing this mornin' on a half-broke bronc."

"It wasn't the colt's fault, son," Smoke said, trying to contain his own chuckle. "He gave you every warnin' he's got. There was a hump in his back a mile high. One of these days you're gonna learn to notice these things."

Cal pushed himself up to his hands and knees, giving Pearlie a scowl downslope for continuing to laugh. "It ain't all that damn funny!" he shouted, until he remembered Sally was there. He gave her a bow of apology. "Sorry for the language, Miz Jensen, but Pearlie hadn't oughta laugh so hard at a man's diffficulties on a cold mornin' like this."

The colt, a gentle-natured animal, stopped bucking to look down at Cal. Most good young horses resisted being broken to a saddle and bridle right at first, a way of showing they were bred with spirit.

Pearlie let out a final guffaw and then pointed to the bay. "See yonder, Cal? That colt's plumb ready to apologize for what he done, turnin' you into a sparrow on the fly when you's all dressed up to be a cowhand. He's sayin' he's sorry by the way he's holdin' his head down like that. Why, it even looks like he's got tears in his eyes."

Cal stood up angrily to retrieve his fallen hat. "If Miz Jensen wasn't listenin' I'd give you a piece of my mind, Pearlie. No need to poke so much fun at an honest mistake."

"Mistakes can git a man killed," Pearlie said seriously. "That young horse is tryin' to teach you a few things about how to stay alive."

"I'm afraid Pearlie's right," Smoke said, watching Cal dust off his Stetson before approaching the colt to grab its loose reins. "A man who wants to stay aboveground in this wild part of the country had better learn to look for the little things, the warnings nature and animals give you. That colt was tellin' you plain as day he wasn't ready for a rider. I've shown you how to lead a young horse off a few steps first-hand, so it gets used to the feel of a cinch. Some of 'em will crow-hop a time or two, just to let you know they ain't happy about the idea of carryin' a rider."

"I remember you showin' me that, boss. I reckon I plumb forgot this mornin'."

Smoke watched Cal lead the bay away from the barn, and to the boy's credit he was paying close attention to the colt's back.

He turned back to Sally and bent down to kiss her gently. "You know I'll miss you," he admitted, before he released her from his embrace.

"I'll miss you too, Smoke. Please remember what I said. If you can, let other men settle their own disputes."

"I'll do it," he promised, starting down the porch steps to mount his Palouse stud, "just so long as they don't wind up involvin' me or my friends or these Hereford yearlings. We've worked hard for two years to get this breedin' pro-gram started and this'll be our first crop to sell. I've got a good feelin' about it . . . that we're gonna be makin' some money on these calves."

He stepped aboard the stud and reined toward the meadow with frosty breath curling from his nose and mouth when he turned in the saddle to say, "Goodbye, Sally. If you need anything, send Johnny to town, and Louis Longmont will do whatever's necessary to see that you get it, includin' helpin' if anybody shows up who don't belong."

Sally nodded. "We can take care of ourselves out here, in case you haven't noticed before. But if I need anything I'll send for Louis."

Smoke knew it was more than just an empty statement to make him feel better. Sally was every bit as good with a gun as she was in the kitchen with a frying pan or a baking tin. Tied behind his saddle, he carried over a dozen warm biscuits she'd made that morning, and almost as many sugary bearclaws. His mouth watered as he thought about them.

"Let's move 'em out," he said, riding up to Pearlie.

Pearlie aimed a thumb at the barn. "Better make sure that young 'un don't git airborne again afore we leave, boss. His feathers wasn't tested all that good a while ago."

Smoke chuckled, looking back to watch Cal mount the bay very carefully with a much shorter grip on the reins. The bay let out a snort; then its back settled, and it responded to the pressure from Cal's heels, moving off toward the herd at an easy walk.

"He's learning," Smoke told Pearlie, casting a glance across the backs of their steers spread over the meadow. "A man can't learn it all at once. Takes time."

Pearlie shrugged. "I'd never let him hear me say it, but he's makin' one helluva fine cowboy. Works hard at everythin' he does an' don't mind long hours or rough conditions, don't matter how cold or hot or muddy it gits. He's a good kid, makin' a man outa hisself in reasonable good time. He still ain't much shakes with a gun, mind you."

"Most men are better off not knowing about guns," Smoke offered as they rode wide to send the herd eastward. "There's some things that just aren't necessary."

Pearlie gave him a puzzled expression. "That's mighty strange advice, comin' from you, Smoke."

"It wasn't my idea to learn how to kill another man. It was circumstances that forced it on me, and Preacher was there to teach me what I needed to know."

"You sound like a feller who's got regrets, boss."

"I've got some, I reckon. Times were different back then. A man did what he had to do to stay alive."

"Can't see how things have changed all that much," Pearlie said. "There's parts of this country still full of bad men who take what they want with a gun."

Smoke sighed. It wasn't really a topic he cared to discuss

at the moment. "That's where men like me can come in handy, if there's a need."

Pearlie looked toward the sunrise as Cal rode up. "I sure hope the need don't arise on this trip," he said offhandedly "I got used to it bein' real peaceful this past summer."

Smoke swung his horse away to sweep some of the steers into a bunch. "No reason to believe we'll have anything different on this ride," he said, wondering. Louis had told him a few tales about some shootings in Dodge City and Abilene that spring, but this was information Smoke had kept from Sally and the others.

Cal was dusting off the front of his mackinaw. "If this here bay colt is any indication of what's in store for us," he said, "we're in for a mighty tough drive. When a man sets out to go some place, an' the first thing happens is he gits bucked off real hard, I don't see it as no good sign."

Pearlie couldn't stifle a chuckle. "If that same feller who got bucked off knowed a thing or two 'bout horses, he wouldn't be tastin' frosty grass first thing in the mornin' for his breakfast."

Cal ignored Pearlie's remark to eye the burlap bag behind Smoke's saddle. "Since it was Pearlie who first brought up the subject of breakfast, how 'bout we eat some of them bearclaws Sally made?"

Pearlie wagged his head like he was disgusted. "She made 'em fer the trail, son. Hell, we ain't hardly more 'n a few hundred yards from the ranch house yet."

"Don't keep me from wantin' one or two," Cal replied, on the defensive.

"I reckon you're gonna tell us gettin' throwed off is such hard work it gave you an appetite," Pearlie said, chuckling again.

"You look fer the worst way to put things, don't you?" Cal asked, turning his colt toward a yearling steer that was reluctant to stop grazing long enough to join the herd.

Smoke grinned. This sort of banter would continue for days, and at night around the campfire. It was Cal and Pearlie's way of showing closeness. They were good men, different as night and day, but men he could count on, and that was what made them so valuable to the Sugarloaf brand.

"Ride point until we get 'em across the valley," Smoke said to Pearlie. "Me and Cal will gather up all the stragglers and be right behind you."

Without a reply Pearlie spurred his sorrel toward the front of the herd to guide the cattle across a winding valley. Smoke was satisfied. The trail drive to Dodge City had begun.

3

Dave Cobbs saw them on the horizon. They came from the east beneath a cloud of dust, too many horsemen to be out in an empty stretch of Kansas prairie without purpose. Dave was sweeping the narrow front porch of his trading post, a little store by a creek without a proper name, calling it simply Cobbs's Trading Post at the Creek, which he had built out of logs and clay mud with his own hands, and with Myra's help. It had been a profitable trading season, the best in eight years of strenuous toil to establish a spot east of Dodge City where cattlemen and farmers could purchase or trade for staples. He had even painted a sign for the roof out front, although the paint had faded some after several winters full of snow and sleet and heavy rains.

He turned to the open doorway and spoke to his wife. "We got riders comin', Myra. A big bunch. Maybe twenty or thirty. They'll probably be wantin' whiskey. Dust off them bottles of corn squeeze an' give the countertop a swipe or two. Wouldn't want to create no bad impression."

There was something about the horsemen, even from a

distance of half a mile or more, that made Dave vaguely uneasy. "They don't look like drovers," he added over his shoulder. "Wonder who the heck they could be."

"Just so they've got money to spend," his wife replied from the log building. "We can't pick an' choose who comes this way. I'll get the children in the back, so they won't be no distraction. Darlene can watch over the little ones . . . give the baby a sugar lump to keep him quiet."

Dave thought about his thirteen-year-old daughter. Darlene was becoming a woman . . . *budding,* it was sometimes called. Men had begun to notice her. "It sure is hard to figure why there's so many of 'em," he said, sweeping faster to rid the hand-cut planks of dust and dirt, one eye on the approaching riders.

"I'll put out the Arbuckles coffee so's they can see it real plain," Myra said. "A bunch that big's liable to need three or four pounds of good coffee. Be sure an' tell 'em these beans are fresh off the wagon from St. Louis."

"I'll mention it," Dave agreed, squinting to keep the sun's glare from his eyes as he finished his sweeping along the porch steps. "From the looks of 'em, I'll bet they're after whiskey. Nearly all of 'em are carryin' guns, rifles booted to their saddles. Maybe they're hide hunters, or somethin' like that. I can't quite figure why they'd be carryin' so many guns otherwise. Hunters is what they'll turn out to be."

"Let's just hope they turn out to have some hard money to spend," Myra called out from the back of the store. "Seems like it's too early for buffalo hunters. Buffalo haven't put on their winter hair yet, accordin' to Mose."

Dave recalled what Mose Baker had said a few weeks back, that this would be a bad year for buffalo hunters because the herds had been thinned by the previous year's hunt to such an extent there were few big bunches wandering the Kansas hills. It was hard to ride in any direction without coming across huge piles of sun-bleached buffalo bones.

"You keep the baby quiet while we got customers," he heard Myra tell Darlene. "Shut the door an' keep it shut. Give the baby a lump of brown sugar if he starts to cry."

Dave thought about his infant son. Dave Junior, a gift he wanted desperately after Myra had given him two daughters. Darlene was much older. The others, Melissa and Davey, hadn't been born until they arrived in Kansas from Chicago to begin building the store, in part because the trip westward had been so hard on Myra, causing several miscarriages along the way. A doctor in Kansas City had said it was the rough ride on a Studebaker wagon seat that caused her to lose the children. Myra's bleeding had scared Dave half to death, because he hadn't known.

"They'll be here in a few minutes," he said, leaning his straw broom against the doorjamb. "I'll put on my clean apron so I'll look like a regular storekeeper. If this is our lucky day we could sell plumb out of whiskey an' coffee and licorice whips to boot. Most hide hunters have got a real sweet tooth. Be sure you tell 'em the Arbuckles has a peppermint stick in every bag. Not just everybody knows that . . ."

Dave's freckled face twisted into a frown when he got a closer look at the horsemen. "Somethin' about 'em don't look just right to me," he added softly, so Myra couldn't hear. He didn't want to worry her. A twelve gauge shotgun was hidden beneath the counter. If these men gave any trouble, Dave was certain he could handle it.

He went inside and put on a clean apron. While Myra was busy dusting off whiskey bottles with a turkey-feather duster, he checked the loads in both barrels of his shotgun, oddly disturbed by the sighting of so many men coming toward his trading post.

"Be sure you tell Darlene to pull the latch shut on the door to the bedroom," he said, moving a glass jar of peppermint sticks closer to the front of the counter. Maybe the strange feelings he was having were misguided. Days would pass without seeing a soul during certain seasons, and he wondered if the loneliness, the emptiness, was eating away at him at that time of year.

"Why'd you say that?" Myra asked, halting in the midst of her dusting chore.

He didn't want to worry her. "Just an ordinary precaution when there's so many of 'em. Wouldn't want some hide hunter to wander into the back by mistake 'cause I know we'll be busy up front, sellin' all sorts of things."

Myra walked to a window, shading her eyes from the sun with a hand. "They *do* have an awful lot of guns, Dave," she said with a trace of worry. "Nearly all of 'em I can see are wearing pistols. They've all got rifles too. Wonder who these men are and what they're doin' here."

"Probably just hungry an' thirsty cowboys," he told her. "I won't judge men by the number of guns they carry. It could be a posse from Wichita lookin' for bad men. You know this part of the Territory can have some dishonest men crossin' on the way to other places. Don't worry, darlin'. Everything's gonna be okay, an' I've got the shotgun loaded. Get those whiskey bottles dusted off so they shine like new."

"I sure don't like the looks of 'em," she said, turning away from the window.

The sounds of horses came on gusts of wind as Dave gave his trading post a final glance, satisfied that everything was ready for new customers. It was with more than a little pride that he gave the interior of his store a look . . . it had taken a year to build the log structure, and all their savings to stock the store with staples, odd items travelers needed, and more. He and Myra were accumulating wealth by means of a swelling selection inside the store, and a small cash savings hidden in a baking soda tin underneath the rear porch.

Dave looked back at the window as dozens of riders came

to a halt at the hitch rails. Smoothing the front of his apron, he came around the counter to welcome the new arrivals, walking out on the freshly swept porch.

A thin man dressed in gray Confederate pants and stovepipe cavalry boots swung down from his horse before the others dismounted. The man wore a battered Confederate cavalry hat, even though the war had been over for several years.

"Howdy, men," Dave said, smiling. "Welcome to the Cobbs Trading Post. What can I do for you, gentlemen?"

The fellow who left his horse ahead of the others had rather odd-colored eyes—gray, almost slate.

"Whiskey," the man replied in a rasping voice, like cold steel pulled across an anvil. He stared at Dave with no sign of friendliness.

"Got plenty of it. Six dollars a bottle an' it's fresh from Kentucky—the best money can buy."

"You got fatback an' beans?" the stranger asked, as his men came down to the ground amid the creak of saddle leather and the rattle of spurs and curb chains.

"We've got plenty of both," Dave replied, "and a fresh shipment of Arbuckles coffee beans."

"We'll take it," the gray-eyed man said. "All of it. You start puttin' it in tow sacks."

"Sorry, mister, but I haven't seen the color of your money yet. You didn't even ask the price of the coffee or beans . . ."

It was then that Dave noticed a brace of pistols tied low around the man's waist.

"Don't care 'bout the price. We wasn't aimin' to pay for none of it anyways."

Dave took a step backward toward the door. "I've got a loaded shotgun inside, mister. You'll pay for the goods you want, or you'll get a taste of buckshot."

Several of the men who were gathered around the porch laughed.

"Buckshot?" a bearded man asked, grinning, like he didn't

believe it. "What the hell is a little bit of buckshot gonna do to keep us from takin' what we want?"

Dave felt a tremor of fear run down his arms. "I'm warning you, gentlemen, I'm a good shot with a scattergun."

The man with the slate eyes spoke as he drew one of his guns from a worn holster. "You ain't gonna have time to fetch that scattergun, boy," he snarled, aiming his gun up at Dave.

"You won't get away with a robbery like this," Dave stammered with his palms spread helplessly.

"Who says?" another rider asked, pulling a pistol from the inside of his coat.

"We've got lawmen over in Dodge City, and a Territorial militia, and United States Marshals. You'll go to jail if you try to rob us."

"You keep sayin' *us*," another newcomer said. "Is somebody else inside?"

"My wife. And my children. Now I'm warning all of you to get back on your horses and ride away from here unless you want serious trouble."

"Serious trouble?" the man in Confederate uniform asked. "I ain't exactly sure what you mean, mister."

"I'll shoot any of you who try to take supplies from our store without paying for them," Dave replied, with courage he did not feel, facing so many armed men.

"Like I said, son, you ain't gonna live long enough to get your hands on that gun. I'll put so many holes in you before you can turn around, you'll leak like a rusty bucket."

Dave tasted fear on the tip of his tongue. "This is the last time I'll warn you. Get back on your horses an' ride off before I'm forced to take drastic measures."

Laughter spread through the group of men standing around Dave's porch, and he sensed now just how deep the trouble was that he found himself in.

"I'm Bill Anderson," the gray-eyed stranger said, his gun

still pointed at Dave's belly. "Maybe you've heard of me an' my boys. Some folks have taken to callin' me Bloody Bill."

Dave's stomach twisted into a knot, and his throat went dry, like sand. Everyone in the Territory knew about Bloody Bill Anderson and his desperadoes, but it was rumored he'd gone south to Texas. No one had spotted him or reported any of his recent exploits to the weekly newspapers—not for more than a year now—and it seemed to Dave it could have been longer. "Word was you went to Texas," he stammered, buying time, edging a little closer to the door. "We don't want no trouble, Mr. Anderson, but you can't just up an' take what's in my store without payin' for it."

Anderson seemed amused. A crooked grin revealed parts of his broken, discolored front teeth. "The hell you say. For a storekeeper you sure as hell can't count. There's twenty-seven of us an' ain't but one of you. I b'lieve they call it 'rithmatic."

Sweat beaded on Dave's forehead, forming on his palms. "I can count," he said weakly, staring briefly into the dark muzzle of Anderson's pistol.

"Let's see what kind of womenfolk you got inside," Anderson said, losing most of his grin now. "Some of my boys ain't been with a woman for quite a spell."

Dave took a brave step backward to block the doorway. "You won't lay a hand on Myra or Darlene!" he screamed, suddenly angry when his family's lives were clearly in danger.

"I'm done talkin'," Anderson snarled, his face becoming a mask of rage.

Dave was wheeling for the inside of his store to make a dive for the shotgun when a gun blast thundered behind him. Something passed through his ribs, and suddenly the front of his clean, white apron exploded, a burst of red showering the countertop and the floor as he began to fall helplessly, unable to control his legs.

He landed hard on his chest, his chin slamming against the floor where tiny droplets of his own blood covered the boards. He heard himself groan, a sound beyond his control as a searing, white pain spread through his body, dulling his brain so that it was hard to think clearly. A scream came from inside the building.

Booted feet stepped over him, all around him, the rattle of spur rowels dragging across floorboards echoing in his ears along with a curious ringing noise.

Dave tried desperately to raise his head as more men walked past him . . . he had to get up and reach his shotgun before these outlaws harmed Myra or Darlene and the other children. His vision was blurred and he couldn't see the men clearly, and neither could he push himself up off the floor. His arms and legs were like lead weights.

Then, as he was losing consciousness, he heard Myra scream at the top of her lungs.

A moment later Dave Cobbs slipped into a dark tunnel. He could feel himself falling, tumbling into a black void.

4

The steers drifted easily across lower Colorado Territory valleys and grasslands, grazing as they traveled, losing little of the weight they'd gained on good pastures at Sugarloaf during the summer.

Smoke stopped on a wooded ridge overlooking Big Sandy Creek southeast of a tiny settlement called Last Chance. They'd been on the trail for three uneventful days, now entering some of lower Colorado's flatlands, where the countryside turned drier, making grass scarce, harder to find. It was also a region where occasional bands of renegade Osage warriors preyed on small wagon trains or widely scattered ranches, although most of the Osages were on reservations down in Indian Territory now. This had once been Ute and Arapaho country, sometimes frequented by roving bands of Cheyenne, until the treaties brought an end to most of the hostilities.

Things hadn't always been so peaceful, Smoke remembered, in the days when he and Preacher had fought, and then made peace with the Shoshones and Utes. He was glad those days were behind him, yet there were times, when he was alone with his thoughts, when he missed that special closeness he felt toward Preacher.

Smoke scanned the valley below, passing an experienced eye along the creek banks. All was quiet. Native birds fluttered among cottonwood and willow branches beside the water, a sure sign no danger was present.

He turned back in the saddle to motion Pearlie and Cal to bring the herd over the ridge, when he spotted Pearlie riding his way at a trot. Smoke pondered the reason why Pearlie would leave his spot riding drag and flank at the back of the herd.

Pearlie rode up and halted his favorite yellow dun gelding. He turned back to the west, squinting, aiming a finger in the same direction. "Seems like we got somethin', or somebody, who's followin' us. Every now an' then the blackbirds rise up all at once, maybe half a mile or so behind us. Then they settle back down till whatever it is moves 'em again. Could be a grizzly, I reckon, or it could be somethin' else. Whatever it is, it damn sure 'ppears to be followin' us the last couple of hours. I had it figured you'd want to know."

Smoke watched for sign of the blackbirds. For a few moments all was still behind them. "Can't see no disturbance now," he said. "Keep your eyes peeled. If it happens again, give me a sharp whistle and I'll ride back to see what's there. It won't be a grizzly in this low country so late in the year. They're headed to the High Lonesome to find places to hibernate for the winter by now. I 'spect it's something else."

"This country ain't known fer rustlers," Pearlie said, as he kept his eyes on treetops north and west. "Accordin' to what Louis told me this summer, hardly a thing happens down here, now that them redskins are cleared out."

"I hadn't heard of any trouble in this part of the Territory either," Smoke agreed. "Maybe it's a cougar. A hungry mountain lion'll sometimes follow a herd of cattle or buffalo for miles hoping to get a chance at a cripple or a calf. Just keep your eyes open and your rifle handy. Whistle if you see any-thing out of the usual."

"If it ain't nothin' but a big cat, I'll take a shot over its head to scare it off. No sense in killin' a graceful animal like that just 'cause it's hungry."

Smoke grinned. "We see things the same way, Pearlie. It was one of a thousand things Preacher taught me . . . never to kill an animal unless I needed the meat, sometimes a rogue grizzly if it gets man-hungry or develops a taste for beef. Same goes for a big cat. Most of 'em'll hide from the scent of a man." He took another look behind them. "That's why I don't think we've got a cougar following us. It would catch our smell an' leave us alone. Same goes for most wild creatures, even a bear. They don't look for man scent. Usu-ally try to get clear of it quick as they can."

"It's the two-legged creatures I worry about," Pearlie said. "Some of them don't scare off so easy."

"You worry too much," Smoke told him, turning his Palouse to ride down toward the creek. "You're gettin' to where you sound more and more like Sally."

Pearlie wanted the last word on the subject. "There's times when things need a dose of worryin' over," he mut-tered, still watching the sky as he started back to the rear of the herd at a slow trot.

Following a gentle slope, Smoke rode to the stream and let his stud drink its fill. A few at a time, the gentle Here-fords came to the water's edge.

Glancing backward, Smoke saw Pearlie and Cal bring the last of the steers over the rise, pushing them toward the creek at an easy gait. All seemed calm, quiet. Pearlie's concerns about being followed had come to nothing.

Suddenly, a swarm of blackbirds swirled into the sky behind them, circling, alarmed by something beneath them. Smoke's full attention remained on the birds for several seconds.

"Something is back there," he said under his breath, reining the stud around, pulling his Winchester .44 rifle from its boot below a stirrup leather.

He heeled the Palouse past water-seeking cattle to gallop to the top of the rise. Smoke found Pearlie on the ridge watching the blackbirds, holding his horse in check.

"That just ain't natural," Pearlie said, keeping an eye on the circling birds. "Somethin' got 'em scared. See how they won't settle back into them trees fer a spell? A blackbird ain't the spooky sort. Somethin's back yonder."

"I'll find out what it is," Smoke said, as Pearlie noticed his rifle resting on the pommel of his saddle. "Keep these steers bunched tight at the creek till I get back. Don't leave 'em for any reason."

Without waiting for a reply, Smoke urged his horse to a lope and rode back along the trail, searching the trees along hillsides and in deep arroyos for any sign of movement, any shape in the forests that did not belong. The blackbirds continued to fly in looping circles above the trees, unwilling to return to their perches.

It won't he a grizzly, Smoke assured himself. *Too late in the year.*

It was his Palouse that sensed trouble first, before he saw anything to cause him alarm. The big stud snorted and pricked its ears forward, slowing its gait, looking straight ahead at something Smoke couldn't see or hear above the rumble of galloping hooves.

Smoke's gaze swept the trees, and he trusted the Palouse's keen sight and hearing. He levered a shell into the firing chamber of his rifle and rested the stock on his thigh.

Four dim shapes, fanned out in an uneven line, appeared and then vanished in forest shadows, men on horses. He pulled the stud to a sliding stop, ready for trouble.

And then he saw clearly the outline of an Indian aboard a pinto pony, coming toward him at a trot, a long-barrel rifle in his hands.

Osage renegades, he thought, when he could see the shaved skull of the Indian, a trademark of the Osage tribe.

All four Indians were visible, coming at him from the trees, and all were carrying rifles. Smoke was out in the open in a grassy meadow, an easy target if he remained in one place.

He wheeled the stud to the left and drummed his heels into its sides, leaning over the Palouse's neck to make him harder to hit with a rifle shot.

The booming report of a heavy-bore gun sounded from a spot between tree trunks. The whistling passage of a lead slug went high above his head.

He rode hard for a stand of juniper, in order to be out of the line of fire. Another gunshot thundered, kicking up a plug of prairie grass in front of the stud's flying hooves.

He reached the pines just as two more shots bellowed from the line of trees. Molten balls of lead, meant for him, went singing among the branches.

Smoke swung to the ground, dropping the stud's reins to find an opening in the pines where he could take aim himself.

A lone Osage warrior, clad in buckskins, his skull shaved clean and painted black and yellow in some design, galloped his pony out of the woods. Smoke shouldered his Winchester, took quick but careful aim, and feathered the trigger.

The concussion of a .44-caliber shell filled the clearing where he'd ground-hitched his Palouse. In almost the same instant a yell echoed across the meadow. The Osage jerked in an odd way atop his racing pony, bending over, clutching a dark red spot in the middle of his chest. He flipped off the pinto's rump in a ball, tumbling, tossing his rifle aside to hold the mortal wound beneath his rib cage.

Another Osage came charging out of the woods, a rifle to his shoulder, screaming a war cry. Smoke calmly levered a cartridge into the chamber, took aim, and fired again.

The top of the Indian's skull seemed to come apart in a sort of slow motion, like syrup on a cold morning. Pieces of skin and bone went skyward, along with a spray of blood. The Osage's heels went up as he fell back across his black pony's croup, and for a time he appeared suspended there, until the rough gait of his horse sent him rolling off to one side.

The Indian landed in the grass limply, arms and legs askew, skidding across tufts of curly mesquite until he slid to a stop near the base of a slender oak tree that was shedding its colorful, fall leaves.

Another round went quickly into the chamber of Smoke's rifle when a third Indian swerved his sorrel pony toward the junipers where Smoke was making his stand.

"Damn fool," Smoke whispered to himself, drawing a bead on the Osage's chest.

When he pulled the trigger, the shock of it rocked him back on his heels a moment, and as a cloud of blue smoke cleared away from the muzzle of the Winchester, he saw the Indian topple over as his pony galloped away.

The fourth Osage brought his pony to a bounding halt more than a hundred yards from the junipers. He looked both ways at his fallen companions, as though he could not quite believe what he was seeing.

Then his head turned, facing Smoke, and the look on his face was one of pure hatred. He lifted his rifle, an old, single-shot musket, and shook it in the air defiantly, throwing back his head while he let out a shrill cry.

"Ayeee!"

Smoke grinned mirthlessly. He stepped around the juniper tree and held his Winchester over his head.

"Ayeee! Ayeee! Suvate!" he shouted, the Ute war song of victory.

As Smoke's cry filled the silent meadow, the Osage suddenly lowered his gun and stared at the white man.

For a time the two men stared at each other, neither moving or making a sound. The Osage was clearly puzzled, how a white man could know the war cry of his old enemy, the Utes.

"Suvate!" Smoke cried again, bringing his rifle down, then to his shoulder.

The Osage remained frozen where he was for a few seconds, then turned his pony around and made a hasty retreat toward the forest from which he had come, his pony's mane and tail flying in the wind until he was out of sight.

From the east, the rhythmic thump of a running horse's hooves came nearer. A moment later, rifle in hand, Pearlie came galloping across a row of low hills, ready to lend a hand in the fight.

Smoke stepped around the juniper so Pearlie could see him, waving his rifle over his head. Pearlie caught a quick glimpse of Smoke and reined his dun in that direction.

Pearlie galloped up and jerked his gelding to a halt.

"What the hell happened, boss? I heard all the shootin', an' I come a-runnin'."

"Four Indians. Osages, by their shaved heads. I dropped three of 'em. One rode off when he saw I wasn't gonna give him any special consideration."

Pearlie looked in the direction in which Smoke inclined his head. "I can see blood on the grass yonder. How come you didn't come after me an' Cal so's we could lend you a hand?"

"Didn't figure I needed any help, Pearlie. But you've got my thanks anyway."

"Damn near any man needs help up against four Injuns," was Pearlie's reply. He let his shoulders drop. "I reckon, knowin' you like I do, you'd be the exception."

"They had old, single-shot rifles. Wasn't much of a fight, really."

Pearlie looked down at Smoke, grinning. "Ain't that just

like you, Smoke Jensen, to make a fight where one man stands up against four Injuns an' he calls it not much of a fight? I'll swear . . ."

"They were young Osage bucks. Inexperienced. They came straight at me. It was like target practice."

Pearlie booted his rifle. "I reckon I'd best git back to the herd, afore you tell me that's where I'm s'pposed to be."

"You took the words right outa my mouth, Pearlie. Me and Sally aren't payin' you wages to sit here and jaw with me about Indians, or how they oughta be fought."

"Yes, sir," Pearlie replied, swinging his dun away from the junipers.

He rode off shaking his head.

5

Cal squatted across the flames of their campfire, watching Pearlie ride slow circles around the steers until they bedded down for the night. Palming a tin cup of coffee to warm his hands in chilly night air, Cal listened to Pearlie sing a creaky version of "Little Joe the Wrangler." Singing, even as bad as Pearlie's voice could be, had a strange calming effect on cattle, a lesson every cowboy learned early on a trail drive.

"I swear, Pearlie sounds worse'n an axle needin' grease," he said. "It's a wonder it don't spook them steers into a stampede all the way to St. Louis."

Smoke grunted, blowing steam from his cup, glancing up at a clear, night sky sprinkled with stars. "It's a fact cows aren't much of a judge when it comes to music. Can't say as I ever heard a cowboy who could carry a tune. It's a blessing that cattle don't get all that particular about a melody, or most trail drives would be in trouble."

Cal looked at Smoke. "While we're on the subject of trouble, boss, tell me 'bout them redskins. Pearlie told me they was Osages, an' that you killed four of 'em."

"Pearlie's always been given over to exaggeration. I shot three that were coming straight at me. The fourth showed good sense an' rode off."

"I knowed we was gonna have trouble on this drive soon as that bay colt throwed me off. It was a message from the Almighty tellin' us to be ready for more'n a few difficulties. I never was all that superstitious 'bout such things, but when that bay pitched me over its head, I could feel it in my bones that we was headed into bad situations."

"What you felt in your bones, son, was the fall you took off that colt's back."

Cal looked down at his cup, a bit embarrassed. "It was more'n that, Mr. Jensen. I had the real clear sensation there was gonna be some shootin' on this drive, an' that whoever it was would be shootin' at us."

Smoke grinned. "If that happens, I'll take care of it. You handle your job with these steers, an' I'll handle any problems we run into."

"You figure that one Osage'll come back with some more of his friends?"

"Not likely. They were young renegades. Probably slipped off the reservation down in the Nations looking to get into a little mischief, maybe rob a rancher or two. They hadn't banked on runnin' into somebody who'd shoot back. I figure we'll have a peaceful drive all the way to Dodge . . . if you don't get bucked off that colt again."

"I sure do wish you wouldn't keep remindin' me. Pearlie still can't stop laughin' about it."

"He's only funnin' you 'cause he cares about you, son. If you can't take a little teasin' once in a while you'll never make it at Sugarloaf."

It was Cal's turn to grin. "I'm gettin' even with Pearlie tonight, boss. Just so you'll know, it's only a joke. He's been ridin' me so hard 'bout gittin' bucked off that I been thinkin' of ways to shut him up. Soon as he comes in from ridin' night herd he'll do what he always does—head straight fer this here coffee pot an' then sit down on his bedroll to pull off his boots. I found this great big cocklebur tangled up in that bay colt's tail whilst I was unsaddlin' him. I combed it out. Soon as Pearlie goes to sleep I'm gonna put that cocklebur in one of his boots. You ever notice the way Pearlie puts 'em on in the mornin'? First he stands up an' then he stomps one foot at a time into his boots. When he lands on that burr, we're gonna find out if Pearlie can dance as good as he can sing."

Smoke chuckled. "He'll try to get even with you. He'll know you put it there."

"I'm countin' on it. Maybe then he'll think twice 'bout remindin' me how high I was flyin' when I got throwed back at the ranch."

"You're liable to be in for a cussword or two. Pearlie knows more than a handful of bad words."

"But it'll be my turn to laugh, boss. My ears are plumb sore from listenin' to him heehaw me over gettin' pitched off that mornin'."

"The two of you are worse'n a couple of kids, like when he mixed castor oil in the syrup tin last year, knowing you'd be the first to cover your flapjacks with it and stuff your mouth full. I laughed so hard myself I nearly broke a rib."

Cal frowned. "Wasn't all that funny, you know. I swallowed a whole bunch of it before I got the taste. I was in the outhouse nearly all that day, seemed like. Miz Jensen took to laughin' every time she seen me runnin' for the two-holer back of the barn. One time I almost didn't make it. She hadn't oughta laughed at me so much. Pearlie never did stop laughin' all day or the next mornin' either."

"It's because they like you, Cal. Sally loves you like you were one of her own. And remember, you got your revenge when you put a dead rattlesnake in his bunk under his blankets. I never heard such a yell as what came from the bunkhouse that night. I bet they heard it all the way to Big Rock."

Cal giggled. "Nearly busted the insides of my ears. Never heard so many cusswords strung together before. He cussed till he ran outa wind."

Smoke's thoughts went back to the ranch, wondering about Sally, wishing he could take her in his arms. It still amazed him that a woman could make him feel that way. He'd been sure he'd spend his life as a bachelor, until he met Sally. She had a power over him no one else ever had, if you didn't count Preacher, and that wasn't the same thing. They had a good life at Sugarloaf, surrounded by good friends and neighbors. It was more than Smoke had ever dreamed of having, after some mighty rough beginnings.

"Seems like you're distracted," Cal said after a bit.

"Thinkin' about Sally and the ranch, is all."

"If you'll pardon me fer sayin' it on account of it's personal, you've gotta be the luckiest man alive, Mr. Jensen, to have found yourself a woman like Miz Jensen. Times, I lay there at night wishin' I could find me a good woman like her. Don't reckon I ever will."

"You're young yet, son. Give it time. I never thought I'd find Sally. I suppose it's fair to say she found me. I was headed down some of the wrong trails when she came along. That little woman brought me up short like she'd put a spade bit in my mouth. Turned my whole life around."

Cal cleared his throat. "Pearlie told me one time that you was a hard-nosed killer beforehand, that you were a shootist with a mean reputation."

"Maybe I was," Smoke allowed. "I never drew a gun on a man who wasn't goin' fer his gun first, if that matters. But I did some things fer the wrong reasons. Sally made me see the error of my ways. She can give a lecture that'd put any preacher in Colorado Territory to shame."

"I know that part real well, boss. When she gits on a mad an' starts shakin' that finger at me when I forgit sometimes to do chores just right, it's the same as bein' whipped with a willow switch. She can hurt a man worse with her tongue an' that finger than any woman I ever run across, even worse'n my ma could."

"Sally can be tempermental," Smoke agreed. "Worst part is, she's always right about things. I keep wishing that, just once, she'd be wrong, so I could remind her of it."

"Then she's got that sweet side, like honey. She'll put her hand on my shoulder, or maybe just give me a certain look, an' I git plumb teary-eyed sometimes. When I had the whoopin' cough that time she mothered me like a hen. Like I said, you oughta count yourself as bein' mighty lucky to have her."

Smoke was truly distracted when, off in the night, Pearlie struck a particular sour note in the middle of a song. "I know how lucky I am, Cal. Never a day passes when I don't think about it. I'm gonna ask Sally to give Pearlie some singin' lessons as soon as we get back. Just now he sounded like a tomcat with his tail caught under a rocking chair."

Cal smiled. "Just wait'll you hear the noise he makes when he sticks his foot into the wrong boot tomorrow mornin'. It'll sound a lot worse than his singin', I promise you."

Smoke drifted toward sleep, entering an unwanted dream from his past. Smoke had been sitting on a rock, eating a cold biscuit, when Kid Austin, as quick-handed a gunfighter as Smoke had ever faced, came striding toward him.

"Get up!" the Kid shouted. "Get on your feet and face me like a man!"

Smoke ate the last of his meager meal; then he rose to his feet. He was smiling.

The Kid kept coming, narrowing the distance, finally stopping about thirty feet away. He hunkered down like he was ready to make his play. "I'll be known as the man who killed Smoke Jensen," he snarled. "Me! Kid Austin!"

Smoke laughed at him.

The Kid flushed. "I done it to your wife, too, Jensen. She liked it so much she asked me to do it to 'er some more. So I obliged her. I took your woman, an' now I'm gonna take you!" He dipped his right hand downward.

Smoke drew his right-hand .44 with blinding speed, drawing, cocking, firing before Austin could realize what was taking place in front of his eyes. Two molten bullets entered the Kid's body—one in his belly, the other just above his ornate, silver belt buckle. The impact of two .44 shells dropped Austin to his knees while shock and then terror twisted his face. He tried in vain to pull his gun clear of its holster.

"I'm . . . Kid Austin," he croaked. "You can't . . . do this to me."

"Looks like I did anyways," Smoke said, turning away from the dying man to walk to his horse. Nicole, Smoke's first wife, and their son were dead by the hand of Kid Austin and his gang. He had tried to live in peace. The men who took what was near and dear to him wouldn't allow it.

He mounted Seven without looking back, until he heard the Kid cry, "It hurts, Momma! Help me!"

Austin was on his knees, rocked back on his haunches with his hands covering his belly, staring up at the sky. None of the other members of his gang were there to hear him begging. A loop of bloody intestine dangled from a hole in his shirtfront. Blood poured over the ground around him.

"Help me, Momma," the Kid said again, weakly this time as blood loss and pain began to claim him.

Smoke knew that Nicole must have begged for the gang members to stop before they killed her. Somehow, hearing the Kid beg for help wasn't enough justice for what he and his men had done to Smoke's family.

"I'm . . . Kid . . . Austin," he gasped, slowly toppling over on his side, curling into a fetal position. His Colt fell out of its holster, clattering on the rocks, glinting in the gauzy sunlight that was filtering into the canyon between the tall timbers.

"You can't . . . do this . . . to me," he groaned again, faint, hard to hear.

Smoke's jaw turned to granite. "Hell, I can't," he spat, his teeth clamped together, holding Seven in check while he gave the gunman a final look.

One of the Kid's feet had begun to twitch in death. Smoke reined Seven away from the scene and started out of the canyon at a walk, his horse's hoofbeats echoing off canyon walls.

Behind him, the canyon was quiet. There was only the soft sighing of the wind passing through treetops where a corpse lay in a pool of crimson.

He rode back to the cabin in the valley and packed up his belongings, covering the pack frame with a ground sheet. He rubbed Seven down and fed him grain and hay.

Smoke cleaned his guns and made camp outside the cabin that night. He could not bear to sleep inside that house of death and torture and rape where Nicole and their son ended their lives.

His sleep had been restless, remaining that way for the week he stayed there, troubled by nightmares in which Nicole called out his name, and sounds of the baby crying.

The second week had been no better, his sleep interrupted by the same nightmare over and over again. Thus, when he kicked out of his blankets on that final morning in the valley, his body was covered with sweat. Smoke knew he could never rest until the men who rode with Kid Austin—the men who had violated Nicole and killed her along with the child—were dead . . . Potter, Stratton, and Richards.

He rode out of the valley, swinging north, bent on vengeance against the others. It had been the beginning of a long trail to track them down. And he was dreaming about it again, even after so many years. He wished the haunting dream would leave him alone.

Later, he awoke with a start when Pearlie came in from night duty with the herd.

"All's quiet, boss," Pearlie said, stripping his saddle off the dun.

"Sure glad to hear how quiet it is," he heard Cal say as the boy mounted to take Pearlie's place. "Sure do hope it stays that way tomorrow mornin'."

Smoke lay back down, grinning, knowing what Cal meant. And he felt good, being awakened from his awful dreams about a past he wanted to forget. Sally and Sugarloaf were his future, and he'd never been happier.

6

False dawn brightened eastern skies when some inner sense awakened Smoke to danger. He reached for his rifle, turning over in his bedroll slowly, blinking sleep from his eyes. He lay for a moment, listening.

Off to his right, Cal rode slowly around the sleeping herd, until Smoke noticed that some of the steers were coming to their feet with ears cocked southward.

Smoke examined the southern skyline, passing a slow glance across each dark hill, every low spot. At first, he heard nothing at all besides the soft rustle of steer hooves on dry grass as more of the Hereford crosses stood up, hind legs first as was a cow's habit.

Cal stopped his horse, standing in his stirrups, also aware that something was wrong, something disturbing the cattle enough to bring them up before dawn.

Then Smoke saw what was frightening the steers. In a swale between two hills, a wolf pack trotted toward the cattle scent. In packs, timber wolves or gray wolves were often able to bring down a calf. Until the clever animals got closer they had no way of knowing the size of the cows they smelled on night winds.

Smoke came to his feet, balancing his Winchester in the crook of his arm. He stepped into his boots quietly, so as not to awaken Pearlie, and walked softly toward Cal.

"It's a wolf pack," he said when he reached the boy. "No need to worry. Soon as those smart creatures see how big our steers are they'll leave 'em alone. A wolf's too smart to take on any kind of animal this size, even when they're traveling in a pack like this bunch."

"There was that lobo a couple of years back, if you recall," Cal said in a quiet voice. "He came right up to the barns like he wasn't scared of nothin'."

Smoke remembered. "A big lobo timber wolf is a bit different. They aren't as afraid of a man's smell. These'll be gray wolves in this flat country. If they get any closer I'll fire a shot over their heads, and that'll be the end of it."

"How come you don't just shoot one of 'em?" Cal asked. "If you shoot one, the others'll sure enough hightail it out of here."

"No reason to kill it," Smoke replied. "They're doing what nature meant fer 'em to do . . . look for food. They scented these cattle on the wind, and to them, it's like a dinner bell. They wouldn't bother steers as big as these anyway."

"Not even in a pack?"

Smoke wagged his head. "They're too smart. A six-hundred-pound steer with a set of horns could kill a wolf easily, if it got the chance and if it was range-bred like ours. Wolves have instincts that tell 'em what to do, and what to avoid."

"They sure do look spooky, trotting across that dark grass the way they are."

Smoke watched the darker outline of the leader of the pack take the others upwind. "To me, they're beautiful animals. All they want is somethin' to eat. That big male will see what he's up against in a minute or two, and he'll signal that the hunt is over. Watch, and you'll learn something about wolves. Unless I'm dead wrong, that big male will stop shortly. He'll size up the situation and turn away. For two reasons. He'll smell men and the smoke from the coals in our firepit. And he'll know these steers are too big to bring down."

Cal looked down from his horse, examining what he could see of Smoke's face in the semi-darkness. "You never are much when it comes to shootin' animals, I've noticed, even somethin' as dangerous as a wolf."

"No need. I suppose it's because I've got respect for all of nature's creatures, even a polecat. A polecat don't have but one weapon, and that's his stink. He won't use it unless he feels threatened."

"But a wolf eats meat, boss."

"Only the meat it can catch and bring down. Keep your eyes on that big male. He's about to call off the hunt. Wait and see if I'm right about it."

Almost at once the heavy male wolf halted in its tracks to sniff the wind, swinging its massive head back and forth to take on more scent. The wolf's tail went up as a silent warning to the others behind it, and just as suddenly, the other wolves came to a stop.

For half a minute or more, the wolves remained frozen to the spot, watching the herd of steers. Then, as Smoke predicted, the big male turned away and trotted off, leading his pack into a dry creek bed west of the herd.

"You sure were right about it," Cal said, a note of amazement in his voice. "They wasn't near as brave as that big lobo that came to the barns."

"A lobo is different," Smoke explained, turning to go back to the fire to start coffee. "He's alone for a reason. He don't think like other wolves, and that's why he doesn't run with a pack like those we just saw. A lobo is dangerous, but he's still real smart. Real hard to kill, in case you've never tried. Some way or another, a lobo can damn near feel a rifle's sights on him."

One of the steers let out a mournful bawl as cattle sometimes do when calling to each other. On the far side of the herd an answering bawl broke the silence.

"These cows don't seem agitated," Cal observed, as more of the steers came to their feet. "I reckon they didn't catch no wolf smell real strong, or they'd be millin' around, actin' like they was nervous about it."

"Sally was right about a Hereford being a gentler breed, an' it shows in the crosses. Takes a lot to spook 'em. Like I told you last night, Sally's right about damn near everything, and a mite too quick to remind me of it."

Cal chuckled, resting his elbow on his saddle horn. "That's about the most halfhearted complaint I ever heard, boss."

"Wasn't a complaint, son, just a simple statement of plain fact."

A shadow moved near the firepit, and a split second later a shrill cry came from a figure hopping up and down on one foot.

"Damn, damn, damn, damn, damn!" Pearlie bellowed, slumping to the ground on his rump. "Feels like a damn porcupine decided to spend the night inside one of my damn boots!"

Cal got a sudden case of the giggles, trying to cover his mouth with one hand while they watched Pearlie struggle to get a boot off. Smoke grinned while witnessing Cal's sweet revenge.

"What the hell?" Pearlie exclaimed, holding something up to his face. Then his head snapped toward the herd where Cal was seated on his night horse. "Where the hell's that young 'un?" he snarled. "When I git my hands 'round his skinny little neck I'm gonna choke him plumb to death. . . ."

Cal could contain himself no longer and burst out laughing. Even Smoke had to chuckle out loud over Pearlie's outburst.

"What happened, Pearlie?" Cal asked as innocently as he was able, between fits of laughter. "Looked like you was dancin' a while ago, only I didn't hear no fiddler playin'. Where's the music?"

"I'm gonna kill you deader'n a gate hinge if'n I can git my hands on you, boy!" Pearlie shouted. "I could be a cripple the rest of my life for what you just done to me. Feels like there's blood in my boot . . . an' my sock's wringin' wet. I'm liable to bleed to death here, an' all on account of some snot-nosed kid who thinks he's done somethin' funny! Damn, damn, damn, that hurts!"

Cal let out a gale of heehaws, then he yelled, "Whoopee! I got you back, Mister Pearlie. Now who's doin' the laughin'?"

Smoke had heard enough, ambling back toward the firepit to get flames going for coffee and breakfast while Pearlie uttered a string of cusswords, rubbing his sore foot, swearing to have his revenge against Cal if it took him the rest of his life.

"Let's get this herd moving," Smoke said, tossing dry wood on the coals when Pearlie ran out of breath. "You boys can have at each other some other time, when we don't have cattle to get to market."

In the beginnings of flickering firelight licking up the sides of the woodpile, Pearlie gave Cal an angry glare. "I'm gonna git that boy next time," he muttered, to have the last word. "I swear I'm gonna fix him good . . . he's got no respect fer his elders, an' I'm gonna learn him some manners."

"Maybe he was remembering all those trips he made to the outhouse a while back," Smoke suggested, grinning.

Pearlie adopted an indignant look. "Have you plumb forgot 'bout that serpent he put in my bed? Any man who'd put a snake in another feller's bunk deserves to be shot. I didn't shoot him that night 'cause we was short-handed at the ranch. Otherwise, I'd have plugged him right then an' there."

Smoke was forced to laugh at Pearlie's mock rage. Pearlie and Cal were as close as brothers when there was work to be done or when the chips were down in a dangerous situation. Anyone who didn't really know them would think they were out to kill each other on a regular basis.

The herd stretched out for a quarter mile, moving slowly, grazing where the steers could find grass. The land yawning before them was empty, not a sign of civilization in this section of southwestern Colorado beyond a few widely scattered wagon ruts where seldom-used trails crisscrossed the countryside. Smoke rode point, guiding the way, using dead reckoning rather than a marked route to follow with the angle of the sun as a guidepost. Other than for the skirmish with the Osages, the trip was going peacefully enough. By Smoke's old standard, shooting three renegades bent on stealing a few beeves was a relatively mild irritation.

Off in the distance he could see a faint, green line, the Arkansas River where it wound its way across territorial boundaries into Kansas. This was land he seldom traveled, and the Kansas prairies were not to his liking—mile after mile of low flint hills without trees in most places, a featureless region where only the most determined settlers tried to establish farms and homesteads, raising a few cattle and sheep, living in sod dugouts, existing on small gardens and what meat they could raise during years when rains came. Thinking on it to pass time, Smoke supposed he'd been spoiled by the raw beauty of the High Lonesome in Colorado. He'd become a man with a kinship to the mountains and high valleys, never quite feeling at home any place else.

An hour later, when the river was in sight, he saw a lone

horseman coming toward them at a long, ground-eating trot as if he were a man in something of a hurry.

"Maybe he's got troubles," Smoke muttered to himself, as the stud flicked his ears back when he heard his master's voice.

A quarter hour more and the rider approached Smoke, slowing his lathered horse a bit until he rode up and came to a halt.

"Howdy, mister," the stranger said, a man dressed in a badly worn business suit and bowler hat, a drummer by his appearance, although he had no packhorse or mule to carry whatever he might be peddling. "I saw your dust as I was crossing the river. I thought I'd warn you." The man carried a shotgun slung from his saddle by a leather shoulder strap, a hunting gun some men called a fowler's piece used for ducks and geese. The slight bulge of a small-caliber pistol showed beneath his coat.

Smoke scowled. "Warn me about what?"

"Robbers," he replied, taking off his hat to sleeve sweat and dust from his forehead. "By way of introduction, I'm Horace Grimes from Springfield. Be cautious as you cross over into Kansas. A gang of thieves and murderers is on the prowl to the east and south of Dodge City. It's an awful story, what happened to me, and to a shopkeeper and his family. I feel lucky to have escaped with my life."

"Tell me about it," Smoke said quietly.

"My personal experience with them was, upon reflection, very fortunate. My mule, along with all my buttons and fasteners, were stolen from my campsite while I was away hunting wild turkey for supper. I got back just in time to see a gang of twenty-five or thirty men stealing my mule. They were hard-looking characters, carrying an assortment of weaponry, so I remained in hiding up on a ridge while they scattered my inventory all over the ground in search of something more valuable, I presume. They took my mule and packsaddle, leaving me no way to carry what I sell. I'm a sales representative with the Springfield Fastener Company. I'm a peaceful man, heading for Dodge City to sell my wares. But the gang of thieves rode off in the direction of Dodge, leaving me no choice but to ride around the city. I've been looking for some sort of military outpost or a peace officer where I can report to the proper authorities what took place. There are no towns and no telegraph lines here. I must confess I'm utterly lost without a map or a road to guide me."

"What was this about a shopkeeper and his family?" Smoke asked, wondering who the thieves might be, traveling together in such large numbers.

Now Grimes's face turned pale. He reached inside his coat for a handkerchief to wipe his face. "Shortly thereafter I came upon a most dreadful sight, while trying to ride in another direction to avoid running headlong into the thieves. At a small stream I found the partially burned remains of a general store. It had been looted and burned. Among the ashes were the bodies of five people, a man and a woman, and the blackened corpses of three children. Some of the building was still smoldering. I must find a place to report this to the authorities as soon as possible."

Smoke gazed across the river into Kansas. "No place behind us, Mr. Grimes. You're welcome to ride with us back to Dodge City to file your report. There's a telegraph and a railroad line. Should be a few peace officers."

"But that was the direction this gang was riding, sir."

Smoke shrugged. "Like I said, you're welcome to stay with us to Dodge. You'll be plenty safe. You've got my word on it."

7

Pearlie and Cal rode up to meet the stranger as the steers were crossing the shallow river . . . they both gave Grimes curious stares during the introductions.

"Name's Pearlie," Pearlie said. "This here's Cal," he added as the men shook hands. Then Pearlie frowned. "You was headed west, an' now you've done changed directions to ride with us. I was just curious about it."

Smoke was urging cattle into the shallows when Grimes gave his reply.

"I ran into a terrible situation," Grimes began. "I'm new to this part of the country, and I was seeking a military post or a town with a peace officer and a telegraph line to report more than one unlawful incident I had the misfortune to be a witness to. I was looking for someone with the legal authority to do something about it."

"That'd be Dodge City," Pearlie said, "only you're ridin' in the wrong direction. It's east."

"I know," Grimes answered, casting a look in the direction from which he had come. "I was heading for Dodge

City when I was set upon by a gang of robbers. They stole my pack mule and left the goods I was carrying scattered all over my campsite. Only that wasn't the worst of it. The gang rode toward Dodge, and I sought another route, hoping to find another town where I could report what had taken place. In the course of my travels, I came to a scene so brutal, so heartless, it rendered me ill. A small trading post beside a stream southeast of Dodge was burned almost to the ground. Among the ruins, I found five bodies, charred beyond recognition. A man and a woman, and three children, two of them hardly more than infants. The store's supplies had been looted. Empty shelves lay among the ashes. It was ghastly— the stuff of nightmares. I'm quite certain it was the same gang of highwaymen who robbed me, only I was more fortunate than members of that tragic family. They lost their lives."

Pearlie glanced over at Smoke. "Did you tell the boss man 'bout this here gang?"

"I did. He invited me to travel with you to Dodge City, so I could report what I saw to the proper authorities. He said there was a railroad and a telegraph there, and certainly a few peace officers. Your boss assured me I'd be safe with you."

Cal chuckled. "That'd be the truth if you ever heard it in your life. Do you know who our boss man is?"

"He did not bother to give me his name. However, he is well armed and he seems quite sure of himself."

"He's none other than Smoke Jensen," Pearlie said.

Grimes frowned. "The name doesn't ring a bell."

"Well sir, it should," Cal said. "He's just about the most dangerous man with a gun in all of Colorado Territory, if he gits pushed. He was a gunfighter some time ago. Lives real peaceful now, runnin' a cow outfit, but I wouldn't wanna be the man who crosses him."

Pearlie nodded. "The name may not ring no bell with you, mister, but it damn sure does in these parts. Just ask around if you got any doubts."

"I'm from Springfield," Grimes said. This was to be my first tour of this area, selling fasteners. While I've never heard of Mr. Smoke Jensen, it does not mean I have any doubts about his ability to protect me. I'm a fairly good judge of character. Mr. Jensen seems quite capable of handling himself. I do, however, have certain reservations. One man, or even the three of you, won't stand a chance against the men who took my mule and packsaddle. These were ruffians, lawless men by the looks of them, and what they most certainly did to that storekeeper and his family makes them cold-blooded murderers as well as thieves."

More cows crossed the river. Pearlie lifted his reins to lend a hand collecting those already on the far side. "Tell us 'bout this gang you mentioned. Did you git a look at 'em?"

"I saw them from a distance. There was so many, I remained hidden until they rode away from my camp with my mule and my packsaddle."

"When you say *so many*, just how many might that have been?"

"Perhaps thirty. Hard-looking men with pistols and rifles. One appeared to be wearing an old Confederate uniform."

"Thirty?" Pearlie asked. "Are you right sure you can count, Mr. Grimes?"

"At least that many. Possibly more. I was too frightened to get a closer look to be certain of their number. I knew I stood no chance against them."

Pearlie rolled his eyes in Cal's direction before he rode off to help Smoke with the strays. "That's a sizeable bunch of bad men," he muttered. "Hard to figure why there'd be so many travelin' together. It's also hard to guess why one of 'em would be wearin' a Confederate uniform so long after the war. That part don't make a lick of sense."

Cal rode up beside Pearlie to push the last of the steers across. "I've got this bad feelin' in the pit of my stomach, Pearlie," Cal said. "Somethin' tells me Smoke is gonna put us right where this outlaw gang is gonna be. You heard that feller say they was headed fer Dodge City, didn't you?"

"I ain't got no extra wax in my ears, Cal," he said with a touch of irritation. "You can damn well bet we're gonna be right square in the middle of a ruckus if them robbers happen to be in Dodge when Smoke Jensen an' the rest of us git there. May as well check the loads in yer pistol an' rifle right now. I can feel a fight comin'."

"I warned you that mornin' I got bucked off, this was gonna be an unlucky trip. I felt it all the way to my bones."

"Them sore bones was on account of your fall, son. But when you ride with Smoke, you can lay long odds that we'll find a peck of trouble some place or 'nother."

"Smoke said this was gonna be a peaceful trip, that all we was gonna do was take these yearlin's to market."

Pearlie made a face. "How many times, when we's gone some place with the boss, have we set out on somethin' peaceful, only to wind up pickin' lead outa our hides?"

"Seems like a bunch."

"Now you've got my drift," Pearlie said, urging a piebald steer into the river. "Ever watch buzzards circlin' in the sky, son? There'll always be somethin' dead underneath 'em. It's a harsh thing to say 'bout a good feller like Smoke, but the same can be said about trouble findin' him. You ain't been with this outfit long as I have. I've seen it a dozen times. We could set out to gather eggs in Miz Jensen's henhouse, an' if Smoke happened to be along, there'd be some owl-hoot with a gun hidin' behind them layin' cages, takin' shots at us."

"You got this tendency to exaggerate, Pearlie," Cal said, reining his bay into the water. "It ain't always that bad, but there's been times when it seemed that way. The boss is tryin' to keep his word to Miz Jensen to stay away from other men's difficulties. He wouldn't intentionally break his word to her for anything. It just seems to happen, like a rainstorm that comes up all of a sudden."

Pearlie urged his dun toward the shallows.

"You ever hear of a magnet, young 'un?"

"Yessir. It draws metal. I seen this feller in Denver on a street corner, peddlin' magnets. He claimed they was magic, that they had magical powers. Made sense to me, 'cause there ain't no other way to explain why one piece of iron would pull another up against it. It's gotta be some kinda magic. That peddler laid out a handful of horseshoe nails on this little table, and when he held that magnet over 'em, they jumped off the table like they was alive and grabbed hold of that magnet like they was stuck with glue. I was gonna buy one, just to show folks I could do magic myself, only they cost two bits an' I didn't have that much money."

"It ain't magic," Pearlie said, when his horse reached belly-deep water. "It's a special kind of metal in 'em. And there's men who've got a special kind of drawin' power when it comes to guns an' gunplay. Smoke draws them hard-nosed types same as a magnet draws other kinds of metal. You wait an' see if I ain't right. I'm bettin' a month's pay that, by the time we git to Dodge, that outlaw bunch will be there, an' Smoke'll find 'em, unless they find him first. There's gonna be more bloodlettin' afore this ride is over."

"But I heard Smoke promise Miz Jensen he wouldn't get in no kinda trouble this time."

Pearlie chuckled, but with a touch of worry in the sound of it. "I'm dead sure he meant it when he gave her that promise, but that don't account for circumstances."

"Circumstances?" Cal asked in a way that made it clear he wasn't sure what Pearlie was talking about.

Pearlie took a deep breath, as though he'd grown frustrated trying to show Cal the logic behind his reasoning. "You think it might be just bad luck that a gang of murderin' thieves is headed fer Dodge same time as we are?"

"But how would they know we was comin', Pearlie? An' how would Smoke know?"

"It's called fate, young 'un. Some men have got the Fates dead set against 'em. Smoke is one of 'em. Most other men can ride all the way from California to Dodge City without havin' so much as a loose horseshoe. Smoke don't hardly ever git that kind of peace. It's the hand of fate that keeps guidin' him toward a fight."

"All he aimed to do was sell these steers," Cal protested as they rode out on the far bank.

Pearlie let it drop, knowing Smoke could hear them now. He rode up and down the riverbank pushing steers into a bunch for the trail running beside the Arkansas River. A road of sorts following the course of the river would take them all the way to Dodge City.

Smoke got the lead steers turned east. Pearlie rode up to him just as the rest of the herd fell in behind the leaders.

"You hear what that feller said 'bout that gang?"

"He told me," Smoke replied quietly, paying more attention to the condition of their cattle, satisfied when he noted their bellies were full and hardly a one was traveling sore-footed in spite of sharp flint rock underneath their hooves.

"Did Grimes also tell you there was thirty of 'em?" Pearlie continued.

"He did," Smoke answered, counting steers as they went past him to see if they'd lost any on the trail—it seemed there were always a few strays that wandered off in the brush on any trail drive, no matter how carefully a group of cowhands tried to keep them together.

"Did he also tell you 'bout that one wearin' a Confederate uniform?"

Smoke stopped counting to look at Pearlie. "He didn't make mention of that part."

A slow recollection of something Louis Longmont told him a few years ago crept into Smoke's thoughts. Louis said there were rumors and occasional newspaper articles in Kansas City and a few Missouri papers that an infamous

raider known as Bloody Bill Anderson had not been killed
shortly after the war, as it was first reported after an incident
at a farmhouse where possemen claimed to have killed Anderson, one of Quantrill's lieutenants, a madman who continued robbing and murdering Union sympathizers after the
war ended. Despite what appeared to have been a positive
identification of the body by men who knew Anderson, there
were reports of sightings all over the Territories long after
his supposed death, and numerous bloody scenes near the
spots where folks claimed to have seen Anderson and his
gang of looters. Louis had said it was hogwash, that Anderson was dead and that someone was merely impersonating
him to shift blame for the raids and killings. Louis felt sure
that Anderson was in his grave and that an imposter was
using his name and reputation to hide his true identity. Louis
Longmont was seldom wrong when it came to history, being
a well-read, highly educated man.

"Louis told me there used to be rumors that Bloody Bill
Anderson was still alive," Smoke told Pearlie, "some killer
who dressed in a Confederate uniform, claiming to be Anderson. Bill Anderson was killed by a posse not too long
after the war, an' men who knew him positively identified
the body. That's what Louis said. I wouldn't pay too much attention to Grimes. It's more likely there were only a dozen
men or so who stole his mule . . . probably a bunch of
drifters and saddle tramps who found easy pickings. Same
goes for the folks who were robbed and killed at that tradin'
post. It's more likely the work of a gang of misfits and cowards. One of 'em just happened to be wearing pieces of an
old Confederate uniform."

"I remember hearin' all about Bloody Bill Anderson and
Quantrill's raiders," Pearlie said. "You said Louis told you
there were rumors he was still alive."

"Louis said they were *rumors*, Pearlie. Stories written up
in a newspaper."

"I sure as hell hope that's *all* they are," Pearlie said as a frown creased his dust-caked forehead. "Him an' Quantrill was supposed to be real mean hombres."

"You pay too much attention to a man's reputation," Smoke said, swinging his Palouse to head for the point position at the front of the herd. "Most times, that's all it is—a batch of made-up stories designed to scare folks. Now let's get these steers to the railhead before they die of old age while you're worrying about other things. Louis told me Bloody Bill Anderson was dead, and that's good enough for me . . . and even if he ain't, he's just another man who bleeds and dies if a bullet hits him in the right spot."

8

"We'll need more mules an' packhorses to haul off the gold an' banknotes," Bill said, holding a half-empty bottle of whiskey by the neck while he stared into the fire, a bottle taken from Dave Cobbs's store. "With two banks, there's gonna be plenty of money needin' to be hauled off in a hurry. We'll head south to Indian Territory an' lay low for a spell, like we was doin' up 'til now. There'll be plenty of law dogs out to hang us, an' the army'll be lookin' for us too. Ain't hardly no law in the west part of Indian Territory. We'll be safe enough if we stay outa sight, send one or two men to the closest settlement to buy the things we need."

"We're gonna be rich," Sammy said, after taking a sip of whiskey from a bottle he shared with his brother. "Won't be no more poor days fer none of us."

Claude nodded in agreement. "It's flat country all the way to Dodge from here, Bill. A few hills. Maybe five miles to the outskirts of town. When I scouted it today, Dodge looked real quiet. Hardly any herds there yet. This train came in from the east, an' I watched it with my field glass. Six soldiers got off the baggage car, carrying cash boxes of loot down to one of the banks, four of 'em did, whilst the others guarded the shipment with rifles. You was right 'bout them banks bein' full. There's money comin' on every train, most likely."

"Maybe we oughta wait a day or two," another man suggested from the far side of the firepit. "If there's money comin' damn near every day, that's more fer us."

"I ain't in the mood for waitin'," Bill said. "We ain't got hardly any cash money an' I'm ready to stuff my pockets full of Yankee gold."

"We never did find that storekeeper's money," Jack Starr said in a sour voice. "The woman wouldn't talk even when I told her I was gonna bust her baby's skull with the butt of my gun 'less she told where it was."

Sammy chuckled. "She was screamin' too loud to talk," he said. "When Claude tore her dress off, 'bout all she would do was scream her head off. Even when ol' Billy Ray was havin' his way with her, all the bitch did was scream an' try to fight them ropes while we was holdin' her legs. She was a lot stronger'n we figured."

Bill took another swallow of whiskey. "We got most of what we needed . . . this here red-eye—twenty bottles of it— an' enough in the way of food to keep us fed for weeks while we're hidin' from the law. Storekeeper like that, he wouldn't have much cash money anyhow."

"He sure did try an' git back up after you shot him, Bill. I never seen a feller try so hard in all my borned days. He come up three or four times, shakin' like a cold pig, only he fell back down from his hands an' knees every time," Claude remembered.

Sammy chimed in. "That sure was a pretty fire, boys. Them flames jumped higher'n hell. Real pretty, too . . . yellow colored with plenty of smoke, making them poppin' noises when the jars of pickled peaches busted. We shouldn't have left so many of them peaches behind."

"Wasn't enough packhorses to carry everything," someone offered. "We got most of the good stuff, like this here bottle of whiskey an' all them others."

Anderson looked up from his idle contemplation of the coals in the pit. "Who's out ridin' guard tonight?" he asked, as if it had suddenly occurred to him that their camp might need watching.

"Lee an' Sonny are up north," Jack Starr replied. "That's where somebody's most likely to stumble onto our camp headed to Dodge. Dewey an' Roy are ridin' circles south, just in case anybody comes from another direction."

"Good idea," Bill said, "only it appeared Roy was too damn drunk to sit in a saddle just before dark. Maybe this cold night air'll sober him up."

Someone belched loudly outside the circle of firelight, a supper of boiled beans and fried fatback not resting well with a bellyful of whiskey.

Claude said, "We hadn't oughta take no chances. If Dewey an' Roy's both drunk, maybe somebody oughta go relieve 'em on night watch."

Bill nodded. "We sure as hell don't need to be takin' no chances, not with all that's at stake in them banks. Two of you boys who can mount a damn horse go fetch Roy an' Dewey back to camp. Don't want no slipups on this job, boys. This'll be the biggest payday of our lives. Any sumbitch don't do his job right an' I'm gonna shoot him myself. I want that understood real clear."

"Let's you an' me go, Sammy," Claude said, coming to his feet slowly, rubbing one knee while he held a bottle of whiskey in the other.

"It's cold out yonder, away from this fire," Sammy protested as his brow formed a frown. "Let somebody else go."

Bill drew his right-hand pistol and aimed it across the fire directly into Sammy's face. "Get on your damn horse," he said, thumbing back the Colt's hammer, "or you ain't gonna notice the cold much longer."

Sammy came abruptly to his feet. "All I was sayin' was, it's cold," he said, backing away from the muzzle of Bill's gun with fear widening his badly crossed eyes. "I sure never said I wouldn't go. No sir, I never said that . . ." He wheeled as he was speaking and hurried off toward the picket lines where their horses were tethered. Claude followed him into the darkness as a silence gripped the camp. Everyone knew that Bill Anderson would shoot one of his own men over the slightest provocation, and as often as not, for no clear reason at all.

Bill put his pistol away. "Some of you boys need to be reminded it takes discipline to hold an outfit together. Well I'm damn sure here to remind any sumbitch who forgets."

As Sammy and Claude were saddling their horses, a sound came from the northwest—horses moving toward the fire at a trot.

"That'll be Lee an' Sonny," a voice said. "Wonder what the hell they's doin' comin' back?"

Bill saw three men outlined against a star-sprinkled sky as they rode over the crest of a rise above the hollow he'd selected for a campsite, where travelers couldn't see the glow of their fire from a distance.

"There's three," another member of the gang said. "Who the hell've they got with 'em?"

"Looks like they've a prisoner," Jack Starr's deep voice answered. "The stranger's got his hands tied behind him. . . . I can see that from here."

Bill stood up, resting one palm on the butt of a pistol, the other hand wrapped around the neck of his whiskey bottle. "Bring the sumbitch to the fire," he said lowly, his right gun hand tensing while his fingers curled around his walnut pistol grips. "I want a damn explanation for why they brung him here. Don't them two fools know we'll have to kill him, now that he knows where we's camped?"

"Must be a reason," Starr muttered under his breath, making his way toward the silhouettes of Lee and Sonny and a newcomer with his hands behind him. Starr drew his Dance revolver and held it at his side.

"Who've you got there?" Starr demanded when the three riders were at the picket ropes.

Sonny's tinny voice resounded from the tether lines as he dismounted. "Just an old man, Jack, but he was headed this way an' we had to stop him or he'd have rode right up on this here fire."

"Pull him down an' bring him over to the light where Bill can see him," Starr replied.

The figure between Bill's night guards was jerked out of the saddle, landing with a grunt on his face and chest near the front hooves of his horse.

"Git up, you ol' geezer," Sonny demanded, "or I'll shoot a hole through the backside of your skull bone."

The man struggled to his feet despite his bindings, and then he was shoved toward the firepit at gunpoint. Sonny held his .44 against the man's spine, prodding him with it.

A slope-shouldered man in his sixties with flowing gray hair came to the fire, his eyes roaming the assortment of hard faces staring at him.

"Who the hell are you?" Bill snapped. "An' what the hell are you doin' out here in the middle of nowhere so late at night on a damn horse?"

The old man refused to answer at first. A bloody gash left a trickle of crimson running down his left cheek into his gray beard.

"Says his name is Smith," the gunman named Lee Wollard said when he walked up to join the others. "Hell, if we was to make ourselves believe every sumbitch who said his name was Smith is a relative of the Smith family, wouldn't be nothin' but Smiths in this whole Territory. I slapped him across the face with the barrel of my gun, only he won't say no more. He just stared up at me, sullen like a damned mule so his jaw won't work when it's supposed to."

"I can loosen that jaw some," Bill snarled, walking slowly around the fire until he stood in front of the old man. "I can put a little grease on it, so to speak."

Having said that, Bill swung his Colt in a wide arc, landing it squarely across the stranger's lips. The old man staggered back and fell down on the seat of his pants, yet he still glared at Bill defiantly, slitting his eyelids.

"He ain't the real talkative sort," Sonny said. "Maybe if I was to stomp on his belly some with these here stovepipe boots he'd find some words inside his mouth."

"Suit yourself," Bill remarked. "Kick the hell out of him a few times. Let's see if it works."

Sonny lifted a booted foot with a silver spur tied to the heel and smashed it into the old man's stomach. A groan came from the downed man's tightly closed lips despite all his efforts to prevent it.

"Kick him again, Sonny," Lee said, grinning in the poor light. "Ask him what the hell he's doin' out here so late. We got a right to know, seein' as this is our camp he was fixin' to ride up on. The bastard ain't got no manners or he'd have rode off in 'nother direction. Kick him real hard this time, so he'll know we mean business."

Sonny, a razor-thin cowboy with deeply bowed legs, swung his foot into the old man's ribs with all his might. A rush of air came from the nostrils of the man who called himself Smith, and still he did not utter a word.

"Tough ol' sumbitch," someone witnessing the affair said when it was clear the man wouldn't talk yet. "You're gonna have to hurt him real bad, I'll bet, afore he says anything."

Bill gazed down at the old man's face. "I'll hand it to you, Mr. Smith. You damn sure know how to take a little pain without complainin' about it. But we ain't done. Before we get through, you'll talk. I'll promise you that much. You see, we gotta know if you was out here spyin' on us. You got no choice but to tell us what we need to know, or you're gonna die. Is that part gettin' through your thick skull?"

Blood oozed from the old man's mouth, dribbling into his beard, falling in tiny damp circles on the ground underneath him, but his lips did not move. He took a deep breath.

"Kick him again, Sonny," Bill demanded. "Make it right near one of his kidneys. In case you ain't never been kicked there, it hurts like hell an' you'll be passin' blood fer days afterward."

Sonny swung his boot toe into the man's lower back, and all who were standing there heard the thud of the blow. Smith winced, twisting his face with pain, until he coughed up a huge mouthful of blood. He said nothing.

Bill looked at the men closest to him. "Some of you boys get mounted. We need to make damn sure this old man was alone, that there ain't others out there lookin' for us. Word of what we done at that tradin' post may have reached the law over in Dodge."

"He was by hisself," Lee insisted, looking to Sonny for agreement. "We checked for half a mile in every direction 'fore we brung him back here."

"I want ten men in saddles," Bill said. "Scour every damn inch of these hills. If word gets to the law dogs in Dodge that we're close to town, they'll form up a posse an' come lookin' for us."

In twos and threes, gunmen left the fire to saddle their horses, spurs clanking across rocky ground.

Bill looked down at the bloody, bearded face resting on the ground near his feet. The old man's eyes were fixed on his in a steady, unwavering stare. "You know we have to kill you, old timer," he said, with what could have been a suggestion of respect in his voice. "You might tell other folks where we are if we let you go. I'll agree you're a tough old son of a bitch, to take that kickin' without spillin' your guts. Just so you'll know, it ain't personal. I'm Bill Anderson. Some have taken to callin' me Bloody Bill. We're gonna rob them banks in Dodge City, an' we can't have the whole damn town expectin' us. This is just business, old man. I gotta make sure your mouth stays shut."

Smith's eyes closed. He nodded once, as though he understood.

Bill aimed down at Smith's forehead and pulled the trigger. The report from his .44 was like a clap of thunder rolling across the Kansas prairie southeast of Dodge.

9

Smoke felt some satisfaction over their crossbred steers and the way they handled the trail. Despite his initial worries that the Hereford blood in them would make them difficult to drive over long distances, their longhorn characteristics prevailed in ways he hadn't expected.

He spoke to Pearlie. "Those short legs don't seem to make all that much difference in the way these steers travel. I had it figured otherwise."

Pearlie nodded as the cattle wandered over a grassy flat, grazing hungrily. "It's that Meskin longhorn in 'em," he said with certainty. "The Hereford makes this bunch gentler, but I'd hate like hell to have to round 'em up if we have a stampede on our hands."

"That don't seem likely," Smoke offered, gazing across the eastern horizon. "These cattle are pretty well trail-broke by now."

"Hearin', or seein', the wrong thing'll spook 'em," Pearlie insisted. "I ain't gonna start countin' no chickens till we got eggs in a basket at Dodge."

"We should be there tomorrow," Smoke said, "if I remember this country right."

Pearlie gave him a sideways look. "You think there's anything to that story Grimes told us 'bout them raiders, an' maybe it bein' Bloody Bill Anderson?"

Smoke gave him an indifferent shrug. "Don't see how it matters to us, so long as whoever it was don't try to steal any of our beeves."

Pearlie looked eastward. "It's after you pocket the money fer these steers I'm worryin' about."

"You worry too much, Pearlie."

"It's my nature. My pappy was a worrier. Momma said it was what put him in an early grave."

Smoke turned back in the saddle. Grimes and Cal were driving the last of the steers over a swell in the prairie. A few steers were limping some after so many miles traveling on flinty soil. "I hope you don't worry yourself to death the way your pappy did," Smoke said absently, his mind on the lame cows bringing up the rear of the herd. "This ground's too damn hard to dig a grave. We'll have to cover you up with your bedroll and leave you on top of one of these hills. We didn't bring a shovel, and I won't dig in this flint with my bare hands. I'll get Cal to say a few words over you, but that's about the best we can do if you cross over here due to worryin'."

"I ain't dead yet," Pearlie growled, "an' I damn sure ain't gonna be happy to have that sneaky young 'un sayin' a damn word over my dead body if it *does* happen. My foot's still sore from that cocklebur. I've been thinkin' real hard about ways to git even with the little runt. If I had any poison, I'd put it in his coffee tonight. A man don't realize how bad he needs two good feet 'til some sneaky little owl-hoot puts a burr in his boot. I swear by the moon an' stars, I'm gonna git even."

"The two of you are like a couple of kids," Smoke said as he urged his stud forward with his heels.

Pearlie wasn't ready to give in. "That boy's got a mean streak. I aim to cure him of bad habits, some way or 'nother. I ain't done with him yet, not by a long shot."

Smoke decided it was time to intervene. "Save your trickery 'til we get these cattle to market, Pearlie. I don't want anything to keep us from getting our beeves sold. On the way back you can have your fun. Meantime, let's get the steers in a bunch and push 'em a little harder. Their flanks have filled out over the last hour or two. We need to make up for lost time as much as we can."

Pearlie spurred his dun to a short lope to circle the lead steers for a push. Smoke headed for the point position while forcing wandering cattle back into a tighter group. If memory served him they were a day and a half west of Dodge City—he had begun to recognize familiar landmarks, a rocky knob to the north and cottonwood groves along the Arkansas River where he'd made camp before.

When the steers were strung out in good trail fashion he allowed himself to relax against the cantle of his saddle. It had begun to seem like the drive would end peacefully, until he heard a distant shout behind him.

Cal was shaking out a loop in his lariat rope, yelling to Pearlie, "Watch out fer that maverick!"

A mottled longhorn cow trotted over a hilltop near the rear of the herd, shaking its massive, six-foot spread of horns. Smoke knew what lay in store unless someone could turn the renegade cow away from the crossbreeds. The wild longhorn, a maverick that had escaped from some earlier trail drive, would frighten the gentler cattle into a stampede. A purebred Mexican longhorn could be among the most unmanageable animals on earth. The big cow coming toward the herd could have been running wild across empty Kansas prairies for years.

Cal spurred his bay into a gallop, swinging his loop over his head. Smoke halted the Palouse, reining around to lend a hand, for he knew the colt that Cal was riding hadn't been taught the finer points of holding a heavy cow at the end of a rope.

He sent the stud into a hard run, taking down his own lariat as he saw Pearlie wheel his horse toward the maverick. Pearlie and Cal would arrive at the hilltop at roughly the same time and Smoke hoped that Pearlie, riding an older ranch horse, would be first to get a noose around the longhorn's neck.

The stud's thundering hooves beat out a rhythm on hard soil as Smoke closed the distance. The spotted longhorn came to a sudden stop, snorting, waving its dangerously sharp horns back and forth as a warning to the approaching cowboys. An old mossy horn of this type could seriously injure a horse or a cowboy if things went wrong. Pearlie would know how to avoid a calamity, but young Cal had little experience with wild range cattle.

It was a blessing when Pearlie reached the longhorn cow first and swung his loop, just when the spotted creature made a turn to escape. Pearlie's noose settled over the cow's horns in expert fashion.

Cal galloped up, slowing the bay at almost the same instant when the wild cow suddenly turned around to charge Pearlie's dun horse.

"Look out!" Cal cried.

Pearlie got his dun stopped a moment too late. The cow made a charge for Pearlie with horns lowered while Pearlie was dallying his lariat around his saddle horn.

The maverick was quick, and wise to the ways of cowboys and ropes. Lunging to one side, it kept coming toward Pearlie at a full charge before Pearlie could collect himself or free the rope from his saddle.

The spotted cow struck Pearlie's dun gelding full tilt, all its power in its hindquarters, driving one horn into the dun's ribs.

Pearlie toppled from his saddle as his horse staggered from the force of impact, a thousand pounds of angry longhorn rushing into the side of the dun.

Smoke asked his Palouse for all the speed it had, drumming his heels into the stud's ribs while shaking out a loop to catch the heels of the maverick—if only he could get there in time to rope the longhorn's back legs before it turned on Pearlie.

But it was Cal who came to the rescue. He threw a loop on the ground just in front of the longhorn's rear hooves as it was goring Pearlie's horse with a razorlike horn, blood squirting from a deep wound in the gelding's side.

Cal jerked the bay around and took off in the opposite direction with his loop securely fastened around the maverick's hocks.

When the bay colt hit the end of the rope it stumbled momentarily, but at the same time the longhorn was pulled backward, freeing its horn from the dun. Pearlie lay helpless on the ground beneath his horse, in real danger of being trampled to death.

Cal yelled, "Pull, you bay son of a bitch!" as he drove his spurs into the colt's hide.

The longhorn bellowed as it was jerked off its feet by the power of the bay's efforts to drag it away from Pearlie and the injured dun. The cow fell over on its side, bawling, swinging a blood-drenched horn back and forth, unable to rise to its feet again as Cal dragged the enraged beast away by its hind legs.

Smoke galloped up on the stud and threw his noose over the cow's horns. The Palouse, with thickly muscled hindquarters and gaskins, had an easy time of it pulling the head of the downed maverick to one side until the animal lay, stretched out between Smoke's rope and Cal's, bellowing for all it was worth, fighting the pull of both ropes in a futile effort to get free.

Smoke quickly examined the dun as Pearlie came staggering to his feet. The horse's wound was serious, but with luck and a bit of careful attention, the gelding would mend.

He turned his attention back to the cow, then to Cal. "Nice work with those heels, son," he cried above the angry roar of the thrashing maverick. "You may have saved Pearlie's life. One of these wild, mossy horns can be damn near as dangerous as a wounded grizzly."

Cal's face was the color of milk. "Didn't know what else I could do, boss," he stammered. "Wasn't no other place I could put a rope 'cept fer them back feet."

Pearlie bent down to pick up his hat, dusting it off quickly before he walked around his dun to inspect its wound. "I owe you, young 'un," he said, frowning, tracing a fingertip over the bloody hole in the gelding's side. Then he turned to Smoke and drew his pistol. "If it's all the same to you, Smoke, I'd like to put a bullet in that damn maverick's brain fer what it done to my best cow pony."

Smoke wagged his head. "We don't need the meat, Pearlie, and what this cow did was what nature intended—tryin' to join our herd when it caught the scent. I've got my rope around its horns, and this stud is heavy enough to drag the cow off for a ways. We ain't gonna shoot it for doin' what came natural to an animal."

"But it damn near killed me an' my dun!" Pearlie exclaimed, with an accusing finger aimed at the cow.

"That isn't what matters, Pearlie," Smoke told him as he swung the stud around to pull the downed longhorn away from the herd. "There's a difference between killin' a dumb animal and a man. Animals act out of instinct—they don't bear grudges or kill for no reason. Same can't be said for some breeds of men. Put the gun away. I'll haul this cow over the hill yonder and take off these ropes. Get back to the herd, or they'll drift all the way to creation."

Pearlie, even as mad as he was, was wise enough to know

when to be quiet. He mounted his horse and gathered up his reins to ride away, holstering his Colt. "I'll tend to this horse's wound as soon as me an' Cal git them cows collected," he said, a change in his voice. Then he looked at Cal. "You done yourself proud, boy, an' I won't forgit it, I was aimin' to git even with you fer that cocklebur, but I reckon we'll call things square, least for now."

Cal gave Pearlie a sheepish grin. "Wasn't you I was tryin' to help, Pearlie," he said. "I got to feelin' real sorry for that yellow dun horse, havin' a horn stuck in him. If that horn had been stuck in the same feller who put castor oil in the syrup tin back at Sugarloaf, I might not have been so inclined to tie my rope to a mad cow."

Pearlie shook his head. "I shoulda knowed it was a waste of perfectly good air to pay you a compliment." He swung his horse back toward the herd, mumbling to himself.

Smoke spoke to Cal. "Shake your loop off this critter's legs, an' I'll yank her out of sight. You're making a right decent cowhand, Cal. That heel loop is mighty hard to throw."

Cal shook slack into his lariat, and the noose opened just enough to allow the longhorn's hind legs freedom.

The Palouse plunged forward when it felt Smoke's heels, and the rope went taut between Smoke's saddle horn and a maverick that could have caused the Sugarloaf brand a stampede.

A few seconds later the longhorn scrambled to its feet and snorted, shaking its head but harkening to the pull of Smoke's rope to keep from choking.

The stud struck a slow trot ahead of the cow, turning its head just enough to keep a wary eye on the horned beast behind it. The Palouse was a seasoned roping horse, bearing the scars of close calls with other wild cattle.

*   *   *

"That was some demonstration," Grimes said at their evening camp fire, waiting for coffee to boil. He was speaking to Smoke when he said it. "The young man named Cal showed courage when he came to Pearlie's rescue."

Smoke was occupied slicing strips of fatback into a small cast-iron skillet on a rock beside the flames as darkness came to the Kansas prairie. "Cal's got the makings of a top cowhand. He lacks a bit of experience, maybe, but that'll come with time. He has what it takes."

Grimes gazed at the pair of pistols belted around Smoke's waist. Smoke saw him from the corner of his eye.

"Your men tell me you are experienced with those sidearms you carry," Grimes said.

It was a subject Smoke didn't care to discuss at the moment. His thoughts were on Dodge City, and cattle buyers he would find there. He ignored the drummer's remark. "Coffee's near 'bout ready, Mr. Grimes. Hand me a couple of those tin cups."

10

Dodge City had grown considerably since Smoke had last seen it a few years earlier, before the railroad line came. A stockyard stretching for half a mile lay beside the end of a railroad spur ending in Dodge. Row upon row of false-fronted, clapboard buildings lined dirt streets in the business district. A few stores and drinking parlors occupied large, canvas tents. Sod houses and wood shacks had been built in virtually every direction around the business sector, but it was easy to see that the heart of Dodge was the cattle market, plank corrals and loading ramps where beef on the hoof could be driven into cattle cars on a number of rail sidings.

Fall winds kicked up dust from nearby barren hills, clouds of alkali chalk sweeping over the town in irregular gusts that swirled across everything. Smoke tugged his hat down to keep it from blowing off as he led the steers toward the west end of the cow pens, where empty corrals would hold his beeves until a price could be struck with a cattle buyer.

It was late, approaching sundown, when he pointed the herd across a rusty set of rails into an alleyway between livestock pens. A couple of young cowboys who worked for the market had begun to open a number of gates so the Sugarloaf cows could be herded into corrals with water troughs and haystacks.

Weary Hereford crosses walked quietly into the alleys and then into the pens, scenting water and sweet prairie hay. The last half-dozen steers at the back, evidencing various stages of sore-footedness, limped into corrals and went straight for the hay and water. A pink-cheeked cowboy with a tally book and a pencil came up to Smoke as he was dismounting from the stud.

"Howdy, mister," the boy said. "I reckon you know the way it's done. You take a head count, an' I'll do the same. If we come up with the same number I'll enter it in the book an' you sign your name to it. Can't be no disagreement over how many you brung that way."

"I understand," Smoke replied, tying off his horse's reins. "I'll start on this end. Should be three hundred an' seven by my count earlier this morning."

"Those sure are fine steers, mister. Don't get many with Hereford breedin'. We've got buyers in town who'll jump at the chance to buy 'em. Ol' Crawford Long is a cranky cuss, but he said one time a drop of Hereford blood in a cow gives it twice as much meat as a longhorn. I figure he'll be your top bidder. I can send word to him when we're done with this count, if you want."

"Sounds good to me," Smoke said, distracted by the sight of Grimes talking to another cowboy working the pens. He could hear part of the conversation.

"They murdered the whole family," Grimes said. "Burned the place to the ground. They stole my mule. Are you certain you haven't seen a gang of rough-looking men coming to Dodge in the last couple of days?"

"No sir, I sure ain't. It's been pretty quiet. The big herds comin' up from Texas ain't arrived yet, so it seems like Dodge is half empty. Everybody woulda noticed if some big gang rode into town. Couldn't hide somethin' like that. But we got us a good City Marshal. Wyatt Earp's his name. He don't act scared of the devil hisself."

"Can you direct me to his office?" Grimes asked. "I need to report my stolen mule and what happened at that trading post east of here."

"The Marshal's gone right now lookin' into some kinda trouble at Cobbs Store. A muleskinner said he saw it got burnt plumb down, just like you said. He didn't say nothin' 'bout findin' no bodies."

Grimes seemed frustrated. "Is there anyone else I can report the theft of my mule to?"

"A deputy by the name of Sims. He can send off a telegram to the army over at Fort Lared . . . tell 'em to be on the lookout for that big gang you told me about."

"Where's the Marshal's office?"

"Right up Main Street, across from Garner's Mercantile. You can't miss it."

Grimes rode off toward the center of town. Smoke began his count of the steers while Pearlie unsaddled to apply another coat of fatback drippings to his dun's wound.

Cal swung down and stretched his legs before he unsaddled his horse to put it in one of the smaller pens.

"Three hundred and seven," the cowboy said, frowning at a page in his tally book. "Just sign your name right here at the bottom of the page."

Smoke scribbled his name and handed back the pencil. "We need a good meal and a decent room for the night," he said as he loosened the cinch on his stud.

"The Drover's Hotel has got the best of both. Best chicken an' dumplin's in the whole world, an' real soft beds. Miz Cox can make the best apple pies you ever ate too. Don't miss out on the pie, if she's got any today. You're kinda early to be comin' with a herd, mister. Be a few more weeks before the big bunches get here, so Miz Cox don't fix as much till more hungry cowboys show up."

"I'll remember to ask for the pie," Smoke told him, swinging his saddle over a fence rail, then taking down his war bag. "You can tell that cattle buyer I'm ready to sell and head back for home."

"Just curious, mister, but where's home?" the cowhand asked as his gaze fell to Smoke's pistols.

"Colorado Territory, at the foot of the Rockies. Can't say as this part of Kansas is nearly so pretty to look at."

The young man shook his head. "There ain't no reason on earth to live here, 'cept for a job. Cold as hell in wintertime an' hotter 'n blazes in summer. There's this sayin' among cowboys who come up from Texas: 'Kansas has got three suns.' "

When no more was offered, Smoke asked for some sort of explanation. "Three suns?"

"Yep. The sun over your head, sunflowers, an' ornery sons of bitches."

The Drover's Hotel was a two-story affair made of wood planks, with peeling white paint. A wooden porch ran the length of the place. Smoke, Pearlie and Cal carried their saddles, gear, and guns up a set of sagging steps to go inside. Smoke could already smell something good coming from a cafe off to one side of the hotel lobby.

"I got wind of chicken an' dumplin's just then," Pearlie said.

"That wrangler at the cow pens said to be sure to try the apple pie," Smoke replied as they walked through a pair of glass-paned doors.

"I'm so hungry I could eat boot leather," Cal said as they rested their saddles on the polished hardwood floor.

Smoke pulled off his hat when an elderly woman came to the desk.

"Do you gentlemen wish to hire a room?" she asked.

"Three of 'em," Smoke answered. "On the second floor, if you don't have no objections."

"None at all," she replied. "Each room is a dollar a night, and it's payable in advance."

He placed three silver dollars on the desk. The woman gave him three keys. Pearlie hesitated before heading for the stairs.

"Ma'am, could that be chicken an' dumplin's I smell?"

"It is indeed. Made this morning, and we have apple pie for dessert."

"Lordy," Pearlie exclaimed, rolling his eyes. "I've done died an' gone to heaven."

Their dinner was delicious, every bit as good as the wrangler said it would be. But when big slices of apple pie— made dark with cinnamon and sugar—were placed in front of them, it was Cal who whistled softly through his teeth.

"It can't be as good as Miz Jensen's, I'll bet, but it looks mighty close."

Smoke had to admit the pie was mighty close to being as good as Sally's, but the thought of a comparison reminded him of how much he missed his wife. He cleaned his dish quickly and took a sip of strong coffee, forcing his thoughts away from Sally and Sugarloaf to the business at hand. "We made it, boys," he said after a moment of silent contemplation.

Pearlie, forgetting his manners, licked his pie plate clean and set it down sorrowfully. He looked at Smoke. "I overheard one of them hands tell Grimes there wasn't no gang of strangers in town. Maybe Lady Luck is gonna smile on us this time. No more shootin' or duckin' lead."

Smoke glanced at a front window as dusk came to Dodge City. "Seems nice and quiet. Come sunrise I'll make the best deal I can for our beeves, draw our money from the bank, and we'll head out. To tell the truth, this flat country just don't suit me none at all."

"Me neither," Cal said, tossing his fork down when the last of his pie was eaten. "Ain't nothin' but dust an' hard rock in Kansas. Can't wait to git back home."

Pearlie's expression turned wary. "We ain't started in the direction yet, young 'un. There's still time for plenty of things to go wrong."

"Like what?" Cal asked, frowning.

Pearlie was watching the front windows.

"Any number of things," he told him.

"But you ain't said what they could be," Cal persisted, as if he needed to know what was on Pearlie's mind. "Them steers can't stampede 'cause they's locked up in corrals. Ain't no redskins gonna ride into Dodge to cause trouble."

Pearlie leaned back in his chair, folding his arms across his belly. "I've got this feelin'," he said quietly. "I sure do hope I'm wrong."

Smoke emptied his coffee cup and pushed back his chair. "Let's check on the steers and our horses before we turn in. After sleepin' on this hard Kansas ground, I'm ready for a bed that's a little softer."

"Sounds mighty good to me," Cal agreed, standing up to rub his stomach. "Only trouble is, I'm so full I may not be able to walk plumb down to them stockyards. Pearlie, I was wonderin' if you'd mind carryin' me part of the way?"

Pearlie grunted, made a face, and walked away from the table without uttering a word, his spurs making a clanking noise over the cafe floor.

Smoke paid for their meal, thinking about the next day. A two-year breeding program at Sugarloaf would be weighed by the price he got for their steers. He hoped Sally wouldn't be disappointed with the result.

Strolling down Dodge City's main street, Cal and Pearlie

were unusually quiet. Off in the distance they could hear a steam locomotive chugging toward town from the east. Smoke had to guess the train was bringing empty cattle cars for the herds coming up from Texas. He felt content, missing Sally more than he expected.

"Train's comin'," Cal said.

"I got ears, boy," Pearlie remarked. The edgy feeling he complained about earlier was showing.

Cal gave Pearlie a look. "Kinda grumpy, ain't you, fer a man with a bellyful of apple pie an' dumplin's?"

Full dark was spreading over the hills and flats by the time they came to the cattle pens. Smoke gave their horses a quick inspection, satisfied. The steers were busy nibbling mounds of hay.

Pearlie had his hands on a top fence plank, taking his own look at the animals. He spoke to the others. "Full bellies all 'round. Us too. But come to think of it, I could sure use a spot of whiskey to settle my nerves before we turn in."

Cal chuckled. "You've sure been havin' plenty of nerve troubles lately. I was the one who was worried 'bout that feelin' in my bones that this trip was gonna be a bad one. It turned out I was plumb wrong."

Smoke swung away from the fence as Pearlie said, "I said it before an' I'm sayin' it again. We ain't got back to Sugarloaf yet with any cow money."

"We'll get back okay," Smoke said as they walked back toward the lights of town. "The only part that ain't clear yet is just how much money I'll be handing over to Sally."

"It'll be plenty," Cal assured him. "Those steers are near fat as ticks on a hound dog. They'll fetch a handsome price from a cow buyer with good sense."

Smoke wasn't ready to agree, not until an offer was made, yet he kept quiet about it.

"Speakin' on the subject of men with or without good sense, I ain't seen that Grimes feller since we got here,"

Pearlie said. "He rode off to the Marshal's office soon as he found out where it was."

"Can't say as I miss him all that much," Cal said. "All he talked about the whole time he was helpin' me ride drag was the button an' fastener business. Can't think of anything I care any less about than buttons or fasteners."

The train was in sight, puffing, pulling a long line of cattle cars with a lone oil lamp on the front of the locomotive, showing the engineer the tracks. Smoke stopped suddenly at the beginning of Main Street, but not because of the train's arrival or anything he could identify. For reasons he couldn't explain, the small hairs on the back of his neck were rising, and it sure as hell wasn't on account of the weather.

11

Smoke drifted off to sleep in a comfortable room at the Drover's Hotel, uneasy for reasons he did not fully understand. And as he slumbered, his dreams were strange, scenes from his boyhood, events that ultimately brought him to where he was now—and the nickname he'd carried with him since he and his father ran across a grizzled old mountain man who simply called himself "Preacher."

Kirby Jensen, at sixteen, found his young mind full of questions his father, Emmett, could not answer. But the old mountain man, Preacher, seemed to understand his curiosity.

It was an odd time to be asking questions, locked as they were in mortal combat in a remote section of northwestern Kansas with a bloodthirsty band of Pawnees, but that did nothing to prevent Kirby from asking Preacher about the Sharps .52-caliber rifle or how to shoot it.

Preacher gave him a terse reply. "Boy, you heeled—so you gonna get in this fight or not?"

"Sir?"

"Heeled! Means you carryin' a gun, so that makes you a man. Ain't you got no rifle 'cept that chunk of scrap iron?"

"No, sir."

"Take your daddy's Sharps, then. You seen him load it, you know how. Take that tin box of tubes, too. You watch out for our backs. Them Pawnees—and they is Pawnees, not Kiowas—is likely to come 'cross that crick. You in wild country, boy. You may as well get bloodied."

"Do it, Kirby," his father said. "And watch yourself. Don't hesitate a second to shoot. Those savages won't show you any mercy, so you do the same."

Kirby, a little pale around the mouth, took up the heavy Sharps and the box of tubes, reloaded the rifle, and made himself as comfortable as possible on the rear slope of the slight incline, overlooking the creek.

"Not there, boy!" Preacher corrected Kirby's position. "Your back is open to the front line of fire. Get behind that tree 'twixt us and you. That way, you won't catch no lead or arrow in the back."

Kirby did as he was told, feeling a bit foolish that he had not thought about his back. Hadn't he read enough dime novels to know that? He chastised himself. Nervous sweat dripped from his forehead as he waited.

And he had to go to the bathroom something awful.

A half hour passed, the only action the always blowing Kansas winds chasing tumbleweeds, the southward-moving waters of the creek, and an occasional slap of a fish on the surface.

"What are they waiting for?" Emmett asked the question without taking his eyes from the ridge.

"For us to get careless," Preacher said. "Don't you fret none . . . they still out there. I been livin' in and round Injuns the better part of fifty year. I know 'em better'n—or at least as good as—any livin' white man. They'll try to wait us out. They got nothin' but time, boys."

"No way we can talk to them?" Emmett asked, and immediately regretted saying it as Preacher laughed.

"Why shore, Emmett," the old mountain man said. "You just stand up, put your hands in the air, and tell 'em you want to palaver some. They'll probably let you speak your piece; they polite about that. A white man can ride right into nearabouts any Injun village. They'll feed you and give you a place to sleep. Course, gettin' out is a problem.

"They ain't like us, Emmett. They don't come close to thinkin' like us. What is fun to them is torture to us. They call it testin' a man's bravery. If'n a man dies good—that is if he don't holler a lot—they make it last as long as possible. Then they'll sing songs about you, praise you for dyin' good. Lots of white folks condemn 'em for that, but it's just they way of life.

"They got all sorts of ways to test a man's bravery an' strength. They might—dependin' on the tribe—strip you, stake you out over a big anthill, then pour honey over you. Then they'll squat back and watch, see how well you die."

Kirby felt sick to his stomach.

"Or they might bury you up to your neck in the ground, slit your eyelids so you can't close 'em, and let the sun blind you. Then, after your eyes is burnt blind, they'll dig you up and turn you loose naked out in the wild . . . trail you for days, seein' how well you die."

Kirby positioned himself better behind the tree and quietly went to the bathroom. If a bean is a bean, the boy thought, what's a pea? A relief.

Preacher just wouldn't shut up about it. "Out in the deserts, now, them Injuns get downright mean with they fun. They'll cut out your eyes, cut off your privates, then slit the tendons in your ankles so's you can't do nothin' but flop around on the sand. They get a big laugh out of that. Or they might hang you upside down over a little fire. The 'Paches like to see hair burn. They a little strange 'bout that.

"Or, if they like you, they might put you through what they call the run of the arrow. I lived through that . . . once. But I was younger. Damned if'n I want to do it again at my age. Want me to tell you 'bout that little game?"

"No!" Emmett said quickly. "I get your point."

"Figured you would. Point is, don't let 'em ever take you alive. Kirby, now, they'd probably keep for work or trade. But that's chancy, he being nearabout a man growed." The mountain man tensed a bit, then said, "Look alive, boy, and stay that way long as you can. Here they come." He winked at Kirby.

"How do you know that, Preacher?" Kirby asked. "I don't see anything."

"Wind just shifted. Smelled 'em. They close, been easin' up through the grass. Get ready."

Kirby wondered how the old man could smell anything over the fumes from his own body.

Emmett, a veteran of four years of continuous war, could not believe an enemy could slip up on him in open daylight. At the sound of Preacher jacking back the hammer of his Henry .44, Emmett shifted his eyes from his perimeter for just a second. When he again looked back at his field of fire, a big, painted-up buck was almost on top of him. Then the open meadow was filled with screaming, charging Indians.

Emmett brought the buck down with a .44 slug through the chest, flinging the Indian backward, the yelling abruptly cut off in his throat.

The air had changed from the peacefulness of summer quiet to a screaming, gunsmoke-filled hell. Preacher looked at Kirby, who was looking at him, his mouth hanging open in shock, fear, and confusion.

"Don't look at me, boy!" Preacher yelled. "Keep them eyes in front of you!"

Kibry swung his gaze to the small creek and the stand of timber that lay behind it. His eyes were beginning to smart from the acrid powder smoke, and his head was aching from the pounding of the Henry .44 and the screaming and yelling. The Sharps he held at the ready was a heavy weapon, and his arms were beginning to ache from the strain.

His head suddenly came up, eyes alert. He had seen movement on the far side of the creek.

"Right there! Yes! he thought. *Someone, or something, was over there!*

I don't want to shoot anyone, the boy thought. *Why can't we be friends with these people?*

And that thought was still throbbing in his brain when a young Indian suddenly sprang from the willows by the creek and lunged into the water, a rifle in his hand, a war cry echoing from his throat.

For what seemed like an eternity, Kirby watched the young brave, a boy about his own age, leap and thrash through the murky water. Kirby jacked back the hammer of the Sharps, sighted in on the brave, and pulled the trigger.

The .52 caliber pounded his shoulder, bruising it, for there wasn't much spare meat on Kirby. When the gun smoke blew away, the young Indian was facedown in the water, his blood staining the stream.

Kirby stared at what he'd done, then fought back waves of sickness.

The boy heard a wild scream and spun around. His father was locked in hand-to-hand combat with two knife-wielding braves.

Too close for the rifle, Kirby clawed his Navy Colt from the leather, vowing he would cut that stupid flap from his holster after this was over.

He shot one brave through the head just as his father buried his Arkansas Toothpick to the hilt in the chest of the other Indian.

And as abruptly as they came, the Indians slipped away,

dragging as many of their dead and wounded with them as they could. Two braves lay dead in front of Preacher; two braves lay dead in the shallow ravine with three others killed in the first attack.

The boy Kirby had shot lay in the creek, arms outstretched, the waters a deep crimson. The body floated slowly downstream as the current carried it away.

Preacher looked at the dead buck in the creek, then at the brave in the wallow with them—the one Kirby had shot. He lifted his eyes to the boy.

"Got your baptism this day, boy," he said. "Did right well, you did."

"Saved my life, son," Emmett said, dumping the bodies of the Indians out of the buffalo wallow. "Can't call you 'boy' no more, I don't reckon. You be a man now, after what you done here today."

A thin finger of smoke lifted from the barrel of the Navy .36 that Kirby held in his hand.

Preacher smiled and spat tobacco juice.

A moment of silence passed, until Preacher spoke as he was looking at Kirby's ash-blond hair. "Yep," he said, taking his own sweet time saying what was on his mind. "Smoke'll suit you just fine."

"Sir?" Kirby finally asked, when he was able to find his voice.

"Smoke," Preacher said again.

Emmett was watching Preacher. "Smoke?" he also asked, as if the word bewildered him.

"Smoke," Preacher drawled for a third time. "That's what I'll call you from now on. Smoke."

Kirby whispered the nickname. "Smoke. Smoke Jensen." He liked the sound of it, and of course he was flattered that the old mountain man thought enough of him to give him a monicker, one that he'd earned by shooting two Pawnees.

Preacher wasn't the sort to show respect for a man unless he'd earned it, and Kirby was only sixteen when Preacher dubbed him with a handle showing bravery in the heat of battle.

"I reckon it suits him," Emmett said, after a moment or two of thought.

"It do for a fact," Preacher remarked. "Judgin' by what the boy showed today, he'll live up to it as time goes by. Some men has got a natural talent with a gun. Seems this boy come to be a man real suddenlike. Be the last time anybody'll call him boy. Like I said, he got his baptism here today. From now on we'll be ridin' with Smoke Jensen, Emmett. He done hisself proud when the chips was down."

Smoke awakened suddenly from a light sleep, turning his gaze to an open hotel window beside the bed, shaking off the memory of that Indian fight with his father and Preacher. That was so long ago, or so it seemed.

He swung his feet off the bed, oddly disturbed by something he couldn't identify. Was it merely the recollection of the dream because it was so vivid? Or was it something else his keen senses detected in the darkness beyond the window?

Smoke went to the windowsill and leaned out, giving the dark outlines of Dodge City a sweeping glance, scenting the wind while he listened to the night sounds.

"Somebody's out there," he told himself quietly. "I can damn near feel it. Or maybe it's like Preacher did that time when he smelled those Pawnees slippin' up on us in the grass."

Yet no matter how carefully he examined the shadows beside every building, the silent streets after the town had gone to bed, he couldn't find anything amiss—nothing he could put a finger on.

Later, he lay back down on the mattress and closed his eyes for a time, still listening to the distant cry of an owl somewhere to the south, the occasional lowing of a cow coming from the cattle pens.

Could be just my imagination, he thought, knowing better. A sixth sense always warned him of danger, and he had that feeling then. No matter how hard he tried he couldn't shake it off or put it to rest.

A slow hour passed, and when he opened his eyes the window was graying with the light of false dawn. It was senseless to lie there, wondering about the odd feeling stirring the hairs at the back of his neck.

Smoke got up and strapped on his pistols, then pulled on his boots. Cradling the Winchester .44 in the crook of an arm, he let himself out into a dark hallway and went quietly down the stairs.

12

Twenty-three-year-old City Marshal Wyatt Earp yawned and stretched when he got out of bed. He'd gotten to bed late after visiting the ruins of Cobbs Trading Post. What he found there was gruesome. Five charred bodies among the remains of the log store, including three children. And when Wyatt got back to send out a burial party early this morning, his deputy told him about the drummer who'd lost his mule to a gang of outlaws too numerous to take lightly, if the report was true. The incident had taken place only a few miles from the trading post.

Probably an exaggeration, he thought, crossing his bachelor quarters behind the jail in his stocking feet to light a lantern, then the potbelly stove so he could boil coffee. Outlaw gangs usually numbered no more than five or ten. Thirty was a ridiculous figure, the result of fear on the part of the drummer. So many men in one bunch would attract too much attention.

He lit the lamp, adjusting its wick to a soft glow, then put kindling in the potbelly and struck a lucifer to it. As soon as he'd blown the flames to life he opened the flue and put water in his coffeepot, then a handful of pan-scorched coffee beans.

Beyond the windowpane of his single room, Dodge City was still dark. And quiet. The tracks of a great many horses had gone south away from Cobbs Trading Post, away from Dodge, he remembered. He'd taken it as a good sign that no trouble was headed this way.

Late the night before, Wyatt had gotten off a telegram to the army about the killings, although he expected little from Fort Larned in the way of action. The army seemed indifferent to all but the most glaring atrocities in Kansas Territory. It was unlikely that the slaying of a storekeeper and his family would be given much attention from the commander at Fort Larned—at best a cursory examination and a meaningless report forwarded to Washington.

Wyatt wondered what he would do if any real trouble came to Dodge. He had two part-time deputies, recently unemployed cowboys who were no great shakes with a gun. Wyatt had his own doubts about facing down a bunch of hardened killers. Most of the troubles in Dodge City came from rowdy cowhands with too much whiskey behind their belts. Senses dimmed by alcohol, they were seldom difficult to control, and most were easily bluffed by Wyatt when he showed his calm exterior, a steely-eyed look and grim determination to settle a dispute or haul a man to jail for the night if he gave too much argument.

He paused at the window again, peering out, when a tall, angular cowboy wearing two pistols and carrying a repeating rifle strode past his office toward the shipping pens.

"He's out early, carryin' enough weapons to fight a war," Wyatt said under his breath. It seemed a strange hour to be on the streets with so many guns.

Simple curiosity got the best of him. He stomped into his boots and strapped on his Colt Peacemaker before shouldering into his coat to walk outside. The stranger was half a block away.

"Hey mister!" Wyatt cried. "Hold up there just a minute!"

Before the first word had left his mouth, the stranger had

begun a rapid turn, one hand close to a pistol. He relaxed when he saw Wyatt standing in front of the marshal's office.

Wyatt started toward him. The man's reactions had been as quick as lightning, and he'd been ready to go for a gun, a sure sign the stranger understood dangerous situations. In the half dark it was hard to see his face until Wyatt walked up to him and halted a few feet away.

"Name's Wyatt Earp. I'm the City Marshal. Just curious as to why you're carryin' so many guns at this hour."

"Smoke Jensen," the big man replied evenly. "I was headed down to check on a herd I brought in yesterday. As to the guns, I rarely go anywhere without 'em. Old habit, I reckon."

Wyatt nodded when he heard the explanation. Jensen was even bigger than he first appeared, looking lean and hard, a tough customer by all outward signs. "It's my job to ask questions now an' then, Mr. Jensen. Like when a stranger comes to town with a good-sized collection of arms. But if you're a cattleman like you say, you'll get my full cooperation. We aim to make sure our peaceful visitors enjoy their stay."

"I'm peaceful," Jensen replied. "Just careful, is all."

Wyatt grinned. "I understand bein' careful. When the big herds come in, a man with a badge don't want to turn his back on anybody."

Jensen understood. "It's a mighty good idea not to turn your back on any stranger . . . 'less you got eyes in the back of yer head."

Wyatt wondered if the stranger might have seen anything at Cobbs Trading Post. "Which way did you come into Dodge?" he asked.

"From the west. Colorado Territory," Jensen replied.

"Did you happen to see a big bunch of riders along any of the trails you took?"

"Hardly a soul, Marshal, 'cept for the drummer who

claimed his mule got stolen. He said somethin' about a sizeable bunch of bad men takin' his mule while he was off hunting. His name was Grimes, best I recall."

Wyatt nodded again. "Grimes filled out a report with one of my deputies. He said a gang of nearly thirty men rode up to his camp an' stole his mule . . . he saw them from a distance an' stayed hid. Then he came upon that burnt-out tradin' post at Cobbs Creek. I rode out there late yesterday to verify the report we got from a muleskinner. Five bodies lyin' in the ashes. A man an' his wife an' three children. I'm sendin' a burial party out this morning. Could be it was the work of that same bunch Grimes reported."

"We didn't see anybody," Jensen said again.

"A gang that big would stick out," Wyatt said. "Be hard as hell to miss 'em, unless that drummer had trouble gettin' the right count. Coulda been 'cause he was scared."

"I didn't question him much on it," Jensen added. "I'm here on business—cattle business. I figured that stolen mule and what he saw at the tradin' post was a job for the law or the cavalry."

"You've got it guessed right," Wyatt agreed, "only I won't get much help from the army. Whoever was responsible is probably headed deep into the Indian Nations by now. It don't seem likely we'll see 'em here in Dodge."

Jensen aimed a glance at the darkened front of the Cattleman's Bank across the street. "If it's outlaws, that many of 'em, a bank full of cattle buyers' money could draw 'em here."

"It's possible," Wyatt said. "We've got two banks in Dodge City, and cattle buyers, along with their money, are beginnin' to arrive on the train."

"I know I'm early," Jensen said, "but I'm from cold country up near the Rockies. Wanted to get my business done and get back to the ranch before the snow flies."

Wyatt turned to head back into the offfice, remembering his coffee. "Enjoy your stay in Dodge, Mr. Jensen. Sorry to have delayed you, but it's a part of my job to be suspicious of any newcomers."

"I understand," Jensen told him, swinging toward the railroad tracks and shipping pens, balancing his rifle in his left hand as he walked off down the street.

Wyatt went back inside, closing the door behind him, left with the distinct impression that Smoke Jensen was a man who could handle himself. Some gents had a way about them, a quiet confidence that was a subtle warning to others who might be inclined to test them.

As he was pouring coffee the front door opened. Jim Bob Watley, one of his deputies, came striding in, wrapped in a green plaid mackinaw.

"Mornin', Wyatt," he said, taking a clean cup from the drainboard. "I just walked past the undertaker's place. Seen Mr. Starnes had five coffins loaded in the back of his wagon, two of 'em real small like you told him. He's takin' Clifford to dig them graves. Had pickaxes an' shovels loaded."

"That's mighty hard ground to dig," Wyatt said, blowing steam from his cup.

Jim Bob poured his own coffee. "Who you reckon coulda done somethin' so awful as that . . . killin' them kids an' all, then get 'em burnt up in a fire?"

"Hard to say, Jim Bob. This territory can be full of men who take what they want by any means available. The tracks went south toward the Nations."

"Then we ain't formin' up no posse to go after 'em?"

"I'm a City Marshal, Jim Bob. That's a job for the army or Federal Marshals. I intend to send a wire to Fort Smith over in Arkansas, to the U.S. Marshal's office there. Trouble is, we got no description of who done it."

"That drummer saw 'em," Jim Bob replied. "He damn sure wants his mule back. But when I asked him if he could identify any of the bunch, he told me he was too far away to see any of their faces."

Wyatt took a sip of scalding coffee. "Probably wouldn't do any good. Like I said, the tracks were headed due south."

"Was there really thirty of 'em?" Jim Bob asked. "I had a hard time makin' myself believe there could be so many."

Wyatt recalled what he'd found on the south side of the creek. "There were plenty of 'em, all right. Maybe not thirty, but a helluva big bunch."

"I'm sure glad they ain't comin' here, Wyatt. Don't know what we'd do if thirty mean-natured men showed up in this town with their minds made up to raise hell."

Wyatt wondered about it. "We'd be badly outgunned, that's for sure."

The front windows of the office brightened as dawn came to eastern skies. Cody Wade, Wyatt's other part-time deputy, walked in as Wyatt was talking to Jim Bob.

"Mornin'," Cody said, his face somewhat ashen in spite of the cold wind. He went over to the stove to warm his hands and get coffee. "Marshal," he said, looking at Wyatt, "I just seen this feller I recognized. He was down at the rail-heads lookin' over a bunch of white-faced cattle."

"Who is he?" Wyatt asked, for it seemed like a number of people were out and about early that morning.

"A gunfighter by the name of Smoke Jensen. A damn killer is what he is. Hails from up in Colorado. It's been ten years since I seen him tangle with a shootist by the name of Sundance. Can't recall no more of Sundance's name."

Wyatt turned to Cody, frowning. "I talked to this Smoke Jensen a half hour ago. He introduced himself and said he was a cattleman."

Cody wagged his head. "Maybe a cattleman is what he's callin' himself now, but back in them days he wasn't nothin' but a hired gun. This Sundance feller, he was supposed to be fast as greased lightnin' with a pistol. Jensen drew on him an' shot off part of his ear . . . before Sundance ever got his gun clear of leather."

"Then Jensen *lied* to me," Wyatt said, his eyelids narrowing as he remembered the stranger, who was wearing two pistols and carrying a rifle.

Cody poured himself a cup of coffee. "All I'm sayin' is, it ain't no good sign that a feller like Smoke Jensen is in Dodge City. We can look for a good-size share of problems if he's of a mind to use them guns of his."

Wyatt put down his cup, glancing over to a gun rack filled with shotguns and rifles near the office door. "Maybe I can talk him out of causin' any trouble," he said, ambling over to the gun rack, taking down a twelve-gauge shotgun, breaking it open to load both tubes.

"Like I said," Cody continued, "that Jensen is meaner'n two mad rattlesnakes. I'd be careful, Marshal, if I was you."

"He didn't seem like he was on the prod," Wyatt answered in a quiet voice, thinking out loud.

"Maybe he ain't. But I figured you'd want to know he was in town."

"I knew he was here . . . I just didn't know who he was or what he was."

"He's a killer, by reputation," Cody assured him. "He ain't no cattleman . . . leastways, he wasn't ten years ago."

"A man can change," Jim Bob offered, sounding like he hoped Wyatt wouldn't ask them to back his move against Jensen.

"An apple don't fall very far from the tree," Wyatt gave as his reply.

Cody seemed perplexed. "Ain't much we can do unless he starts somethin', is there?"

"I can warn him," Wyatt replied, sauntering over to the door with the shotgun aimed at the floor.

Cody looked at Jim Bob, and it was clear that the same thought was in each deputy's mind.

"You want us to go with you?" Cody asked.

Wyatt shook his head. "I can handle it. If he's a cattleman

like he claims to be, there won't be any trouble. But if he's a paid shootist who has his sights on the money in both of our banks, then that's another matter. I recall he *did* make some mention of the bank across the street."

"One man ain't gonna try an' rob the Cattleman's Bank," Jim Bob said. "It'd take at least three or four."

Wyatt opened the door and stepped out into a coming sunrise. "I'll find out if he's got anybody with him," he said, starting off down the boardwalk in front of the office, aiming for the cow pens beside the railyard.

13

Smoke leaned against a corral plank, examining the condition of his steers as the first rays of sunlight beamed above the horizon. The cows' flanks were full. They were in almost perfect, market-ready flesh. Sally had been right about how a Hereford crossed with a longhorn. These were beefy cattle, the type any meat company would want to buy, and despite Smoke's earlier misgivings, they trailed well, covering distance while staying in good shape.

Just thinking about Sally made him lonely, and when he felt it, that emptiness, he chuckled softly to himself. He would not have dreamed of missing a woman in his early years. It was proof of how much he had changed—how much she had changed him.

He heard footsteps behind him. Marshal Earp was coming to the shipping pens, and now he carried a double-barrel shotgun.

Smoke turned away from the fence, wondering why Earp would be headed in his direction.

Earp walked up, the shotgun's barrels aimed at the ground in a way that helped Smoke relax the hand he held near one of his pistols.

"Mr. Jensen," Earp said when he came to a halt a few yards away, "one of my deputies said he recognized you . . . that you're a gunslick—a hired gun."

Smoke didn't like the sound of Earp's voice. "That might've been true of me some years back," he said.

Earp seemed uneasy, his gaze flickering from the pair of Colts around Smoke's waist to the Winchester he held loosely in the palm of one hand. "We don't tolerate any gunplay in Dodge City," the Marshal said.

"I'm not here to use a gun," Smoke answered. "These are my crossbred steers. I'm here to sell 'em, get my money, and ride back to Colorado Territory. Ain't no law against that in Dodge, is there?"

"No, sir, there ain't," Earp replied, "but my deputy said you were a dangerous man. He did make mention of some incident he saw a few years ago . . . maybe he said it was five years, give or take."

"What incident was that, Marshal?"

"I reckon it was a shootout of some kind. Some guy called Sundance. I believe he told me the gent's last name was Morgan, just before I left the office to come down here an' ask you about it."

"I did have a little difficulty with Sundance Morgan. He came after me with a gun. I put a little notch in his ear, just to remind him it was a mistake."

"Then you're sayin' it was self-defense?"

"That's exactly what it was. He brought up this gang of gunnies from the Mexican border, offerin' 'em money to bring me down. Him and his boys weren't particularly good at what they set out to do."

"When we talked earlier," Earp continued, "you made

some mention of the bank. It would be a natural conclusion on my part if I wondered about you takin' a notion to rob it, seein' as you have this mean reputation as a shooter an' all."

Smoke felt he understood the Marshal's concerns. However, he wasn't going to be pushed. "The only thing I'm interested in at that bank is the money a cattle buyer is gonna pay me for these pens full of steers. I've never taken a dime of money that wasn't mine." Smoke took a shallow breath, one eye on Earp's gun hand, and the other on the shotgun. "Your deputy was right to tell you I'd tangled with Sundance, but that was quite a spell in the past. I came to Dodge with steers to sell. I mind my own business these days. Don't stick my nose in another man's troubles, and my guns ain't for hire. I don't rob banks for a livin' and I've never drawn a gun on a man who didn't draw on me first, if it'll put your mind to rest."

Earp appeared to relax some. "I've never been one to hold a man's past against him, Mr. Jensen. I've been in a scrape or two that could have been called a killin', or self-defense. There's times when a man has to do what his gut tells him, or he's liable to wind up dead."

"It was the same with Sundance Morgan," Smoke told him. "It was him an' his boys, or me. I did what I had to do, and the Sheriff at Big Rock in Colorado can verify my side of things. I caused a lot of blood to be shed, but Morgan and his shootists didn't leave me with no selection."

Earp nodded. "I reckon that's good enough for me. It's just that report we had about outlaws and the drummer's stolen mule, on top of the killings at Cobbs Trading Post, that've got me on edge a little. There was a bunch of tracks leadin' south where that family got massacred."

"Grimes told me about it. Grimes told one of my cowboys he saw a man with 'em who wore an old Confederate uniform, and there was some talk that it could have been Bloody Bill Anderson. I've been told Anderson was killed over in Missouri long years back. You know how folks can worry when a rumor starts."

The muscles in Earp's jaw tightened some. "We've had one or two reports come down the wires that Anderson was sighted, only nobody could verify it, and that was a year or two ago. Could be somebody wantin' folks to think it's him. But there was truth to the stories about raids in southeastern Kansas last year. A town got sacked, and more'n a dozen citizens were killed by a gang of misfits. The army looked into it and couldn't find a trace. A handful of survivors swore the leader looked like Bill Anderson, but folks get scared when lead's flyin', and sometimes they can't be all that sure of what they saw."

Smoke knew that eyewitness reports were often unreliable. "I can vouch for that. A man who's scared don't always see what he thinks he sees."

Earp made a half turn to leave. "I'm still curious as to why you're out an' about so early, totin' that rifle. It's like you're expectin' some kind of trouble."

Smoke decided he would confide in the Marshal, even though he had no basis for his worries. "I woke up early with a feelin' in my gut that something wasn't quite right. I've learned to trust that feelin' over the years. Appears it wasn't anything, just my nature to be suspicious when somethin' gnaws on me like it did last night and this morning."

Earp gave Dodge City and its surrounds a passing glance as buildings and the hills beyond brightened with dawn. "Seems real peaceful to me, Mr. Jensen. Hard to ask for a town to be any quieter."

He didn't want to concern Earp, since he really didn't have anything solid to base his vague uneasiness on. "Maybe that was it," he said, giving the hills his own careful examination. "It may be too quiet. I suppose I'm accustomed to noisy towns, and when a town ain't noisy, it don't seem natural."

"Just wait a few weeks," Earp told him, giving a weak grin. "Soon as the big herds start comin' in, you'll get all the noise your ears can stand. After a bunch of cowboys have been on the trail for weeks without seein' a woman or havin' a bottle of whiskey, they get a little carried away when they ride into Dodge an' find plenty of both. A man can't hardly sleep at night for all the music and hell-raisin', but for the most part it's just honest cowhands lettin' off steam."

"To tell the truth, I'm glad I won't be here to see it," he said. "I've gotten used to the peace and quiet up in the High Lonesome."

Earp gave Smoke a curious stare. "You don't sound like a man who used to throw lead for a livin'. If my deputy hadn't recognized you, I'd've never guessed it."

Smoke leaned back against the fence. "Plenty of men've taken the wrong fork in the road, Marshal. 'Specially when they were younger."

The Marshal was still looking at him, sizing him up, or so it seemed. "What was it changed you, if you don't mind me askin' you?"

Smoke grinned. "A woman."

"A woman?" he asked, clearly surprised. "I was expectin' you to say you'd done a little jail time, or maybe had a run-in with the law someplace."

"A woman came along, a real special woman. She's my wife now."

Earp shrugged. "Can't say as I've ever met a woman who'd make much of a change in me," he said.

"I was lucky. I've thought about it plenty. I was headed for an early grave, most likely, until Sally came along. It don't matter how careful a man is when he's in the gunfighter's trade—he's always got a backside."

Earp was grinning again. "Same goes for a man who wears a badge. Some son of a bitch decides to come gunnin' for you, it ain't possible to hide from it for long. Best thing to do is face up to it. You gotta hope you're just a fraction faster with a gun."

Smoke offered his opinion on the subject. "Bein' fast ain't all there is to it, in my estimation."

The Marshal frowned. "It can make the difference between livin' and dyin', if you ask me."

Smoke wagged his head. "Gettin' off the first shot don't amount to much if you can't hit what you're aiming at. If I had to chose between bein' fast and having the best aim, I'll take the latter every time. Course, it helps if you got both speed and accuracy."

"Sounds like you figure you've got both," Earp replied as he shouldered his shotgun for the walk back to his office.

"I get by," was all Smoke said as Earp took off toward the center of town.

He watched the young Marshal walk away with a mixture of impressions. Earp had nerve—it was easy to see that. Most men wouldn't have walked up to Smoke looking for a confrontation as to his gunfighter's reputation—not anyone who knew about his past. But there was also something about the way Earp carried himself that showed he lacked some confidence, as if in his own mind he hadn't been fully tested yet.

Smoke turned back to the cow pens when he heard a man wearing spurs clanking down an alleyway between corrals. He appeared to be checking float valves on water troughs, filled by several windmills on both sides of the shipping pens, that filled a storage tank beside the railroad tracks.

Satisfied that all was as it should have been with the herd, Smoke pushed away from the fence to find a place where he could buy coffee and breakfast.

A gust of wind swept across Dodge as daylight came, and when it did, Smoke paused to look at the southern horizon. A lone horseman sat on a hilltop more than a mile away as though he were watching the town.

"Wonder why he ain't moving," Smoke whispered, unable to make out any detail from such a distance. A rider headed for Dodge wouldn't be sitting still like that, he reasoned.

Smoke stood frozen, watching the horseman for almost half a minute before the rider turned away and rode out of sight.

The feeling returned, stronger than ever, that something was looming beyond the horizon, and he'd just seen possible proof of it. Could the raiders who struck Cobbs Trading Post be setting their sights on a town the size of Dodge?

It could only mean one thing, if this were true; the gang was as big as Grimes said it was, perhaps as many as thirty men. It would take a small army to strike a town of this size with any hopes of shooting their way in and out, exchanging gunfire with armed citizens and lawmen. A handful of men, no matter how well armed or brazen they might be, could never pull it off.

Smoke continued up Main Street when no one else appeared on the hills south of town, wondering if he might be jumping to conclusions. Lengthening his strides to make the hotel so he could wake up Cal and Pearlie, he halted again when he saw Marshal Earp standing on the boardwalk in front of his office, looking south.

Earp spoke to him. "Did you notice that gent way out yonder on the top of a hill, Mr. Jensen?" he asked.

"I did," Smoke replied. "Seemed kinda outa the ordinary to me, that he wasn't headed into town. He sat there for about a minute an' then turned back."

"I was thinkin' the same thing," Earp offered, with his gaze fixed on the hills.

"Could be a lookout," Smoke suggested.

"We're in agreement on the possibility. Just to be on the safe side I'll tell my deputies to load their rifles and side-arms. Don't hurt to be careful."

"I'll have my two wranglers climb outa bed and strap on

their pistols," Smoke said. "They've got Winchesters and plenty of shells."

He noticed that Earp swallowed hard . . . his Adam's apple rose and fell.

"I sure hope we're both wrong about it," Earp said, as he turned for his office door.

"Same goes for me," Smoke agreed, walking on with a bit more haste to reach the hotel.

"Wake up, Pearlie," Smoke said. "Get dressed and check the loads in your pistol and rifle. Then get Cal out of bed and tell him to do the same."

Pearlie sat up in bed quickly, rubbing his eyes. "We got trouble?" he asked.

"Can't say for sure," Smoke answered. "All the same, I intend to be ready if there is any."

14

Bill Anderson addressed his men in the pale gray of dawn as they sat their horses in a swale southeast of Dodge City. Bill could feel his heart pumping. "Pass out the ammunition, Claude, an' make damn sure everybody has extra shells. I want every gun fully loaded. Don't spare no lead when we get to town. Shoot any sumbitch who ain't runnin' for cover. Kill anybody who's got a gun out if he's actin' the least little bit like he's ready to use it."

Claude stepped down from his sorrel and went to a pack-horse to begin passing out cartridges. Solemn-faced men began loading weapons—pistols, shotguns, rifles of every description, depending upon the preferences of the men who used them.

"We'll split into two parties," Bill continued. "Jack's gonna lead the bunch comin' from the north. We'll give him half an hour before ten to get around. Then we ride in slow, like we ain't up to nothin'. Folks won't be none the wiser 'til we get to them banks an' start shootin', most likely. But if some sumbitch yells or makes a fuss, kill him right where he stands.

Jack's gonna take four men in one bank with him while me an' Sonny an' a couple more hit the other bank, the one on the west side of that main street. That'll leave nine or ten men outside to cover us. Jack'll have a packhorse an' that mule to load the money on. We'll have two packhorses. I want Claude leadin' the string of packhorses that comes with us. Dewey's gonna lead the other horse an' the mule. Six men stay with each string of packhorses to guard the rear whilst we're clearin' out of Dodge City. There's gonna be a helluva lot of lead flyin', so stay low in the saddle an' keep your eyes open. We start ridin' into town at ten o'clock so the bank vaults'll be open."

"What about that Marshal?" Sammy asked. "I thought we was gonna stay an' string him up, then set the whole damn town on fire."

Bill gave Sammy a look. "That fire's your job, Sammy, you an' Roy. Find some kerosene an' toss it on some of them walls. Strike a match to it an' then get mounted. The wind blowin' like it is, Dodge is gonna burn plumb to the ground."

Jack thumbed cartridges into his spare pistol and stuck it in his belt before he loaded his sawed-off shotgun. "If we kill enough of 'em real early, the rest are gonna run like rabbits," he said.

"Jack's right," Bill agreed. "Don't show no bashfulness when it comes to the killin' part. I want them streets to turn red with blood."

Lee Wollard, a lantern-jawed man from Mississippi, holstered his Colt .44 and took a lariat rope from his saddle horn. "Me an' Sammy an' Buster can ride up to the law dog's office an' blast him out. I'll put this here rope round his neck, an' we'll drag him to the closest tree to string him up, if we don't have to kill the bastard first. Come to think of it, we'll hang him anyway 'cause he's gonna wind up dead, one way or another."

Some of the men chuckled while they were putting rounds into their weapons.

"I'm puttin' you in charge of the marshal, Lee," Dill said, before he took a swallow of whiskey. "Kill the sumbitch any way you have to, but just make damn sure he's dead."

The click of loading gates on all manner of weaponry filled a moment of silence. Brass-jacketed shells clattered while going into place.

Bill looked at his father's pocketwatch. "It's near seven right now. Pick out the men you want, Jack, an' get headed up to the north. Stay out of sight behind these hills. Don't want 'em to know we're comin' if we can help it. Harley said the town looked real quiet. No train's due 'til noon, if it's on schedule like it has been all week."

Harley Woods urged his horse closer to Bill's. "Hardly no sign of life on them streets. Most of them cow pens is empty, only I did see some real strange-lookin' cattle. White heads, damn near every one, an' the rest of their bodies was solid color or they had stripes on their hides."

Bill opened his Greener shotgun and made sure both ten-gauge tubes were loaded. "We ain't interested in cows, Harley. It's them banks we're after. Who the hell cares what color a damn cow is, anyways?"

"They was just unusual," Harley said quietly, like he wished he hadn't mentioned it.

Bill snapped his shotgun closed, booting it at the front of his saddle in a sleeve that was tied to the cantle. "All right, boys," he said. His Winchester came out of a boot beneath a stirrup leather as he spoke, jacking a cartridge into the firing chamber. "Let's move out."

Jack Starr led fourteen men in a circle, heading back down the swale. The metallic sound of armament, bits, and spurs was the only noise accompanying the whisper of hooves through dry grass as they moved away.

"Pass out the whiskey," Bill said, taking another swallow from the bottle he held in his fist. "Don't want none of you runnin' out of nerve when the shootin' starts."

Claude walked among the mounted men, passing out fresh jugs of whiskey. He paused when he passed Bill's horse.

"You want a new one, Bill?" he asked.

Bill examined the contents of his bottle. "I'm okay for now I reckon. We've got plenty of time. Them banks won't open 'til ten. We gotta make sure we don't kill nobody inside 'til them vaults are open."

Claude moved on, handing bottles up to several more men. He felt confident of his plan to take Dodge by storm, Bill did, and his instincts were seldom wrong. Surprise would be a part of their success that morning, but overwhelming fire-power would be the most important thing. City folk weren't usually inclined to shoot back when they were being shot at.

Homer Suggins swung his dappled gray over to talk to Bill. "One thing would be a help, Bill," he said, his face twisted in thought. "If some of us rode up to the back of them buildings an' got up on the roof where we could shoot down at the street, we'd be able to keep any local heroes from makin' a run fer one of them banks while the men are inside."

"Good idea," Bill said. "You an' Sikes are good shots with a rifle. Take him an' get up on a couple of rooftops. You'll have cover, an' any sumbitch who comes out in the street'll be a sittin' duck."

"Just thought it made good sense, Bill."

"It does for a fact. Soon as you boys see the money is on our packhorses, climb down an' head out to the south. Jack's gonna help cover our escape with heavy doses of lead. You ride down them alleys an' join us quick as you can."

Homer smiled. "It's gonna be like old times again, ain't it? Like when me an' Sikes was with Quantrill when we hit Lawrence. We shot every man an' boy in sight. Them newspapers claimed we killed a hundred an' fifty in Lawrence. If you recall, Frank James was with us then."

I remember," Bill said. "That was before Jesse, when he was just turned seventeen, joined up with us. Jesse an' Frank

James rode with me when we hit Centralia, Missouri, in '64, an' that was when we stopped that Wabash an' Pacific train by puttin' cross ties on the rails."

"I heard you got three thousand dollars off'n that train, afore you gunned down twenty-five Yankee soldiers."

"That's when Jesse James shot the Union commander right off his goddamn horse," Bill said.

"Wasn't no better fights than them two—Lawrence and down at Centralia," Homer agreed.

Bill's face turned hard. "It was that damn Order number eleven that done it," he said.

"We burned more houses an' barns in this Territory an' Missouri when we come across Yankee sympathizers than any other outfit. Damn proud of it, too. If it hadn't been for Bobby Lee givin' up so quick, we'd've won that war a piece at a time."

"You ever hear from Jesse or Frank?" Homer asked.

Bill wagged his head. "They both think I'm dead. They shot the wrong man over in Missouri, them Yankees did, an' somebody did me a favor."

"A favor?"

"They claimed it was me. Somebody said he was positive it was me they killed. I owe that feller."

"Jesse an' Frank an' them Younger boys have sure made a name for themselves."

"We're liable to do the same thing," Bill promised, "after we pull off this robbery in Dodge. It's gonna be in all the newspapers."

" 'Specially if we hang that Marshal," Homer said, with an eye to the north where Dodge lay just beyond a string of low hills. "They'll sure as hell talk 'bout that, the way they's talkin' 'bout Jesse an' Frank an' Cole."

"We're fixin' to make news," Bill said, taking a swallow of whiskey. "It's time we quit hidin' from them blue belly sons of bitches."

Homer scowled a little. "They'll come after us hard, Bill. We ain't got enough men or guns to hold 'em off like we done in the old days."

Bill thought about it. "We'll hire us some gunmen from down in Mexico with part of this bank loot, Homer. With money, we can buy the best gunmen there is, south of the border, if we make the right offer."

"I never did trust Meskins much."

Bill shrugged. "Don't have to trust 'em. Pay 'em good wages an' kill the sons of bitches who don't take orders from me like they should."

Homer's scowl softened. "Down in Lawrence we couldn't miss with a bullet, Bill. There was folks all over the place, runnin' like hell in every direction. All a man had to do was shoot in the general direction an' somebody'd go down. I still remember it like it was yesterday. Seemed like we killed more'n a hundred an' fifty. Maybe them newshounds can't count all that good."

"We're gonna have us some more of them good times," Bill said. "Startin' in about two hours . . ."

Homer lowered his voice. "We've got a few with us who ain't so good with a gun, Bill, an' some of 'em don't have much in the way of backbone." He said it quietly, after making sure no one was listening.

Bill glanced over his shoulder. "Some men get more backbone when they've got a bellyful of whiskey. That's why I had Claude pass them bottles around."

"Maybe, then, they can't shoot straight?" Homer wondered aloud as he took a drink of whiskey himself.

Bill gave Homer the eye. "What the hell difference does it make if we lose a few? Some of these farm boys ain't worth the gunpowder it'd take to kill 'em. Like Tom the other night—a goddamn crybaby. I was glad to be rid of him."

"I can hardly wait for the shootin' to start," Homer said with a wistful expression glazing his eyes. "I can hear them city folks screamin' right now, when they see us ride off with their money."

"It's gonna be easy," Bill said. "We ride in shootin' every sumbitch in sight. Jump down an' clean out them safes. Then we ride like hell for the Nations."

"The army's gonna follow us."

Bill's mouth drew tight across his teeth. "Let 'em come. I got a plan for that, too."

"What sorta plan, Bill?"

"You'll see, when the time comes. There's this place down in Choctaw country, a real narrow canyon."

Homer grinned. "We'll get up on the rim an' shoot 'em down like caged turkeys. Right?"

"They'll follow our tracks, an' we'll make 'em real plain so they can't miss us. We can settle a few scores for the stars an' bars, even if the damn war is over."

"Sounds like a good plan to me."

Homer had been with Bill since the war, and he trusted him in tight spots. "You keep one eye on Jack Starr," he said, keeping his voice low.

"Why's that, Bill?" Homer asked.

"It's simple enough. We're gonna have us four horses loaded with Union money. There's lots of men who'd shoot a man in the back for that much loot. Jack was born natural mean. He can't be trusted plumb to the core when there's too much hard money at stake."

"He ain't never showed no sign of bein' a snake. . . ."

"That's on account of us not havin' enough to be worth takin' the chance. All that's about to change."

"You figure he'd shoot you in the back? Honest?"

"He might. You keep an eye on him after we pull this job. Be ready to kill him if'n he so much as touches his gun when he's around me or that money."

Homer let a bubbling swallow of whiskey slide down his

throat. Then he sighed, sleeving his lips dry. "I'll kill him if'n he does, Bill. You can count on it."

"I knowed I could trust you, Homer. You been sidin' with me since the war. Ain't many in this outfit I'd say the same thing about."

Homer looked around them before he said any more. "There might be more'n one who'd get greedy," he said. "I never did trust Dewey or Roy all that much."

"When there's a pile of money involved, not many men can be trusted. You remember that, Homer."

15

Crawford Long, a dapper man in a business suit and silk vest, introduced himself to Smoke at nine o'clock sharp down at the shipping yards while Pearlie and Cal kept an uneasy watch in all directions from a top rail of a corral fence, rifles resting on their laps.

"Pleased to meet you, Jensen," Long said, passing his eye over Smoke's offering of steers after they shook hands. "These are top-notch cattle. I come to Dodge City early every year to get my pick of what comes in. I'm with Chicago Beef Company, and I can assure you I'll pay top prices for your steers."

"How much might that be?" Smoke asked, his rifle leaning against a corral post within easy reach, just in case the trouble he sensed early that morning, after seeing the lone rider turn away from the horizon, actually arrived.

Long, in his fifties with a paunch straining the buttons on his vest, screwed his face into a frown. "An ordinary longhorn in good flesh fetches eight or nine dollars a head. I'll double that for this bunch. How many have you got?"

"Three hundred and seven," Smoke answered. "That's what's in the railyard tally book."

"I'll stick my neck out an' pay eighteen dollars apiece," Long offered.

"I'm holding out for twenty, but I appreciate your offer," Smoke told him. "I'll show them to a couple more buyers, and if your offer is tops, then I'll sell to you. On the way down here I was guessing they'd bring twenty-five a head. It's choice beef, and any experienced cattleman can see that. Not much waste on a carcass."

Long chewed his fleshy bottom lip a moment. "I'll pay the twenty, then. That comes to six thousand one hundred and eighty dollars, by my calculations."

Smoke quickly did the numbers in his head. "Sounds right to me, Mr. Long."

Long turned away from the fence. "Then we'll shake hands on it an' our bargain is sealed. As soon as the Cattleman's Bank opens we'll go draw your money. I'll write out a bill of sale while we're at the bank. Sheldon Herring, the bank president, is a friend of mine. We can use his office to finish our business. I come here every year since the rail spur was built. I'll start arranging for cattle cars right away. I'd like to get these cows to Chicago as quickly as I can."

Smoke shook with Long, thinking how pleased Sally would be when she heard the news. Their Hereford crosses had more than doubled their income from beef production over previous years. "It's done, then," Smoke said. "We've got a deal at twenty per head."

"It's a pleasure doing business with you, Jensen," Long said with a smile. "I'll meet you in front of the bank at ten. In the meantime I'll check with the yard foreman to get cars ready for the three o'clock train back east. The locomotive gets here at noon, usually. Then it takes time to make that turnaround and fill the boiler. After you pocket your money, the yard foreman can start pulling empty cattle cars to the loading chutes with teams of mules. See you at the bank, Jensen."

Crawford Long hurried off, his head bent into the wind to keep from losing his bowler hat.

When Long was out of earshot, Pearlie said, "That's one fine price fer a batch of steers, boss." He squinted in the sun's early glare, watching the hills a moment. "It sure don't appear them owl-hoots are gonna show up in Dodge today. Maybe that feller you saw was just some drifter. . . ."

"The day ain't over yet, Pearlie," Smoke said. "I've still got this funny feelin' down the back of my neck."

Smoke ran across Marshal Earp and his two deputies on Main Street—the three lawmen were walking around Dodge carrying shotguns, and one deputy had a Winchester rifle. Smoke left Cal and Pearlie to watch the herd.

Earp spoke to Smoke first. "No sign of any strangers or anything unusual goin' on. Seems real quiet."

"It does for a fact," Smoke agreed.

"Did you get your cattle sold?" Earp asked.

Smoke nodded. "Made a deal with Crawford Long from the Chicago Beef Company just now. Soon as the bank opens I'll draw my money and we'll be headed back home."

Earp gave his deputies a sideways glance. "Just to be on the safe side, I'm puttin' a deputy at the front door of both banks armed with shotguns and pistols, while I keep movin' around with an eye out for strangers."

"Good idea," Smoke said, although he felt sure that experienced bank robbers would make short work of two deputies standing out in plain sight, making easy targets. "My men are down at the cow pens keeping an eye on things until my business with Long is finished."

"Can your cowboys shoot?" Earp asked.

"I was about to ask you the same thing about these two deputies," Smoke replied.

Earp seemed a little embarrassed. "I'd say they're fair hands with a gun."

Smoke wasn't all that impressed with the looks of either one, and yet he kept his opinion to himself. As he was about to leave the Marshal, he happened to spot a pair of cowboys riding along the railroad tracks, coming from the east, still almost a mile away. "Here comes a pair of newcomers," he said. "Maybe they're just passin' through, but it wouldn't hurt to keep one eye on 'em until we know what they're up to."

"We get saddle tramps passin' through all the time," Earp said, "and there ain't but two. No sign of that big bunch the drummer told us about."

Smoke slitted his eyes to keep out the sun, still watching the pair. "They might come in quiet, in twos an' threes. It'll pay to watch 'em."

"You've got a suspicious nature, Mr. Jensen."

Smoke nodded. "It's what has kept me alive all these years, Marshal."

He strode off down a side street, a knot forming in his gut, telling him something was about to go wrong.

At a corner where he had a view of open land to the east, he stopped long enough to watch the two riders approaching Dodge by following the rails.

"Unusual," he said to himself, his voice lost on a gust of wind.

Playing a hunch, he walked back a dozen paces and slipped into an alley running between rows of buildings in the business district. As it was early, shadows offered him a place to stay out of sight.

Pausing near the back wall of a harness shop, he rested against the boards, waiting, holding his rifle down beside his leg.

A quarter hour later one of the cowboys he'd seen reined his horse into the alleyway. He stopped his mount, gave a look toward the rooftop above his head, and drew a rifle, stepping to the ground, tying off his brown gelding to a rain gutter. The stranger looked both ways up and down the alley; then he pushed an empty flour barrel against the building and began climbing up on the roof.

He's going to cover the street, Smoke thought, *while the bank is being robbed.*

There wasn't time to alert Pearlie or Cal or Marshal Earp to what was going on. . . .

Hatless so as not to show himself, a rawboned cowboy lay on his belly peering over the false front of a dry-goods store with a view of Main Street. Smoke crept up behind him on the balls of his feet, pulling his gleaming Arkansas Toothpick from a sheath inside his right boot. The cowboy's rifle lay beside him, next to his battered Stetson.

"Nice view, ain't it?" Smoke whispered, when he was a yard or two away.

A square-jawed man whirled around, clawing for a pistol he had buckled to his waist, his eyes rounded with surprise.

A ten-inch blade sliced into Clifton Sikes' chest, snapping cartilage and bone. His mouth flew open to cry out in pain when a huge hand covered his face, smothering his shout.

Sikes arched his back, trembling, his gun hand clamped around the butt of a Walker Colt .44. Blood squirted from the knife blade when Smoke pushed it all the way to the hilt into the gunman's ribs.

"Stings a little, don't it?" Smoke asked, a mirthless grin twisting the corners of his mouth, his palm still covering the man's quivering lips, silencing the sound bubbling in his throat.

The gunman's eyelids batted, then closed. His body relaxed on the rooftop. Blood pooled around him as Smoke took out his knife, leaving a gaping wound over Sikes's heart.

"One more," Smoke said, ducked down behind the false front of the store, wiping blood off the blade before inching backward to climb down to the alley.

He broke into a run when his feet touched ground, heading for the side street where he had left his rifle hidden behind a barrel of trash. Smoke rounded the corner at a dead run, aiming for Main Street.

He saw Marshal Earp standing next to a hitch rail with his face turned northward. "Marshal!" he cried, running as hard as he could, rifle in one hand, bloody knife in the other.

Earp wheeled at the sound of his name. He saw Smoke coming toward him.

"What the hell? . . . Where'd you get all that blood on your sleeve?" Earp asked, eyeing the knife.

Smoke raced over to him, slightly out of breath. "One of those strangers we saw followin' the tracks into Dodge climbed up on that roof yonder with a rifle. He was gonna cover this street while the bank's bein' robbed."

Earp tensed, pointing to the hills north of town. "I see a dust cloud comin'. Takes plenty of horses to kick up so much dust."

"They're comin' for the bank, whoever it is," Smoke warned as he sheathed his bowie. "There's one more of 'em somewhere on a rooftop. I killed the first one I found. Tell your deputies to get to cover—and you'd better do the same!"

Earp appeared frozen momentarily. He looked across the road at the bank. "The Cattleman's just opened. I'd better warn them to close the safe an' get to a safe place."

Smoke gave the dust sign a closer look. "If it's as many as old man Grimes said there was, no place is gonna be safe, Marshal. Tell 'em to lay down on the floor behind somethin' while I find that other owl-hoot who's gonna cover the street from a roof somewheres."

"Son of a bitch," Earp sighed, his face gone white. "Here it is, a goddamn bank robbery in Dodge, an' I've got just two green deputies."

Smoke turned away, sighting along the rooflines of stores and shops on Main. "I'll help all I can, Marshal," he said over his shoulder as he broke into a run, turning down another side street to reach an alley across from the smaller Dodge City Savings Bank farther down the road.

Homer Suggins took a drink of whiskey and set the bottle down beside him, removing his sweat-stained Confederate cavalry hat to peek over the wood front of Martha's Eatery. He'd been very careful crossing the roof, so as not to make noise that would alert anyone inside. He put his Henry repeating rifle by his side, rising up on his elbows to see what was happening on the street below.

He saw a sign reading, "The Dodge City Savings Bank" and quickly lowered his head. He had a perfect view of the front, which would allow him to kill anyone who challenged Jack Starr or any of his men when they went inside for the robbery—and of far more importance, to cover them when they came out.

Homer felt a strange tingling of excitement in his chest, like he did back when William Clark Quantrill signaled that a raid was about to begin. That was so many years ago, and he'd missed the feeling, the rattle of guns, the screams of wounded and dying men all around him. Bill Anderson was too cautious, staying far from any chance of a real showdown. This raid on Dodge was more like it.

He thought he heard the whisper of feet behind him, although he knew it wasn't possible—hell, he was hidden up on a roof, and no one had seen him climb up that pile of wooden crates at a back corner.

Homer glanced over his shoulder, merely to satisfy himself that it was his imagination.

What he saw made his blood run cold. A towering giant of a man loomed above him, a bloody Arkansas Toothpick in one hand and a pistol in the other.

"Let me guess," the tall stranger said, his voice like a horseshoer's rasp across an anvil, grating. "You came up here with that rifle to go bird huntin'. I've heard it's a good time of year for whitewing doves."

Homer's heart stopped beating altogether for a moment or two, as he heard the deadly tone behind the wisecrack this big man had just made.

"I . . . I was gonna fix a leak in this roof," Homer explained with his voice breaking. "Honest, I was. . . ."

In a blinding movement the stranger's blade penetrated Homer's belly. White-hot pain raced through his chest and abdomen when the blade twisted. Something popped inside him, and it hurt like hell.

"I never met a man who fixed leaky roofs with a rifle an' a bottle of whiskey," the same voice said, as Homer felt himself slipping into a black void. The stranger's shape was fuzzy, indistinct.

His eyes closed. Then Homer Suggins began the long sleep.

16

Smoke saw dust rise above hills south of Dodge as he wiped blood off his Toothpick on the dead man's pants leg. "Comin' from two directions," he muttered, wheeling in a crouch to hurry back across the rooftop and to climb down to the alley. He needed to warn Marshal Earp and to have him clear the streets. Otherwise any number of innocent citizens could have been killed.

He dropped to the ground and took off in a run, rounding a corner where he spied Earp on Main Street, positioning Deputy Cody Wade in front of the Dodge City Savings Bank.

"Get everybody inside!" Smoke yelled, causing Earp to swing around suddenly. "Another bunch is comin' from the south!"

Earp looked southward as Smoke ran up to him.

"Son of a bitch!" Earp exclaimed. "Two bunches!" He turned to Deputy Wade. "You an' Jim Bob start yellin' for everybody to take cover inside some place. I'll tell both bankers to close their safes an' get to cover. This is gonna be a war,

Cody, an' I want you an' Jim Bob inside one of these build-ings so you don't get shot all to pieces!"

"I'll go fetch my men," Smoke said, breaking into a run for the cow pens. He cried over his shoulder, "We'll get up on the rooftops like they aimed to do and shoot down at 'em!"

He didn't wait for Earp's reply, running hard until he sighted Pearlie and Cal at a corral fence. Both men were looking at the dust rising from hills south of town.

"Bring your rifles!" Smoke bellowed, waving them away from the rail yard. "Hurry it up! Trouble's comin'!"

Cal and Pearlie took off in awkward runs with Winches-ters clamped in their fists. Cal was the first to reach Smoke.

"Is it that big gang Grimes told us about?" Cal asked, out of breath from his sprint.

"Looks like it. You boys get extra boxes of shells from our gear and climb up on one of them roofs with a false front, so you'll have some protection from a bullet. I'll get on that roof across from the savings bank. The minute any shooting starts, be damn sure you aim for a bank robber. Don't take no chances if you can't be sure your target is one of 'em."

"Lordy," Pearlie said, glancing over his shoulder. "I knew this wasn't gonna be no peaceful trip. . . ."

"So did I," Cal added, swallowing hard, "right after that bay throwed me off."

"Get going!" Smoke commanded. "Bring me some spare shells an' we'll pick out the best places where you can shoot."

As Pearlie and Cal took off for the hotel, Smoke saw Crawford Long heading into the Cattleman's Bank. He shouted across the road at the cattle buyer. "Find some cover, Mr. Long! Me an' the marshal think there's a gang of bank robbers headed this way. Stay out of sight 'til it's over. We'll conduct our cow business soon as we can settle this."

Long's face went slack. "Right!" he cried, making a fast

turn away from the bank, hurrying as quickly as his chubby legs could move down the boardwalk, entering a smaller hotel named the Palace, with his coattails fluttering in the breeze.

Now Deputies Wade and Watley were shouting to everyone to get off the streets. Women and children and men of every description made dashes for doorways on either side of Main Street.

Cal burst out of the hotel cradling extra boxes of cartridges against his chest. All of their Winchesters were .44s, and the same shells fit the cylinders of the pistols they carried.

Smoke took a box of shells as Marshal Earp trotted up with his shotgun. Pearlie came clumping out of the Drover's Hotel as Smoke was speaking to the others.

"I'll get back up on the roof of Martha's Eatery," he said, "on account of it gives me the best view of the Dodge City Bank. I want you an' Pearlie across the road an' get up where you can cover the front of the Cattleman's. An' watch your backsides when the shootin' starts, so nobody can slip up behind you. We'll have 'em caught in a cross fire when they ride into town. If they don't know we're ready for 'em, maybe we can drop a good-sized handful before they get the wiser."

"What about our steers, boss?" Pearlie asked, pushing brass cartridges into the loading gate of his rifle until the tube was full, jacking one into the firing chamber.

"They ain't after cows, Pearlie. They've come for the money we aimed to get for our herd, an' every cent that's in them bank vaults besides. We ain't gonna let 'em just ride in an' take the profit out of a year's worth of ranching at Sugarloaf. Soon as the first shot gets fired, start killin' outlaws . . . only remember to stay down so you don't wind up dead or wounded."

Pearlie and Cal hurried across the street as the dust to the north and south grew thicker, moving closer rapidly. In minutes the gangs would be in sight.

Marshal Earp spoke. "I'll take up a position inside my office, along with Cody, so we'll have a good view of the street in both directions. I told Jim Bob to hide behind that brick wall next to the blacksmith's shop. He's got plenty of ammunition, an' he don't have to be all that good a shot, usin' a double scattergun."

Smoke nodded, preparing to run back to the alleyway to get on the roof of the cafe. "Just keep your heads down. I'll get as many as I can, maybe move around a bit if they find cover in town instead of pullin' out."

Earp gave him a weak grin. "I sure hope you're as good with a gun as Jim Bob said you was, Mr. Jensen. We're gonna need all the help we can get."

Smoke took off without a word, his mind focused on what was to come. A battle was about to be waged in the streets of Dodge City, if he was any judge of such matters. He could feel it coming as he ran into the alley to make the climb to the roof of Martha's Eatery.

He found the dead outlaw just where he had left him, a few feet behind the false front of the building. Blood encircled the corpse and already the blowflies were feeding on it, buzzing over the body in swirling black clouds.

Ignoring the green-backed flies, Smoke took off his hat and rested against the wooden front of the building, only his eyes visible above the boards where a sign was painted, with the words: "The Best Grub in Dodge."

Now there was nothing to do but wait, and see what kind of move the bank robbers made when they hit town. It would depend on how experienced they were, how much savvy they had.

In the back of his mind he wondered if this bunch could be led by Bloody Bill Anderson. Louis had been so sure of the report that Anderson had been killed in Missouri many years ago, not long after the war was over. But Smoke found himself with a nagging feeling of doubt, until he decided it really did not matter either way. He'd been up against men with tall reputations before, and most of them had turned out to be ordinary men who died just as quickly as nameless gents with guns. The trick was to be first with a bullet in a critical spot, something Smoke had learned before he was old enough to shave—he'd had one hell of a good teacher, a withered old mountain man who understood the business of living and dying better than anyone he'd ever known.

He thought of his promise to Sally the day they left the ranch with the herd—to swing wide of trouble whenever he was able. She'd understand this sudden turn of events, he told himself. How could he have known a gang of bank robbers had planned to strike Dodge City at the same time they arrived to sell their steers? It was the luck of the draw, a coincidence.

Peering above the boards, he could see riders now, more than a dozen heading for Dodge at an easy trot from the north. To the south, where more hills stretched to the horizon, all he could see was dust, thickening, like storm clouds moving over Kansas prairies.

Brushing blowflies away from his face, he studied the men riding toward town. By being watchful, paying attention to things out of the ordinary, he'd been able to kill two of them before the robbery attempt had begun. Like so many parts of his nature that were regular habits, he'd learned this watchfulness from Preacher.

As Smoke gazed south, a line of horsemen appeared below the dust, maybe fourteen or fifteen men, spread out in a ragged line. It was plain that these riders were after something, splitting into two groups, arriving at the same time.

Keeping his rifle barrel hidden behind the planks so that sunlight wouldn't reflect off it, giving him away, he settled in to see what would happen next.

Sounds from the street below quieted as everyone in the business district of Dodge hid behind closed doors. And in the silence, Smoke could hear the distant drum of hoofbeats coming closer to town.

"There's gonna be a lot of blood spilled here," Smoke said under his breath, sure of it. A gang of this size would not be easily discouraged.

The most important factor in evening the odds against them would be to wait until all the robbers were in range. If anyone fired a shot too early, the raiders would be warned and their plans might change. If they spread out across the town, killing and looting, Smoke and his cowboys and Earp and his deputies would stand little chance of thinning the outlaws' ranks.

"Here they come!" someone cried from down Main Street. It sounded like Deputy Watley. The deputy was too green to know how to win a fight like this.

Smoke took a chance, raising his head slightly above the top of the roof. "Stay quiet!" he yelled as loudly as he could. "We don't want 'em to know we're ready!"

As the sound of his voice faded away, an eerie silence came to Dodge. Only the constant buzzing of the flies hovering over the corpse behind Smoke reached his ears, save for the distant rumble of approaching horses.

Hidden in the shadow that was cast by the false front of Martha's Eatery, he could lean away from the boards to get a view of the riders coming from the south. When he slitted his eyes to dim the sun's glare, he saw a man riding at the front, wearing an old Confederate cavalry officer's hat and a gray tunic.

"Maybe it's some gent tryin' to make folks think he's Bill Anderson," Smoke said to himself. "Damn near every Southern soldier's got parts of an old Rebel uniform."

And Smoke could also make out the rifles and shotguns these men were carrying, evidence they were headed into Dodge without a peaceful purpose.

"It won't be long now," he whispered, as a change came over him. It was always like this before he engaged in a fight—the tingling down his arms, his tongue going dry, the slight increase in the beat of his heart when his muscles tensed, ready to do battle with an enemy.

The horseman in the gray hat and tunic was clearer now, at a distance of less than a quarter mile. He rode with a stiff spine, in soldier fashion.

"Maybe it is Bloody Bill," he whispered. "It don't make a damn bit of difference to me who he is. . . ."

The gang picked up speed, urging their horses to a lope as they neared the outskirts of town. Smoke raised his Winchester to his shoulder, keeping the muzzle low, out of sight.

"Welcome to Dodge, Mister Bloody Bill Anderson, or whoever the hell you are," he hissed, clamping his teeth, cords of hard muscle standing out in his neck. "We've got a little surprise waitin' for you."

The men rode past small houses and shacks at the edge of the business district. The raiders coming from the north were entering the other side of town—Smoke could hear their horses pounding hard ground with shod hooves.

Only a minute or two more, Smoke thought, drawing back out of sight behind the planks.

Suddenly, the roar of a shotgun blasted from the far side of Main Street, probably an edgy deputy of Earp's who couldn't wait for the right moment.

"Damn!" Smoke snapped, his hands gripping the stock of his Winchester. Someone had given their ambush away to the gang of highwaymen, too soon to give them the benefit of the element of surprise.

As Smoke rose up to join the fight, a deafening series of gunshots filled Main Street, thundering off buildings lining the roadway. Guns began cracking and popping from so many directions, it was impossible to tell who was doing the shooting, although it was clear the shots came from the street and buildings on both sides.

A horse screamed when shotgun pellets riddled its hide. A sorrel fell over in front of the Dodge City Savings Bank, pinning its rider's left leg.

Smoke found a target, a man on a rearing horse with a rifle in his hands. Aiming quickly, Smoke fired a .44-caliber slug into the man's ribs, sending him toppling from the saddle.

A brass cartridge case tinkled hollowly near his feet when he worked the Winchester's lever . . . he scarcely noticed it in the melee.

A scattergun exploded from a window of the Marshal's office, sending another raider plunging off his horse with his face a red mass of pulpy tissue and blood.

Smoke heard a rifle crack from a rooftop across the street, where Pearlie was making his stand. A gunman with a flop-brim hat let out a yell and rolled backward off the rump of his steed.

The fight was on. Smoke fired at a slender rider aboard a pinto gelding. The man disappeared into a cloud of dust churned up by so many horses' hooves.

17

A storekeeper ran out on the porch in front of Burns Hat & Boot Shop, shouldering a long-barrel goose gun, taking aim at the first riders to come up Main from the south. Just when he had his feet planted and was ready to fire, a woman's voice shrieked, "No, Henry! Come back inside!"

The concussion of a shotgun blast bellowed from a gun in the hands of a raider on the back of a galloping, black stud. Smoke was too far away to return fire accurately and he didn't want to give his position away yet, not until he had plenty of targets he knew he could fell.

Henry Burns was torn from his feet, his shopkeeper's apron shredded by shotgun pellets, bloodied when a full charge struck him in the chest and face. His goose gun flew from his hands as he toppled off the porch, clutching his belly, landing in the dirt on his side, screaming in pain, his feet kicking helplessly while he thrashed about at the edge of the road.

"Damn," Smoke whispered, wondering why anyone would run out to face a gang as large as this, armed only with a hunting gun. Some would call it courage—Smoke classed it as stupidity when the odds were so long.

Suddenly the leader of the raiders spurred his horse into a full-tilt charge, headed for the front of the Cattleman's Bank at top speed, his men spurring their mounts behind him. One of the raiders fired a sawed-off shotgun into a storefront window, and the sounds of shattering glass accompanied the thunder of hooves echoing off buildings lining the road. Inside the Ladies Fine Dress Shop, a woman wailed at the top of her lungs when glass fragments and a pair of dress dummies were blown into the interior of the building. In another part of town a child began to cry incessantly, frightened by the explosions.

Smoke raised his head and shoulders above the false front of the cafe, aiming for the leader of the bunch aboard a racing sorrel gelding. His sights came to rest on the center of the man's gray Confederate tunic when fate took a hand. The sorrel stumbled, then quickly regained its footing just as a raider on a chestnut moved between the leader and Smoke. Too late, Smoke triggered off a reflexive shot, feeling the Winchester's stock slam into his shoulder.

A bearded bandit atop the chestnut jolted when Smoke's slug passed through him. He teetered dangerously in the saddle and then fell off to one side, where he was trampled by running horses behind him, his limp body twisting and turning every time a flying hoof struck him.

Smoke levered another round into the chamber as rapidly as he could, but the raiders had him pinpointed. Pistols and rifles fired up at the roof of Martha's place, forcing Smoke to duck for cover.

Splintering boards and the crack of dry wood announced the impact of a dozen bullets meant for him. The element of surprise was gone for Smoke and the others trying to defend the town and its banks. Things would quickly settle into a game of hide-and-seek, with death as a reward for the loser.

Moving on his haunches, he crept to another spot on the roof as guns opened up across the road, the unmistakable bang of a .44-caliber rifle amid the roar of several shotguns. Answering fire came from the street until the air was filled with the noise made by dozens of pounding guns—the whine of lead passing overhead was hard to hear above the sounds of exploding gunpowder.

From the north, pistols chattered and rifles popped when the second group of robbers hit town. Now and then a stray bullet would strike the storefront where Smoke was hidden, some glancing off, others becoming embedded in sun-warped planking. Smoke was too wary to rise up again until the time was right—he'd have been a fool to have made a target of himself again. The time would soon come when the fully loaded guns in the raiders' hands were empty. Then Smoke could make each shot count from his perch above the cafe.

A shotgun thundered close by. A window just beneath Smoke was blasted to pieces, bits of glass tinkling to the boardwalk below like tiny musical chimes.

"Son of a bitch!" a muffled voice cried from somewhere in the cafe; then the sounds of scurrying feet moved toward the back of the place.

A lessening in the booming gunfire brought Smoke's head up just in time to see Marshal Earp's deputy, Jim Bob Watley, rise above his hiding place behind the brick wall at the blacksmith's shop to aim his shotgun. He fired point-blank into the side of a running horse, knocking the animal off its feet, sending it crashing down on its side, legs flailing, kicking up dust while its rider raced for cover with a rifle in his hands. But before the robber could make the corner of the telegraph office, a pop came from Pearlie's rifle on a rooftop. The outlaw staggered, trying to keep his balance and run at the same time, until he sank to his knees with blood pumping from the front of his shirt. He dropped his rifle to clutch his wound in a feeble effort to stem the flow of blood.

Smoke came up quickly, turning his Winchester on a man in a stained leather vest, leading a pair of packhorses. Smoke fired at precisely the right moment, when his gun sights were steady. The cowboy flew forward over the pommel of his saddle, diving headfirst toward the ground with a pistol still clamped in his fist. His gun went off when his skull landed in a dry wagon rut, the bullet plowing a furrow in the dirt near him. He collapsed in a heap with his head twisted at an odd angle after he fell, lying still.

Smoke ducked just in time to escape a hail of bullets coming from the street when some of the raiders heard his gun. The pop and crack of lead riddled the boards above Smoke's head for a time, until more gunfire from another rooftop took their attention away.

Smashing glass at the front of the Dodge City Savings Bank forced Smoke to peek over the planks again. Three robbers were down off their horses, shooting out the bank's front windows with shotguns. Women were screaming inside the building; then a man cried out in agony a split second after another shotgun blast.

Smoke watched the outlaws rush in, climbing over a brick ledge that had once supported big panes of glass. He couldn't see what was going on inside, or hear any more voices when a lull in the shooting abruptly ended.

"They're inside," he growled angrily. "They'll kill everyone in the bank, or take some as hostages. . . ."

Marshal Earp fired sporadically from a broken window of his office, wounding another horse when he downed a raider with the shotgun. Two wounded, dying horses lay in the street. Smoke counted the bodies of five bank robbers sprawled in the dust and dirt. One wounded outlaw was crawling toward safety behind a water trough, leaving a trail of red in his wake.

The leader of the gang was nowhere in sight. Guns thundered in front of the Cattleman's Bank as more robbers tried to shoot their way in.

He heard Cal open up with his rifle, firing five shots in quick succession down into the street. Tiny wisps of gunsmoke lifted from the boy's firing position.

He finally found his nerve, Smoke thought with no rancor. A boy like Cal had never been in the midst of a war like the one going on in Dodge City then.

Smoke backed away from the edge of the roof to move again, to the far side of the cafe in order to keep the gunmen who were in the road guessing where he was. Inching across the roof, he could not help thinking about what must be going on inside the Dodge City Savings Bank, where hapless citizens of the town had made the mistake of doing their banking business that morning. Smoke was sure that members of the gang would be smart enough to take hostages, probably women, believing that no one would take a shot at them if the women were used as human shields.

He came to the corner and glanced over his breastwork of planks to see what was going on. Gunfire rattled and boomed up and down Main Street with no signs of lessening.

We're badly outgunned, he thought, spotting loose horses trailing their reins and galloping in every direction. Some of the raiders were on foot, making them easier to stalk—easier to kill when he came down off the roof to go after them one or two at a time.

One thing was in their favor: he and his cowboys, and Earp and his deputies, had been as ready as they could be for the robbery—behind cover with plenty of ammunition. Things would likely have been over already had it been otherwise. But the truth was, the fight to save Dodge City's money was far from being won or lost. It was a pitched battle, one-sided as hell, yet Smoke had not begun to thin the robbers' ranks, as he had planned to do, when opportunity came.

A heavy-bodied raider jumped off his nervous, brown mare to make a run for the broken front windows of the bank. He stood at a hitch rail to tie his horse in front of the building just long enough for Smoke to draw a bead on his head.

The Winchester spat out its deadly load, banging so near Smoke's right ear that he was deafened for a moment. The gunman was midway through looping his reins around the hitch post when he stiffened his spine. His left foot came off the ground in a most curious way, suspended as though he intended to remain balanced on his right leg. His Stetson flew off amid a cloud of crimson mist, and it appeared that a plug of his long, black hair went with his hat.

"Gotcha, asshole," Smoke whispered, dropping back down out of sight at the same time the gunman's right knee buckled. He sank to the roadway, arms windmilling, his right shirtsleeve bloodied. He dropped the shotgun he carried and went over on his face, his chin landing hard on the boardwalk in front of the bank's shattered windows.

Smoke was barely ahead of answering fire from the street below. Bullets thudded into the boards between him and the war going on beneath him, some slugs sizzling over his head.

His senses warned him before his ringing ears actually heard the sound behind him. Whirling around, clawing for a pistol, he was just in time to fire at a head that was peering over the back of the rooftop.

His bullet struck a bearded outlaw in the throat. Pale blue eyes bulged in their sockets, eyes locked on Smoke's. For a time the man seemed frozen, gulping mouthfuls of his own blood, until he let out a groan and fell to the alleyway below, making a deep, thudding noise when he landed, followed by another groan that was louder than the first.

I've got to move, Smoke thought. The robbers were closing in on his position.

Bent over in a crouch, he ran to the back of the cafe, only to find another gunslick staring up at him.

Smoke's Colt belched flame and lead. His aim was true, in spite of the fraction of a second he had to shoot his adversary while staring into the dark muzzles of a shotgun.

A sandy-haired cowboy flinched when a ball of lead entered his forehead, knocking his hat to the ground. The outlaw took a half step back, still gazing up at the roof with a blank look in his eyes while the rear portion of his head came apart. Pieces of skull bone and twists of hair spiraled away from a spot just above his shirt collar. Bloody droplets splattered over the dirt alley where he stood; then suddenly his shotgun discharged. A swarm of speeding buckshot went skyward harmlessly, making a soft, whistling noise after the roar from both barrels filled the space between the rears of several buildings.

As if an anvil had been dropped on his chest, the raider was driven flat on his back in the alleyway, a delayed reaction to the fatal wound that had split his head open. His lips moved, trying to speak, although no words came out—only more blood coursing down his cheeks.

Smoke swung over the cave, letting himself down slowly, with his rifle tucked between his knees. The steady bang of guns had lessened somewhat up and down Main by the time he reached the ground.

Instinct kept him still for a moment, until he was certain no one was watching him from either end of the alley. On nothing but a hunch, he ran north, toward the rear of the harness shop, leaving two dead men in his wake.

At the corner leading into a side street, he paused to look and listen, getting his bearings, when he caught a glimpse of a rider spurring relentlessly away from the battle that was raging from one end of Dodge City to the other. A bandit wearing a Confederate infantryman's cap urged his horse to greater speed, looking back over his shoulder with a revolver gripped in his fist.

"Drop the gun!" Smoke shouted. "You can leave yer friends, but you ain't taking any guns with you."

The outlaw whirled around in the saddle to face the voice he heard, and just as quickly he swung his pistol in Smoke's direction.

Smoke fired his rifle as the words "I warned you!" came loud and clear from his mouth. The Winchester thudded with all the power of a .44, its recoil jarring Smoke's right thigh as the bullet rocketed from the barrel in a spit of orange flame and a cloud of gun smoke.

The robber's horse shied as the loud report clapped in front of it, and in the same instant a Confederate soldier's cap went into the air as the head on which it had been perched was driven backward. The man fell twisting, tumbling to the street.

A woman in a blue, ankle-length dress tried to escape out a side door of Brown's Bakery at a corner on the far side of Main. One of the raiders fired his pistol from atop a prancing horse, shooting her in the back before he spurred out of sight.

Sudden rage filled Smoke when he saw the woman go down. It was time to send these yellow bastards a message.

18

Bill Anderson ducked into the Dodge City Savings Bank with a pistol in his right hand, a twin-barrel sawed-off shotgun in his left. Lee, Sonny and Dewey were positioned behind a polished, oak counter next to the door of a massive safe. Lee held a gun to the head of a trembling, balding man in front of the vault, obviously the banker in charge of things. The vault was closed. Sonny had a woman in front of him, his fingers wound into her long, dark hair so that her head was pulled back. Her palms were raised, and they shook uncontrollably. Outside, at a hitch rail, a gunman called Lucky held both nervous packhorses, trying to calm them in the midst of all the shooting while staying hunkered down, to be out of the line of fire while Dewey and the others were inside the bank.

"He won't open it, Bill!" Lee growled, glancing out broken front windows when another wave of gunfire filled the street. "I swore I'd kill the sumbitch if he don't."

Bill noticed two bodies on the floor—a farmer dressed in overalls surrounded by blood, and an elderly woman in a faded, calico dress, her deeply wrinkled face pockmarked by shotgun pellet wounds oozing more blood onto waxed hardwood flooring. It appeared that the woman was still alive—he heard her soft whimpering above the thunder of gunshots outside.

"What's your name?" Bill asked, looking at the banker. He didn't like what he saw—a pampered man with fear written all over his face.

"F . . . Feagin," the banker stammered. "David Feagin. I'm the only one who knows the combination to the safe . . . and I . . . won't open it. The money belongs to the townspeople of Dodge City."

Bill crossed a floor that was covered with broken glass and bloodstains, walking around the counter. He went up to Feagin with a snarl widening his lips. "Then I'm gonna have to kill you an' dynamite your vault. . . ." His gaze wandered to the woman with her hands raised in the air. Sonny held a gun against her ribs. "Or I can shoot this pretty lady, Mr. Feagin. You can watch her die, an' then I'll give you one last chance to open your vault. You ever see a woman die from a bullet hole right before your very eyes? There'll be this big hole, plumb through her, and her blood's gonna run all over this here floor. She'll scream real loud right at first, an' then she'll make softer noises after she falls on the floor. Her blood's gonna be on your hands, Feagin, unless you open that goddamn safe right now."

"Dear God," Feagin whispered, sweat running down his pale cheeks, dribbling on the front of his brown suit coat and vest. "You wouldn't simply execute her . . . would you?"

Bill nodded as the rattle of guns quieted briefly out in the road. "We sure will, Mr. Banker, 'less you open that damn iron box real quick."

A sudden blast of shotgun fire bellowed from a spot not far from the bank.

"What the hell was that?" Bill demanded, inclining his head toward the windows. "See what it was, Dewey."

Dewey stepped cautiously to a shattered window. He stood still for a moment, peering out. "It's Jack an' Sammy an' a few more boys. They just shot their way into that other bank up the street. Yonder's some kid, maybe fourteen or so, runnin' with his hands coverin' his bloody face. Appears he caught a faceful of buckshot. Acts like he's blind. He just fell over a water trough outside, an' he can't stand up no more." Dewey gave the south end of Main a closer examination. "Somebody musta shot ol' Claude, 'cause the packhorse an' that mule is wanderin' loose, draggin' lead ropes. There's sure a bunch of dead folks layin' all over the place. . . ."

"May the Lord have mercy on us!" Feagin said, as if he knew his time had come. "Please don't kill any more people! Order your men to stop shooting, and I'll open the safe. Please don't kill any more women or children."

At that precise moment a shotgun erupted; then a shrill woman's voice screamed farther down Main.

"Roy shot this woman in the back of her head," Dewey said tonelessly. "She was tryin' to run from that store across from the bank. I swear, if it don't look like Roy shot her head plumb off . . . I didn't know we was gonna kill womenfolk this time."

"Please ask them to stop!" Feagin cried. "You can have all the money! Please don't kill anyone else."

"Start twistin' that dial," Bill snapped. "Soon as it's open, maybe I'll think about havin' my men stop shootin'. The longer you wait, the more folks is gonna die."

Two pounding shotgun blasts came from the Marshal's office, almost in unison. Then a wall of answering fire boomed from all directions, bullets cracking against the front of the building in a staccato of ear-splitting noises.

As Feagin began working the combination dial on the front of the safe, an eerie quiet settled over Dodge for a moment. Not a gun sounded for several seconds. The silence caught Bill's attention until another noise came from a rooftop almost directly across the street.

It sounded like a charging buffalo bull's roar at first, as a man stood up behind the false front of a bullet-riddled cafe called Martha's Eatery, hoisting what appeared to be a lifeless body over his head. He made the roaring sound with his head thrown back, then, demonstrating tremendous strength, threw the body over the wooden front of the building and disappeared.

The body landed on Main Street will a dull thud. Bloody Bill Anderson's eyelids narrowed, staring at the prone form. "Goddamn!" he exclaimed bitterly. "That's Homer! Some son of a bitch went an' killed Homer Suggins!"

Dewey blinked. "That is Homer," he said softly, with a note of disbelief. "Homer was 'bout the most careful feller I ever knowed in my whole life . . . how the hell did anybody git up on that roof behind him without him knowin' it? Homer could hear a damn sewin' needle drop."

"He's damn sure dead," Lee said, his gun jammed into the woman's ribs while he glanced out the glassless windows. "He ain't so much as moved a muscle."

Anderson's jaw clamped. He looked up at the rooftop of the cafe. "One of you go find that half-breed scout, Scar Face. Tell Scar Face to hunt down that son of a bitch who killed Homer an' bring me his goddamn scalp. Tell that breed the bastard's up on that roof yonder. Run an' fetch that breed, Dewey, an' tell him what I said. While you're out there, have somebody grab up the pack mule an' that horse so we can haul our loot outa the Cattleman's Bank."

"What about Claude?" Dewey asked.

"Who cares about Claude?" Bill said. "Get goin'."

Dewey stepped carefully over a low windowsill and turned up the street, hunkered down with his gun aimed in front of him, not taking any chances that a stray bullet might hit him.

Dill turned back to Feagin, fighting the fury he felt inside for losing a good man like Homer Suggins, one of the few in his band he truly trusted. Homer had been with him since the war, and he'd always carried his share of the load. "Get that safe open!" he shouted. "Or you'll be the next sumbitch lyin' out there in that road dead as a fence post."

Feagin's fingers quivered, turning the dial as Bill wondered who the brazen bastard was who tossed Homer's body down to the street—an act of outright defiance. And there was that strange yell he gave to attract attention to himself while he did it, a man who needed to be taught manners.

A rifle cracked from a rooftop near the Cattleman's Bank, and the sound made Bill grin. Sikes was still up there, gunning down resistance. Losing Homer wasn't good news, but they had another expert marksman firing from a good position, keeping any lawmen in town pinned down.

"Hurry up!" Bill said to the banker, when the safe had not yet been opened.

The crackle of pistol fire came from inside the Cattleman's Bank. Jack Starr was probably after revenge for what had happened to Homer, Bill thought, killing townspeople unlucky enough to be in the bank when it was being robbed. And Scar Face, the half-breed Pawnee, would take care of the loudmouth on top of the cafe in a short while. The breed was good at stalking . . . not much at long-distance shooting, Bill remembered. Scar Face could read horse sign the way some men read a book. He'd find that big, murdering bastard who had somehow slipped up behind Homer. Throwing his body down in the street was a form of insult that Bill wouldn't take without exacting revenge.

Feagin said, "I must have gotten part of the combination wrong. It won't open. I'll have to try again."

Bill whirled around, showing his teeth. He spoke to Lee. "Give Mr. Feagin a reminder of what'll happen if he gets it wrong again."

Lee drew back his pistol and whacked the banker on the top of his head. Feagin's eyes rolled upward, and he sank to the floor, out cold.

"Goddamn, Lee!" Bill cried. "Why the hell'd you hit him so hard? We ain't never gonna get that money 'til he wakes up."

"Sorry," Lee muttered, reaching down to pick Feagin up by his coat lapels. "I'll slap his face 'til he comes around."

Lee backhanded the banker's left and right cheeks several times, yet nothing seemed to revive Feagin at the moment. Lee gave Bill a quizzical stare. "What do you want me to do with him now?" he asked.

Bill cocked his .44 angrily. "I've got no use for a man who's too damn stupid to know what to do," he said, and at the same time, he pulled the trigger.

A bullet tore through Lee Wollard's left ear, coming out the other side amid a splash of crimson that spattered all over the door of the vault. Lee was slammed against the wall beside the safe as though he'd been kicked in the head by a mule. He slid down to the floor with his eyes wide open and his lips moving, trying to form the word *no*.

Sonny flinched when he saw Bill shoot Lee through the head, but he held his tongue when Bill glared at him. Lee let out a final groan and went still.

"Ask the bitch real nice if she wants to live," Bill said, struggling to control his temper. "If she opens that safe I'll spare her life. Otherwise, we're gonna kill her right here an' now."

"You heard what Bill said," Sonny snapped, punching the barrel of his gun a little deeper into her side. "Open it, or we'll kill you."

"I . . . don't . . . know . . . the combination," the woman stuttered, her eyes about to pop from her face. "I swear before God, I do not know how . . . to open it."

"You want I should shoot her?" Sonny asked.

Bill looked down at Feagin. "Let's try one more time to wake this bastard up. This is takin' way too long. We should already be headed out of town by now. Put the bitch on the floor an' find a pitcher of water. There's gotta be some water round here some place."

Sonny shoved the terrified woman to the floor and stalked off to locate a pitcher of water, entering an office to one side of the bank lobby. He came back a few moments later, as Bill was listening to the slackening gunshots up and down Main Street, a sure sign that Dodge City's lawmen were already dead, or pulling back when they saw that the odds were against them.

"Here's some water," Sonny said, carrying a small ceramic pitcher over to Feagin. He bent down and splashed the water on the banker's face. "Wake up, you son of a bitch!" Sonny snarled before he tossed the pitcher to the floor, smashing it, drawing his pistol again.

Feagin's eyelids fluttered. "What . . . happened?" he asked in a groggy voice.

"You went to sleep," Sonny replied, showing the banker the muzzle of his Colt. "Now git up an' open that safe or I'll kill the woman yonder. Better make it quick, too."

Feagin shook his head. He came slowly, unsteadily, to his feet, swaying dizzily, reaching for the combination lock once again. "Please don't kill Miss Peabody," he croaked, twirling the dial. "She doesn't deserve to die. She's only an employee of the bank."

Sonny waved his gun barrel near the banker's face. "But she is gonna die 'less you git this open."

"I'm doing the best I can."

While Feagin twisted the lock, Bill sauntered over near one of the front windows, glancing up at the roof of Martha's Eatery. It was all he could do to control himself, his blinding rage, when he saw Homer's body lying in the street. Gunshots were fewer now in Dodge, and he consoled himself with that fact. They had taken the town by storm, and soon they would empty every pocket in the entire place by cleaning out the two vaults.

"It's open," Sonny said, passing a quick look over Lee's motionless form. "We're gonna need some help gettin' all this money outside into them packs."

Bill saw Scar Face trotting down the boardwalk in front of a small harness shop. He ignored Sonny for a moment, going to the window to catch the half-breed's eye with a wave. When Scar Face saw him, he came to a halt.

Bill pointed to the roof of Martha's Eatery. Scar Face gave a nod in return and headed down a side street toward an alleyway.

He spoke to Lucky, who was holding the horses outside. "Tie 'em off an' get in here to help us load this money. Most of the shootin's stopped anyhow."

Scar Face turned into the alley with a bowie knife gleaming in one hand, a Colt pistol in the other. Bill gave a grin without any humor behind it. "That'll teach the sumbitch, whoever he is, not to tangle with Bloody Bill Anderson," he added softly.

19

Wyatt knelt beside the remnants of an office window, being very careful when he peered over the sill to see what was going on at the Cattleman's Bank. Cody lay on the floor, groaning, his left shoulder seeping blood around the bandanna Wyatt had tied over his wound. For several minutes Cody had been unable to shoot, in a state of mild shock after the bullet had grazed his flesh, peeling his skin open so it looked like a gash made by a knife.

"I'm seein' stars, Marshal," Cody whispered, blinking. "It feels like I'm gonna faint."

"You'll be okay," Wyatt said. The shooting had all but stopped on Main Street. Half a dozen bandits were inside the bank. Three more were outside, hidden behind stone water troughs with rifles and shotguns. All seemed lost. There weren't enough guns in Dodge to halt a bank-robbing gang of this size, and with the corpses of innocent women and the Wilkins boy lying in the road in spreading pools of blood, it was unlikely that any civic-minded citizens would rush to their aid with hunting rifles or shotguns. Henry Burns lay dead in front of his store. The bodies of four outlaws lay farther to the south, although one appeared to be alive, barely able to crawl, trying to reach safety.

He wondered about Jim Bob. Watley's shotgun had been silent for several minutes. Every now and then, one of Jensen's cowhands would fire a shot at a robber from a rooftop. Neither man seemed to be much of a marksman.

"Jesus, this hurts," Cody sighed, resting his head on the floor, watching the fly-specked ceiling through pain-hooded eyes. "Wish I could get over to Doc Sanders' house."

"Ain't no back door," Wyatt reminded him, seeing shadows move inside the bank. Suddenly, coming from the north, a bandit came down the street leading a horse and a mule bearing packsaddles.

Wyatt raised his shotgun over the windowsill and thumbed back both hammers, determined to stop the pack animals from hauling off the money if he could. But the bandit walked between the pair of animals, using them as shields, preventing Wyatt from taking a shot that wouldn't harm the four-legged creatures.

"Hellfire," he said quietly, waiting for the right opportunity. "I can't shoot him without hurtin' the horse or the mule. I reckon I oughta shoot 'em anyways, so they can't carry off the money. Seems a damn shame. . . ."

A rifle cracked from a rooftop up the street, kicking up a cloud of dust in front of the bandit who was leading the animals. And at the same time, a terrific shotgun blast came from Jim Bob's position behind the wall at Joe's Blacksmith Shop.

The mule brayed, lunging forward as shotgun pellets struck its rump. It jerked the lead rope free of the bandit's hand and took off down Main at a gallop.

The bandit quickly put himself behind the plunging, rear-

ing, bay packhorse, trying to settle it so he would be safe stand
ing behind it. Two men rushed out of the bank with rifles before the horse calmed down.

One raider took aim at Jim Bob's hiding place and fired a
Winchester .44 in Watley's direction. The boom of the outlaw's gun echoed off buildings while the second robber aimed
for the same spot.

Another rifle cracked from a rooftop. One bandit staggered and went down on one knee, dropping his rifle to grip
his right thigh muscles. Wyatt wasted no time. He pulled the
trigger on one barrel of his Stevens twelve-gauge.

The kneeling robber was swept off the roadway by a
swarm of heavy buckshot, spinning him around like a child's
top while his dust-covered, gray hat was torn to shreds, flying off his head in bits and pieces. The outlaw's face appeared
to melt, changing shape as skin and blood were ripped off
his skull while he was twisting in the air. Before he fell he
became a ghostly apparition, a man with a grinning skull for
a head, toppling over on his back between a pair of dry
wagon ruts.

Wyatt ducked down just in time. Four or five rifles banged
away at his ruined office windows, sending singsong balls of
lead speeding through the office until they struck the rear
wall, where dozens of wanted posters were nailed up around
a doorway that led to jail cells at the back. A slug pinged into
the potbelly stove, bouncing harmlessly to the wood floor.
Another shattered the globe on Wyatt's desk lantern, sending
tiny glass shards all over his desktop and the floor. Then the
shooting died down and finally ended, bringing on another
moment of quiet, which Wyatt guessed would be short-lived.

"We're gonna git killed, Wyatt," Cody said in a high-
pitched voice. "They's gonna storm this jail, an' then we's
done for."

Wyatt was annoyed, despite his young deputy's lack of
experience. "It'd be a help if you got up an' fired out one of

these windows once in a while. Two guns are sure as hell better than one. You ain't hurt so bad you can't shoot, an' it might discourage 'em from rushin' us."

There were tears in Cody's eyes when he came trembling to his hands and knees. "I'm scared, Marshal," he whimpered, taking up his shotgun again. "No sense denyin' it . . . I'm scared I'm gonna die."

"Shoot at 'em every once in a while an' then get back down out of sight," he said. "It ain't over yet. That big feller, Jensen, has killed the hell outa four or five. He just tossed one off the roof at Martha's, an' you never heard such a yell as when he done it. Jensen may be every bit as mean as you said he was. He damn sure don't act like he's scared of nothin' . . ."

Wyatt fell silent when he saw an Indian dressed in buckskin leggings and a sleeveless vest hurry around a corner farther up Main. The redskin wore a derby hat with a feather stuck in the hatband, and he was carrying a long knife and a pistol. "Looks like they've sent somebody after Jensen," he said, keeping his head low near a corner of the sill. "He'll be headed to that alley behind the cafe so he can climb up to where he's got a shot at Jensen. No tellin' how many of 'em Jensen's killed. Sure don't seem there's near so many robbers as there was when they rode in. Jensen sure must be a quiet feller on his feet, to be so big. He slipped right up on them two who came in ahead of the others to get on rooftops. Killed 'em both with that huge knife he's got. The blade had blood all over it, an' so did Jensen's shirtsleeve."

Cody winced when he put the shotgun to his right shoulder, even though his wound was to the other arm. "Jensen used to be one bad hombre, Marshal. Sundance Morgan an' his gang wasn't no bunch of greenhorns. I heard later on that Jensen killed damn near every one of 'em, before it was over. Maybe Jensen's a little older now, but I still wouldn't care to tangle with him. Sure as hell am glad he's on our side, him an' his two cowboys, only it ain't likely to be enough. I counted damn near thirty men ridin' into town a while ago. To my way of thinkin', we don't stand a chance against so many, not even with Smoke Jensen sidin' with us."

Wyatt took a quick look at the Cattleman's Bank before pulling back. "The real tough part is gonna be when they try to ride outa here with the money," he said, thinking out loud, reloading the spent tube in his Stevens. "We'll have to kill as many as we can without bein' killed ourselves . . . maybe scare 'em into leavin' some of the money behind. With Jensen an' his men shootin' down from the roofs, an' Jim Bob doin' the best he can along with the two of us, maybe we can make a difference." His face twisted in a frown. "That is, if that damn redskin don't get Jensen first with that knife or the gun."

"You seen a redskin with 'em?" Cody asked.

Wyatt nodded. "At least a part-blood. He was wearin' this ol' derby hat with a feather in it, an' deerskin leggin's. I saw this big scar down one side of his face."

Cody turned, facing the back wall. "Holy cow, Marshal!" he exclaimed, pointing to a wanted poster that was fluttering in a soft wind that was coming through broken window-panes. "That'll be a gent they call Scar Face Parker. We got his reward poster last month, if you'll remember. Came from the U.S. Marshal's office over in Fort Smith on the train, along with a handful of others. He's wanted for murder in Indian Territory. Seems like that poster said he was a half Pawnee. Said he'd be armed an' dangerous to catch . . . that he killed two Deputy Marshals from ambush while they was on his trail some place down in the Nations."

Wyatt pursed his lips. "It don't make a damn who he is, Cody. Right now he's got a knife an' a gun, an' he's headed for the roof where Jensen tossed down that body. Could be we're about to find out if Mr. Smoke Jensen is as dangerous as you say he is, if the redskin I saw is this Scar Face Parker."

Cody turned back to the window, peeking above the sill. "He won't be no match for Jensen, Marshal, if Jensen's the same man he used to be."

"Time's gonna tell," Wyatt replied, taking his own quick look at the front of the bank. "They've got one packhorse tied to the rail over yonder. Best we can do is shoot any son of a bitch who comes out carryin' bags of money. Smoke Jensen'll have to take care of himself."

A shotgun roared from Jim Bob's spot behind the wall, and the clatter of pellets rattled off the front of the bank harmlessly.

"Jim Bob couldn't hit the side of a barn," Wyatt muttered. "I wish we had one or two more men who could shoot straight."

Now Cody's cheeks began to turn red. "It ain't so much that my aim is bad, Marshal. I'm just afraid of dyin', is all. I got two kids to feed, hardly more'n babies yet. Beth wouldn't know what do to fer money if I wasn't here to help her raise 'em up like I'm supposed to, bein' their daddy."

"I understand, Cody," Wyatt told him quietly. "Just do the best you can. The more lead we throw at 'em, even if it ain't all that true, will be a help."

"My arm's hurtin' somethin' awful," Cody added, as though he needed to explain.

Wyatt let it drop, bending his head around an edge of the window frame to see what was going on.

A muffled pistol shot came from inside the bank, and right after that a woman's voice let out a mournful wail.

"That was Miz Meeks," Cody said. "Wonder if they shot her? Can't see no reason why they'd shoot a nice ol' lady like Miz Meeks."

"They didn't shoot *her*," Wyatt explained. "She's frightened. I imagine they shot Sheldon Herring for some reason or another. Maybe he tried to argue with 'em over takin' away all the bank's money."

"Lordy," Cody sighed. "Now they've gone an' killed the president of the bank. Whoever this bunch of outlaws is, they's sure as hell bad men."

Wyatt thought about it. "I figure we've just had a visit by Bloody Bill Anderson, even though some folks believe he's been dead since the war. It's just a guess, but it looks like we've got proof on our hands that Bloody Bill is still alive, robbin' an' killin', just like he used to. It would explain what happened to Dave Cobbs an' his family down at the tradin' post the other day. It was easy to see that the store was looted before they burned it plumb to the ground, an' they killed Cobbs an' his whole family so there wouldn't be no witnesses alive to talk, to tell who done it."

Cody bowed his head, fingering traces of tears from his eyelids. "Beth's been tellin' me all along I hadn't oughta took this job. She said I could find work at the shippin' pens durin' the trail drive season, an' that we'd live off what we could grow in our garden between times. Right about now I sure do wish I'd listened a little bit closer to what she was sayin'."

"It's too late for regrets now, Cody. Just keep your head down an' shoot as careful as you can when there's a target. If we're careful, we'll make it out of this alive."

Cody wagged his head. "I ain't so sure, Marshal," he said in a hoarse, dry whisper. "When it comes to luck, mine ain't been all that good, usually."

A noise somewhere to the north made Wyatt jump—the sound of a gun. He'd gotten accustomed to the quiet, all the while knowing it wouldn't last much longer. "Maybe the other bunch is comin' out of the Dodge City Savings Bank," he said, risking yet another quick look around the window frame.

He saw another body lying near a brown mare that was

tied in front of the bank owned by David Feagin, and several more horses, two with packsaddles, tied out front.

Maybe Jensen got another one, he thought, wondering if Smoke Jensen could possibly be as deadly as Cody believed he was. Cody was young, impressionable, not the sort to be accurate about any number of things.

"What was it?" Cody asked. "Did they shoot somebody else?"

"There's a body in front of Mr. Feagin's bank, but it could've been there all along. The gent wasn't movin'."

"No tellin' how many bodies we're gonna find when this is over," Cody whispered, "if we're alive after it's over to make a count. I know Beth's at home, worried to death hearin' all this shootin'. She'll be cryin', figurin' I was the first one to get killed."

"Then she'll be twice as glad to see you when you get home," Wyatt said, wishing Cody would shut the hell up with all his damn worrying.

He wondered about the Indian . . . if it truly was Scar Face Parker, and what would happen when the man ran into the tall cowman from Colorado . . . unless the gunshot they had just heard meant that Jensen was already dead.

20

Catlike, moving soundlessly on the balls of his feet, Smoke stepped across to another rooftop, bending low to keep from being seen from the street. Every instinct he had was sharpened, keened by anger over the senseless killing of women, and the boy who was blinded by buckshot. It was not uncommon, for men who had bad intentions, to kill or maim others who could defend themselves in a contest with weapons. But when cold-blooded murder occurred, with the victims being women and children—killing for the sake of killing alone—Smoke couldn't bridle his temper, no matter what kind of promise he'd given Sally.

And as he moved farther away from the cafe roof, he was sure someone would be coming after him. Throwing the body down where every bank robber in the gang could see it was a form of challenge that men who believed they were tough couldn't ignore. And with this in mind, Smoke was certain he had lured one or two more outlaws up on the roofs on the east side of Main Street, men who had been sent to hunt him down and kill him. In the fit of rage he found himself in, he was looking forward to this contest with more anticipation than he had experienced in years. Like in the old days, when killing was little more than a day's work.

He crept to the rear of a roof over a narrow building in between the cafe and a cobbler's shop, looking cautiously into the alley, for it was from the alleyway that manhunters would be most likely to come, like the two before who wound up with a slug through the neck, and another with a shattered skull.

"Come on up, boys," Smoke whispered, mouthing the words silently. He knew he had to be back in a good firing position with a view of Main when the robbers tried to make a getaway with their loot.

While this wasn't Smoke's natural range, being caught inside a town, without mountains or trees or underbrush to give him cover from enemy fire, he knew lawless men well enough. His surroundings would make little difference, like the time he and Preacher tangled with Casey and the TC Riders; that time reminded him of the standoff he was in, with men inside buildings, protected from bullets by walls his guns couldn't penetrate, facing overwhelming odds with no choice but to dig, or lure, or burn his enemies out. . . .

Stopping in a stand of timber a couple of hundred yards from the ranch house, Preacher said, "There she is. Got any plans on yer mind?"

"Start shooting," was all Smoke said in reply.

"The house an' the outbuildin's?"

"Burn 'em to the ground," Smoke answered.

"You a hard young 'un, Smoke."

"I suppose I am." He smiled at Preacher. "But I had a good teacher, didn't I?"

"The best around," the mountain man replied.

The house and bunkhouse were built of logs, with sod

roofs. *Burn easy,* Smoke thought. He yelled, "Casey! Get out here!"

"Who're you?" a shout came from the house.

"Smoke Jensen!"

A rifle bullet wanged through the trees. High.

"Lousy shot," Preacher muttered.

The rifle cracked again, the slug humming closer.

"They might git lucky and hit one of the horses," Preacher said.

"You tuck them in that ravine over there," Smoke said, dismounting. "I think I'll ease around to the back, just to see if it looks any easier."

Preacher slid off his mustang. "I'll stay here and worry 'em some. You be careful now."

"Don't worry."

"Course not," the old man replied sarcastically. "Why in the world would I do that?" He glanced up at the sky. "Seven, maybe eight hours till dark."

"We'll be through before then." Smoke slipped into an arroyo that half circled the house, ending at the rear of the ranch house.

Fifty yards behind the house, he found cover in a small clump of trees and settled down to pick his targets.

A man got careless inside the house and offered part of his forearm on a sill. Smoke shattered it with one round from his Henry. In front of the house, Preacher found a target and cut loose with his Henry. From the screams of pain drifting to Smoke, someone had been hit hard.

"You hands!" Smoke called. "You sure you want to die for Casey? A couple of your buddies already bought it a few miles back. One of them wearing a black shirt."

Silence for a few moments. "Your Daddy ride with Mosby?" a voice yelled from the house.

"That's right."

"Your brother named Luke?"

"Yeah. He was shot in the back, and the gold he was guarding got stolen."

"Potter shot him . . . not me! You got no call to do this, so ride out an' forgit it."

Smoke's reply to that was to put several rounds of .44s through the windows of the house.

Wild cursing came from inside.

"Jensen? The name's Barry. I come from Nevada. Didn't have nothin' to do with no war. Never been no further east than the Ladder in Kansas. 'other feller here is the same as me. We herd cattle . . . don't git no fightin' wages. You let us ride outa here!"

"Get your horses and clear out!" Smoke cried.

Barry and his partner made it to the center of the backyard before they were shot in the back by someone in the ranch house. One of them died hard, screaming his life away in the dust of southeast Colorado.

"Nice folks in there," Preacher muttered as he crept up to Smoke's firing position, motioning for Smoke to continue his stalking of the men forted up inside the log house.

Smoke followed the arroyo until the bunkhouse was between him and the main house. In a pile behind the bunkhouse, he found sticks and rags. In the empty bunkhouse he found a jar of coal oil.

He tied the rags around a stick, soaked them in oil, lighted them, then tossed the stick onto the roof of the ranch house. He waited, Henry at the ready, watching the house slowly catch on fire.

Shouts and hard coughing came from inside the ranch house as the logs caught and smoldered, the rooms filling with smoke and fumes. One man broke from the cabin, and

Preacher cut him down in the front yard. Another raced from the back door, and Smoke doubled him over with a .44 slug in the guts.

Only one man still appeared to be shooting from the house. There were two on the range nearby, at least two hit in the cabin, and two in the yard. While he and Preacher had begun that affair badly outnumbered, the odds were swinging their way.

"All right, Casey!" he shouted over the crackling of burning wood. "Burn to death, shot, or hung—it's up to you!"

Casey waited until the roof was caving in before he stumbled into the yard, eyes blind from swirls of smoke inside. He fired wildly as he staggered about, hitting nothing but earth and air. When his pistol was empty, Smoke walked up to the man and knocked him down, tying his hands behind him with rawhide.

"What do you figure on doin' with him?" Preacher asked as he walked up, shoving fresh loads into his Henry.

"I intend to take him just outside of town, by that creek we rode past, and hang him."

"I just can't figure where you got that mean streak, boy. Seein' as how you was raised . . . partly . . . by a gentle man like me."

Despite the death he had brought, and the destruction wrought, Smoke had to laugh at that. Preacher was known throughout the West as one of the most dangerous men ever to roam the high country and vast Plains. The mountain man had once spent two years of his life tracking down—and killing, one by one—a group of men who had ambushed and killed a friend of his, taking the man's furs.

"Course, you never went on the hunt for anyone yourself?" Smoke asked, dumping the unconscious Casey across a saddled horse before tying him down.

The house was engulfed in flames, black smoke spewing into the endless sky.

"Well . . . mayhaps once or twice," Preacher responded, "but that was years back. I've mellowed some."

"Sure," Smoke said, grinning. Preacher was still as mean as a cornered puma.

They mounted and rode slowly away from the flaming ranch, with black smoke spiraling into a cloudless sky. That had been a time when killing meant nothing to Smoke, something akin to swatting a fly.

Smoke glanced up and down the alley, finding nothing, yet his senses told him someone was there. Two bloodied bodies lay behind the cafe, but that was not the reason for his concern. A voice inside his head warned that someone was coming for him, a man he couldn't see at present.

He walked quietly over to an eave of the building and lay down, resting his Winchester beside him as he drew his Arkansas Toothpick. This was likely to be a job requiring a silent kill, a job for a knife.

Then a shadow moved farther south down the alley, near the spot where he'd killed the two robbers who tried to come up on the roof after him. A pair of horses still stood ground-hitched near the bodies of both men, a piebald gelding snorting at the scent of blood puddling around one of the corpses.

Smoke's eyes narrowed, fixed on the shape he saw moving a moment before. And there it was—the faint outline of a man in a derby hat staying close to the rear of a building.

Even in the slanted sunlight of early morning, Smoke saw the glint of a knife blade in the man's hand.

So, he thought, reaching for his own Arkansas Toothpick, drawing it slowly out of his boot . . . it was to be a duel of steel and nerves. It suited Smoke, never one to complain about an opponent's choice of weapons. One factor would force the fight to be short and sweet; in minutes, perhaps even now, the gang of bank robbers would be attempting a break with the town's money, tied to packsaddles.

Frozen, evidencing the patience Preacher taught him so long ago, Smoke waited for the shadowy stalker to make his next move. In most any form of combat the one who struck first had a better chance of victory—in particular, when the battle was fought with guns, or in a fistfight, even a war with knives. But when there was a game of cat-and-mouse, a stalker and his prey, it was often best to be patient, waiting for the right opportunity. The man who moved first gave his position away.

Time seemed to stand still. Smoke watched the figure in the alley, remaining motionless. He could see the shape of a feather protruding from the man's hatband.

An Indian, he thought. *He'll be careful.*

The shadow moved again, inching down the back of one building and then another, coming closer to the spot below the roof where Smoke was hidden.

"A little bit more," Smoke breathed. The man in the derby was within easy rifle range, yet the movement of a barrel in sunlight might alert him to the danger.

Out in the street, an angry voice shouted, "We're comin' out, an' we've got prisoners! Women! Any sumbitch shoots, we'll blow these women to pieces!"

Time was running short. Smoke needed to be back facing Main Street with his rifle ready in order to stand any chance of saving the women and Dodge City's money. But there was an Indian to be dealt with first, creeping toward him where shadows hid his progress.

A shotgun blasted somewhere on Main, the first shot to be fired in several minutes.

"I done warned you!" the same thick voice cried. "Just to show you we mean business, we're gonna shoot one of these here women an' shove her out where everybody can see her!"

A pistol shot cracked, followed by a muffled woman's scream and then dry laughter, faint, hard to hear.

"The bastards," Smoke hissed. He'd wasted too much time waiting for the Indian in the derby to make his move.

Slipping his rifle forward until it rested against his left shoulder, the offside he avoided when firing a rifle, Smoke pulled the hammer back on the Winchester as silently as he knew how.

"You dirty sons of bitches!" a high-pitched voice cried from the roadway behind Smoke. "Any yellow bastard who'd shoot a woman like that oughta be hung!"

"Come try an' hang us!" the first man shouted. "You'll be the next one to die!"

Smoke couldn't wait any longer. Sighting along the barrel of his rifle, he did something he rarely ever allowed—he pulled a trigger on a man first.

The Winchester exploded, rocking hard against Smoke's upper arm and shoulder. The man in the derby jumped, both feet leaving the ground before he fell over on his back, kicking furiously as Smoke pulled back away from the eave.

He ran across the roof, bent over like a man in pain, until he had a view of Main Street. He levered a fresh cartridge into his rifle, certain that the man lying in the alley was out of the fight forever.

21

Jack Starr was worried. Three men defending Dodge City had good aim and iron nerves. One was in the Marshal's office with a shotgun. Another was down the street, across from the Dodge City Bank, picking his shots carefully. One more kept moving from rooftop to rooftop, the bastard who threw Homer Suggins down in front of the cafe.

Jack had other concerns. Anderson had been wrong about the amount of resistance they would face in robbing the banks. Someone had known they were coming.

"Take a look outside, Sammy," Jack said, holding his Dance .44 beneath the trembling chin of a woman who was employed by the bank. "We've lost too goddamn many men already. Make damn sure nobody's out there, an' look real close up on them roofs across the street."

Jack couldn't have cared less if cross-eyed Sammy McCoy got shot peering outside. Claude, his brother, was a far better marksman and his nerves were like ice. And Claude's brain was twice the size of Sammy's.

"Somebody's liable to shoot me," Sammy protested, taking a rifle with him to a spot near a busted front window-pane. "If it's all the same to you, Jack, I'd just as soon not git shot takin' a look outside."

"I'll kill you myself if you don't do like I say," Jack snarled. "You ain't got near the big balls your brother Claude has got."

Sammy swallowed hard. He saw bodies of his friends lying all over the street.

Sammy knew Jack meant what he said, that he would kill him if he didn't follow orders. He wondered which was better—to be shot in the back by a member of his own gang or to die by another man's bullet. Winding up dead was the result, either way. He made up his mind that it did not make all that much difference.

"Do it!" Jack snapped.

Sammy went closer to the windowsill and looked out cautiously. "It sure as hell seems okay to me, only there's two guys in the Marshal's office who fire off shotguns every now an' then. I wish there was some way fer some of us to shut them shotguns up afore we git killed."

Jack's attention was taken away from the window when the man who ran the bank groaned. Scar Face Parker had stuck a knife in the banker's belly when he reached in a desk drawer for a small-caliber pistol. The banker was losing a lot of blood, and the vault was still closed. Jack turned to the woman he held by the back of her navy blue dress. "I'm gonna give you one more chance to open that goddamn safe, bitch," he said. "If you don't do it, I swear I'll kill you."

"No . . . one else knows . . . the combination," she said, blue eyes bulging with fear when she felt a nudge in the soft flesh of her neck from Jack's gun barrel.

"You're lyin'!" Jack cried. "There has to be somebody else who knows the combination, an' I figure that's gotta be you." He jacked back the hammer on his .44. "This is it, you ol' bitch. Open the safe or I'll blow your damn head off."

"I swear I can't do it," she cried.

"Then say your damn prayers, woman. Your body's gonna be fillin' a casket 'less you open that vault right now. There's gonna be a funeral procession in Dodge tomorrow, an' it's gonna be fer you."

"I can try," she whimpered. "I think I remember the first number is ten, after two spins clockwise to clear the lock. Then I believe the next number is eighteen. . . ."

Jack shoved her over to the safe. "You get just this one chance," he said. "If it don't open, you're the same as dead. You can count on it."

The woman put a shaky hand on the combination dial and spun it clockwise two times. Tears streamed down her slightly wrinkled cheeks. "I can't recall the last number," she said. "It may be twenty. Please don't kill me. When Mr. Herring wakes up he'll tell you what you want to know, if he doesn't bleed to death beforehand."

"He shouldn't've gone fer that gun," Jack said. "He was a damn fool to try that."

"He won't refuse you now. Please give him a chance to tell me what the last number is."

Jack looked over at Tinker Barnes. "Rouse that banker, an' ask him what the last number of the combination is. If he don't give you no answer, then shoot the son of a bitch."

"Somebody's movin' outside," Sammy said from his spot near the window. "He ran across the road just now. Make's two of 'em behind that brick wall in front of the blacksmith's shop, if I got 'em counted right."

"How come you didn't shoot the son of a bitch?" Jack wanted to know.

"He was runnin' real fast," Sammy answered, "an' I seen he had a rifle."

"You yellow, gotch-eyed bastard!" Jack snapped. "If we wasn't already short of men I'd put a hole through you big enough to fit a man's fist."

"Don't shoot me, Jack," Sammy said, tightening his grip on his Winchester. "I'll do whatever you say. I need my share of that money bad as you do."

"I oughta kill you anyways, Sammy. You ain't showed not one bit of backbone, hidin' behind that window."

Sweat beaded on Sammy's face and neck. "I'm just wantin' to make sure I live to spend the money, Jack."

"Where's Scar Face?" Jack demanded. "He shoulda been back by now."

"He went after that sumbitch up on the roof," Frankie Weaver said. "Bill gave the order hisself."

Jack wondered what was taking the half-breed so long to get a simple job done. Some local citizen with a rifle had gotten up on top of the cafe, probably catching Homer by surprise. Jack had never completely trusted Homer. He was a suckass, shining up to Bill whenever he had the opportunity.

Frankie stepped over to another broken pane of glass. He looked out for a moment. "If we use them pack animals as a kind of shield, we can git cleared out of here with the money without bein' shot all to hell."

Jack scowled at the woman trying to open the safe. "First thing is to get our hands on the money. If this ol' bitch don't open the door on this here vault, I'm gonna scatter her damn brains all over the front of it."

"Please don't shoot me," the woman begged. "I'm doing the best I can."

"It ain't good enough 'cause it ain't open yet," Jack said bitterly.

Frankie kicked the wounded bank president in the stomach, producing a groan.

"Kick him again," Dave Watkins cried, his face the color of milk. "Like Jack said, we's runnin' out of time."

Frankie obliged, kicking Sheldon Herring in the gut just above his bleeding wound. Herring's eyes fluttered open. He gave the bank lobby a distant stare.

"What's the last number of the combination?" Dave demanded with his boot cocked, ready to deliver another swift kick to the banker's groin.

"Twenty-two," Herring sighed, closing his eyes again with a look of pain wrinkling his face.

"You heard him," Jack snarled to the woman. "Use twenty-two for the last number. If this vault door don't open I'm gonna put a bullet through you."

She gave the lock another spin, trying the sequence of numbers. Tumblers clicked into place, and the door swung open a few inches.

"That'll do it," Jack said, suddenly swinging his pistol barrel down on top of the woman's head, making a dull thud when it landed.

She fell to the floor, unconscious.

Jack pulled the safe door open. Sacks of currency and coins filled almost every shelf. "Start loadin' this stuff on them pack animals, boys," he said. "We're rich as six foot up a bull's ass now. Soon as the money's loaded, we're clearin' out of here."

"What about Bill an' them boys down the street?" Frankie asked.

Jack didn't need much time to think about it. "They're on their own," he said.

Sammy gave him a questioning look. "You mean we's gonna leave 'em?"

"You heard what I said."

"But Bill's gonna be mad as hell."

"Maybe he won't be around to get mad," Jack replied. "Our job is to clean out this here vault. His job is to take care of the other bank. So long as everybody does his own job, we got no problems."

"But Bill's trapped. That bastard up on the roof has got him pinned down," Frankie argued.

Jack aimed a chilly stare in Frankie's direction. "That's Bill's problem now," he said. "We empty this safe like he told us to, an' we'll be followin' his orders."

Sammy hesitated. "He'll kill every damn one of us if'n we ride off an' leave 'em there, Jack."

"A dead man ain't gonna kill nobody," Jack replied.

"That sure as hell is cold," Frankie muttered. "If it was me down there, I'd sure want somebody to help me git out." But as Frankie said it, he headed over to the vault to begin taking out sacks of money.

A thundering shotgun blast rattled the front door of the Cattleman's Bank. It came from across the road.

"We gotta git rid of them bastards holed up inside the Marshal's office," Sammy declared, as he, too, walked over quickly to help Frankie take bags from the safe.

"Wish to hell Scar Face would get back," Jack said, with an eye on the street. "Wonder what's keepin' him?"

"Maybe that jasper up on top of the cafe went an' killed *him* too," Frankie said, pushing bulging sacks of currency into packs they would tie to the animals out front.

"Scar Face Parker ain't gonna be easy to kill," Jack said under his breath, wondering. The half-breed was sneaky, good in a tight spot, always careful.

"Just 'cause a man ain't easy to kill don't mean he's gonna live forever," Frankie added, when one side of a pack was full of banknotes.

"My money's on Scar Face," Jack said, shoving the crying old woman out of the way. "He knows his business, an' his business is killin' folks, when he ain't down off a horse readin' sign for us to follow."

"I sure hope you're right," Dave Watkins remarked, his face near the window. "Our biggest problem's gonna be them two sons of bitches in the Marshal's office. We git past them, an' we've got a chance to git outa here with our skins."

"You're a born worrier, Dave," Jack said.

"I'm still alive," was Dave's only reply, looking the other way down Main Street.

"Hurry up, damn it!" Jack snapped, when it appeared Frankie and Sammy were taking too long loading the second set of packs with money.

"I'm loadin' as fast as I can," Sammy replied.

"Me too," Frankie insisted, although he stuffed a few more of the bags into a pack pocket hurriedly, forgetting to tie it shut in his haste.

"Let's get ready to ride," Jack said, ambling over to the front doors before he peeked out.

The street was littered with the bodies of men and horses, and women. Blood lay in crimson pools from one end of Main to the other. Flies had begun to gather at the corpses, and the noise made Jack angry. "Hurry the hell up!" he shouted over his shoulder. "Looks like they've got Bill surrounded."

Jack did not really mind leaving Bill Anderson behind with gunmen all around him. Of late, Bill had begun to ramble, and it seemed his mind wandered back to the past, to the war, as if he were still living it.

"We're damn near ready," Frankie said, "only what the hell we gonna do 'bout them two shotguns over at the lawman's office when we run outside?"

"Stay low," Jack told him. It made no difference to him if the shotguns brought Frankie and Sammy down.

"They'll sure be shootin'," Sammy promised. "Every damn time somethin' moves out yonder, one of them shotguns goes off real loud."

Jack grinned, intending no humor. "Are you scared of loud noises, Sammy?"

"I'm sure as hell scared of dyin'."

"You ain't gonna die. Just git that money on the backs of

them horses yonder. We're all gonna be filthy rich soon as we git clear of Dodge."

"It's gettin' clear of Dodge that's worryin' me," Frankie said, hoisting a pack over his shoulder.

"Like I said before, you worry too much," Jack answered in a dry voice.

"Somebody cover me," Frankie said as he went over to the front door.

Jack grinned. "I've got you covered, an' who's any better at coverin' a man's ass 'n me?"

22

Wayland Burke crouched down behind the brick wall across the front of the blacksmith's shop. Jim Bob Watley was sweating, and with shotgun shells lying around his boots, he seemed out of place somehow. He didn't look like a deputy or a man who belonged in a deadly shoot-out with outlaws.

"I fetched my scattergun," Wayland said, blinking furiously as he gazed across the street at the Cattleman's Bank. "Somebody's gotta help you an' Marshal Earp an' Cody. Don't seem nobody else is willin'."

"We're obliged fer your help," Jim Bob said, "only you gotta remember one thing—the Marshal said to keep our heads down an' only to shoot when we git a chance without gittin' our own heads blowed off. With so darned much lead flyin' all over the place, it ain't been so easy to do what Marshal Earp said."

"I'll be real careful," Wayland told him, wondering. "Who the hell woulda believed so many bank robbers would show up in Dodge at the same time? My wife said I gotta help the Marshal keep our money safe, 'cause nearly everything we've got is over yonder in that vault of Mr. Herring's. Our little store don't make all that much money, but we need every cent of it in order to keep on livin' here."

Jim Bob watched one of the outlaws peer out a shattered bank window, and with an opportunity like that he knew that Marshal Earp expected him to shoot. Thumbing back the hammer on his Stevens twelve-gauge double barrel, he took quick aim and fired.

The kick of his shotgun drove Jim Bob back a half step at almost the same instant a yell came from the Cattleman's Bank.

The outlaw standing at the window frame threw both hands to his face and fell out of sight.

"You got him!" Wayland cried, rising up just high enough to take a shot of his own. With nothing to shoot at besides a bare window at the front of the building, he pulled one trigger on his scattergun, the explosion making him wince, shutting both eyes until a cloud of blue smoke cleared. He grinned as soon as he opened his eyelids again, blinking, trying to see if he'd been able to hit one of the robbers himself.

"Git down, Mr. Burke!" Jim Bob shouted. His warning came too late.

The roar of a rifle thundered from the front of the bank. Wayland's head jerked backward, and his best beaver-felt derby hat went flying off his scalp, twirling, wobbling as it fell to the ground behind him, fluttering there like a wounded bird. A dark mass squirted out of the rear of his skull, a twist of his black hair moving just ahead of a thick stream of blood.

Jim Bob cowered behind the brick wall, watching Wayland make a slow half turn in his direction with an odd expression on his face, a look of surprise. Then Jim Bob noticed a hole below the storekeeper's right eye, a hole the size of a man's thumb.

"Git down, Mr. Burke!" Jim Bob said again, softer when

he realized what the hole in Burke's face (and the stream of blood) meant. "Jesus, Mr. Burke! How come you didn't git back down behind this here wall?"

Wayland's lips were moving as if he were trying to answer Jim Bob's question, but no sounds came from his mouth. Pinkish foam began bubbling from his throat, rolling off his tongue as his knees slowly buckled.

His shotgun fell to the dirt, butt first, causing the second barrel to discharge with a tremendous blast. A sizzling load of buckshot tore off Wayland's right arm, sending it into the air with his coat sleeve covering it the way it had when he had put it on that morning. Blood showered over the brick wall where Wayland was standing, and over the brim and crown of Jim Bob's hat, pattering down like red rain all over Jim Bob and the place where he hid behind the wall.

Wayland sank to his knees, the stump of his missing arm pumping blood. He toppled over on his face and lay still until one of his booted feet began to twitch.

"Jesus," Jim Bob said again, turning away from the grisly sight, retching up his breakfast, gagging desperately to breathe. "Oh, dear Jesus. . . ."

From one of the rooftops, a rifle cracked twice, yet Jim Bob was afraid to look over the wall to see if the shots had done any damage. Neither could he force himself to look at Mr. Burke then, thinking only of what he'd unwittingly seen when the rifle shot had torn through Wayland's head, and then when his hunting gun had blown his arm away.

"Take that, you son of a bitch!" a young voice yelled from the roof. Jim Bob recognized it as coming from the young cowboy who rode with Smoke Jensen.

Jim Bob had also seen Jensen stand up on the rooftop of the cafe not long after the fight had begun, throwing a dead man off the building. Jensen had guts—either that, or he was crazy as all hell. Cody claimed Smoke Jensen was an honest-to-goodness gunslick. Maybe he was, after all. He sure had been willing to throw in with the Marshal to help defend the town when it wasn't none of his affair.

Jim Bob risked a quick look over the top of the wall. A shadow moved inside the bank, only an outline because of the slant of the sun. Then a man ran outside carrying canvas bags of money, heading for a packhorse that was tied at the hitch rail directly in front of the bank.

Jim Bob shouldered his shotgun quickly and sent a charge blasting across the road. The outlaw carrying the money staggered and slumped down beside the packhorse just as pellets of stray buckshot struck the horse's rump.

The animal lunged out of the way, fighting the pull of its halter rope, trying to break free. The horse's sudden movement gave Jim Bob another shot at the downed outlaw. He jacked back the second hammer and fired again.

The robber flipped over on his back, screaming with pain as the money sacks fell to the dirt beside him. One of the bags opened, and in gusts of wind sweeping down Main Street, a swirl of paper currency tumbled down the road like giant snowflakes.

A rifle popped as Jim Bob was ducking down to reload, and he felt something sting the top of his head. His Stetson, still red with Wayland Burke's blood, was swept away before he could make a grab for it.

The stinging sensation became a sharper pain. He touched the spot with his fingertips, feeling something wet in his hair. And there was more he couldn't see . . . his fingers traced a deep gash running from the front of his scalp to the back of his head.

He glanced at his fingertips and found them dripping blood, and then blood ran from his hairline down his forehead into his eyes.

"I'm shot!" he gasped, feeling suddenly dizzy. "Son of a bitch! I'm shot!"

He fell against the bricks, too shocked to think of reloading at the moment. The pain across the top of his skull was worsening. Blood began to pour down his cheeks, staining the front of his shirt.

"No," he whispered, trembling from head to toe, still staring at his bloody fingers. He was sure he would bleed to death unless someone came to help him.

"I'm shot, Marshal Earp!" he yelled at the top of his lungs, overcome by fear of dying. "Somebody come help me afore I bleed to death!"

No one answered him.

"Marshal! Can't you hear me? I'm shot right on top of my head, an' I'm bleedin' somethin' awful!"

Again, no voice answered his plea for assistance.

"Don't leave me here to die! Somebody's gotta come over here an' help me git to the doctor's house!"

He could hear someone groaning near the front of the bank during a moment of quiet. Then suddenly, two shotguns opened up from the marshal's office—four thundering blasts in quick succession.

"I'm gonna die," Jim Bob whispered. Right then, more than anything else, he feared dying alone. And he was thirsty. It seemed an odd time to want water.

"I hope you die real slow!" a voice cried from the bank, a thin voice filled with anger. "You done went an' shot Frankie down, you son of a bitch!"

A strange calm spread over Dodge City. Even though two banks were being robbed, not a sound could be heard from either end of Main Street. Jim Bob wiped blood away from his face; then his gaze happened to fall on Wayland Burke's body. Clouds of dark flies hovered over his corpse, making a noise like swarming bees.

"We're all gonna die," Jim Bob said, swallowing the bitter bile that was rising in his throat. "Every last one of us is gonna die on account of that money." He thought about his mother back in Clay County, Missouri, wishing she could be there with him then before he bled to death.

He hadn't wanted the deputy's job in the first place, but in the absence of any other employment until the big herds came up from Texas, he felt he had no choice. It was becoming a deputy, or cleaning out spittoons and mopping floors at one of the town's saloons. Being a part-time deputy, he earned less than twenty dollars a month.

"I'm gonna die over a twenty-dollar-a-month job," he said to himself, touching the tear in his scalp again. He shuddered when he felt bare skull where his skin was parted, and the pain had intensified. "I shoulda took that damn job down at the livery shovelin' out horse stalls fer ten bucks a month." At least he'd have been alive, and his head wouldn't have hurt like it did then; a pain like someone had put a hot branding iron against the top of his skull.

"We're comin' out!" a deep voice announced from the bank's windows. "Any sumbitch takes a shot at us, we're gonna kill him an' every friend he's got. We'll burn this whole goddamn town plumb to the ground! I hope all you sons of bitches are listenin', 'cause we damn sure mean what we say!"

Buzzing flies around Wayland Burke's body took Jim Bob's attention away from what was being said, but only for a moment, until he heard another voice farther down the street, coming from the savings bank.

"We're comin' out, too! The first gunshot I hear, I'm gonna blow this little woman's head clean off. Her name's Sara Jane Peabody. Any you sons of bitches want Miss Peabody's death on yer conscience, you start shootin'."

Jim Bob closed his eyes. Miss Peabody was about the most gentle woman in Dodge City; she played the foot-pump organ at the First Baptist Church every Sunday morning. For some bank robber to be willing to kill her seemed too cruel for him to think about right then.

A rifle exploded from the other end of Main, and at the moment Jim Bob didn't care. His head was throbbing now, and he couldn't clear his brain of a creeping fog.

"I done warned you!" the man shouted.

A gun went off, booming, followed by a woman's shriek.

"Jesus," Jim Bob mumbled, fighting to stay awake while the stabbing pains inside his head got worse. Someone—one of the bank robbers—had shot Miss Peabody.

It isn't fair, he thought, remembering Smoke Jensen for reasons he couldn't explain—what Cody had said, about how he was a really dangerous man with a six-gun. If Jensen was the kind of expert with weapons that Cody had said he was, then what was he doing to save the town?

"Next sumbitch we's gonna kill is this banker feller!" the same voice bellowed. "Name's Feagin. He's the next one to die unless all the shootin' stops!"

Jim Bob was losing consciousness. The gray fog was creeping closer to him, enveloping him like a blanket, and no matter how hard he tried, he couldn't keep his eyes open.

He slid down the brick wall, resting his bleeding head on the cool surface. His thoughts drifted back to Clay County and all the troubles in that part of Missouri after the war.

A gang of mounted Rebels led by a fellow named Quantrill had come blazing through Missouri and Kansas, killing Union sympathizers, burning their homes and barns to the ground. Among them was a man calling himself Bloody Bill Anderson, and opinions differed as to whether or not Bloody Bill had been killed right after the war was over. In far western Kansas Territory, all sorts of reports surfaced about Anderson and a gang of cutthroats still pillaging carpetbagger holdings. Someone had mentioned the possibility that Anderson might come to Dodge City on one of his raids.

Jim Bob's eyes batted shut. He wasn't thinking about Bill Anderson then. In a type of dream, he saw himself sitting by the edge of a muddy creek, holding a fishing pole, until he heard the sound of his mother's voice.

"Time fer supper!"

And then Jim Bob felt hungry as well as thirsty. He wished for some of his mother's sweet cornbread, covered with butter and a splash of cane syrup.

The rattle of guns brought him back from his dream with a start. The din of gunfire seemed endless.

In a daze he opened his shotgun, fumbling to pull out the spent shells, knowing he was expected to help Marshal Earp and the others to win this fight. But when he tried to put fresh loads into his gun, his fingers felt numb and they wouldn't work right.

The last sound he heard was a scream, and he couldn't be altogether sure it wasn't his own. . . .

23

Smoke listened to the young deputy's cries for help. He had no way to go to the man's aid without exposing himself to gunfire on two sides. Many times, the innocent became the most tragic of all victims in duels between men with guns. A gun was no better than the man who used it . . . the amount of savvy he had, knowing when to shoot and when to wait for the odds to change in his favor.

The odds were still long against Smoke and his cowboys, and the lawmen sworn to protect Dodge City, although Smoke had done his part to change things. Leaving three men dead in an alley behind the bank, his latest victim being an Indian with a long knife scar on his face, he made his way to a side street with his rifle, pausing at the corner of a building to listen to a voice that was shouting demands to everyone in town who was in hearing distance, a warning to anyone who shot at the raiders, when they left the bank with the loot, that they would be killed.

The bank robbers were coming out, no doubt with the money from both vaults. Smoke hoped Cal and Pearlie had the good sense to wait for an opportunity. When the gang tried to leave town they would be exposed to riflemen on rooftops, and to Marshal Earp, along with his remaining deputy . . . if the last deputy were still alive and able to shoot.

Looking down the side street, Smoke saw two bodies. Blood had pooled around both raiders, attracting flies. The wind was picking up from the northwest. In a matter of minutes the gang would ride out of Dodge with every cent both banks had, including the money Smoke had come all the way from Sugarloaf to bring back to Sally, the profits from their cross-breeding program. And as he thought about this, he decided he'd be damned if he'd let them do it . . . not without a fight. He'd given them as much fight as he could without risking his life in a careless fashion, but as it became clear that the bank robbers were close to making their escape, it was high time he gave those land pirates a lesson in mountain-man justice.

Bent over, rifle at the ready, Smoke made his way cautiously to Main Street, where he hesitated at a corner of the town's lone barbershop. A red and white barber's pole out front told him what was inside the building.

Okay, boys, he thought, *I'm ready for you to make your move to pull out.* He had seven shells in his Winchester, and a dozen more in a pair of pistols. By making sure of every shot, he had a chance to make them pay dearly for the spoils they hoped to take from Dodge.

Someone was moaning near the front of the Cattleman's Bank, a quiet sound, full of the misery of a serious wound. And on the far side of Main, he could hear one of Earp's deputies crying out for his mother, a not-all-that-uncommon occurrence when men were dying.

Tilting his head, he gave the rooftop where Pearlie lay hidden a glance; then his eyes wandered down to Cal's position before he returned his attention to Main Street.

"Let's go, boys," he whispered, growing more impatient as each minute passed, ready for the killing to begin.

A shuffling noise forced Smoke to take a look around the corner of the barbershop. Two men came out of the bank, laden with sacks of money. It was a shot too good to pass up, and he took it quickly, firing his rifle twice, as fast as he could pull the trigger and work the ejection lever.

A man in a fringed buckskin coat yelped when Smoke's first slug hit him in the ribs. He flung four bags of money over his head and fell off the boardwalk, reaching for his right side with both hands.

Smoke's second bullet struck a slope-shouldered cowboy who was wearing a bandanna over his face, catching him between his shirt pockets while he made an attempt to load bags of money onto a nervous bay. He dropped in the dirt as though he'd been hit on the head with an axe handle.

"I done warned you!" an angry voice shouted from inside the bank. "You jest got yer bank president killed!"

A tall, thin man in a vest and blue suit coat was pushed out on the boardwalk, staggering to maintain his balance just seconds before a shotgun blast caught him between his shoulderblades. He dove off the walkway shrieking with pain, arms outstretched as if he meant to embrace a loved one, with tiny tufts of blue material swirling from the back of his coat where shotgun pellets shredded it. His cry echoed up and down Main until he landed on his face, bouncing limply, and then he was silent, still.

"The yellow bastards," Smoke hissed, jaw muscles working furiously. One of the outlaws had shot another unarmed citizen of Dodge.

He pulled back behind the barbershop, feeling white-hot rage swell in his chest. Without knowing how many more innocent people were held hostage inside either of the banks, shooting at the outlaws would be too costly in human lives. He was sure of what Preacher would have done in the same situation, trying to do battle with men inside a town! He would wait until the robbers rode off with their ill-gotten gains, and then he would go after them in surroundings where the advantage would change on behalf of a man who knew wild country, its secrets, and the ways of stalking men who knew less about staying alive with no buildings to protect them. It wouldn't matter to Preacher if there were no mountains to hide him as he went about seeking revenge. Preacher was a man who had mastered the art of hiding in plain sight, a fact known only briefly to many of his enemies before he took their lives. And this was a gift Preacher had given young Kirby Jensen so many years ago—careful instruction in the stalking of men.

Smoke decided it would save lives to let the raiders leave Dodge in peace. Then he would go after them, killing them off a few at a time.

He rested his rifle against the building and cupped his hands around his mouth, facing the Marshal's office. "Marshal Earp!" he yelled. "This is Smoke Jensen! Let 'em ride out with the money! Too much blood's already been spilled!"

No answer came from Earp's office for several seconds, and then a voice shouted back. "Whatever you say, Jensen! My deputy an' me are layin' down our guns!"

Smoke added a message to his cowboys. "Pearlie! Cal! Don't shoot when they come outside! Let 'em go!"

He didn't need an answer from Cal or Pearlie to know they would follow his instructions. For a time he waited, listening to wounded men and women moan and groan in the street, until a harsh voice spoke to everyone in Dodge.

"This better not be no trick! We got us a woman here, an' we'll blow her goddamn head off if anybody shoots at us. We're comin' out!"

Smoke drew back, turning for the alley so he could get back up on the roof. He wanted to see what direction the outlaws went while Cal and Pearlie were fetching his horse.

He raced back up the alleyway, jumping atop the empty flour keg to climb up on the roof of the cafe. He gave the three men he had killed only a passing glance before he started up to the rooftop.

Removing his hat, he peered over the false front of Martha's as several men came cautiously from the front door of the bank, a woman being shoved in front of one gunman who was holding a pistol to the back of her head.

A heavily muscled man with a black beard glanced up at the rooftops holding a rifle while five or six men began loading bags of money onto a horse and a brown mule. Turning to the front of the savings bank, he saw eight or nine men move cautiously out on the boardwalk with guns and more bags of money.

One man in particular stood out, an older gent wearing a Confederate cavalryman's hat and a gray tunic. His pants were stuffed into the stovepipe tops of cavalry boots. His long hair had turned silver with age, and his face had a craggy look about it. He wore a curious yellow Confederate officer's sash around his waist, and below it he carried a pair of low-slung pistols in cutaway holsters.

I reckon that could be Bloody Bill Anderson, Smoke thought, not really caring either way.

"Sooner or later I'm gonna kill him for what he done here," he whispered savagely, passing one quick glance across the bloody bodies of two women and a boy with his face drenched in blood, the kid couldn't have been more than fifteen or sixteen. Farther down the street a storekeeper lay in front of his hat-and-boot shop wearing a blood-soaked apron. And in front of the bank, the bank president lay on his chest with a swarm of blowflies feeding on dozens of tiny, bloody holes in his back. There was so much blood in the street and on various boardwalks, it appeared that someone had meant to paint the town and its main road a dark red color. At some rendezvous point away from Dodge City, Smoke intended to add a splash of the same color to whatever ground happened to be occupied by this outlaw gang—when he caught up to them and began killing them one or two at a time, as many as he could before he moved to another position to start killing again. He could scarcely control his anger then, looking down upon what the raiders had done to unarmed folks. He would make them pay when the time and circumstances were right.

A few outlaws were gathering up loose horses, still wary, keeping their guns at the ready while they went about bringing mounts to the front of each bank. Some of the robbers began to mount up, covering the rooftops and the front of the Marshal's office with shotguns and pistols and rifles.

I hope Marshal Earp and his deputy are smart enough to let them ride out without taking a shot, Smoke thought. Earp would likely send a telegram to the army post at Fort Larned, asking for their help. Smoke's experience with soldiers had convinced him that, in most cases, the cavalry was virtually useless. By the time they got to a particular spot where there had been some trouble, the troublemakers were usually long gone.

But in this instance, another revenge-seeker would take up the outlaws' trail long before a company of cavalrymen could get to Dodge—a man who understood how to exact vengeance.

The last bank robber was in the saddle, and the silver-haired gent in the Confederate uniform gave a signal to the others to start riding, proving he was leader of the bunch, as Smoke had known all along.

The rumble of galloping hooves passed beneath the cafe as Smoke dropped out of sight; then he rose just enough to get a quick count of the men he would be after.

"Less than fifteen," he said. "Closer to fourteen, maybe a few less." Between Smoke and his men, and Marshal Earp, they had thinned the robbers' ranks considerably. Not that it gave Smoke that much satisfaction. He wouldn't be satisfied until the last outlaw was dead, and the money was back in the bank vaults.

Earp's face was waxy white when he met Smoke in the middle of Main Street. He spoke first. "I sent Cody to the telegraph office to get off a wire to Fort Larned," he said, passing a sad look across the wounded and dead who had been citizens of Dodge. "Cody took a slug in his shoulder. Jim Bob's over yonder unconscious with a wound to his head. We'll need the doc quick as he can get here. What folks are still alive are hurt real bad. Timmy, the boy with blood all over his face, lost both of his eyes when they got him with a shotgun."

Smoke nodded, watching Pearlie and Cal hurry toward him from a side street. "We didn't have no choice, Marshal," he said in a tired voice. "They were killin' too many innocent people."

"The army'll catch 'em sooner or later," Earp said, sounding convinced of it.

Smoke turned his gaze to the south, watching the dust cloud rising above the fleeing outlaws. His eyes slitted. "Not if I get to 'em first," he said, barely raising his voice.

"You aim to go after 'em yourself?" Earp asked. "Why, you ain't got but two men to help you."

"They won't go with me," Smoke replied. "I'm leavin' them to watch over our cow herd."

"You can't be serious," Earp said.

"Dead serious," Smoke told him, never taking his eyes from the dust on the southern horizon.

"There's too many of 'em," Earp stated flatly, like he did not fully believe Smoke's intentions.

"Depends," Smoke said, just as Cal and Pearlie trotted up to him.

"What you want us to do, boss?" Pearlie asked, balancing his rifle in one hand.

"Keep a close eye on our cows. Make damn sure they get lots of hay an' water till I get back."

"I just knowed you was gonna say that," Pearlie exclaimed, with a look toward Cal for agreement. "You aim to track 'em down an' kill 'em."

"That's right," Smoke replied, only a hoarse whisper. "Every last one of 'em, includin' that gent wearing the gray uniform."

"I figure that was Bloody Bill Anderson," Pearlie said.

"I don't give a damn who he is," Smoke told him; then his jaw turned to granite.

"I don't believe this," Marshal Earp said, "that just one man would set out after more'n a dozen armed outlaws. You won't stand a chance."

"Maybe not," Smoke answered quietly, as the dust sign moved farther away. "Won't know till I get there, don't reckon."

24

Cal hurried up beside Smoke as he was headed down to the cow pens beside the railroad tracks to saddle his Palouse. Smoke's mind was on something else—tracking the bank robbers wherever they were going—and he hardly noticed the boy walking next to him; not until Cal spoke.

"Wanted to ask you somethin', Mr. Jensen."

"Ask," was all Smoke said.

"Pearlie told me there come a time back when you was a whole lot younger'n me, when Preacher took you off with him to tangle with a bunch of honest-to-goodness bad men."

"I was some younger," Smoke answered, walking past the store where the man in the bloody apron lay on his back, his wife at his side, crying. "It wasn't of my choosing. Things happened. I didn't have much selection when the time came. I reckon you could say it was us or them."

"Then I say it's time you took me with you now," Cal said. "I give you my word I won't git in the way an' that I'll be a help catchin' them crooks."

"Too many of 'em this time," Smoke told the boy gently. "If it wasn't gonna be so one-sided, I might take you along. This ain't exactly the right sort of situation for you to cut your teeth on."

"Don't matter how many there is," Cal argued. "I want to go, an' I know I'm ready. I won't let you down—honest, I won't. I can carry my share of the load, an' I'm a right decent shot with a rifle."

"There's some things about slippin' up on a man you ain't learned yet."

"You can teach me now. Couldn't be no better chance than right now."

"Sally would kill me if something happened to you."

"Ain't nothin' gonna happen. I'll do exactly like you say, an' won't give you no argument."

Smoke gave it some consideration. He hadn't been as old as Cal when he and Preacher and Emmett had tangled with that bunch up in the northwest part of Kansas Territory. But Cal was awkward at times, careless, like when he forgot to look for the hump in the bay colt's back when they left Sugar-loaf, and a mistake like that could get him killed.

"It's real clear them outlaws've got plenty of experience under 'em," Smoke said, lengthening his strides, forcing Cal to break into a trot to stay up with him. "This would be the wrong bunch for you to cross trails with."

"I ain't scared, Mr. Jensen."

"Being scared's got nothing to do with it."

"I'm nearly beggin' fer the chance. I shot down one of them robbers when they rode in. Hit a movin' target with this here rifle. That oughta be worth somethin', an' I done swore I'd do just what you said to do."

They got to the corral fence, where their horses grazed on a mound of prairie hay. Smoke couldn't quite make up his mind about Cal's request. In most respects the boy was old enough to take care of himself in a tight spot. However, the spot where they met up with this batch of bad men might get tighter than what was ordinary.

"Pearlie could use your help here," he said, knowing that the excuse sounded weak.

"Pearlie's able to take care of these here cows without no help from me, an' you know it, Mr. Jensen. How come you ain't got no faith I can handle myself?"

He halted and turned to the young cowboy. "I *do* have faith in you, son. That isn't what's eatin' at me. The men we'll be after are seasoned to being hunted . . . especially if it's Bloody Bill Anderson's boys. They've been hounded all over the middle of this country by lawmen and the cavalry. They won't be easy to catch unawares. They'll be expectin' somebody to be close on their heels. This job's gonna take a man who's done this sort of thing before."

Cal looked him straight in the eye. "I can do it," he said, a promise Smoke knew he truly meant. "You just gotta give me a chance to prove myself."

What Cal said struck a chord deep within Smoke. There had been a time when Preacher had given him the chance to prove he was a man—a fighting man. But when Smoke thought about what Sally would say, he hesitated. If anything happened to Cal he would have hell to pay with the woman he loved. Cal had become, in a sense, like the son they never had. If Smoke brought him back to Sugarloaf in a pine box, or with a debilitating injury that left him a cripple for the rest of his life, Sally would never forgive him.

"I figure I've earned the chance," Cal said, standing as tall as he knew how. "I've done everything you an' Miz Jensen ever asked me to do, an' a time or two I've showed I had nerve when it comes to handlin' a gun."

"It won't be nerves you'll need. This is mostly open land to the south of here, till we strike the Nations. You need the know-how when it comes to slippin' up on a man where there ain't enough natural cover."

"You can learn me. I'm willin' to do whatever it takes to learn how." He glanced back at the main street through Dodge City. "I've seen my share of blood. Them poor folks who got shot back yonder deserve some justice. I hadn't wanted to say nothin' about it, but seems like you an' Miz Jensen don't never aim to stop treatin' me like a little kid. I'm darn near full-growed. Time I learned a few things 'bout stayin' alive, like when Preacher showed you how."

He stared into Cal's eyes, wondering. "There's no doubt you can learn it, son. You've got plenty of smarts. A time or two you've showed a tendency toward distractions. Like when that bay colt tossed you off."

"That was different. Wasn't no reason to be so all fired careful then."

Smoke's expression turned to a scowl. "That's where you're wrong. There's always a good reason to be careful. A man never knows what's out there lookin' to end his days. You can't use that one on me."

Cal tilted his head a little. "How 'bout the real reason I want to go?" he asked.

"And what's this real reason?" Smoke wondered aloud.

"Makin' them sorry sons of bitches pay. I was lookin' right down on that kid they shot in the face. Marshal Earp said the boy was stone blind on account of it. It sticks in my craw like sand when some owl-hoot with a gun shoots a man who ain't armed, an' that was just a youngster."

"Made you mad, did it?"

"Yessir, it did. Makes me wanna take a gun to the rotten bastard who done it. It don't seem right he can just blind that boy an' ride off with sackfuls of money. If we don't catch up to 'em, they'll hide down in Injun Territory, an' won't nobody ever make the bastard who shot that kid's eyeballs out of his head pay."

"Justice is a job for the law, Cal. We don't carry badges or have any legal jurisdiction in this affair."

"You know darned well nobody's gonna catch 'em 'less we do, and we gotta git on their trail damned quick."

Smoke let out a deep sigh. Sally was as much of a concern as the boy's safety. If Sally found out he had taken Cal with him after more than a dozen killers, Smoke could count on sleeping out in the bunkhouse with Pearlie all the next winter, and maybe well into the next spring. But there was something about the way Cal said what was on his mind that touched an inner part of Smoke's soul. He understood as well as any man what it was like to want justice for folks who couldn't defend themselves.

"Please let me go, Mr. Jensen," Cal begged. "It's somethin' I just gotta do. . . ."

"All right, Cal. Get your horse saddled and bring our gear and our saddlebags down from the hotel. Make sure we've got some coffee an' fatback. We could be on the trail of these robbers for a week or more."

Cal's entire face lit up with a grin. "I'll be back afore you knowed I was gone," he said, breaking into a run toward the hotel. He glanced back over his shoulder. "I'll tell Pearlie what we aim to do."

Smoke turned back to the corral fence, hoping he'd made the right choice. *Boys have to come of age sometime,* he thought, realizing that some of them did it earlier than others. But if Cal got himself in trouble during this manhunt, Smoke knew he would never be able to forgive himself. And a little woman up in Colorado Territory would be even less likely to overlook what he'd done, no matter what reasons or explanations he gave her. She had taken to Cal almost from the first day he went to Sugarloaf, and she mothered him like her own child.

Pearlie gave him a wary look. "You ain't really gonna let that young 'un go with you, is you?"

Cal was across the corral saddling the stud and his bay gelding. "He sorta begged me into it, Pearlie. I reckon he's old enough."

"What he ain't got enough of is good sense," Pearlie exclaimed. "He ain't smart enough to pour his own water outta his boot."

Behind them, the town of Dodge City was attending to its dead and wounded, and the sounds of sobbing and groaning reached Smoke's ears before he replied. "He was smart enough to put a cocklebur in *your* boot, Pearlie."

"You know danged well that's different, boss. Cal ain't hardly more'n out of diapers."

"He's old enough. High time he learned how to survive when he's up against tough situations."

Pearlie made a disgusted face, and Smoke knew it was because he cared for the boy. "This is a helluva lot more'n a tough situation. Them's some genuine bad hombres, an' they proved it here today."

Smoke disagreed, although he knew the robbers were hard types. "They didn't show me much. Yellow bastards shot down unarmed women an' kids an' the banker, besides that old man who came out with his goose gun. Don't take a lot of courage or savvy with a firearm to do what they did. They're just a bunch of greedy men who had an advantage. Leastways, that's what they figured. I aim to show 'em just how wrong they were."

Pearlie watched Cal leading both horses through a corral gate toward them. "I won't sleep a damn wink the whole time you two is gone," he grumbled.

Smoke was sticking by his decision, even if he did have some reservations. "I doubt we'll get a helluva lot of sleep ourselves, Pearlie. Those boys are gonna be hard to catch in this open country without them knowin' we're back there."

Pearlie lowered his voice, like what he was about to say embarrassed him. "Just watch out fer that young 'un best you can, Smoke. Only, don't tell him I said so."

"Showing you've got a soft side, Pearlie?" he asked with a grin.

"Hell no. Just worried 'bout what Miz Jensen's gonna say if'n he don't come back in one piece."

"He has to grow up one of these days. I'm hoping Sally'll understand."

"She ain't got no understandin' when it comes to that there young 'un. She quit fixin' me bearclaws fer a whole damn month one time after I got on him fer leavin' that south pasture gate open so them weaned calves got back with the cows. Never was so hungry in all my borned days."

Cal walked up, leading the Palouse stud and his bay. He had his rifle booted, with their saddlebags tied behind the cantles of their saddles.

"Ready to ride," Cal said, handing Smoke his reins.

Pearlie wagged his head like he was disgusted. "You's ready to ride into a mess," he said. "You ain't plumb dry behind them ears yet. I'm against what you're doin', only it don't make one damn bit of difference to me if'n you're hardheaded enough to want to do it anyhow."

Cal glanced at Smoke. "I'm doin' it anyhow," he said, as he put a boot in his left stirrup to mount.

Smoke booted his Winchester and climbed aboard the stud with a final glance at the crowds on Main Street. "Take good care of our steers, Pearlie," he said. "We'll be back quick as we can get this job done."

Pearlie looked down at his boots a moment. "Sure do hope the two of you can git it done."

"We'll manage," Smoke answered, reining his Palouse toward the south. "Tell Marshal Earp we'll be back with the town's money, soon as we find the right spot to take it back from those yellow bastards."

"I'll tell him what you said," Pearlie remarked, scuffing one boot toe in the dirt, unable to look directly at Cal when the boy swung his leg over the colt.

Smoke led Cal away from the cattle pens, across two sets

of railroad tracks, heading due south. They urged their horses to a gallop.

"Pearlie sure did act strange just now," Cal said above the rattle of iron horseshoes across flinty soil.

"He was just worried," Smoke replied.

"Worried 'bout what?" Cal asked. "He don't think I can take care of myself?"

"That wasn't it," Smoke said. "Pearlie's just a born worrier, is all it was."

25

Marshal Earp came down the street toward Pearlie, watching Smoke and Cal ride off. Pearlie heard his footsteps and turned around.

"I was aimin' to tell Mr. Jensen we couldn't get that wire through to Fort Larned. Somebody must've cut the telegraph line some place east of here. Clifford Barnes at the telegraph office has been tryin' to put a message through ever since those outlaws came to town."

"Don't take no real deep thinker to figure who it was," Pearlie said. "Them bank robbers done it. Accordin' to the way Smoke feels 'bout the cavalry, wouldn't've done no helluva lot of good nohow."

Earp watched the silhouettes of Jensen and his cowboy ride toward the southern horizon. "I ain't got much faith in the army neither," he said. "That leaves Mr. Jensen and your pardner to handle things by themselves. No offense to Mr. Jensen intended, but I ain't got much faith in them two havin' a chance against so many shootists. Your boss man an' your pardner are liable to get killed."

Pearlie shook his head. "Won't worry Smoke none at all, Marshal. Fact is, he'd rather do the job all by his lonesome, anyways. A cavalry outfit would only git in his way."

Earp slitted his eyelids against dust that was borne on a gust of wind, and coming at his face. "Is Jensen really that tough a customer?" he asked.

"Toughest I ever knowed. An' he was worse 'bout killin' men back when he was younger, afore he settled down."

"Looks like he killed three men back in that alley behind the cafe, and I saw him shoot down several more. Then there was that pair he got while he was on them roofs. It don't seem all that natural, how just one man can be so all-fired good at killin' folks. I'm sure this robbery was the doings of Bloody Bill Anderson, an' he's got one helluva bad reputation for killin' folks himself. If them two meet up south of here, even as tough as you say Smoke Jensen is, he won't stand a snowball's chance in hell against so many hard-nosed killers as them."

"You could be eatin' them words," Pearlie told him as he saw Smoke and Cal disappear over a rolling hill. "My money's on Smoke an' the boy, only I sure do hope that young 'un don't jump in front of no bullet when Smoke ain't around to see after him like he oughta."

"The boy did look a bit green," Earp agreed.

"He's young yet, only he's got the best teacher he could have."

Earp wheeled like he was headed back to town, then took a moment's pause. "Even if Jensen is every bit as good as you say, there's too many of Anderson's men. Hope this won't be the last time I set eyes on your boss man. He's taken on one helluva big bite this time."

"He can chew it," Pearlie replied. "I've seen him come out of worse messes than this one without a scratch. It may take him some time, but he'll be back with the town's money sure as snuff makes spit."

"I'll try to form up a posse, only I don't figure there's many who'll ride with me. Most folks who live here are businessmen or out-of-work cowboys, waitin' for the herds to come up the Chisholm. Not many who can shoot straight. One of my deputies is hurt bad, an' the other's got a notch in his arm that won't let him sit a horse. That don't leave me too many choices."

"I'd go," Pearlie said, "only Smoke told me to stay with the herd. One thing I ain't gonna do is go against none of Smoke's orders. Sorry, Marshal, but I'd sooner tangle with a grizzly as face Smoke Jensen if I didn't do like he told me to."

"I understand," Earp said, starting off toward Main Street. "Maybe Clifford can find where that wire's been cut. Right now I'd better see to helpin' the wounded over to the doc's place. That boy Timmy is blind as a bat, an' there's others bad hurt. No tellin' how many are dead. Hadn't had time to start a count yet."

Pearlie knew that the death toll would be high. It was small consolation, but there was also a goodly number of Anderson's gang decorating the streets and alleys across Dodge. Bloody Bill had paid a high price to empty out two bank vaults, but he was about to pay the highest price of all, in Pearlie's estimation, for making the mistake of pulling a raid on Dodge City's banks while Smoke was in town.

26

Jack Starr was waiting for an opportunity, although he knew Bill would be expecting something from any one of his men. As they pushed their horses south Jack counted thirteen survivors of the raid, a damned unlucky number for a man who was superstitious. But two of Bill's most loyal followers died in the fight that day, and that would be a help. Homer Suggins and Scar Face had been killed trying to bring down the big cowboy who kept moving around on Dodge City's rooftops. Jack wondered who the guy was, and how come he was so damned hard to kill. Somebody calling himself Smoke Jensen had yelled across the street to the City Marshal, telling him to stop shooting. If Jensen was the man who had killed Homer and Scar Face Parker, it was a name Jack didn't recognize.

One or two more steadfast supporters of Bloody Bill remained alive, riding on either flank. It would be hard to shoot Bill in the back with both of them underlings around, so close to Bill, but killing Bill was a chore that needed to be done. Bill had been losing his mind the last year or two, getting badly drunk, rambling on about the old days, the war. His plan to escape into the Nations was a stupid move, and it meant they'd be living on beans and fry bread for months, instead of heading out to California or some place where they could enjoy the money they'd just stolen. Bill was living in the past, believing that all they needed to do was hide from the army and the law. But the law had gotten a helluva lot smarter lately, and there were telegraph wires and railroad lines running all over the place now. With their ranks so dangerously thin, they couldn't fight off a big company of cavalry or a posse of any size. It was time to take Bill out of the picture, so his damned foolish hardheadedness wouldn't get all of them killed or caught.

Joe Lucas rode off to Bill's right. Lucas was dangerous, a man with eyes in the back of his head. Shorty Russel was the type who'd kill a man in his sleep if Bill gave the order, and he was on Bill's left as Bill led the gang and four pack animals loaded with money toward the Kansas line.

What Jack needed most was an ally, someone he could trust when he shot Bill and Lucas and Russel off their horses, a man who would watch his backside while he told the rest of the gang what his plan was—to cut up the money in equal shares and split up, making them that much harder to track down. But Jack wasn't quite sure who to trust among the survivors. He rode at the rear with big Buster Young and was a quiet man whom nobody knew much about, yet he had been with them for several years and never once shirked a job or his responsibility. If Jack remembered right, Buster was from Texas.

He decided to take Buster into his confidence. Leaning out of the saddle, he spoke to Buster in a hushed voice, ready to kill him if he made like he meant to warn Anderson of his plan.

"The army's gonna come after us hard, Buster," he said as their horses trotted over a rocky knob fifty yards behind the others. "We ain't got enough men left to put up much of a fight if they catch us. I've tried to talk Bill into splittin' up the money an' splittin' up the gang fer a spell. He won't listen to a word I say."

Buster glanced over his shoulder, the same shoulder where he carried a sawed-off Greener shotgun on a leather strap. He wore a Colt pistol in a cross-pull holster. "We all damn near got killed back yonder," Buster said. "That son of a bitch shootin' down from that little cafe damn near got me 'fore I could git in the bank with Bill. Bill was talkin' plumb crazy inside there. He shot Lee Wollard hisself when Lee hit that banker too hard over the head. Said he didn't have no use fer a man without good sense. I got to thinkin', maybe Bill aimed to kill us all. His eyes got this funny look to 'em."

"Bill ain't right in the head no more," Jack said. "He's liable to turn on every one of us an' shoot us down for our shares of the money. Lucas an' Russel will back his play if he decides he wants a bigger share. I been keepin' my eyes on Bill since we rode out of town. He don't act right."

"He damn sure don't," Buster agreed.

Jack let a silence pass. "One thing *we* could do is make sure Bill don't shoot us."

"How'd we do that?" Buster asked.

Jack spoke very softly. "We could shoot him down first, afore he kills us. Most of the rest of the boys would go along with cuttin' up the money now an' ridin' different directions, maybe in pairs. You an' me could take our shares an' head out to California, or maybe to Texas an' cross over the Mexican border where the law can't touch us."

Buster frowned. "Maybe that ain't such a bad idea, Jack, only we'd best be damn sure we done it right. Bill an' Joe an' Shorty'll kill both of us quicker'n we can sneeze if we don't git 'em first. Mexico would be the safest place to hide. We'd have enough money to live like kings down there."

Jack hoped he could trust Buster to keep up his end of the

bargain. "We'd better do it quick," he said, taking the hammer thong off his Dance revolver for an easy, quick pull. "We'll ride up behind 'em like we need to talk about somethin'. I'll shoot Bill soon as I'm close enough. You take Shorty with that scattergun, an' I'll go for Lucas whilst you cover everybody else with your second barrel an' pistol. Then I'll explain what we's aimin' to do. We'll find us a low spot so nobody can skyline us an' we'll count the money an' cut it up ten ways, 'less we have to shoot one or two more."

Buster swelled, rubbing beard stubble and his square jaw. "It's gonna be risky as hell, but I'll go along with it. You ride up behind Bill, 'cause he's gonna be the most dangerous. I can stay off to one side an' blow Shorty plumb outta his saddle 'fore I wheel around an' cover the rest. But watch out Lucas don't git you. He's fast as hell, an' he's got a nose fer trouble when it's behind him."

"Let's do it," Jack said, urging his horse to a faster gait, with his heart pumping. Bill Anderson would be wary, but then he trusted Jack and he wasn't likely to suspect anything was wrong until it was too late.

Jogging past the other raiders and the heavily laden pack animals, Jack kept his hand away from his gun. He wouldn't reach for his Dance until he was close . . . very close.

He noticed that Sammy McCoy was sobbing quietly, and he knew it was over his brother Claude. A lot of good men had died back in Dodge that day—some better than others. Jack hadn't known that Bill had gunned Lee Wollard down until Buster told him. It was just one more reason to kill Bill before his mind left him completely.

He came within twenty or thirty feet of Bill's back before Bill and Joe Lucas both glanced backward. Jack grinned and gave them both a nod. From the corner of his eye he saw Buster riding a little bit behind and to his right.

Bill and Joe turned their gazes toward Buster, and then

Bill gave a silent nod. The gesture bewildered Jack, taking him by surprise.

Jack heard the dull metallic click of a shotgun being cocked, and he looked quickly over at Buster. Buster had his Greener aimed directly at *him.*

The blast swept Jack out of his saddle like a hurricane-force wind, a fiery, hot wind that made his face and chest and belly burn. He felt himself sailing toward the ground as his horse spooked, galloping out of the way.

Jack landed on his side in the dirt, opening his mouth to yell, when several of his teeth fell out, rolling off his tongue. He tried to move, to escape the most awful pain he'd ever known, but he found he was paralyzed.

"He was gonna shoot you in the back, Bill," he heard Buster say, "just like you said he was plannin' to do. He wanted me to help him do it."

"You'll get half of his share along with yours, Buster," he heard Bill growl. "I never did trust the sumbitch. Just leave him there to die. Fetch his horse an' let's keep pushin'."

Jack's last conscious thought was one of anger, because he'd been double-crossed by Buster Young. If he'd been able, Jack would have gotten up and killed them all, the rotten bastards.

His eyes closed.

27

Their trail was easy to follow—shod horses crossing barren ground, tracks spread some distance apart, indicating that the outlaws were pushing their horses as hard as they could. Smoke kept an eye on the horizon. Far to the south, when they rode higher hills, he could see scattered trees in the distance. Near the Kansas border they would come to the Cimarron River, and beyond it they would be in Indian Territory. Anderson was running for the most lawless stretch of land he could find, where a handful of Federal Marshals tried to keep peace in lands given to various Indian tribes after the big treaty at Medicine Lodge.

Cal was studying the hoofprints. "They been keepin' their horses in a long trot, Mr. Jensen. Won't be long 'til they have to stop an' rest 'em."

"They'll pick a low place where they'll be harder to see," he told Cal. "We'll have to be careful we don't ride up on 'em unawares."

"I got it figured they'll keep rear guards posted, 'cause they know somebody'll come after 'em."

"That's a fact," he said. "Might give us a chance to take a few of 'em on, that rear guard you called it. If they stray too far from the main bunch, I might be able to slip up behind 'em."

"But there ain't no cover," Cal protested, giving Smoke a look.

"There's plenty of cover out here," he replied, "if a man knows how to use it."

Cal gave their surroundings another examination. "Just some brush an' tumbleweeds."

"It's enough."

"Then you'll slip up on 'em on foot?" the boy asked.

"Be the easiest way, if they're far enough from the rest of the gang so I can get behind 'em."

Cal shook his head. "Don't seem like nearly enough places to hide to me."

Smoke knew that the youngster wanted an explanation. "It's what some Indian tribes use, son. A white man, unless he's been shown a few tricks, is lookin' for the shape of a man on a horse, or a man walking upright. Most men are lookin' for what they expect to see, and they aren't ready for somethin' else."

"You aim to crawl on your belly?"

"Depends," Smoke said. "I'll have to wait an' see what they give me."

"If they're smart they won't give you much."

"Most men aren't as smart as they think. You learn to use any kind of cover there is, cover that'll hide a man."

"That's some of what Preacher taught you?"

"Some. There's a whole lot more to it. You've got to learn it a little bit at a time. Takes some practice to get it right an' not make any fatal mistakes."

Cal still seemed puzzled. "Even a man crawlin' on his belly in this brush won't be hid from a pair of good eyes, seems like to me."

"That's because you know what I'm aimin' to do, son.

These boys we're after expect a posse, or the cavalry, to come ridin' hell-for-leather on their tracks. They won't be lookin' for one man on foot who understands how a pair of eyes can play tricks on the one doin' the lookin'.'"

"I'm not real sure I understand, Mr. Jensen, but I'll pay real close attention . . . so I can learn."

"That's the reason I brought you along, Cal. If my wife had any idea what I was doin' she'd yell so loud we'd hear her all the way from Sugarloaf to Kansas."

They rode up on the body, warned by circling buzzards that something dead awaited them—a fresh kill of some kind. When Smoke saw the corpse, he recognized him as one of the bank robbers.

"Appears they've already had some kind of disagreement," he said, halting the stud a few yards from blood-soaked ground where a bearded man lay sprawled on his back, his upper body riddled by buckshot.

Cal's cheeks weren't as dark as they had been. He gazed down at the dead man a few moments. "Shot at real close range," he finally said. "Tore the hell outta his face. Why would they shoot one of their own, Mr. Jensen?"

"Can't say for sure, but maybe this one got greedy. Wanted a bigger share."

Cal swallowed. "A shotgun makes one helluva mess, don't it?"

"It's good for close-quarters fighting, but it don't have much range."

"You hardly ever use one," Cal continued, unable to take his eyes off the body, "but you git real close to the men you're after, sometimes, an' then it seems like you always use a knife on 'em."

"A knife's quieter. Kinda depends on how many of 'em there is."

"You gonna use a knife on them rear guards when we find 'em?" he asked.

With his eyes, Smoke followed the tracks made by more than a dozen horses. "The situation will tell me what to use. If I can, I'll do it quiet. If I can't, I'll do it any way I can and change positions real quick."

"Change positions? That's so the rest of the gang won't come to the sound of your gun?"

He took a deep breath and collected his reins to ride off along the tracks. "Most times. But once in a while you *want to* draw somebody else to the sounds you make . . . only you gotta be ready for 'em when they show up."

Cal was reading Smoke's face. "How come you don't ever act scared, Mr. Jensen? Don't seem like you show no fear, even when you go up against a big bunch of killers."

Smoke nudged his stud with his boot heels. They rode away from the corpse side by side.

"Fear's a funny thing, Cal. It can do a feller some good if he understands what fear is. It's a warning. So long as you don't let it get the best of you, it can be a help."

"A help? Tell me how bein' afraid can help when it makes a feller nervous."

"You pay more attention to little things . . . the sounds around you—the smells, the way a bird flys, or the way a good range-bred horse behaves when it smells somethin' unfamiliar. It's nature's way of tellin' you to be careful."

Cal frowned, chewing his bottom lip. "I think I understand, Mr. Jensen, only sometimes, when I git scared of somethin', it gives me the shivers. All I can think about is gettin' the hell away from wherever I'm at."

"Most often," Smoke told him in a soft voice, "that's the smartest thing to do. It takes a few years before you know when to run and when to hold your ground."

*   *   *

"Yonder they are," Cal whispered, lying on his belly in a clump of sagebrush, overlooking a dry streambed that wound its way from east to west. "Looks like they's passin' around bottles of whiskey."

Smoke was intent upon what he saw below the hilltop, and he didn't answer for a spell. "All the better," he said. "Whiskey robs a man of the best edges on his senses. A man who's half drunk don't hear or see nearly so good."

"I still can't see no rear guard, like you figured they'd have," Cal continued.

"There's two of 'em," Smoke said. "Back this way about a quarter mile."

Cal focused all his attention on the land between the hill and the dry creek. "I still don't see a damn thing, Mr. Jensen. Not a single thing nowhere."

"Look to the left of that big rock," Smoke whispered. "See how the brush in back of it is layin' down? That's where a pair of careless men walked up to that rock to keep an eye on things while the main bunch rested their horses an' had a little drink or two."

Cal narrowed his eyes in the afternoon sun. "I see what looks like a trail of some kind leadin' up to that rock, but I can't see nobody. Nary a soul."

"That's because they've hid behind the rock," Smoke said as he pushed back on his belly off the crest of the hill. "All you can see is the trail they left behind while they got to that spot on foot."

Smoke straightened up when he was out of sight behind the hill. He walked down to the Palouse and hung his Stetson on his saddle horn.

"Are you goin' after 'em?" Cal asked, watching Smoke take off his boots to put on a pair of Pawnee moccasins he removed from his saddlebags.

"I'll see if I can slip up on 'em before they move," he said, taking his Arkansas Toothpick from the sheath inside his right boot. "You stay here an' hold the horses. Don't look over that hilltop, no matter what you hear. Don't matter what happens, you stay put. You hear?"

"Yessir. I'll be right here, waitin' on you.

He stared into the young cowboy's eyes a moment, thinking of Sally and the closeness both of them felt toward Cal. "If you hear a gunshot, climb on this bay an' head back to Dodge just as fast as these horses can travel."

"I won't leave you if'n yer in trouble, no matter what," he answered.

"I admire that in you, son, but this is one time when you do exactly what I tell you to do. If you hear a gun, it'll mean they saw me before I got to them. Don't give me no argument. You get up on that horse and ride."

Cal wouldn't look at him. "Yessir," was all he said as Smoke wheeled around on soundless feet to walk toward low ground east of the hillside.

Dewey Hyde tipped back the bottle of whiskey and took a thirsty pull. Sammy McCoy was awaiting his turn with the jug as they sat behind a boulder, watching the amber fluid drain down Dewey's throat.

"Buster sure did blow ol' Jack in half," Sammy said, his crossed eyes fixed on Dewey's face. "How did Bill know Jack was aimin' to double-cross him like that?"

Dewey ran his sleeve across his lips before he gave the bottle to Sammy. "It was easy, I reckon. Jack kept talkin' about going west to California . . . how much he didn't like the notion we'd hide in the Nations fer a spell. Bill put two an' two together. I heard Bill tell Buster to keep an' eye on Jack for him. Bill said the same thing to Homer Suggins, only that crazy sumbitch on top of the cafe got to Homer first, afore Buster did."

"Bill don't hardly trust nobody."

Dewey took a look over the rim of the boulder. "I reckon that's how come he's still alive, Sammy. He don't sleep like most men do. I swear, he keeps one eye open all night."

Sammy took the bottle and drank deeply. He let out a breath and belched. "There's three of us who'd do damn near anything Bill told 'em to."

"That'd be Shorty an' Joe an' Buster."

"Right," Sammy said, taking another swallow. "Buster don't worry me all that much, not the way Jack Starr did. But with him bein' dead now, I'd keep an eye on Joe Lucas. He kinda scares me sometimes."

"Bill Anderson scares me all the time," Dewey said, pulling back when he saw nothing behind them. "Shorty's a bad ass with a blade, all right, but Joe's the one to watch. If Bill thinks you're fixin' to double-cross him, he'll have Joe put a bullet plumb through your heart."

Sammy thought about it, drinking again. "Shorty would kill a man in his bedroll. Joe'd do it whilst you was lookin' at him square in the eye."

A soft noise distracted both men. Dewey reached for his pistol, although he kept it holstered. "What was that yonder?" he asked.

"It made a little rattlin' sound," Sammy replied. "Maybe it was a rattlesnake."

"Didn't sound like no goddamn rattler," Dewey growled, his eyes locked on a cluster of brush to the west, where a setting sun made things harder to see. "Damn near sounded like somebody took a little rock an' chunked it off in them bushes."

"You're hearin' things, Dewey," Sammy said. "It was a snake."

They were looking toward a late-day sun, at brush close to the rock where they were hidden, when a razor-sharp steel blade slashed across Dewey's windpipe. Sammy heard a noise, a gurgle when Dewey's blood spilled down the front of his shirt.

Sammy whirled, clawing for his Colt, staring up at a huge figure crouched behind him. "Who the hell're you?" he blurted out, jerking his pistol free of its leather berth, intent upon shooting the stranger.

A bowie knife plunged into his heart with tremendous force, and he felt bones crack inside him—a pain that was so intense he could not breathe, pinned him to the ground.

"Afternoon, gents," a soft voice whispered, and then the blade made a sucking sound when the stranger pulled it out, dripping wet with Sammy's blood.

Dewey made strangling noises, coughing, choking when he fell over on his face. Sammy wasn't listening. His head dropped back, and he saw the sky for a moment, until a cloud above him began to look fuzzy, indistinct, like a swirling bowl of cotton.

28

Joe Lucas stared down at the bodies. His horse snorted when it became edgy over standing so close to the scent of death. Joe turned in the saddle to speak to Bill Anderson. Bill's face was tight with anger.

"Whoever done it had to be slick." He gave the brush-lands a sweeping glance, his rifle butt resting on his thigh. "This is damn hard country to slip up on a man. The sumbitch has to be part Indian."

Bill grunted. "If we had the time, I'd have everybody fan out an' hunt him down," he said bitterly. "He's got a horse hid somewheres. Can't be far. I'll hand him one more thing—he's a gutsy bastard, gettin' close enough to use a knife so's the rest of us wouldn't hear him."

Shorty Russel spat tobacco juice off one side of his red sorrel gelding. "Hell, I ain't worried. Means two more shares fer the rest of us. Dewey was dumber'n a rock, if you ask me, an' Sammy was damn near an idiot, with them gotch eyes. We ain't no worse off without 'em."

Bill was looking north. "I think I know who it is. That big

son of a bitch who throwed Homer off that roof done this. I got this feelin' he's the one."

Lucas gave the skyline his own inspection. "He ain't got no posse with him, or they'd be ridin' down on us. Havin' just one sumbitch behind us proves he's crazy, whoever he is. Prob'ly some goddamn pig farmer who lost all his money when we robbed the banks . . . gonna be a hero an' try to git everybody's money back."

"We can't afford the time to look fer him," Bill said, after another look at Dewey and Sammy. "He'll come back. He won't give up, not after he got this done so easy. Sammy an' Dewey was drunk, or this couldn't've happened. Ain't no place to hide in this miserable country. The thing to worry 'bout is if he's got a Sharps so he can shoot us from long range, a few at a time. We ain't got no long guns with us."

"I'll ride back an' track him down," Lucas said, levering a cartridge into the firing chamber of his Winchester. "The rest of you keep headin' south. I'll catch up soon as I've killed this sneaky bastard."

"Maybe I oughta go too," Russel said, "case there's more'n just one."

Bill gave it some thought. Wind whipped around their horses in gusts, swirling the animals' manes and tails, causing the brim of Bill's cavalry hat to flutter. "I reckon that's a good idea," he said after a bit. "Two'd be better 'n one lookin' fer him. I owe the son of a bitch, if it's the same feller who killed Homer an' Sikes."

"I figure he got Scar Face Parker likewise," Russel said around a ball of chewing tobacco.

"We got proof he ain't no tinhorn," Lucas agreed. "All the same, he can't outrun no bullet. He ain't gonna git close enough to use no knife on me. Won't be the same as slippin' up on Dewey an' Sammy."

"Find him," Bill snarled, "and kill him. Bring me his god-damm head so I can tie it to my saddle horn. Homer'd been ridin' with me since the war. I don't take it lightly when somebody kills my friends."

"We'll find him," Lucas said, reining his horse around the bodies "Just make sure the boys save me an' Shorty some of that whiskey."

Shorty Russel hurried his sorrel up beside Lucas's yellow dun as Bill turned back to rejoin the others. They rode toward the crest of a hill, with rifles ready.

A moment later, Russel glanced over his shoulder to make sure Bill was out of earshot before he spoke to Lucas. "How come you volunteered us fer this job, Joe? Looks like me an' you oughta be playin' it safe so we can live to spend our share of that money."

"I figure this *is* safer," he said, scanning the brush as they rode at a slow walk. "It's gonna be dark in a few hours. If this sneaky son of a bitch is as good as he appears to be, he'll come fer us after sundown. But if we find him first an' kill him, won't be no reason to worry 'bout the dark."

"I don't figure he's really all that good," Russel said. "Sammy McCoy's eyes was so bad crossed he couldn't see a buffalo bull chargin' straight at him. Dewey Hyde was just plain dumb. Homer was gittin' old hisself, an' Sikes never struck me as near careful enough. That breed, on the other hand, woulda been hard to kill fer might' near anybody. If this same feller got Scar Face, we could have our hands full bringin' him down."

"Bill's worried," Lucas remarked, as they neared the top of a rise. "He had robbin' them banks figured as bein' easy, only we lost damn near half of them that come with us."

"Bill wasn't helpin' things none, shootin' Lee like he did. Bill's temper's been real bad lately. He don't act quite right sometimes."

"He's still smarter'n most an' dangerous as hell too. He knowed Jack was gonna try an' double-cross him. He sent Buster back to keep an eye on Jack. Bill can smell a rat, same as he always could. I'll grant you, he ain't the same as he was, but I'd have to give it a helluva lot of thought 'fore I tried to cross him."

"Me too," Russel agreed, stopping his horse when they could see what lay beyond the rise—more of the same empty hills. "I did think about it once, that night he shot my pardner Curly Boyd whilst we was plannin' this job. Curly an' me went back a few years. Wasn't no call to gun Curly down when all he done was ask a question."

Lucas nodded and urged his horse forward again. "We've both been with Bill a long time, Shorty, an' we know how crazy mean he can git at times. After we git our shares of the money, maybe you an' me oughta light outta here . . . head fer Arizona or some other place. After pullin' a job big as this, the law dogs an' the cavalry are gonna be turnin' over every rock lookin' fer us. There'll be plenty of 'em out to hang us, fer sure."

"I ain't lookin' to stretch no rope. That's a good idea, Joe, to head west when we collect our money."

"I've sure been thinkin' on it aplenty," Lucas said, guiding his dun into a shallow ravine.

Lucas jerked his horse to a halt in a clump of sagebrush and broomweed. He pointed to something with the barrel of his rifle. "Yonder he is, Shorty."

Russel stopped his sorrel, stood in his stirrups, and grinned wide. "I'll be damned," he said. "The fool's just sittin' out yonder on his horse, leading a spare, one of them spotted Palouse Indian ponies from up in Idaho country. The dumb sumbitch ain't even tryin' to run fer it now that he sees us. He's just sittin' there like he was froze or somethin'."

"Don't seem quite right," Lucas wondered aloud. "Spread out an' we'll rush him. Shoot both them horses if we can, so he'll be afoot. Let's ride!"

Lucas and Russel spurred their horses into a hard gallop toward the lone rider, who was leading an extra horse. Lucas was puzzled when the horseman made no move to turn and run, sitting motionless while they came charging at him. Russel rode off to the left, bringing his rifle to his shoulder, waiting for the right range. Wind gusted through the broom-weed and brush, creating waves across the prairie hills that surrounded a cowboy with two horses, who simply sat there, waiting for them.

In the back of Joe Lucas's mind, a warning sounded that something was wrong.

Smoke drew a bead on a lanky gunman who was wearing a black cowboy hat and racing toward Cal with a rifle at his shoulder. It was a calculated risk that neither man would be able to get off a shot at Cal before Smoke killed them. But a man on a running horse had more difficulty steadying a pistol or a rifle. A man living on his belly, peering through a tangle of broomweed, resting his elbows on the ground, had a distinct advantage—better still, when that rifleman understood guns and the nature of a rifle slug's drop at greater distances.

He feathered the Winchester's trigger very gently and did not wait to see the result of his shot before he levered another round into the chamber, the crack of his gun carried away on the winds.

The man in the black hat appeared to run into an invisible rope or a wire while his dun was at full speed. The gunman's head was jerked backward, and the rest of him went along off the rump of his charging mount. He sailed through the air, flinging his rifle away, clawing wildly for his throat as he began to tumble downward.

Smoke fired again, feeling the hard jolt of the rifle butt

against his shoulder. A stocky gunman atop a bounding sorrel did a circus flip out of his saddle, folded over, knees tucked under his chin. He appeared to be suspended there while his horse ran off without him.

He landed in curious fashion, on the back of his neck with his butt sticking straight up, while his legs flopped over his head. Somehow he'd managed to hang on to his rifle, and it discharged the moment he fell, a muffled pop from a distance of at least two hundred and fifty yards, a difficult target for even the best marksman at that range.

Smoke came slowly to his feet as his second empty cartridge flew from the rifle's chamber. He had to make sure both gunmen were dead. When he saw Cal start riding off the hill to investigate for himself, Smoke waved him back, unwilling to take any form of chance with the boy's life.

He walked up on the first man he shot, and what he saw left him satisfied. A slack-jawed man in his middle thirties with deep brown hair lay on his back with his throat torn open where a slug had gone through. He was still breathing shallowly, blood pumping from the gaping hole in his throat to form a spreading, red stain around his head and shoulders. His eyes, as black as coal, filled with a mixture of pain, surprise, and hatred, turned on Smoke when Smoke's shadow fell across his face.

"If you see Anderson again, which ain't likely," Smoke said tonelessly, "tell him his men make real good target practice. I heard Bloody Bill Anderson rode with some of the toughest gunmen west of the Mississippi. You can tell him for me it just ain't so. I haven't met up with a tough one yet."

"Bastard . . ." the dying man croaked through a torn windpipe, his empty hands making claws in the dirt.

"That's a real bad reflection on my mother," Smoke told him without a trace of inflection in his voice. "Under damn

near any other circumstances, I'd make you sorry you said
that. But it looks like I'd be wastin' my time showin' you the
error of your ways. You'll be dead in a minute or two."

Smoke walked away to find the other bank robber, with
his rifle cocked, ready. Remembering the way the shorter
gunman had fallen on his neck, it wasn't likely he would
need a gun.

The man lay in an odd pose, with his butt up, feet over his
head, as if he'd meant to land that way.

"This one's dead," Smoke muttered, turning to Cal, beck-
oning to him, lowering the hammer on his Winchester. Like
he'd set out to do, he was making Bill Anderson and his
killers pay for what they'd done to unarmed citizens of Dodge,
and for emptying both banks of their money.

Cal came galloping up, leading the Palouse. He reined to
a halt a few yards from the gunman.

"Right unusual way to die," Cal said, staring at the body,
the blood from a chest wound around it.

Smoke took the stud's reins and mounted quickly. "Let's
get clear of this spot," he said, swinging southwest. "No
tellin' if there's some comin' behind these two."

"Beats anything I ever saw, Mr. Jensen," Cal said as they
hit a steady trot away from the scene, "how you killed two
men afore they ever fired a shot. They didn't even know you
was there."

"We baited 'em, son," Smoke said, booting his rifle. "Like
putting a worm on a fishin' hook."

"How's that?" Cal asked.

"It's simple enough. I hope you'll remember it. They saw
you on that hill where I told you to wait. That drew 'em to
you like a bear comes to honey. They weren't expectin' anybody else to be there figurin' you had to be the one who got
them others with a knife. They didn't do a helluva lotta
thinkin' just now. They thought they saw what they expected
to see. That can be a man's biggest weakness when he goes

lookin' for somethin' special because he believes it's gonna be there. Learn from it, Cal. Never trust yer eyes without makin' sure of everything around you."

"You said we was gonna trick 'em, only you didn't explain how. I understand, Mr. Jensen. They didn't look close enough at little things, like when I saw sunlight shine off your rifle barrel just a second or two afore you shot 'em. On top of that, they should have done even more thinkin'. I was sittin' up there with a spare horse, but it was also wearin' a saddle. A man don't take two saddles when he rides cross-country with a fresh mount. No need for but one saddle if it's just one man."

"You've got the idea," Smoke told him as they circled a knob to ride into an arroyo. "It's the little things that often make the difference between livin' and dyin'. It's better to be sure of things before you make your play."

Cal was gazing south. "You sure showed 'em," he said in a low voice. "Hasn't been but a couple of hours, an' you've already killed four of 'em. If they've got a lick of sense, the rest'll be worried by now."

"We'll send them a little message," Smoke said, halting his stud, pointing to the gunmen's riderless horses, which were grazing farther down the ravine. "Go fetch up those two geldings and hand me your lariat rope. You just gave me an idea. . . ."

29

Bill stood on a rock ledge just before dusk, watching their back trail with his field glasses. He and Buster Young talked as Bill studied the horizon from the highest point they could find, while the men waited in a draw, resting and drinking whiskey to pass time or dress a few minor flesh wounds that three of his gang had taken during the robbery. It had been a hard push to cover so much ground—hard on horses as well as on men. And there was a problem of another sort—a man, or several men, who kept following them, killing Dewey and Sammy with a knife in a spot where they should have been able to see someone stalking them. Bill had watched closely for dust sign to the rear, and he'd seen nothing all day—not so much as a wisp of trail dust. What was happening didn't make a hell of a lot of sense. He'd been running from lawmen and Union cavalry for so many years he was sure he knew all the tricks of the game. Until then. And for reasons he couldn't explain, he felt it was the work of just one man, and that was even more puzzling. Who would go alone after a gang the size of his? Only a madman, or one crazy son of a bitch.

"Joe an' Shorty ain't comin'," Buster said. "The guy who got Dewey an' Sammy got them, too."

"Not Joe Lucas," Bill answered. "He's too damn careful to get bushwhacked. It's just takin' 'em more time than they had it figgered."

"This gent's slippery," Buster argued. "He could even be the feller who got Scar Face. Maybe he's got some others with him . . . a posse. That'd explain why it's takin' Joe an' Shorty so long to git back. They coulda run into a whole bunch of guns back yonder."

"We'd've seen some dust if it was a posse," Bill said, passing his glasses along the crests of hills, then along the low places between them. "It's that sumbitch who flung Homer off the roof who's responsible. I've got this feelin' about it, about how it's him."

"It can't be no good feelin', if it's just one man," Buster told him, frowning. "It just don't figger why some tough son of a bitch would be in Dodge this time of year. The gent who got Homer wasn't no lawman. Big feller . . . real tall, from what I seen of him. I remember one more thing. He yelled real loud when he throwed Homer's body, like he wanted us to know it was him an' that he was up there. Damn near like he was darin' somebody to shoot at him. Could be he's crazy."

"Crazy like a fox," Bill replied angrily, still reading the horizon through his lenses. "A genuine crazy man woulda showed hisself by now. I seen a few crazies durin' the war, when they seen too much blood, too much dyin'. They'd come runnin' at our lines like they was bulletproof, screamin' their damn fool heads off 'til a bullet shot 'em down. Some of 'em would get right back up an' come chargin' at us again whilst they was dyin'. It was a helluva sight to see. But this bastard who's followin' us ain't that kind of crazy. Somehow, he's able to sneak up on us without showin' hisself . . . which is damn hard to do in this open country. But I still don't figger he got Joe. Shorty, maybe, but not Joe Lucas."

"Ain't no man bulletproof, not even Joe," Buster said after a pause.

Bill's glasses found movement on a distant hill. A pair of horses came trotting into view. Bill let out a sigh. "Yonder they come. Both of 'em," he told Buster. "I can see both their horses—a sorrel an' Joe's big buckskin."

"Let's hope they killed the sumbitch," Buster remarked. "If they did, we can quit worryin'."

Bill watched the horses a little longer, because something about them seemed wrong, and yet he couldn't put a finger on just what it was. Dusky darkness made it hard to see detail. Long black shadows fell away from the hills in places, preventing him from seeing Joe and Shorty clearly.

He waited while the horses came closer, holding a slow trot along a trail of horse droppings and hoofprints his gang had left in their wake. Bill was in too much of a hurry to make the alabaster caves west of old Fort Supply, where they could hide out, and there wasn't time to be careful about leaving a trail to follow until they crossed over the Kansas line at the Cimarron River. In the river, they could ride downstream in the shallows and lose any possemen or cavalry when the current washed out their horse tracks.

"I can see 'em now," Buster said, squinting. "Two horses, only they sure as hell are comin' real slow. Looks like they'd be in a hurry to bring good news. Maybe they couldn't find the sneaky son of a bitch."

The pair of horses rounded a low hill, and Bill could see them plainly enough. His jaw muscles went taut when his teeth were gritted in anger. "Damn!" he said, taking one last look before he lowered his field glasses, hands gripping them so tightly his knuckles were white.

"What the hell's wrong, Bill?" Buster asked, unable to see all of what Bill had seen, without magnification.

"He got 'em," Bill snapped.

"What the hell're you talkin' about?" Buster wanted to know, glancing back to the horses that were approaching the ledge where they stood. "Yonder they come. That's Joe's yeller dun, an' that's Shorty's sorrel, ain't it?"

Bill's rage almost prevented him from answering Buster. A moment passed before he could control himself. "It's the right horses," he growled. "Shorty an' Joe are tied across their saddles. Means they're dead."

"Dead? Why would the bastard take the time to tie Shorty an' Joe to their saddles?"

"He's sendin' us a warning," was all Bill could say right then, fuming.

Buster frowned at the horses a third time. "Son of a bitch," he said softly, unconsciously touching the butt of his pistol when he said it. "They *are* dead. I can see their arms danglin' loose." He turned to Bill. "What kind of crazy son of a bitch would do that?"

Bill tried to cool his anger long enough to think. "A man who don't give up easy. He aims to dog our trail all the way to the Nations. Can't figure why, only it's real clear he ain't in no mood to give up."

"I ain't so sure it's one man, Bill. One man couldn't've handled Joe an' Shorty so quick. I say there's a bunch of 'em back yonder. Damn near has to be."

"I've got this feelin' you're wrong," Bill said, swinging off the ledge, taking long, purposeful strides down to the spot where his men rested. "But there's eleven of us left, an' we'll be more careful from here on," he added.

"We've lost some of our best shooters," Buster reminded him, when he saw the men waiting for them in the draw.

Bill was in the wrong humor to discuss it. "Send a couple

of men out to fetch Joe an' Shorty back here. Their horses'ıu comin' too slow, followin' the scent of these others. I'll have everybody get mounted. Maybe we can lose that bastard when we come to the river."

Pete Woods and Stormy Sommers led the horses, with bodies lashed to saddles, over to Bill. Stormy's face wasn't the right color.

"Joe's got a hole blowed plumb through his neck," Pete said while jerking a thumb in Joe Lucas's direction. "Shorty caught one in the chest right near his heart."

Bill paid no attention to the swarm of blowflies that were clinging to both bodies, wondering how anyone could have taken Joe Lucas by surprise. "Cut 'em down an' leave 'em here. We'll use their horses for fresh mounts. See if there's any money in their pants pockets. Don't leave nothin' valuable behind."

"Whew, but they sure do stink!" Pete said, climbing down to cut pieces of rope that were holding the corpses in place. Shorty's body fell limply to the dirt. Joe slid out of his blood-soaked saddle to the ground with a sickening thump. "God-damn flies been eatin' on 'em, on the blood."

Bill didn't care to hear about the smell. "Search their pockets like I told you," he said. "Time we cleared outa here quick. Been here too long. We oughta hit the river close to midnight."

"Who you reckon done this?" Charlie Waller asked, fingering his rifle in a nervous way.

"A crazy man," Buster answered, when Bill said nothing. "He has to be outta his goddamn mind."

Bill wheeled his horse, heading south onto a darkening prairie, leading ten men and four pack animals loaded with bags of money toward the Cimarron.

In the back of his mind he wondered what kind of man

was following them. Unlike Buster, Bill wasn't quite so sure the stalker was crazy. *Deadly* might be a better word.

And to make matters worse, the man on their trail seemed to be enjoying himself, in a way. Why else would he have sent the bodies back, unless he wanted fear to cause Bill and his gang to make another careless mistake?

Smoke led Cal down a series of winding dry washes, staying off the hilltops, where they might be seen. It took longer to travel this way, yet time was unimportant to Smoke. Facing far superior numbers, his best weapon was caution.

Cal rode up beside him, peering into the dark. "How come you don't act worried they'll ambush us, now that there ain't no light?" he asked.

"This Palouse'll warn us. A tribe of Indians up in the far northwest bred an' raised the Palouse for special reasons. First off, they're tough. Got more stamina than any other breed of horse. On top of that, they've got real unusual noses an' the best ears ever attached to horseflesh. They can smell a man or another horse from half a mile away, if the wind's right, an' the slightest sound'll make this stud's ears prick up."

"How come everybody don't ride a Palouse?" Cal asked. "Do most folks know how they're special?"

"Ain't many of 'em left, son. When the army captured Chief Joseph an' the rest of the Nez Perce tribe, they killed off most of their spotted ponies."

"That's mighty cold-blooded, to kill horses fer what a tribe of Indians done."

"Another reason I've got damn little respect for the army. An outfit that kills horses for no reason other than they're better than most is the act of cowards."

"I always wondered why you favored that stud an' his colts so much."

"I want the best animal I can find between my knees when I strap a saddle on."

Cal glanced up at a cloudless, moonless sky. "Them bank robbers'll be more careful now. How do you aim to git the rest of 'em?"

"They'll give me my chances."

"You sound mighty sure of it, Mr. Jensen."

"It's the nature of men on the run. When they feel somebody close, they make mistakes. Get in too big a hurry."

Cal nodded. "I've been payin' real close attention to most everythin' you do. So I can learn from it. You ride low country, an' you always keep your eyes movin'. You don't never look at one spot fer long."

"Old habit, I reckon."

Cal seemed to be pondering something. "Does it ever bother you that you've killed a bunch of men?"

"I used to think about it some, until I met Sally. Since we got married, I've tried to live peaceful, only there's been times when my past catches up to me."

"Old enemies, from before you hitched up with Miz Jensen?"

"Mostly. I still have trouble passin' up a one-sided fight where someone who's in the right is facing men who mean to do them wrong."

"Like the folks who live in Dodge City, maybe," Cal said, thinking. "If you hadn't been there, more of 'em would have died tryin' to save their money."

"I told Marshal Earp it was time to let 'em ride out of town with what they came for. This way's better. It's just us and them. Nobody else gets hurt or killed."

"I reckon I hadn't oughta tell you this, but I was scared when all that shootin' was goin' on. I stayed hid behind the front of that roof most of the time. Couldn't hardly make myself rise up an' shoot nearly as regular as I shoulda."

"You played it smart. No need to apologize for it. You did

a right decent job of shootin' when you had the chance, and that's all anyone can expect from you."

"Didn't do as much shootin' as you or Pearlie. I was just too scared."

"Fear can be a good thing," Smoke explained. "Until you know a little more about fighting, it's better to take it slow and easy. You'll learn as you get older. Experience is the best teacher. I suppose that's why I brought you along, but I don't want you to take any big chances. Leave that to me."

"One of these days I aim to be as good as you when it comes to fightin'," he said. "I'm real determined to learn it."

"There's a lot better things for a young man your age to spend his time learning. Like the cow business, and horses. Leave the fightin' to them that have a knack for it."

"Like you, Mr. Jensen."

Smoke couldn't offer much argument, even though it hadn't been his choice to learn how to kill.

30

The clatter of horseshoes on rock announced their arrival at the Cimarron River. Beyond the sluggishy, late-fall current, trees grew in abundance, which suited Bill Anderson just fine. More places to hide in the all-but-total darkness of a night without a moon.

Buster rode up next to him while they halted on the riverbank to look things over.

"Seems quiet enough," Buster observed.

Bill wasn't satisfied. He gave the far bank a close look, listening.

"You act real edgy, Bill," Buster said. "That bastard can't get ahead of us, hard as we been pushin' these horses. I say we get across quick."

Bill had been thinking about what had happened to Joe, Shorty, Dewey, and Sammy, for the last few hours. "I've done give up on tryin' to predict what he'll do. But once we get in the river, we're gonna ride down it maybe a mile or two. It'll make it harder for him to find where we came out.

We'll look for a stretch of rock north of them alabaster caves to ride out. Can't no man track a horse on them hard rocks."

"This ain't like you, Bill, to act worried 'bout one or two men, however many there is. We used to ride off like we was in a damn parade every time we pulled a job. Seems like we're runnin' with our tails between our legs now, an' all on account of one or two gents chasin' us."

Bill scowled at the forests beyond the Cimarron. "Things have started to change, Buster. This land ain't empty like it was before. An' the sumbitch behind us—maybe it is two or three—has proved to be pretty damn good."

"That ol' fort is abandoned. We could ride for it hard an' be there by daylight. No matter who's behind us, we can stand 'em off there real easy."

"It's gettin' across this river that's got me playin' things safe. Send a couple of men down to the water ahead of us. If nobody shoots at 'em, we'll bring the money down."

Buster turned back in the saddle, picking out less-experienced men. "Floyd, you an' Chuck ride down to the river, an' keep your rifles handy."

Two younger members of the gang spurred their trail-weary horses past the others to ride down a rocky embankment to the water's edge. Both men approached cautiously, slowing their mounts to a walk.

Bill waited until no shots were fired at his men. "Let's go," he said, sending his horse downslope.

Floyd Devers turned to Chuck Mabry. Beads of sweat glistened on Floyd's face. "Looks safe enough," he said to his cousin from Fort Smith.

As Chuck was about to speak, a rifle cracked from the opposite bank, accompanied by a blossom of white light from a muzzle flash.

Mabry, at the tender age of nineteen, the newest member of Bill Anderson's gang, fell off his horse like he'd been poleaxed. Floyd's horse bolted away from the shallows when it was spooked by the explosion.

Floyd was clinging to his saddle horn when a bullet struck him in the right hip. "Yec-oow!" he cried, letting his rifle slip from his fingers. Pain like nothing he'd ever known before raced down his leg, causing him to let go of the saddle and to slide slowly off to one side.

Floyd landed in the water with a splash, thrashing about, making a terrible racket, yelling his head off about the pain.

From Bill Anderson's men, half a dozen guns opened up on the muzzle flash. The banging of guns rattled for several seconds more, until the shooting slowed, then stopped.

Bill turned his horse quickly to ride back behind the bank of the river, out of the line of fire.

"Goddamn!" Buster yelled, trying to calm his plunging, rearing horse. "How'd that bastard get across ahead of us?" he wondered at the top of his voice.

Bill was furious. He knew he should have sent an advance scouting party ahead to get the lay of things at the river, but with fatigue tugging at his eyelids, he'd forgotten to do it until it was too late.

He could hear Floyd thrashing about in the water, making all manner of noise. The kid, Chuck, fell down like he was dead the moment the bullet hit him.

"This don't make no sense," Bill said, when Buster got his horse stilled. "We've been ridin' as hard as these damn horses could carry us an' he still beat us to the river."

"Give me two men," Buster said, "an' I'll ride upstream an' cross over so we can get behind him. He won't be expectin' that from us."

Bill knew men as well as he knew anything on earth. "This son of a bitch, whoever he is, has got us outguessed with every move we make."

"We can't just sit here all night, Bill."

"Wasn't aimin' to," Bill replied. "We'll swing to the east

and ride hard as we can. Let's test his horse, see if he can stay up."

"He sure as hell ain't had no trouble so far," Buster said before he reined his mount around.

"Make sure you stay close to the money," Bill added in a quiet voice. "If one of our own decides to get rich while all this is goin' on, shoot him."

"I'll stand by you, Bill. Always have. But this gent we got shootin' us a few at a time is smart. You'll have to hand him that. We need to stay together. It's when we split up that he cuts some of us down."

"Numbers don't appear to make no difference to this son of a bitch," Bill answered. "Just do like I say. Stay close to the packhorses. We'll ride the riverbank for a ways an' see what he does next."

"We need to make it over to them trees, Bill," Buster told him. "Out here in the open, he's got a clear shot at us damn near every time. We'll be a helluva lot safer on the other side. We keep on this way, he's gonna bushwhack us all."

"I've got eyes, Buster, an' I don't need no help countin' the men he's killed. Start ridin'."

"Hold on a minute, Bill!" Pete Woods cried, pointing down to the river. "Listen to Floyd yonder. He's hurt real bad, an' he needs somebody to go an' fetch him outta that water."

Bill aimed a hard-eyed look at Pete. "You go fetch him out, if you want," he said. "I ain't gonna make no target out of myself. Floyd can figure his own way out."

"He's just shot in the leg!" Pete protested.

Bill had grown tired of the useless banter. "You could get shot in the head if you run down there, Pete. This was a chance every one of us took when we decided to rob them banks. Men get bullet holes in 'em sometimes when they take what ain't theirs. But if you're so damn softhearted, you ride right on down to that river an' lend Floyd a hand."

"Sure seems hard," Pete said, quieter.

"Robbin' folks of their money ain't no church picnic," Bill said.

Pete lowered his head, unwilling to challenge Bill over it any longer.

Bill rode off in the lead, and beyond the lip of the river-bank he could hear Floyd crying out for help. It reminded him of the war, when no one had been there to save all the brave soldiers from Missouri or Tennessee when they begged for assistance.

Someone near the loaded pack animals began to gag, and Bill knew it was the kid, Stormy Sommers. He ignored the sound and spoke to Buster. "High time some of the little boys learned a thing or two about robbery. If it was easy, every son of a bitch who owned a gun would take up the profession."

Buster sounded a touch worried. "Don't leave us with but nine men, Bill."

"Nine?" Bill asked, his voice rising. "You don't think nine men stack up right?"

"Whoever's doin' the shootin' at us has been real good, or real lucky today," Buster answered.

"Luck is all it is," Bill said.

Another rifle shot boomed from across the river, and Bill pulled his horse to a stop, turning his head to listen. He heard another painful cry coming from the Cimarron.

"Damn! Damn!"

It was Pete Woods's voice.

"Pete was dumb to ride down there so soon," Buster said with his head turned toward the sound. "He shoulda waited for a spell to see if things was clear."

"We don't need no careless men," Bill anounced to the men around him. "Pete wasn't thinkin' straight, or he'd've knowed to wait, like Buster said."

Stormy continued to gag, gripping his sides. Bill's nerves

were on edge, and he had to do something to calm them. "Shut the hell up, Stormy, or I'll kill you myself. If you ain't got the stomach for robbin' banks, then ride the hell away from here an' do it now!" Bill's right hand was on the grips of one revolver when he said it.

"We're all gonna die," Stormy whimpered. "That feller who's follerin' us ain't no ordinary man."

Bill didn't want Stormy's fear to infect the others. He took out his Colt .44, cocked it, and fired directly at Stormy's head.

Stormy's horse bolted away from the banging noise as he went off one side of it. He landed with a grunt, falling on his back, staring up at the stars.

"Anybody else don't like the way I'm runnin' things?" Bill asked defiantly.

When not another word was said, he reined his horse to ride east, spurring his horse to a trot. He hadn't wanted to kill any more of his own men, like he'd had to do when Lee Wollard pulled that damn fool stunt inside the bank, hitting the banker so hard it knocked him out. But there were important things for men to learn if they aimed to stay outside the law, and one was when to take orders and follow them to the letter. A leader couldn't run a military outfit any other way.

Keeping his men and their precious cargo well out of rifle range from the far side of the Cimarron, Bill led his men east at a gallop, determined to make a crossing into the Nations as soon as he felt it was safe.

Smoke and Cal rode across the river, finding it shallow that time of year, until they reached the wounded outlaw, who was holding his bleeding leg on a flat rock, moaning softly. When the robber saw them coming, he threw up his hands.

"Don't shoot me no more!" he begged, showing that his hands were empty. "I give up! I swear, I do! My leg's killin' me, an' I gotta git to a doctor real soon, or I'm gonna bleed to death."

Smoke swung down beside him, holstering the Colt he held in his right hand. "It's high, your wound is," he said. "If we tie a rag around it real tight an' catch one of these loose horses, you can sit a saddle back to Dodge. Give yourself up to Marshal Wyatt Earp, an' he'll see to it you get medical attention."

"You gonna trust me like that, mister?"

"If you aren't in Dodge when we get back, I'll come lookin' for you."

"Sweet Jesus, but my leg hurts. I'll do like you say. Don't want no more of Bloody Bill or this bank robbin' business anyhow. I'm done with it for good."

Smoke glanced at the other three motionless bodies before he knelt next to the raider. He was hardly more than a kid, nearly Cal's age. "What's your name, son?" he asked, taking a faded, blue bandanna from his neck to tie around the wound.

"Floyd. Floyd Devers. I been ridin' with Bloody Bill fer a couple of years, only there never was nothin' like this. We never shot no unarmed folks, nor no women an' kids before. Made me belly sick."

"Where is Anderson headed with the money?" Smoke asked as he tied the cloth tight over Floyd's bullet wound.

"It's near this abandoned fort named Fort Supply. The army give it up years ago. There's these deep caves where we hid our horses when the law came lookin' fer us. The big one is where a fork comes in a dry riverbed. But watch out, mister, 'cause he'll have guards all round."

"We'll be careful," Smoke said, finishing the knot in the dark, doing it by feel. He turned to Cal. "Catch one of them horses, an' we'll put this boy on it."

Cal rode off toward a black gelding that was grazing up-river a few hundred yards. Smoke helped the young outlaw to his feet.

"You got Bloody Bill mighty worried," Floyd said, wincing when he put weight on his bad leg. "He can't figure out who'd be slick enough to slip up on us a few at a time like you two've been doin'. He figures there's just one of you. You're the same feller who tossed Homer Suggins off that roof, ain't you?"

"Never did know the dead man's name," Smoke replied.

Floyd nodded once. "I tol' my pardner Chuck we oughta cut out before we got our own selves killed. That's Chuck layin' over yonder."

"Who's the other man?" Smoke asked. "I only fired at three of you."

"That's Stormy Sommers. I saw Bill shoot him down 'cause he wouldn't stop actin' scared. Makes two of us Bill went an' killed. He shot Lee inside the bank 'cause he hit that banker too hard an' knocked him cold. Bill's been actin' crazy as hell lately."

"We'll find him and get the money back," Smoke said as Cal came up, leading the horse.

"I'll turn myself in to the Marshal just like you said, only I can't tell the Marshal who it was ordered me to do it 'less you give me your name."

"Tell him Smoke Jensen sent you, an' that I said to take you to the doctor. Just make damn sure you show up in Dodge, or I'll track you down."

"Yes, sir, Mr. Jensen. You got no worries 'bout that," Floyd said as Smoke helped him climb into the saddle seat.

31

Four men sat huddled around a small fire, deep within a rock cavern with curious, glistening walls of solid alabaster. Bill was chewing a mouthful of jerky, washing it down with whiskey. Deeper into the cave, their horses and pack animals were hobbled and fed what little grain the gang had left in tow sacks. Bags of money lay near the fire, and piles of currency, along with gleaming gold and silver coins, were stacked in neat rows. Bill watched Walter Blackwell count the money.

"More'n forty thousand so far, Bill," said Walter, a quiet, retiring man who was a remarkably good shot with a pistol.

"We're rich," Bill said, cocking an ear toward the entrance into the cavern where Buster, Billy Riley, and Cletus Miller were standing guard. "Best of all, we gave that sneaky bastard the slip, so our troubles're over. He'll never find us here. Hell, the cavalry an' dozens of U.S. Marshals from Fort Smith've been ridin' past these caves for years. Hardly nobody knows they're here. We lay low for a little while, maybe five or six weeks, an' then we ride out free as birds."

He gave Walter a stare. "Keep on countin'. You ain't hardly more'n half done. There's gonna be sixty thousand dollars, the way I figure."

Tad Younger, a cousin to Cole and his famous outlaw bunch, was frowning. "Sure do hope whoever's been behind us don't show up. He's made a habit out of showin' up when he ain't supposed to."

Bill wagged his head. "We lost him. Can't no Indian or white man find a horse's tracks where we just rode. Slabs of rock don't leave no horse sign."

"Here's ten thousand more," Walter said, adding a stack of banknotes to the counted money.

Bill grinned. "Maybe there's gonna be seventy thousand after all. . . ." He abruptly ended his remark when a series of loud explosions came from the mouth of the cave.

Bill leapt to his feet, clawing both six-guns from his holsters, shattering the bottle of whiskey he'd been holding.

A scream of agony came from the tunnel, followed by a much louder bellowing string of cusswords that was Buster Young's voice.

Bill took off in a run for the entrance, leveling his pistols in front of him, almost tripping in the dark. Then two more heavy gun blasts sounded, and he recognized Cletus Miller's cry of pain.

Racing up to the opening, caught in a wild fury beyond his control when he knew the man who'd been tracking them had showed up at the cave in spite of all his precautions, he stopped when he saw three dark shapes lying behind a pile of boulders where his guards had been hiding. Big Buster Young was writhing back and forth, holding his belly, gasping for air, his face twisted in a grimace.

Billy Riley lay face down on the rocks in a pool of blood, and he wasn't moving. Cletus sat against a big stone, a shotgun resting in his lap, arms dangling limply at his sides while his mouth hung open, drooling blood on his shirt.

And when Bill saw this—all three of his men dead or dying from three well-placed shots—he tasted fear for the first time in his life. Gazing out at the darkness, where only dim light from the stars showed any detail of his surroundings, something inside him stirred—a knot of terror forming in his chest that had never been there before. And he noticed that the hands holding his pistols were shaking so badly that he knew his aim would be way off target . . . if he could find anything to shoot at.

"Come on out, Anderson!" a deep voice shouted. "Got you cornered! There ain't gonna be no escape!"

Bill crouched down. In spite of the night chill, sweat poured from his hatband into his eyes. "You're gonna have to kill us!" he yelled back. "You ain't takin' none of us alive!"

"Suits the hell outta me!" the voice answered.

Bill heard soft footsteps coming up behind him. He didn't bother to turn around to see who it was. "Get your rifles," he said in a whisper. "We'll gather up the money an' shoot our way out of here."

"He'll kill us!" Walter Blackwell said.

"Like hell he will," Bill snapped. "Just do like I say, an' get rifles ready. Tell the others to saddle our horses an' put the money on them packsaddles."

Walter, always soft-spoken, said, "I've never disobeyed an order from you, Bill. But this is different. It'll be like we killed ourselves if we try to ride out. Whoever that feller is, he don't miss."

Bill's fear turned to anger. "Shut the hell up, Walter, an' do what I ordered!"

"I won't do it," Walter said very quietly.

Bill turned an angry glance over his shoulder, staring up at Walter's dark shape standing right behind him. "You what?" he demanded.

Bill heard a soft click while Walter spoke. "I won't let you get the rest of us killed," he whispered.

The sudden realization of what Walter meant to do struck Bill Anderson a split second before the hammer fell on a Mason Colt .44/.40 conversion. A roar filled the cave mouth, and Bill's ears, when it felt like a sledgehammer had hit him squarely in the middle of his forehead.

He was slammed against a cavern wall, with his ears ringing, until the noise made by the gunshot died away. Then he heard Walter shout from the entrance.

"I just shot Bloody Bill! Don't shoot at us no more! We give up! You can have the money, only don't kill no more of us! We're done runnin' from you!"

Bill saw two more dim shapes walk outside the cave behind Walter. All three had their hands in the air. Someone else, a voice he didn't recognize, said, "Please don't shoot. We ain't carryin' guns, an' Bill Anderson's dead!"

Bill wondered if he could be dying. He couldn't move his arms to touch the painful place in the center of his head. A growing weakness rendered him helpless, yet he was still listening when he heard Walter ask, "We sure have been curious 'bout who you was, mister. Never had nobody on our trail so hot an' heavy before this."

"Smoke Jensen," a coarse voice said from farther away. "I don't see how names make any difference now. . . ."

Bill's eyelids fluttered shut. He found a dream creeping up on him, a recollection of the war, back when he was with the best of them all, William Quantrill. Quantrill and his soldiers were invincible then. Nobody ever rode them down.

He saw burning farmhouses and heard women and children screaming when the flames consumed them. He heard the pop of cap and ball pistols and the louder crack of muskets when they led a raid on an unprotected farm.

Then he saw another scene, the terrible, stinking trenches at Franklin, Tennessee, when the Army of Tennessee was being commanded by General John Bell Hood from Texas, one of the bravest men ever to lead a battle charge. Eight thousand Confederates died at Franklin, with twice that many wounded who would die later from gangrene, dysentery, and infection. Death always seemed to ride with the Confederate Army, and Bill Anderson had been proud to be one who had lived through it all.

But an inner voice told him he was dying, although he had some satisfaction: He was dying a rich man.

A black thought struck him, as he recalled what had happened as the shooting had started in front of the cave. Walter, one of his own men, had refused a direct order and betrayed him with a bullet to the head. He never would have guessed it from Walter.

He felt sleepy, yet he still wondered about this man named Smoke Jensen. Just who the hell was he? And how could he be so clever as a manhunter?

Bill wished that Smoke Jensen had been riding with them when they had hit the banks in Dodge. That was the reason this robbery failed—because he couldn't trust his own men to get the job done.

At last, he slipped away into a dreamless sleep.

"Tie their hands real good," Smoke told Cal, keeping a Colt aimed at the three survivors of the Dodge City raid. "Then we'll go in the cave an' fetch the money out."

Cal was busy tying knots with cut strips of Smoke's lariat rope. "Sure was unusual that one of his own men went an' shot him for us," Cal said.

One man spoke. "We got tired of followin' stupid orders. I shot him. Can't say as I'm one bit sorry."

"Maybe the judge'll go light on you at your trial," Smoke said.

"I'm hopin' he will."

Another outlaw asked a question. "Where'd you learn to track a man like you been doin' all day an' tonight?"

"From an old mountain man up in the High Lonesome of Colorado Territory."

"Never saw nothin' like it before, mister. You killed some mighty tough men since we came to Dodge."

"Sometimes being tough isn't enough," Smoke told him as Cal finished the last knot on an outlaw's wrists. "Now walk in front of me, boys, while we go down for that money. Don't reckon I have to warn none of you that if you try anything, I'll kill you so quick, you won't have time to blink."

"You won't git no more trouble out of us," one man said as they turned for the mouth of the cavern with their hands tied.

As Smoke walked past Bloody Bill Anderson, he gave the old Confederate a passing glance. Anderson had met his end at the hands of a Judas, and somehow it seemed fitting.

"What about these here bodies?" Cal asked as they went down into a dark tunnel. "We gonna bury 'em?"

"Leave 'em," Smoke replied. "The buzzards an' coyotes'll scatter their remains. I'd give an honest man a decent burial, but I never was inclined to dig graves for them that don't have it coming."

When Smoke and the others were out of sight, Bill Anderson's eyes blinked open briefly.

Their return to Dodge City with three prisoners and four pack animals loaded with money ended a long funeral procession on its way out to the city cemetery. Marshal Earp and Pearlie rode out on the prairie south of town at a gallop to meet them.

Earp looked at the three packhorses and the mule first, a surprised expression on his face. "You got all the money back?" he asked. "Where's Anderson and the rest of his gang?"

"Had to kill a few," Smoke replied.

"One of Anderson's own men shot him," Cal said. "We

had 'em trapped inside this cave, an' there wasn't no way out. Anderson still wanted a fight, until this feller over on the left settled it hisself by shootin' Bloody Bill in the head."

"One of 'em came to town with a hole in his leg to give himself up," Earp said. "He told us a little about what had happened on their way to the river." He shook his head and gave Smoke a one-sided grin. "You're every bit as good with a gun as we heard you were, Mr. Jensen. Hard to believe you came back with our money . . . just the two of you."

Pearlie was giving Cal a close inspection. "I reckon this young 'un ain't got no scratches on him that'll upset Miz Jensen when we git back."

"Cal was a big help," Smoke said, before his mate could speak. "He showed a lot of nerve."

"It wasn't his nerves I was worried 'bout," Pearlie said, and then his face turned red when he realized he had admitted to worrying about Cal. "Not that I was really all *that* worried 'bout him."

"Let's get this money back in the vaults," Smoke said to Earp. "Then me an' Cal need a few hours of shut-eye before I finish that cattle deal with Mr. Crawford Long. It's high time we got back to our home range, where things are quieter."

32

Bill awakened slowly. He found Buster Young sitting beside him. Buster's belly was leaking blood, and despite his great size, he seemed small, childlike, and afraid.

"I'm dyin', Bill," Buster said.

It required a moment for Bill's head to clear. He gave big Buster a vacant stare.

"You hear me, Bill?"

"I . . . hear . . . you."

"I'm gut-shot. Worst way to die there is."

"What . . . happened to . . . my head?"

"Walter shot you, only the slug grazed across the top of your skull. Looks like you're gonna live, only you're bleedin' bad as I am."

Bill raised an arm and touched his scalp tenderly. A slice of skin and hair went all the way to the bone. "I don't remember much."

"There ain't but one horse," Buster whispered, twisting his face with pain. "If I can git to a doctor. . . ."

"One horse?"

"Down yonder, grazin' on short grass."

"I need it," Bill said.

"So do I, Bill. I'm gonna die 'less some sawbones can stop this blood."

"One horse can't . . . carry the both of us."

Buster appeared to be near passing out. Bill tried to focus his eyes. A sorrel wearing a saddle, trailing its reins, grazed a few hundred yards from the cave.

"I can go fetch help," Bill said.

Buster's head wagged. "You won't come back for me, Bill. I know you."

Bill's hand moved to a pistol that was lying on the rock near his left leg. His choice seemed easy, crystal clear. "Then I'm gonna have to take the horse," he said, wrapping his palm around the butt of the Colt.

Buster looked up at him. "You'd leave me here to die?"

"No choice," Bill told him, lifting the .44, cocking it with a trembling thumb. "Sorry, Buster. Wish it didn't have to be this way."

The sharp report of a gun echoed up and down the dry riverbed. Buster's head was driven back against the rock where he was sitting. A crimson splash spread across the alabaster stone like a ball of fire.

Buster relaxed his grip on his belly. His thick arms fell to his sides.

Bill sleeved blood from his eyes, his head throbbing with unimaginable pain; then he came unsteadily to his feet while his head cleared.

"To hell with you, Buster," he said, hoarse, strangled. "I got to get to a doctor myself."

Staggering, almost falling, he made his way slowly to the red sorrel gelding and caught its reins.

After a moment of rest he managed to pull himself across the saddle.

He rode off, leaving a trail of blood spots on the rock at the bottom of the dry river.

33

Gray clouds cloaked the mountaintops. Spits of light snow came sweeping down mountain valleys. Bundled in their coats, Smoke, Cal, and Pearlie sighted the ranch house, and when they did, Cal let out a yell.

"Yahoo! Sure feels good to be home."

Pearlie gave the sky a look. "We's just gittin' here ahead of a powerful storm. My ol' bunk sure is gonna feel nice an' warm tonight."

Smoke couldn't suppress a grin when he saw the house—the barns and corrals, all the product of his own labors, his and Sally's. And he couldn't remember when he had longed to see Sally so badly. This trip had been about the worst when it came to missing her.

He noticed that Johnny North had put plenty of hay out in the pens for cattle and horses. Everything looked like it was in order.

"It does feel good to set eyes on this place again," Smoke said, when the stud's strides lengthened to a faster trot. It was ready to be back in its own stall after weeks of hard miles and wet saddle blankets.

A figure came out on the porch of the ranch house, and Smoke recognized Sally at once. He touched his heels to the Palouse's ribs and said, "I've got a kiss or two to deliver to that woman yonder, not to mention a saddlebag full of money. See you boys at the supper table."

He let the stud strike a gallop toward the front porch, and even from a distance, he saw the smile on Sally's face.

Smoke pulled the stud to a halt at the porch rail and swung down with his saddlebags, a grin crinkling his sun-weathered face before he reached the porch steps.

"Howdy, stranger," Sally said, beaming, opening her arms to him.

He went into her embrace, dropping the saddlebags on the floor. Then he wrapped his arms around her and bent down to give her a lingering kiss, feeling the warmth of her body come through the front of his shirt where his mackinaw was unbuttoned.

"Damn, but it's good to see you, woman," he said, staring into her eyes.

"I've missed you so much, Smoke."

"You wouldn't believe me if I told you how much I've missed you. This time it was different, for some reason or other. I got a bad case of lonely while I was gone."

"We can make up for lost time tonight," she said, smiling coyly, and he knew what she meant.

"Howdy, Miz Jensen!" Cal shouted as he rode past the house toward the barns at a steady trot.

"Howdy-do, Miz Jensen," Pearlie cried, tipping his battered felt hat politely.

"Hello, boys," she said. "As soon as you've put your horses away I've got two apple pies on the kitchen table. I made them yesterday. I'll be warming them up for you."

"Lordy, Lordy!" Pearlie exclaimed, grinning from ear to ear. "Did you hear that, young 'un? Two apple pies. One's fer me, an' you gotta share the other with the boss man."

"Like heck I do!" Cal replied, wearing his own wide grin. "I always git my very own pie. Just ask Miz Jensen if that ain't so."

Pearlie bent down when he rode up to the stud, gathering the Palouse's reins. "I'll feed him good an' rub him down, boss, only don't let that boy with the tapeworm git too much apple pie afore I git there."

"I'll make sure we save you plenty," Sally said, turning back to Smoke. "Now tell me how the steers did, and if you had any difficulties along the way. Come inside. I've got coffee on the stove."

He followed her through the front door, to a warm, familiar room and a fireplace full of flaming wood, which was throwing off wonderful heat. "The steers trailed better than I ever expected," he said as she led him into the kitchen. "And they fetched a price I'd never've dreamed they'd bring." He placed the saddlebags on the kitchen table, pointing to them. "There's better'n six thousand dollars. A buyer came early, and he paid my price quick as I could ask it."

"Why, that's almost twenty dollars a head," Sally exclaimed as she poured him coffee.

"That's exactly what it was . . . twenty a head for three hundred and seven steers. Just over six thousand dollars for a crossbred yearling calf crop. I'd say we had a mighty good year this year."

She gave him his coffee and kissed his cheek, still beaming after she heard the cow price. "It'll get better every year from now on, Smoke," she said. "This spring's calves already look heavier. We'll be showin' a nice profit next fall, too."

"I knew you'd be happy," he said, warming his insides

with the contents of his cup before he sweetened it with brown sugar. "You were right about a Hereford making a good cross with our longhorns, but then you claim to be right about everything."

She sat down beside him and took one of his callused hands in her own. "I was right about you, wasn't I? How many women would have taken a chance by marrying a gun-fighter like the man you were when we met?"

He sipped more coffee, grinning behind the lip of his cup. "I knew it when I met my match. Only a fool takes on a con-test he knows he can't win."

Her face darkened a little. "Was there any difficulty on the way? Any trouble?"

Smoke knew he couldn't lie to her—she could read his mind any time she wanted. "We ran across a few renegade Osages on the way to Dodge."

She searched his eyes. "There's more, isn't there?"

"A little. Both banks got robbed while we were in town, and I lent the City Marshal a hand gettin' the money back, seein' as some of it was our money, money for our steers."

"You got in a gunfight, didn't you?"

He shrugged. "Some might call it that."

"Oh, Smoke. When will you ever stop?"

"I didn't have a choice, Sally. Several innocent citizens of Dodge City were wounded or killed, including women and kids. You know I can't turn my back on that sort of thing."

She let out a sigh. "I suppose not. I don't suppose you ever will."

He thought about it. "This time, I really didn't have a way out."

"And you killed some men," she said—a statement and not a question.

"A few. What's in a number anyway?"

"I suppose I don't really want to know, do I?"

"It'd be better if you didn't. Now open those saddlebags and take a look at all that pretty money. The only thing on this earth that's any prettier right now is you."

Sally smiled, unbuckling a strap over one of the saddlebags. She pulled out a canvas bag with THE CATTLEMAN'S BANK printed on it.

When she opened the sack, her eyes rounded. "This is an awful lot of money!" she said. "It'll buy everything we need, with plenty to spare." She pulled bundles of wrapped currency out of the bag and placed them in front of her on the tabletop.

But then she ignored the money to look at him, and he knew that look on her face. "I wouldn't trade all the money in the world for you, Smoke Jensen. That's why I keep hopin' that one of these days, when you leave the ranch, you'll leave yer guns at home."

"Maybe that time ain't far off," he said. "Things are changin' in this part of the West. But until they do, I'll keep on carryin' my guns. I won't let anybody take what's rightfully ours. We worked hard to build this ranch an' stock it with the best animals we could find. What we make is ours to keep."

"I know," she said softly, squeezing his hand. "And I know I can't change that part of you that won't let you pass up a wrong. Maybe that's a part of why I love you, only I can't help it if I worry."

They were interrupted when Cal and Pearlie came stomping through the back door. Cal was first to eye the pair of apple pies, and he promptly licked his lips.

"Prettiest sight I ever saw, one of your apple pies," he said. "That one on the left's mine, Miz Jensen, if you've got no objections."

"Ain't fair," Pearlie complained, hanging his hat on a peg near the door. "One cowboy don't git a whole pie to eat all by hisself."

Sally got up to bring plates to the table. "Cal's a growing boy, Pearlie," she said, smiling. "Let him eat as much as he wants. I've got bearclaws under that linen over on the drainboard. There's plenty to go around."

Pearlie gave Cal a satisfied smirk. "See there, young 'un. Miz Jensen made them bearclaws fer me. Go ahead an' stuff yerself with pie, so you'll grow. I hope you bust wide open at the belly, so we have to haul you to town in the wagon to see the doctor. I think you'd look good with stitches across yer middle. Maybe the doc can put one of them newfangle zippers in yer belly so's we can open you up afore you bust open every time you sit down to eat."

Smoke accepted his slice of pie with a nod, sipping coffee, thinking how lucky he was to have Sally and good men like Cal and Pearlie and Johnny around him. Things hadn't always been this good for Kirby Jensen—not in the beginning, not until he changed his ways.

Then he reckoned he hadn't played much part in the changes. Sally deserved the credit. He found himself looking forward to sundown, when he could crawl into bed beside her and forget about the bloodshed in Kansas.

CODE OF THE
MOUNTAIN MAN

I acknowledge the Furies, I believe in them, I have heard the disastrous beating of their wings.

Theodore Dreiser

1

No one knew why the outlaws chose to attack the town of Big Rock. It was a very stupid thing for outlaws to attack any western town. For those who inhabited the towns of the West were veterans of the War Between the States, veterans of Indian wars, buffalo hunters—men who had lived with guns all their lives. But Big Rock, located in the high-up country of northern Colorado, was known to be off-limits to anyone who sought trouble.

And most trouble-hunters were as careful to avoid Big Rock as they were to keep from sticking their hands into a nest of rattlers.

Perhaps the outlaws who struck Big Rock that day hit it because the West was taming somewhat. The bad old days were not gone entirely, but they were calming down. Maybe the outlaws felt they could pull it off. They would have fared much better had they pulled off their boots and stuck their bare feet into a bucket filled with scorpions.

"Good morning, Abigail," Sally Jensen said to the woman behind the counter.

"Good morning, Sally," the shopkeeper's wife said. "And how are things out at the Sugarloaf?"

The Sugarloaf was the name of their ranch. "They" being Smoke and Sally Jensen.

Both women turned at the sounds of hooves pounding the earth. A lot of horses. Sounded like fifty or more.

"What on earth? . . ." Sally said.

A bullet busted a window of the store and tore through cans of peaches. A second bullet hit Sally on the arm and knocked her down. A child and her dog were trampled under the steel-shod hooves of the galloping horses.

It didn't take the rampaging outlaws long to discover they'd struck the wrong town as men reached for their pistols and rifles and emptied a few saddles. They raced out of town, whooping and hollering and shooting. But the damage had been done.

"Four people dead," Judge Proctor said grimly. "Including a little girl. Half a dozen more wounded. Couple of them seriously. Somebody ride for the Sugarloaf and fetch Smoke. Sally's been hit."

"Lord God Amighty!" a citizen breathed. "Them outlaws don't know it, but they just opened the gates to Hell!"

He waited until he was absolutely certain that Sally was not seriously injured. A neighbor lady would stay with her, tending to her. The hands who worked the Sugarloaf range would make damn sure no one tried to attack the ranch.

"Now you be careful," Sally told her husband. "And don't you worry about me. I'm just fine."

He bent down and kissed her lips. "I'll see you when I get back." He walked out of the house and stepped into the saddle.

Sally made no attempt to dissuade her husband. This was the West, and a man had to do what a man had to do. They were bound by unwritten yet strictly obeyed codes. Especially a man like Smoke Jensen.

He rode a big buckskin that he'd caught wild in the mountains and gentled. Because of the way he'd worked with the horse, and the bond that had been established between horse and rider, Smoke was the only human the buckskin would allow on its back.

Smoke was tall, with wide shoulders, heavily muscled arms, and lean hipped. His wrists were huge, and his big hands were as powerful as they could be gentle. His hair was ash-blond, cut short, and his eyes were a cold, unforgiving brown that rarely showed any emotion except when he was with his wife and children.

He wore two guns, the left-hand gun worn butt-forward, the right-hand gun low and tied down. He was just as fast with one gun as he was with the other. Some said he was the fastest man with a gun who ever lived, but he never sought out attention or bragged that he was a gunfighter. He was just a man one did not push. He carried a long-bladed knife that he usually shaved with on the trail. Or fought with, whichever was the most important at the time. He'd been raised among old mountain men and some called him the last mountain man. His clothing was earth-tones, his hat brown and flat-brimmed. A Winchester rifle was in the saddle boot.

Leadville was behind him and the Gunnison River just a few hours ahead. He would make the small town just about dark. There was a hotel there, and there he would bed down for the night.

He was in no hurry. He knew he would find the outlaws that had ridden into Big Rock and shot it up, killing and wounding innocent people. If their intentions had been to rob the bank, they had failed miserably. But they had left behind them a bloody main street and sorrow in the hearts of those who had to bury their dead and watch the suffering of those wounded by the indiscriminate bullets.

The sheriff of Big Rock, Monte Carson, had been wounded during the bloody battle, and could not lead the posse that went after the outlaws. Went after them, but finally had to return empty-handed.

The man on the mean-eyed buckskin didn't need a posse. Didn't want to be hampered by one. He knew the difference between right and wrong, and he sure as hell didn't need some fancy-talking lawyer to explain it. As far as he was concerned, lawyers should stick to writing wills and drawing up deeds and such. Keep their noses out of a man's private business. That was part of the problems facing the world today: too damn many lawyers.

He had kissed his wife goodbye, provisioned up, and ridden out from their ranch in the high lonesome of northern Colorado. Alone.

Nobody attacked Big Rock. Nobody. Not and got away with it. Smoke didn't believe in cowboys hoorahing a town. People got hurt doing that. A gun was not a toy, and when a man grew up, he put boyhood behind him and accepted the responsibilities of being a man.

Smoke had helped found Big Rock; his blood and sweat and time and effort were ingrained in the streets and buildings. And those outlaws had shot his wife. Nobody shot his wife. Ever. Not and lived to brag about it.

One lawyer, straight from the East and new to Big Rock, had said the outlaws probably had a poor childhood, and that was what caused them to behave in such a barbarous manner. They really shouldn't be blamed for their actions.

Smoke had slapped him down in the street, jerked him up by the seat of his britches and his shirt collar and dumped him in a horse trough.

Preacher Morrow had tried to talk him out of tracking the outlaws. So had Dr. Colton Spalding and some of the others in the town.

"It's the 1880s, Smoke," Judge Proctor said. "You just can't take the law into your own hands anymore."

The big man who stood by the big buckskin looked at the judge. Judge Proctor backed up, away from those terribly hard eyes.

"I'll be back," Smoke said, then swung into the saddle.

He swung down from the saddle in front of the livery stable in the small town by the Gunnison River and led the buckskin inside, stripping the saddle and bridle from him and stabling the animal.

"Feed him good," he told the boy who had appeared out of the gloom of the cavernous building. "Rub him down. Give him a bag of grain." He looked at the boy. "You sleep in this place?"

"Yes, sir. I got me a room back yonder." He pointed. The man looked familiar, but the boy just couldn't place him. He took the coin the man offered him. It was a silver dollar.

"Don't you have a home, boy?"

"Yes, sir. But my ma lets me stay here during the night so's I can earn extra money to help out."

"I'll leave my saddle here. You look after my gear."

"Yes, sir!"

"Any strangers in town?"

"Three men rode in late this afternoon. They was too cheap to use the livery. They picketed their horses down by the river. They looked like hardcases. Guns tied down low. They just looked mean to me."

"How'd they smell?"

"Sir?"

"Did you get close enough to them to smell them?"

"Yes, sir. I did, come to think of it. They sure did smell bad."

"That's not the only thing that's really bad about them. Did they bathe?"

The boy looked at the tall man with the wide shoulders and the massive arms that bulged his shirt with muscles. "Bathe? Ah . . . no, sir."

"So they still stink?"

"Ah . . . yes, sir. I reckon so, sir."

"I feel sorry for the undertaker."

The tall man with the two guns walked out of the livery stable, moving like a great hunting cat, his spurs jingling as he moved. He carried his rifle with him as he crossed the wide street and walked toward the hotel.

The boy hung a nose-bag on the buckskin and began currying the horse as he ate a bite of grain. The boy suddenly stopped his brushing as a coldness washed over him. "Oh, my God!" he whispered, finally placing the big man with the cold eyes. "Oh, my God!"

"Good evening, sir!" the desk clerk called. "It certainly is a quiet evening in our town."

It won't be for long, Smoke thought, as he signed the register.

The desk clerk looked at the name on the register and gripped the edge of the counter. His mouth dropped open and worked up and down like a fish. "Ah, bah, bah, bah . . ." He cleared his throat. "The dining room just closed, sir. But I can get you a plate of food sent up to your room if you wish."

"I wish. Thank you."

"We're a very modern hostelry, sir. We have the finest in up to date water closets."

"Good. Give me the key to my room, have the tub in the facilities filled with hot water, and put a fresh bar of soap in there. Lots of towels. I like lots of clean towels."

"Yes, sir. Right away, sir. And I'm sure that room I assigned you has fresh sheets. As a matter of fact, I know it does. It's such a pleasure having you here with . . ."

Those cold eyes stopped his chatter. It was like looking into a frozen hell.

The tall man turned and walked up the stairs.

The desk clerk beat on the bell until a man appeared. "Get the marshal—right now! Tell him to deputize the boys. We got big trouble." Or somebody has, he thought, recalling those three hardcases who rode into town that day.

When the tall man walked down the stairs, four of the men the marshal had deputized took one look at him and exited the lobby, fading into the night. They wanted no part of this hombre. They weren't cowards; they were all good, solid men who had used a gun on more than one occasion against outlaws or Indians. But they were intelligent men.

"You got business in this town, mister?" the marshal asked.

"Oh, yes," Smoke replied. "But it's my business."

"Maybe I'll make it mine." The marshal stood his ground.

"That's your job. But I have a better suggestion."

"I'm listening."

"Go home. Make yourself a fresh pot of coffee. Talk to your wife and family. Tell your men to go home and gather their families around them. Get the citizens off the street."

"I don't take orders from you."

"I didn't give you any orders."

The marshal nodded his head. That was a fact. What Jensen was doing was giving him an out, to save face. The desk clerk was all ears, hanging on every word. Whatever happened here would be all over town in ten minutes. "I'm not afraid of you, Jensen."

The desk clerk gasped.

"I can see that. You're a good man, Marshal. The town should be proud to have you behind that star, and the city council should give you a raise."

The marshal cut his eyes. He was alone. His newly deputized men had gone. "Come to think of it, my wife just baked a fresh apple pie. It'd still be warm."

"Man shouldn't pass that up," Smoke said. "Might insult his wife. My wife was insulted the other day when the gang those punks in the saloon was ridin' with shot her."

The marshal's eyes narrowed. No man harmed a woman in the West. Just to jostle one on the street was grounds for a good butt-whipping. "She bad hurt?"

"Caught her in the arm. They killed a little girl."

"You have a good evening, Mr. Jensen."

"Thank you, Marshal. I plan to."

The marshal left the hotel lobby. The palms of his hands were sweaty. He wiped them on his britches. He was a good, tough lawman, having gunned down Bad Jack Summers on the main street of this very town only a few months back. But Bad Jack couldn't shine Smoke Jensen's boots. The marshal sighed. Come to think of it, a wedge of pie would taste mighty good.

Smoke stepped out of the lobby and moved to the shadows, standing for a moment. He worked his guns in and out of leather a few times. The grips of the .44s seemed to leap into his big hands. He stepped off the boardwalk and into the street, walking to the saloon. He stood for a moment at the batwings, looking in, allowing his eyes to adjust to the lantern light of the interior. He pushed open the batwings, stepped inside, and walked to the end of the bar.

"Whiskey," he told the pale-faced barkeep. "Out of the good bottle. I don't like snake heads."

"Yes, sir."

Some people who made their own whiskey would drop snake heads into the barrel for added flavor.

Smoke was not much for strong drink, but he did enjoy a sip every now and then. The saloon was empty except for Smoke, the barkeep, and three unshaven and dirty men seated around a table next to a wall.

The barkeep poured a shot glass full. "That's the best in the house, sir."

"Thank you." Smoke did not touch his liquor. "Where's all your business this evening?"

"Everybody left sort of sudden-like a few minutes ago."

"Is that right? Well, I can sure understand why."

"Oh?" The barkeep was getting jumpy.

"Stinks in here. Smells like a bunch of damn sorry punks whose mothers didn't teach them to bathe regularly. Like that stinking bunch of crap over there at the table."

That made the barkeep real nervous. He moved farther away from the tall, well-built man with the cold eyes and the big hands with flat knuckles. Fighter's hands.

"What's that?" one of the men at the table said.

"You heard me, punk. I said you stink."

The man pushed back his chair and walked toward the bar, the big California spurs jangling. "You're pushin', mister. You ain't got no call to say somethin' like that."

"I've been around skunks that smell better than you three," Smoke told him. He lifted the shot glass with his left hand and took a small sip. It was good whiskey.

One of the men at the table laughed. "Take him, Bob."

Smoke chuckled, but the sound was void of humor. "Yeah, Bob. Why don't you take me?"

Bob looked back at his buddies. This wasn't going like it usually did. He'd been a bully all his life, and folks usually backed up and took water when he prodded them. This tall man just laughed at him. Funny kind of laugh. Guy looked familiar, too. He'd seen that face somewheres before.

The tall man turned to face Bob. Dirty, unshaven, and smelly. Smoke grimaced at the body odor. "It wouldn't be right for you to meet your Maker smelling like an overused outhouse. Why don't you boys find a horse trough and take a bath?"

"Huh! What are you talkin' about, mister? I ain't a-goin' to meet my Maker."

"Oh yes, you are." Smoke set the shot glass on the bar. "All three of you."

"You seem right sure of that," one of the men seated at the table said.

"I'm positive of it."

The men at the table smiled. "Three of us and one of you You're either drunk or crazy."

"I'm neither. But I'll tell you boys that you made a bad mistake getting tied up with Lee Slater and that pack of rabid hyenas that run with him. You made the next to the worst mistake of your lives when you attacked Big Rock the other day and shot those women and kids."

The third man cleared his throat and asked, "You the law, mister?"

"I don't need the law to take care of scummy punks like you three."

The man flushed deeply. But he kept his mouth shut. There was something about this tall man that worried at him. He and most of Slater's men were west coast outlaws, working from the Canadian border down to Mexico. He didn't know a whole lot about Colorado and the men who lived there. This tall man with muscles bunching his shirt was just too damn confident. Too calm. He was clean-shaven and smelling like bath soap. Neatly dressed and his hair trimmed. But he was no dandy. The outlaw could sense that. Those guns of his'n had seen a lot of use.

"We ain't with Lee Slater now," the second man said.

"You were."

"You said 'next' to the worst mistake," the punk standing in front of him said. "So that means we made a worser one."

"You certainly did."

The three waited. The tall man stood by the bar, half turned, smiling coldly at them. The barkeep was poised, ready to hit the floor.

"Well, damnit!" the second man threw a greasy deck of cards to the table. "Are you going to tell us, or not?"

"One of the women you shot was my wife," Smoke said.

The third man sighed.

"And who might you be, mister?" the punk facing Smoke asked, a nasty grin on his face.

"Smoke Jensen." Smoke followed that with a hard left fist that smashed into the punk's face. It sounded like someone swinging a nine-pound sledge against a side of freshly butchered beef. The punk's nose exploded in a gush of blood, and the blow knocked him to the floor.

Smoke straightened up with his right hand full of .44 just as the pair at the table jumped to their feet, dragging iron. He shot the two, cocking and firing so fast the twin shots sounded like one report. One was hit in the center of the chest, dead before he hit the sawdusted floor. The second was struck in the throat, the .44 slug making a terrible mess.

The punk he'd punched on the beak was moaning and crawling to his knees when Smoke jerked him up and threw him against a wall, next to the batwings. The punk screamed as ribs popped from the impact. His eyes were filled with fear as they watched the big man walk toward him, those brown eyes filled with revenge.

The punk staggered out the batwings and fell off the boardwalk, landing in the street. "Help!" he squalled. "Somebody come help me!"

The dark street remained as quiet as the grave he would soon be in.

Smoke had holstered his .44. He stood on the boardwalk and stared at the gunslick. "You think you're bad, boy." The words were chipped ice flying from his mouth. "Then draw, you sorry piece of crap!"

"You ain't no badge-toter!" The punk slobbered the words. "I got a right to a trial and all that. You can't take the law into your own hands."

Smoke stared at him, his eyes burning with a glow that the young man on the street had never seen coming from any man. It was eerie and unnatural. A dark stain appeared on the front of the young man's dirty jeans.

"You gonna let me git up, Jensen?" he yelled.

"Get up."

The punk tried to fake Smoke out, drawing as he was getting to his boots. Smoke drew and shot him in the belly. His second shot shattered the punk's six-gun. Smoke turned and walked back into the saloon, leaving the outlaw in the dirt, hollerin' and bellerin' for his mother.

"You got an undertaker in this town?" he asked the barkeep.

"Ye . . . ye . . . yes, sir!" the barkeep stammered. "Got us a right good one."

"Get him."

"Right now, Mr. Smoke. You bet. I'm gone."

Smoke reloaded and finished his drink.

"Ain't much to this bunch of trash," the undertaker griped. "I'm gonna have to sell their gear to make any money."

"You do that."

"You know their names?"

"Nope."

"Well, I got to have something to put on the markers."

"You can carve on it, 'they should have bathed more often.' "

2

The marshal walked into the hotel's dining room early the next morning and over to Smoke's table. He pointed to a chair, and Smoke pushed it out with the toe of his boot.

The marshal ordered breakfast—the same thing Smoke and everybody else in the dining room was having: beef, fried potatoes, and fried eggs—and laid several sheets of paper on the table. "These may help you."

They were flyers, wanted posters sent out by various law enforcement agencies west of the Mississippi River, and by the federal government. One was of Lee Slater.

Lee had to be the ugliest man Smoke had ever seen in his life. Ugly and mean-looking. "He sure isn't much for looks, is he?"

The marshal chuckled. "He probably didn't win any pretty-baby contests, for sure. But he's a bad one, Smoke. Vicious. He likes to hurt people. Kills for no reason. These others ride with him. Deke Carey and Curt Holt. They're both wanted for rape and murder. Everyone in his gang is facing either long prison sentences or a rope."

"So I heard. His gang was cut down by half a dozen when they hit Big Rock. But it's still a big gang."

"The biggest still operating in the West, Smoke. Fifty at least and some place it at closer to seventy-five. He's always run big bunches. I'll tell you what I know about him, and then I wish to God you'd leave our town before some punk huntin' a reputation learns you're here."

Smoke did not take umbrage. "I'll do my best, Marshal."

"Mind if I ask you a question?"

"Not at all."

"If you'd never seen him before, how'd you know it was Lee Slater who hit your town?"

"The sheriff recognized him. Monte Carson."

The marshal smiled. "Ol' Monte was a rounder in his day. But he was never a crook. Just a bad man to fool with."

"Marriage settled him right down."

"It usually does. Ask you a few more questions?"

"Sure."

"How old are you? Early thirties?"

"That's close enough."

"I heard what happened to your first wife and baby boy. I'm sorry. I won't dwell on that. Now you've married again—and a fine lady she is, too, so I'm told—but you're still apt to go on the prod ever' now and then. Why?"

Smoke shook his head. "Louis Longmont asked me that a couple of years ago and then answered his own question. Maybe I am the last mountain man, Marshal. There's something in me that screams out for the high lonesome. Something in me that can't tolerate punks and thugs and bullies and the like. Back in the hardscrabble hills of Missouri, while my daddy was off in the war, I kept body and soul together by eating turnips—when the garden came up, that is—and berries and what game I could kill. Many's the time I went to sleep with my belly growling. But I never stole. I never took what wasn't mine. And I won't tolerate them that do. Louis said that some people think I have a Robin Hood complex. But that's not true. I just don't like the way laws are changing, Marshal. They're not getting better, they're getting worse. I honest to God read in a Chicago newspaper a couple of months ago that a man shot a burglar breaking into his home and the police put the homeowner in jail! Can you believe that? What in the hell is this world coming to?"

"I know. I read about it myself. But it's the 1880s now, Smoke. You got to change with the times."

Smoke shook his head. "Not me, Marshal. Somebody does me a hurt, I'll hunt him down and settle it. Eyeball to eyeball. Man kills for no reason, or kills trying to take what isn't his, hang him. 'Cause he's no good. Now I read where the country is spending money building prisons." He shook his head. "It's a mistake, Marshal. A hundred years from now, people will see that it's a mistake. But it'll be too late then. A man who'll lie and cheat and steal and hurt people and kill at fifteen will do the same damn thing when he's fifty. I don't care if this nation builds ten thousand prisons . . . it won't matter. It won't stop them. But a bullet will."

Everybody in the restaurant had stopped eating and was listening to the most famous gunfighter in the world.

"I sass my daddy when I was a kid, he'd a-knocked me slap to the floor. Now we got so-called smart folks back East saying that you shouldn't whip your children. If that silliness continues and catches hold, can you imagine what it'll be like in the 1980s? There'll be no discipline, no respect for law and order. I whip my children, then I hug them to show them I love them and I tell them why I just put a belt to their rears.

"I respect the laws of God, Marshal. I'm an Old Testament man. Eye for an eye and a tooth for a tooth. Hurt me or mine and I'm comin' after you. And man's laws be damned!"

The marshal sighed and ate his breakfast. "I hope to God I'm not the lawman who ever has to come after you, Smoke."

"That day's coming, Marshal," Smoke admitted. "'Cause I'll never change. Someday, a posse will come after me, hunting me down like an old lobo wolf. And when they do, the land's going to run red with blood. Because I won't go down easy.

"Marshal, if a man is hungry, can't feed his family, he can just come to me and I'll give him food. If they're down on their luck and really want to work, I'll give them a job, find one for them, or give them money to keep on hunting for work and eat while they're doing it. But if I catch someone stealing from me, or hurting my family, or threatening me, he's dead on the spot.

"It's a funny thing about laws and lawyers, Marshal. You take a small town that just has one lawyer, he can make a living and that's just about it. Let a second lawyer move in, and damned if they don't both get rich."

Smoke pulled out and rode past the graveyard, located on a barren hilltop just out of town. Three mounds of earth were waiting to be shoveled in the holes.

The marshal had told him some names of men who rode with Lee Slater: Curly Rogers, Dirty Jackson, Ed Malone, Boots Pierson . . . to name just a few. They were all trash and scum. Back shooters and torturers. He had asked if Smoke planned to take on the whole gang by himself.

"Just one gang, isn't it?"

Smoke headed south, staying between the Cebolla and Cochetopa Rivers. Although the outlaws' trail was days old, it was not that difficult to follow. Their campsites were trashy reminders of just how sorry a bunch of people he was tracking. Tin cans and bottles and bloody bandages and torn, worn-out clothing clearly marked each night's site.

With San Luis Peak still to the south of him, Smoke came up on a woman sitting in front of a burned-out cabin. Only the chimney remained. He noticed several fresh-dug graves by the side of the charred ruins. The graves had not been filled in.

The woman's face bore the results of a savage beating. She looked up at him through eyes that were swollen slits. "You be the law, mister?"

"No. As far as I know there is no law within a hundred miles of here." He swung down from the saddle and walked to her. She had fixed her torn dress as best she could, but it was little more than rags. "You had anything to eat?"

"A biscuit I had in my pocket. The outlaws tooken everything else. Before they put the house to the torch. I ain't able to move."

Smoke took a packet of food from his saddlebags and gave it to her. "I'll get you a dipper of water from the well."

"I wouldn't," she told him. "They killed my kids' dogs and dumped them in the well."

"Then I'll get you some water from the creek."

"I'd appreciate it. I tried to get around, but I can't. They kicked my ribs in. Left me for dead. I don't think I got long 'fore I join my husband and girls. Ribs busted off and tore up a lung. Hurts."

He found a jug and rinsed it out, filling it up with water from the creek. Looking at the woman, he could see that she was standing in death's door. Sheer determination had kept her hanging on, waiting for help, or more probably, he guessed, someone to come along that would avenge this terrible act.

"Who dug the graves, ma'am?"

"I did. The outlaws made me. Then they used my husband for target practice. Made me and my girls watch. He suffered a long time. My girls was ten and twelve years old. They raped me and made them watch. Then they raped the girls and made me watch. Then they thought they had kicked me to death. I lay real still and fooled them. They done horrible things to me and the girls. Things I won't talk about. Unnatural things. I been sittin' here for three days, prayin' and passin' out from the pain, prayin' and passin' out. Wishin' to God somebody would come along and hear my story."

"I'm here, ma'am."

She drifted off, not unconscious, but babbling. Some of her words made sense, most didn't. Smoke bathed her face and waited. The woman's face was hot to the touch, burning with fever. While she babbled, Smoke unsaddled Buck and let him roll and water.

"Who you be?" she asked suddenly, snapping out of her delirium.

"Smoke Jensen."

"Praise God!" she said. "Thank you, God. You sent me a warrior. I thank you."

"Lee Slater's gang did this?"

"That's him. I heard names. Harry Jennings, Blackjack Simpson, Thumbs Morton, Bell Harrison, Al Martine. They was a Pedro and a Lopez and a Tom Post." She coughed up blood and slipped back into delirium.

Smoke took that time to walk to the graves and look at the shallow pits. His stomach did a slow rollover. The man had been shot to ribbons. His wife had been right: he died hard over a long period of time. The naked bodies of the children would sicken a buzzard. The kids had been used badly and savagely. People who would do this deserved no pity, no mercy . . . and the only justice they were going to get from Smoke Jensen was a bullet.

He filled in the holes and took a small Bible from his saddlebags. He read from the Old Testament and then set about making some crosses. He made four, for he knew the woman wasn't going to last much longer.

"Them names was burned in my head," the woman said. "I made myself memorize them. They was Crown and Zack. Reed and Dumas and Mac. They was a Ray and a Sandy and some young punks called themselves Pecos, Carson, and

Hudson. Three more pimply faced punks hung with them three. They was all savages. Just as mean and vicious as any man amongst 'em. They was called Concho, Bull, and Jeff."

Smoke rolled one of his rare cigarettes and waited, squatting down beside the dying woman.

"I recollect hearin' a man they called Lake and another man they called Taylor. Dear God in Heaven it was a long two days they stayed here." She looked at him. Her eyes were unusually bright and clear. "Did I dream it, or did you put dirt over my family?"

"I buried them and read words from the Bible."

"Thank you. I'm sorry, but I don't remember no more names of them outlaws."

"I'll find out who the rest of them were. Did they all . . . ah? . . ." He didn't know quite how to say it. But the woman did.

"Yes. Several times. One of my girls died while they was abusin' her. You got kids of your own, Mr. Smoke?"

"Yes."

"Then you know how I must feel."

"I believe so."

"I heard them say they was goin' to take over part of Colorado."

"The only thing they're going to take over is a grave, ma'am."

"That's good. You got a hole dug for me?"

"Yes."

"I reckon it's about time then." She closed her eyes, smiled, and said, "Thank you, God, for sending me a warrior." Then the woman leaned her head back and died.

Smoke buried the woman and moved on, making camp a few miles from the scene of cruelty and savageness. He would try that little town on the Rio Grande, on the southern edges of the La Garita Mountains; see if any of the scum had ridden in there. What was the name of that place? Yeah, it came to him. Somebody had named it Gap.

Wasn't much to Gap, Smoke thought, as he approached the town from the north. A saloon, a little hotel, a general store, a cafe and barbershop. Maybe two dozen houses. He swung down in front of the small livery and looked at the man sitting in a cane-bottomed chair in front of the place.

"That horse has got a mean eye on him," the man said.

"Feed him, curry him, and take care of him," Smoke said, dropping the reins. "Give him all the grain he wants. And don't get behind him. He'll kick the crap out of you."

"Gonna cost you extra for me to take care of that wall-eyed bastard."

Buck lilted his head and showed the man his big teeth.

"Don't call him names. He's sensitive about that."

"I'll make a deal with you," the man said. "You stable and feed him, and I'll just charge you for what he eats."

"That's fair enough. Livery looks full."

"Bunch of lawmen in here, U-nited States Marshals, stayin' over to the ho-tel. Chasin' some gang, they is." He squinted his eyes. "Don't I know you?"

"Never been here before in my life."

"You shore look familiar. I seen your pitcher somewhere. Maybe on a wanted poster?"

Smoke laughed. "Not likely. I ranch up north of here, outside of Big Rock."

"That's Smoke Jensen's country. He's kilt a thousand men."

"Not quite that many."

"You know him?"

"I know him. You got a marshal in this town?"

"Yep. Right over there's his office." The man pointed. "Name is Bradley."

Smoke took his gear and checked in at the hotel. He got the last room available. He registered as Jen Sen.

"Funny name," the desk clerk said. Then he looked into the coldest eyes he'd ever seen. "No offense meant, mister."

"You been in this country long?" Smoke asked.

"Just got in from Maryland a few months back."

"Then learn this: you belittle a man's name out here, and you'd best be ready to back it up with guns or fists."

"Here, now!" a man said. "There'll be none of that around me."

Smoke turned. A man stood before him with a big badge on his chest that read: "Deputy U. S. Marshal."

Smoke took in his high top lace-up boots and eastern clothes. He wore a pistol in a flap holster. Smoke looked at the other men. They were all dressed much the same.

"Who in the hell do you think you are?" Smoke said, taking an immediate dislike for the man.

"United States Marshal Mills Walsdorf."

"Come to bring peace to the wilderness?" Smoke said with a smile.

"I do not find law enforcement a humorous matter, sir. It's very serious business."

"I'd say so. That's what that woman told me, in so many words, just before I buried her a couple of days ago."

"What? What? Where did this take place?"

"North of here. Gang of scum rode through and shot her husband to ribbons. Then raped the woman and her two children. Same gang of trash that shot up Big Rock."

"Did the woman identify the gang?"

"She did."

Mills waited. Tapped his foot impatiently. "Well, speak up, man! Who were they?"

"Lee Slater's pack of filth."

"Scoundrels!" one of Walsdorf's men muttered darkly.

"Which direction did they head, man?" Walsdorf demanded in a tone that told Smoke the man was accustomed to getting his way, when he wanted it.

"South."

"Oh, say, now!" another Fed said. "I find that hard to believe. We've been here several days and have seen no sign of them."

He didn't exactly call him a liar, so Smoke let the remark slide and leaned against the front desk. "Where are you boys from?"

"From the Washington, D.C., and Chicago offices," Walsdorf replied.

Smoke sized up Mills Walsdorf. About his own age, and about his size, although not as heavily muscled in the arms and shoulders. His hands were big and flat knuckled and looked like he'd used them in fights more than once.

"You look familiar," Mills said. "I've seen you somewhere."

"I do get around."

Mills spun the register book and snorted at Smoke's name. "Jen Sen. That's obviously a phony name. Are you running from the authorities?"

"If you represent the authority, I wouldn't see any need in it."

"I think, sir, that I do not care for your attitude."

"I think, sir, that I do not give a damn what you care for."

Mills drew himself up and stared Smoke in the eye. "You need to be taught a lesson in manners, sir."

"And you think you're just the man to do that, huh?"

"I've thrashed better men than you more than once."

"Cut your bulldog loose, Walsdorf," Smoke said easily. "Just any time you feel lucky."

Jen Sen, the desk clerk was musing. Jen Sen. Jensen. Smoke Jensen! "That's Smoke Jensen, Marshal," he said softly.

The color drained out of Walsdorf's face. A sigh passed his lips.

"Hear me well, Mr. U.S. Marshal," Smoke said. "Lee Slater and his gang attacked Big Rock about ten days ago. They killed several people, including a little girl. And they wounded my wife, Sally. The former Sally Reynolds. You've probably heard the name, since her family owns most of New England. Nobody shoots my wife, Walsdorf, and gets away with it. Nobody. Not Lee Slater's bunch, not a marshal, not a sheriff, not the president of the United States. There's a little town up on the Gunnison, where the Taylor River feeds into it. I found three of Slater's men there. I hope somebody buried them shortly after I rode out 'cause they damn sure smelled bad alive.

"Now I'm going to find the rest of that gang, Walsdorf. And I'm going to kill them. All of them. And I don't need some fancy-pants U.S. Marshal from back East stumbling around screwing up what trail there is left. You understand me?"

Mills drew back in astonishment. Nobody, nobody had ever spoken to him in such a manner. He shook his finger in Smoke's face. "Now, you listen to me, Mr. Smoke Jensen. I realize that you have some reputation, but the West is changing. Your kind is on the way out, and it's past due in coming. Now I . . ."

"Jensen!" the shout came from the street. "Smoke Jensen! Step out here and die!"

"Albert," Mills said, "step out there and see what that man is bellowing about."

A man filled the doorway, paused, then stepped inside. He wore a badge pinned to his shirt. He looked at Smoke. "That's Chris Mathers. He's a local troublemaker. Pretty good with a gun. Better than I am. You killed his big brother several years ago. He used to ride for a scum named Davidson."

"I remember Davidson. Ran an outlaw town. I killed him and his personal bodyguard, man by the name of Dagget. I don't remember any Mathers."

"Smoke Jensen!" the shout came. "You're a coward, Jensen. A dirty little boot-lickin' coward."

Smoke slipped the hammer thong from his guns.

"There'll be none of this!" Mills said.

"There's no law against it." The local marshal shut him up. Momentarily. "This ain't back East where you kiss every punk's butt that comes along. So why don't you just close your mouth and see how we do it in the West?"

Smoke stepped out onto the boardwalk. "I don't have any quarrel with you, boy," he told the young man in the street. "So why don't you just go on home, and we'll forget you calling me out?"

"Big tough man!" Mathers sneered. "I always knowed you was yellow."

"He's givin' you a chance to live, boy," the local marshal told him, standing well to one side. "Take it. You'll never get another one after this day."

"You shut up," Mathers told him, without taking his eyes from Smoke. "Make your play, gunfighter."

Smoke just stood and looked at him.

"I said draw, damn you!" Mathers screamed.

"I got nothing against you, boy. Far as I know, the marshal has no charges against you. So you're not wanted. Go get your horse and ride on out of here."

"He's giving him every chance," Albert said, watching from the hotel lobby's right front window.

"Yes, he is," Mills agreed. "He's a tough man, but seems to be a fair one."

"I'll kill you where you stand, Jensen!" Mathers shouted. His hands hovered over his guns. "Draw."

"I'll not sign your death certificate, boy," Smoke told him. "You'll have to draw on me."

"Are you ready to die, Jensen?" Mathers shouted.

"No man is ever ready to die, boy."

Mills grunted, arching an eyebrow at the philosophical uttering from the mouth of the West's most famous gun handler. He just didn't understand these Western men. They could be incredibly crude, then turn about and quote Shakespeare. They could brand cattle and endure the squalls of pain from the cow, then turn right around and shoot somebody who tried to hurt their pet dog.

Mills reluctantly concluded that he just might have a lot to learn about the West and the people who lived here.

"Now!" Mathers yelled, and grabbed for iron.

Smoke's right-hand Colt seemed to leap into his hand. Mathers felt the slug strike him. His own gun was still in leather. The bullet shattered his breastbone and sent bone splinters into his heart. The young man looked up at the clear blue of the sky. He was on his back and could not understand how he got in that position.

"Holy Mother of God!" Albert muttered. "He's fast as a snake."

Townspeople began gathering around the fallen young man.

"I'll pray for you, young man," the local minister said, clutching his Bible and leaning over Chris Mathers.

But he was talking to a corpse.

Smoke punched out the empty and let it drop to the boardwalk. It bounced and rolled off into the dirt.

"I didn't come into your town to cause trouble, Marshal."

"I know that. What you probably done was save me a lot of trouble. Mathers was born to it and had a killing coming."

Smoke's smile was a grim one. "A hundred years from now, that very statement will come back into the minds of a lot of good, decent, law-abiding people, Marshal." He walked back into the hotel.

Mills Walsdorf had stepped out onto the boardwalk. He

cocked his head to one side and had a puzzled expression on his face upon hearing Smoke's words. "Now . . . what in the world did he mean by that?"

"I could try to explain it to you, Mills," the local marshal said. "But people like you never seem to understand until it's just too damn late."

3

Smoke lingered over his coffee after breakfast, pondering his next move. He didn't want to pull out and have Mills Walsdorf and his Eastern U.S. Marshals tagging along behind him. For the life of him he couldn't understand why the government would send men from the big cities out West to catch Western born and reared outlaws. It just didn't make any sense.

Of course, there were a lot of things the federal government did that didn't make any sense to Smoke.

Like sending seven U.S. Marshals out to round up a gang of fifty or sixty outlaws. That wasn't a dumb move; that was just plain ignorant. Especially when the marshals didn't know the country, weren't familiar with Western ways, and rode their horses like a bunch of English lords and dukes out on a foxhunt.

"May I join you?" Mills broke into his musings.

Smoke pointed to a chair.

"I can't get used to having no menu," Mills said.

"It's on the chalkboard over there," Smoke replied, cutting his eyes.

"I know where it is! I'm not blind." He paused, then said, "I'm afraid we got off on the wrong foot yesterday afternoon, Mr. Jensen. I should like to make amends and offer you some employment."

"The first part is fine with me. Forget the job offer."

"You would be doing your country a great service by joining us and helping to bring an end to this reign of terror put upon the land by Lee Slater and his men."

"I intend to put an end to it, Mills. Permanently."

"The men deserve a fair trial."

"They deserve a bullet, and that is what they're going to get."

"You're going to force me to stop you, Mr. Jensen."

Smoke's eyes were amused as he gazed at the man. "I'd be right interested in knowing how you plan on doing that, Mills."

"By arresting you for obstruction of justice, that's how."

Smoke chuckled. "First you better get yourself a federal warrant for my arrest. Nearest telegraph station is south of here, across the San Juan Mountains. The federal judge is in Denver. I know him. You'll play hell getting him to sign a warrant against me. And if you get another to sign it, I'll get the judge in Denver to cancel it. But that's only part of your problem. The biggest problem facing you would be trying to arrest me."

"You're very sure of yourself, aren't you, Mr. Jensen?"

"The name is Smoke. And yes, I am. You ever heard of the Silver Camp Shoot-out?"

"Yes. That was the setting in one of those penny dreadfuls written about you. Pure fiction, of course."

"Wrong, Mills. Pure fact. There were fifteen salty outlaws in that town when I went in. There were fifteen dead men when I rode out. I wasn't much more than a boy—in age. You ever seen a cornered puma, Mills?"

"No."

"You ever try to brace me, Mills, and you'll see one."

"Are you threatening me?"

"Nope. Just telling you the way it'll be."

"I can have a hundred U.S. Marshals in here in a week, Smoke."

"You'll need them. I was raised by mountain men, Mills. I know areas in this country that still haven't been viewed by white men. I'll get you so damn lost you'll have a beard a foot long before you find your way out. I know where to ride, and where not to ride. And that last part is far more important than the first. And as for you and your boys taking me in, forget it. You'd have to pay too terrible a price. I've had as many as five slugs in me, and stayed on my feet shooting. The men who put those slugs in me are rotting in the grave. I'm sitting here drinking coffee. I'd think about that if I was you."

"I don't think you'd draw on an officer of the law, Smoke."

"I wouldn't want to do it. I surely wouldn't. Most of them just get out of my way and leave me alone. They know I'm not a criminal; they know I work hard and try to live right. Western lawmen also know that you got to put a rabid animal down. There is no cure for what they've got."

"Men are not animals, Smoke."

"You're right. Many men aren't nearly as good as animals. Animals don't kill for no reason. They kill to protect their mate or their cubs. They fight for territory and food. Only man kills for the fun of it. And there are lots of species of animals who won't tolerate a rogue animal. One of their kind goes bad, the others will drive it out or kill it."

"I can't make you understand," Mills said, shaking his head.

"One of us can't," Smoke said. He stood up and walked out of the dining room, climbing the stairs to his room.

"Keep an eye on his room," Mills said, after waving one of his men over. "Just sit right there in the lobby. It's the only way out."

Smoke had paid in advance, as was the custom, and in his room, he gathered up his gear, slung the saddlebags over his shoulder, and climbed out the window, swinging up to the roof. He jumped over to the next building, climbed down, and walked through the alley to the livery, entering the back way.

"Figured you'd be along shortly," the stable man said, walking back to meet him. "Heard them Eastern lawmen want to capture Lee and his bunch alive for a fair trial and all that."

"That's their plan." Smoke threw a saddle on Buck and secured his gear.

The man spat in the dirt. "I'll go get you a poke of food for the trail."

Smoke tried to give him money. The man shook his head. "This one's on me. I'll be right back."

By the time Mills Walsdorf discovered that Smoke was gone, Smoke was halfway between Gap and Beaver Creek.

"He's what?" Mills jumped up.

"He's gone," Winston said glumly. "Liveryman said he pulled out this morning."

"How?" Mills yelled.

"On his damn horse, I suppose!" the marshal said.

"Oh! . . ." Mills brushed the man aside and ran up the stairs to Smoke's room. It was empty. "Climbed out the window, up to the roof, and went down into the alley. Damn! Tell the men to provision up and get mounted. We're pulling out. We have got to see that justice is done. It's our sworn duty. This lawlessness has got to stop. And by God, I intend to be the one to stop it."

"Yes, sir."

* * *

Smoke cooked his supper, rested, and then wiped out all signs of his camp before moving on several miles to make his night's camp. He made a cold camp, not wanting to attract any visitors by building a fire. As he lay rolled up in his blankets, his saddle for a pillow, his thoughts were busy ones.

Was he wrong for being what many called out of step with the times? Was he too eager to kill? Had he reached that point that many men good with a gun feared: had he stepped over the line and begun to enjoy killing?

He rolled over on his back and stared at the stars.

He knew the answer to the last question. No, he did not enjoy killing. He did not enjoy seeing the light fade from a man's eyes as the soul departed.

Was he too eager to kill? He didn't think so, but that might be iffy. He had killed a lot of men since those days when he and his father had left that hardscrabble rocky farm back in Missouri and headed west. But they were men who had pushed him, tried to kill him, or had done him or a loved one harm. What was that line from Thoreau that Sally loved to quote to him? Yes. He recalled it. "If a man does not keep pace with his companions, perhaps it is because he hears a different drummer. Let him step to the music which he hears, however measured or far away."

But is my drummer beating out the right tattoo? he wondered. Am I marching toward the wrong side of the law? What would I really do if Mills Walsdorf tried to arrest me? Would I draw on a badge?

He drifted off to sleep before an answer came to him.

He slept soundly and was up before dawn, waiting until the sun broke over the horizon before building a small fire to boil his coffee and fry his bacon. He sopped out the grease with part of a loaf of bread the liveryman had put in his poke and then broke camp.

He crossed Beaver Creek and would stay to the east of Wolf Creek Pass and Park Creek. This time of the year, early spring, Wolf Creek Pass would be chancy. He was pretty sure Slater and his pack of hyenas would stay clear of Pagosa Springs—which means "Indian healing waters." The town was not a new one, and was populated by men who would not look kindly upon outlaws coming in and raising hell.

And Pagosa Springs was also where Smoke, when he was about nineteen years old and still running with the old mountain man, Preacher, had gunned down Thompson and Haywood. A few days prior to that, he had put lead in two men in a tough mining town named Rico.

The name Smoke Jensen was legend in Colorado and those states bordering it to the west, north, and south.

It was wild and beautiful country he was riding through. Still wild and beautiful despite the onslaught of settlers from the East. This was not farming country, although a few were running cattle in the area. There was a little bit of a town down near Mix Lake, just north of the Alamosa River. That would be ideal for Slater and his crud to hit.

Faint tracks indicated that Slater and his bunch had split up into small groups, but they were all heading in a southeasterly direction. More south than east. That would put the little settlement directly in their path.

And since Smoke had learned that the bunch had worked the west coast for most of their outlaw careers, and really knew little about this country, he had one up on them there. For he had traveled this country since a teenager, and knew shortcuts that only mountain men and Indians knew of.

He turned south and put Del Norte Peak to his right, riding right through some of the most rugged country the state had to offer . . . and that was saying a mouthful. He climbed higher and higher and nooned with a spectacular view for his dessert.

Uncasing his field glasses, he began a slow careful sweep

of the area. He spotted half a dozen smokes from cook fires, all well to the north of his location. He smiled. Slater and his bunch were hopelessly tangled up, taking the rough and rugged way to the settlement.

Smoke smiled as he chewed on a biscuit filled with roast beef. Come on, Slater, he thought. I'll be waiting for you.

The settlement was still half a day's ride ahead of him when he ran into two unshaven and thoroughly mistrustful-looking men riding down the narrow road.

The riders eyeballed him suspiciously as they neared where Smoke sat his horse, his right hand resting near the butt of his .44.

"You boys look like you been riding hard," Smoke said. "Plumb tuckered out."

"You figure that's any of your business?" one asked.

"My, aren't we grouchy today? Just trying to be friendly, boys."

The other rider muttered curses under his breath.

"Heading down to the settlement, boys?"

The pair reined up. "You got a nose problem, you know that, mister?" one said.

"I don't have near the problems you boys are about to have."

"Huh? What do you mean by that?"

"What I mean is, if you boys think the reception you got up in Big Rock was hostile, you're about to learn that was a picnic compared to what's looking at you now."

The outlaws had moved their horses so that they both faced Smoke.

"I think, mister," the bigger of the two said, "that you got a big fat mouth. And I think I'll just close it—permanently."

"Before you do that, I got a message for you."

"From who?"

"From that woman and her two daughters you raped and killed up north of here."

The two men sat their horses and stared at Smoke.

"And from her husband that you trash used for target practice."

"You're about ten seconds away from dyin', mister."

Smoke turned Buck, giving him a better field of fire. "Enjoy all the comforts of hell, boys." Smoke spoke softly.

"What's your damn name, mister?" the other punk asked.

"Smoke Jensen."

The outlaws grabbed for their guns, and Smoke emptied two saddles. The bigger of the two scum hit the ground and tried to lift his pistol. Smoke shot him between the eyes, shifted the muzzle of his .44, and put another slug in the second man's chest.

The dying man said, "You'll never leave this part of the country alive, Jensen."

"Maybe," Smoke told him. "But that isn't doing you much good right now, is it?"

The outlaw cussed him.

"Tsk, tsk," Smoke said. "Such language while on the way to meet the Lord."

The outlaw died in the dirt, a curse on his lips.

Smoke stripped the saddles from the horses and turned them loose. He took the men's guns and money and shoved the dead over the side of the mountain road. Several miles down the road, he came to a cabin and halloed it.

A man, a woman, and two wide-eyed kids peeked around the corner of the cabin that was set well off the road in a thick stand of timber.

"I'm friendly," he told him. "Can I water my horse?"

"You can," the man told him. "I'll not turn no man away from this house who's in need."

"Thanks kindly. Some outlaws tried to rob me up the road

a piece. They weren't very good at their work." He placed the rifles and pistols on a bench next to the house. "They're part of a much larger gang that'll be coming along this road shortly, I'm thinking." He handed the man a wad of greenbacks he'd taken from the dead outlaws. The eyes of the man and woman widened in shock. "I took this off the dead men, figuring I'd run into someone who needed it more than me. You folks look like you've hit some hard times here."

"You're a saint, mister," the woman said. "There must be several hundred dollars there."

"Probably. I didn't count it. And I'm no saint, ma'am. Was I you folks, I'd pack me some food and bedding and take off for the deep timber until the trouble is over. Get those kids out of harm's way."

"We'll do that, mister. You the law?"

"No. I've been tracking these outlaws since they rode into a town near where I live and shot it up. One of the people they shot was my wife."

"What's your name?" the woman asked.

"Jensen, ma'am. Smoke Jensen."

They were still standing with their mouths hanging open when Smoke rode away.

Smoke made the settlement by late afternoon and stabled his horse at the livery.

"They got rooms for let over the saloon," the liveryman told him. "They ain't much, but they're better than nothin'. Bonnie's Cafe serves right good food if the cook ain't drunk." He peered at Smoke. "Don't I know you?"

"I doubt it. First time I've ever been here. This town have a name?"

"It's had three or four. Right now we're 'twixt and 'tween."

"You got a marshal?"

"Nope. Had one but he left 'cause we couldn't pay him . . . among other reasons. Had a bank but it closed. Got one stage a week comes through. Heads north. You wanna go south, you're in trouble. Starts out in Monte Vista and makes a big circle. Alamosa, Conejos, through here, and back up the grade."

"You ever heard of the Lee Slater gang?"

"Nope."

"You will." Smoke gathered his gear and walked to the saloon, dumping his saddlebags on the bar.

"Got a room for a few days?" he asked the barkeep.

"Take your choice. They're all empty. The best in the house will cost you a dollar a night. Dollar and a half for clean sheets."

Smoke tossed some coins on the bar. "Change the sheets. I want a room facing the street."

"You got it. Number one. Top of the stairs and turn right. You cain't miss it," he added drily.

"Tubs inside?" Smoke asked hopefully.

"You got to be kidding! Tubs behind the barbershop. Want me to have one filled up?"

"Please."

"Fifty cents."

Smoke paid him and stowed his gear in the room. He walked over to the barbershop and bathed, then had the barber shave him and cut his hair.

"Lilac water?" the barber asked. "Two bits and you'll smell so good the ladies'll be knockin' on your door tonight."

Smoke handed him a quarter. "How many people in this town?"

"Sixty-five, at last count. We're a growin' little community, for sure. Got us the bes' general store within fifty miles. Freight wagons jus' run yesterday, and she's stocked to the overflowin'."

Perfect for Slater and his bunch, Smoke thought. They might not get much money out of this place, but they could take enough provisions to last them a month or better while they raided towns, then disappeared back into the mountains.

"Any strangers been riding through?"

"Yeah, they has been, come to think of it. Yesterday, as a matter of fact. Some real hard-lookin' ol' boys. Stopped over to the saloon and had them a taste, then looked the town over real careful-like. Made me kind of edgy."

"Who runs this town?"

"Mayor and town council. Why?"

" 'Cause you got a big bunch of outlaws probably planning to hit this place within the next few days. I've been on their trail for several weeks. Lee Slater's bunch out of California. They hit my town up north of here and killed several people."

"Lord have mercy! And us without no marshal."

"You want a lawman?"

"Sure. But we can't pay no decent wage."

"You go get the mayor and the town council. Tell them I'll work as marshal for a time—free."

"You got any qualifications to do the job?"

"I think so."

"You sit right there. Here's a paper from Denver. It ain't but three weeks old. I'll be right back."

The mayor was the owner of the general store, and the town council was the blacksmith, the saloon keeper, and the liveryman.

They listened to Smoke and shook their heads, the mayor saying, "That many outlaws would destroy this town. You figure that you'd do any good stoppin' them, mister?"

"I think so."

"You ain't but one man," the saloon keeper said. "Hell, we don't even know your name."

"Smoke Jensen."

The barber sat down in his chair, his mouth open in shock. The liveryman cackled with glee.

"Here's the badge and raise your right hand, sir," the mayor said, after he found his voice.

4

Smoke was leaning up against an awning post in front of the saloon when Mills Walsdorf and his men rode slowly into town. Three very boring and totally uneventful days had passed with no sign of any of the Slater gang. Mills gave Smoke a very disgusted look as he noticed the star pinned to Smoke's chest. He turned his horse and stopped at the hitch rail.

He dismounted and sighed as his boots touched the ground. The horse looked as tired as he did.

"Have a good ride, Mills?" Smoke asked.

"Very funny, Jensen," the federal man said. "Did you kill those two men we found off the side of the road a few miles back?"

"Yes. I did. They accosted me on the trail, and I was forced to defend myself."

"My God, man! You could have at least given them a decent burial."

"They weren't decent people."

"You're disgusting, Jensen. The vultures had picked at them."

"They probably flew off somewhere and died."

Mills ignored that. "Did you really think you could lose us?"

"Only if I wanted to. You may be city boys, but you probably know how to use a compass."

"To be sure. I'm curious about that badge you're wearing."

"I think it's made of tin."

A pained look passed Mills' face. He sighed. "You are a very difficult man to speak with, Jensen. I meant . . ."

"I know what you meant. I believe the Slater gang is heading this way. The town didn't have a marshal. I volunteered and they accepted my unpaid services."

"Well, we're here now, so you can feel free to resign."

"Oh, well, hell, Mills. That makes me feel so much better. What are you going to do when the Slater gang hits town, talk them to death?"

A flash of irritation passed the federal marshal's face. He cleared his throat and said, "I intend to arrest them, Jensen. Then we'll try them and see that they get long prison sentences."

"How about a rope?"

"I don't believe in capital punishment."

"Oh, Lord!" Smoke said, looking heavenward. "What have I done for you to send this down on me?"

Mills laughed at Smoke. "Oh, come now, man! You're obviously a fellow of some intelligence. You surely know that the death penalty doesn't work . . ."

"The hell it doesn't!" Smoke said. "They'll damn sure not come back from the grave to commit more crimes ."

"That's not what I mean. It isn't a deterrent for others not to commit the same acts of mayhem."

"Now, what bright fellow thought up that crap?"

"Very learned people in some of our finest eastern universities."

Smoke said a few very ugly words, which summed up his opinion of very learned people back East. He turned and walked toward the batwings, pausing for a moment and calling over his shoulder. "There're rooms upstairs here, Mills. Take your baths across the street behind the barbershop. Don't try supper at Bonnie's Cafe this evening. The cook's drunk. That apple, turnip, and carrot stew he fixed for lunch was rough."

Mills and his marshals were sitting at one table in the saloon, Smoke sitting alone at another playing solitaire when the batwings shoved open and half a dozen men crowded into the saloon, heading for the bar. They eyeballed the U.S. Marshals and grinned at their high-top lace-up boots, their trousers tucked in.

Mills cut his eyes to Smoke. The gunfighter had merely looked up from his game, given the newcomers the briefest of glances, and apparently dismissed them.

The men lined up at the bar and ordered whiskey. "Hear you got some law in this town now." A big cowboy shot off his mouth. "I reckon me and the boys will have to mind our P's and Q's. We sure wouldn't want to run afoul of the law."

The cowboys laughed, but it was not a good-natured laugh. More like a sarcastic, go-to-hell braying of men who looked for trouble and did not give a damn about the rights of anyone else. Smoke didn't know if they were outlaws or not. But they damn sure were hardcases. Standing very close to the outlaw line.

"Evenin', Luttie," the barkeep said.

Smoke had been briefed on the men. The one with the biggest mouth was Luttie Charles, owner of the Seven Slash Ranch. The foreman was named Jake. Neither man was very likeable, and both were bullies, as were the dozen or so hands the ranch kept on the payroll.

"Yeah," Jake said, after tossing back his whiskey.

"Where is this new marshal? I want to size him up and maybe have some fun."

Smoke had also learned that the last marshal the town hired had left not because the town couldn't pay him, but because he'd been savagely beaten by men from the Seven Slash, although low pay had played a part in it.

"I hope it ain't one of these pretty boys," a hand said, turning and sneering at Mills and his men. "That wouldn't be no contest a-tall."

I wouldn't sell Mills and his men short, Smoke thought. I got a hunch those badge-toters have a hell of a lot more sand and gravel in them than appears. They've been dealing with big city punks and shoulder-strikers and foot-padders for a long time. You boys just might be in for a surprise if you crowd them. Especially Mills. He's no pansy.

Luttie turned to stare at Smoke, sitting close to the shadows in the room. "You, there!" he brayed. "What are you doing?"

"Minding my own business," Smoke said in a quiet voice. "Why don't you do the same?"

To a man, the Seven Slash riders turned, looking at the partially obscured figure at the table.

"You got a smart mouth on you, mister," Luttie said. "Maybe you don't know who I am."

"I don't particularly care who you are."

The Seven Slash riders looked at one another, grinning. This might turn out to be a fun evening after all. It was always fun to beat hell out of someone.

"Git up!" Luttie gave the command to Smoke.

Smoke, in a quiet voice, told him where he could put his order—sideways.

Luttie shook his head. Nobody talked to him like that.

Nobody. Ever. "Who in the hell do you think you are?" Luttie roared across the room.

"The new town marshal," Smoke told him, shuffling the deck of cards.

"Maybe he's sittin' over there in the dark 'cause he's so ugly," a hand suggested.

"Why don't we just drag him out in the light and have a look at him?" another said.

"And then we'll stomp him," another laughed.

"That's Smoke Jensen," the barkeep said.

The hands became very silent, and very still. They watched as Smoke stood up from the table. Seemed like he just kept on gettin' up. He laid the deck of cards down on the table and walked out of the shadows, his spurs softly jingling as he walked across the floor. He stopped in front of Luttie.

Luttie was no coward, but neither was he a fool. He knew Smoke Jensen's reputation, and knew it to be true. As he looked into those icy brown eyes, he felt a trickle of sweat slide down the center of his back.

"If there is any stomping to be done in this town," Smoke told the rancher, "I'll do it. And I just might decide to start with you. I don't like bullies. And you're a bully. I don't like bigmouthed fatheads. And you're a bigmouthed fathead. And you're also packin' iron. Now use it, or shut your goddamn mouth!"

Luttie was good with a gun, better than most. He knew that. But he was facing the man who had killed some of the West's most notorious gunfighters. And also a man who was as good with his fists as he was with a six-shooter.

"I got no quarrel with you," Luttie said sullenly. "The boys was just funnin' some."

"No, they weren't," Smoke told him. "And you know it. They're all bullies, just like you. I've heard all about how you and your crew come into this town, intimidating and bullying other people. I've heard how you like to pick fights and hurt people. You want to fight me, Luttie? How about it? No guns. Just fists. You want that, Luttie?"

"I shall ensure it is a fair fight," Mills said quietly, opening his jacket to show his badge.

"Luttie," Jake said. "Them Eastern dudes is U.S. Marshals."

The rancher's sigh was audible. Something big was up, and he didn't know what. But he knew the odds were hard against him on his evening. "We'll be going, boys," he said.

Luttie and his crew paid up and left the saloon, walking without swagger. The crew knew the boss was mad as hornets, but none blamed him for not tangling with Smoke Jensen. That would have been a very dumb move. There was always another day.

"What the hell's he doin' here?" Jake questioned, as they stood by their horses.

"I don't know," Luttie said. "And what about them U.S. Marshals? You reckon they're on to us?"

"How could they be?" another hand asked, surprise and anger in his eyes. "Not even the sheriff suspects anything."

"I don't like it," Jake said.

"Well, hell! How do you think I feel about it? Come on. Let's ride."

"You push hard, Mr. Jensen," Mills said. "There might have been a killing."

"You figure his death would be a great crushing blow to humanity?"

Mills chuckled. "Sometimes your speech is so homey it's sickening. Other times it appears to come straight from the classics. I'm new to the West, Mr. Jensen . . ."

"Smoke. Just Smoke."

"Very well. Smoke. I have much to learn about the West and its people."

"We saddle our own horses and kill our own snakes."

"And the law?"

"We obey it for the most part. Where there is law. But when you come up on people rustling your stock, a man don't usually have the time to ride fifty miles to get a sheriff. Things tend to get hot and heavy real quick. Someone starts shooting at you, you shoot back."

"I can understand that," Mills said. He smiled at Smoke's startled expression. "I'm not the legal stickler you think I am, Smoke. There are times when a person must defend himself. I understand that. But there are other times when men knowingly take the law into their own hands, and that's what I'm opposed to."

"Like you think I'm doing?"

Mills smiled. "As you have been doing," he corrected. "Now you are sworn in as an officer of the law. That makes all the difference."

"And you really believe that?"

"In most cases, yes. In your case, no."

Smoke laughed.

"You became legal—in a manner of speaking—simply as a means to achieve an end. The end of Lee Slater and his gang. What would you do should Lee and his men attack this town, right now?"

"Empty a lot of saddles."

"And be killed doing it?"

"Not likely. I'm no Viking berserker. Anyway, I don't think he's going to attack this town."

"Oh? When did you change your mind?"

"During the course of the day."

"And what do you think he's going to do?"

"I have an idea. But it's just a thought. I'll let you know when I have it all worked out. And I will let you in on it, Mills. You have my word."

"Fair enough."

"Are some of you going to be in town tomorrow?"

"Yes. We're waiting on word from the home office. We sent word where we'd be from that little settlement on the Rio Grande. The stage runs in a couple of days."

"I appreciate you staying close. I'll pull out early in the morning to do some snooping. Be back late tomorrow night."

Smoke could tell the man had a dozen questions he would like to ask. But he held them in check. "I'll see you then."

Smoke pulled out several hours before dawn, pointing Buck's nose toward the east, staying on the south side of the Alamosa River. Luttie's Seven Slash Ranch lay about twenty miles south of the town.

Luttie was up to something besides ranching. Those hands of his were more than cowboys; Smoke had a hunch they were drawing fighting wages. If that was true, who were they fighting, and why?

At the first coloring of dawn, Smoke was on a hill overlooking Luttie's ranch house. He studied the men as they exited the bunkhouse heading for chow in a building next to it. He counted fifteen men. Say three or four were not in yet from night herding; that was a hell of a lot of cowboys for a spread this size.

So what was Luttie up to?

Smoke stayed on the ridges as long as he dared, looking things over through field glasses. For a working ranch, there didn't seem to be much going on. And he found that odd.

Come to think of it, he hadn't seen any cattle on his way in. What he had seen were a lot of signs proclaiming this area to be "posted" and "no trespassing allowed." Odd. Too many odd things cropping up about the Seven Slash Ranch.

It was time to move on; his position on the ridge was just too vulnerable. He tightened the cinch and swung into the saddle. He hadn't learned much, but he had learned that something very odd was going on at the Seven Slash Ranch. And Smoke didn't think it had a damn thing to do with cattle.

"So what is going on?" Mills asked.

The men were sitting on the boardwalk in front of the saloon, enjoying the night air. Mills was contentedly puffing on his pipe, and Smoke had rolled a cigarette.

"I don't know. Luttie could say he stripped his range during roundup, and a range detective would probably accept that. But he hasn't run any cattle in several years on the ground that I covered today. Any cattleman could see that. So why does he have the big crew, all of them fighting men?" Smoke smiled. "Maybe I know."

"Share it with me?"

"It's just a guess."

"A lot of good police work starts right there."

"It might be that he's hit a silver strike and wants it all for himself, mining it out in secret. But a better guess is that he's running a front for stolen goods."

"I like the second one. But I have some questions about that theory. Why? is one. He's a rancher who has done very well, from all indications. He is a reasonably monied man. I suppose we could chalk it up to greed; however, I think, assuming you're correct, there must be other reasons."

"Why, after all the years of outlawing on the west coast, would Lee Slater put together a gang and come to Colorado?" Smoke questioned. "The west coast is where all his contacts and hiding places would be."

"Where are you going with this, Smoke?"

"I don't know. I'm just trying to put all the pieces together. I may be completely off-base and accusing an innocent man of a crime. All I've got is gut hunches. Can you do some background work?"

"Certainly. But on whom?"

"Luttie Charles and Lee Slater."

That got Mills' attention. He took the pipe out of his mouth and stared at Smoke. "How could they be connected?"

"Maybe by blood."

The Lee Slater gang seemed to have dropped off the face of the earth. Five days went by with no word of any outlaw activity in the area.

The sheriff of the county and two of his deputies rode into town, and Sheriff Silva almost had a heart attack when he learned that Smoke Jensen was the new town marshal.

"By God, it is you!" he said, standing in the door to the town marshal's small office. He frowned. "But why here, of all places?"

Smoke laid it out for the man, but said nothing of his suspicions of Luttie Charles.

The sheriff nodded his head. "We heard he was in this area. If he is, he's found him a dandy hidey-hole."

Smoke had him an idea just where that might be. But he kept that to himself. "Can you make me a deputy sheriff of this county?"

"Sure can. It'd be an honor. Stand up and raise your right hand."

After being sworn in, Smoke and Sheriff Dick Silva sat in the office and drank coffee and chatted. Mills and his men were out of town, roaming around, looking for signs of the Slater gang.

"It could be," the sheriff said, "that Slater learned about the new silver strikes to the north and east of here. The big one's up around Creede, but we've got some dandy smaller ones in this area."

"Any gold?"

"A few producing mines, yeah. The stage line is putting on more people, and they'll be running through here every other day commencin' shortly. This town'll boom for a while. But you know how that goes."

Smoke nodded his head. The rotting ruins of former boom towns dotted the landscape of the West. They flourished for a few months or a few years, until the gold or silver ran out, and then died or were reduced to only a few hangers-on, scratching in the earth for the precious metals.

"I've seen a few boom towns in my life."

"You rode with ol' Preacher, didn't you, Smoke?"

"Yes. He raised me after my dad was killed. I knew all the old mountain men. Beartooth, Dupree, Greybull, Nighthawk, Tenneysee, Pugh, Audie, Matt, Deadlead. Hell of a breed of men, they were. I hated to see them vanish."

One left, the sheriff thought, taking in the awesome size of the man seated before him. Smoke's wrists were as large as some men's arms. If he hit you with everything he had, the blow would do some terrible damage to a man's face.

"Tell me everything that's on your mind, son," the sheriff urged in a quiet tone. "You've been steppin' around something for an hour."

Dick Silva was no fool, Smoke thought. He's a good lawman who can read between the lines. But what if he's a friend of Luttie's, or on his payroll? How to phrase this?

"I had a little run-in with Luttie Charles the other night," he said, figuring that was the best way to open up.

The sheriff spat and clanged the cuspidor. "I don't have much use for Luttie. When he first come into this country, years back, he was a hard-workin' man. I didn't approve of the way he built up his ranch—he was one of them homesteader burners, if they got in his way—but the sheriff back then was easy bought and in his pocket. I ain't," he said flatly. "Luttie steps cautious-like around me."

"I took a ride over to his place the other day. He appears to be a man who don't like visitors."

"All them posted signs?"

Smoke nodded.

"They went up about five years ago. 'Bout the same time

the bottom dropped out of the beef market—for a while—and Luttie took to hirin' hardcases to ride for him. I've run off or jailed a few of his hands. But he's got some bad ones workin' for him."

"And no cattle." Smoke dropped that in.

"You noticed too," the sheriff said with a smile.

"Of course, there is no law that says a man has to run cattle on his ranch if he doesn't want to."

"Exactly. But it sure makes me awful curious about just how he's earnin' a livin'." He shook his head. "I know where you're goin' with this, Smoke. But I have no authority to go bustin' up onto his property demandin' to know how he earns his livelihood. And a judge would throw me out of his chambers if I tried to get a search warrant based on our gut hunches."

"Oh, I know."

"Say it all, Smoke." Sheriff Silva smiled. "You're one of my deputies now. You can't hold back from the boss."

"I've got a hunch there is some connection between Slater and Luttie. I've asked a U.S. Marshal to check their backgrounds. He's doing that now. Probably be a week or more before anything comes back in."

"You'd make a good lawman, Smoke."

"I've toted a badge more than once," he replied with a smile. "County, state, and federal. Mills Walsdorf doesn't know that, though."

"What do you think of the man?"

"I like him. I thought he was a pompus, stuffed-shirt windbag when I first met him. But he sort of grows on you. He sure has some funny ideas about enforcing the law. He doesn't believe in the death penalty."

The sheriff almost choked on his chew. "What?"

"Says it's barbaric and doesn't accomplish anything. Says criminals aren't really to blame for what they do."

"Say what?"

"Says it's home life and pressure from friends and so forth that cause criminals. Rejection and things like that. Says all sorts of real smart folks back in fine Eastern universities thought all this out."

Sheriff Silva shook his head. "I hope them thoughts of his don't never catch on. In a hundred years, criminals would be runnin' the country."

5

It was a very weary and dejected-looking band of U.S. Marshals that rode back into town late in the afternoon. After a bath and a shave, Mills walked over to Smoke's office. He was almost dragging his boots in the dirt from exhaustion.

"Cover a lot of ground, did you?" Smoke asked, pouring the man a cup of coffee from the battered pot on the stove.

"More than I care to repeat any time soon." Mills sat down with a sigh and accepted the cup of coffee. "And didn't accomplish a damned thing."

"No," Smoke corrected. "Don't look at it like that. You accomplished a great deal, in fact."

"I'd like to know what."

"You saw the country, and if you're just half as smart as I think you are, you committed it to memory. You know where good water is now. You found some box canyons and now know to stay out of them. You found good places to bed down for the night. You found where outlaws might hole up. You know where good river and stream crossings are located. And you saw some of the most beautiful country in all the world."

Slowly, a smile crinkled the marshal's mouth. "Yes. You're right on all counts, Smoke." He peered over the rim of his coffee cup at the new gold badge on Smoke's chest. "Say, now. Where did that come from?"

Smoke told him of Sheriff Silva's visit.

"The sheriff checks out as a good, honest lawman. He's a rancher that got caught up in the market bust years back and turned to police work. His ranch rebounded, but he was hooked on police work by that time, and the people of the county like him. He earns enough money from both vocations to ensure he can't be bought."

"Find out anything about Luttie Charles?"

"A few things. The people around here don't like him and don't trust him. He says he came here from Texas, but people doubt that. Oklahoma Territory seems to be the general consensus. Early on he let it slip that he's fairly knowledgeable about that part of the country."

"So why would he lie about it?"

"You know the answer to that as well as I do. He's hiding something in his past. But he could be running away from a wife. It's certainly happened to other men."

"With Luttie, it's more like a rope he's running from."

"Agreed. But proving it is another matter. I have feelers out. It'll take some time."

"You'd better get some rest. You look like you're all in."

"Yes. I'll see you in the morning."

Smoke did some paperwork, then locked up the office and stepped out into the gathering dusk of evening. He began his walking of the settlement's streets. That didn't take long, and he headed for Bonnie's Cafe for a cup of coffee.

Movement at the edge of town stopped him. Smoke stepped into a weed-grown space between the empty bank building and the general store and waited.

There it was again. But at this distance, he couldn't tell if the movement was human or animal. He removed his spurs and put them in his pocket while he waited and watched, not staring directly at the mysterious shape, for some people can sense being watched. The form began to take shape as it drew nearer, staying in the shadows. It was a man, no doubt about that, and moving slowly and furtively.

The man ducked down the far side of Bonnie's Cafe, and Smoke took that time to run silently across the street and into the alley that ran between the combination saddle building and the saloon.

Staying close to the building, but not brushing against it, he pulled iron and eased the hammer back just as the man stepped into the rear of the alley.

Smoke dropped down to one knee and said, "You looking for someone, partner?"

The man fired, the muzzle blast stabbing the darkness with a lance of flame. The bullet slammed into the building, a foot above Smoke's head.

Smoke let the hammer down, and his slug brought a scream of pain and doubled the man over. A rifle barked from across the street, and that slug howled past Smoke's head. Smoke flattened on the ground and rolled under the building, hoping a rattlesnake was not under there and irritated at being disturbed.

The rifle barked again, just as lamps were turned up in the homes and businesses of the settlement.

"Goddamnit, Jesse!" the man Smoke had shot screamed. "You done killed me!" He moaned once and said no more.

Running footsteps reached Smoke, followed by the sounds of galloping hooves. He rolled out from under the building just as Mills and his men came running out of the saloon, in various stages of dress, or undress. Mills had jerked on his high-top boots, not laced up, and put on his hat. He was dressed in hat, boots, and long-handles.

"Bring a lamp over here," Smoke called. "One's down in the alley."

"Don King," the barber said, as the dead man was rolled over onto his back. "Rides for Luttie Charles."

"He don't no more," Bonnie said, peering over the man's shoulder.

"I heard him yell that someone named Jesse shot him," Mills said.

"He put the second slug in him," Smoke said. He looked at the barber. "You act as the undertaker?"

"Yes, sir, Mr. Smoke. I do a right nice job, too, if I do say so myself."

"Leastwise, he ain't never had no customers complain," Bonnie said.

"Stretch him out in your place, then," Smoke told the man. "It's cool enough so he'll keep for a day. Mills, you and me will take a ride out to break the sad news to Luttie Charles first thing in the morning."

"I'll be up at five."

They left before dawn and were on Seven Slash range as the sun was chasing away the last of the shadows of night. They stopped at a wooden, hand-painted sign nailed to a tree.

TRESPASSERS WILL BE SHOT.

"Certainly gives a person a warm feeling of being wanted, doesn't it?" Mills said drily.

Smoke laughed. Despite their differences of opinion concerning law and order, he liked the federal marshal. He was looking forward to seeing the man get into action. He had a hunch Mills would be hard to handle if you made him mad.

Mills shifted his badge to the front of his coat. "So they'll be sure to see it," he said.

"Makes a dandy target," Smoke told him. "Might stop a bullet if it was fired from a far enough distance."

"You're so full of good cheer early in the morning."

"Thank you."

"Just hold it right there, boys," the voice came from be-hind them. "And keep them hands in sight."

"I'm a United States Marshal," Mills said, without look-ing around. "And this is Deputy Jensen. I have six of my men fifteen minutes behind us . . ."

Pretty good liar, Smoke thought. Quick, too.

". . . Cease and desist and come forward."

"Do what?"

"Get your butt around here so's we can see you." Smoke made it plainer.

"I don't take orders from you."

"You think you can get both of us?" Smoke asked. "If you do, you're a fool."

"Just sit your saddles." The man walked around to face them.

"Now you've seen me," Smoke told him. "If you ever again put iron on me, I'll kill you. Now put that rifle away."

"Just pointing that weapon at me could mean prison for you," Mills told him.

"All right, all right!" the hardcase said, lowering the muz-zle. "I'm just following orders from the boss. What do you want here?"

"To see your boss," Smoke told him. "Let's go."

"He ain't up yet. He don't get up 'til eight. Likes to work at night."

Smoke smiled.

"Jesus Christ!" Luttie hollered, as Smoke grabbed him by the ankle and dragged him out of bed. "What the hell's goin' on here?" Luttie's butt bounced on the floor, and he came up in his long johns swinging both fists.

Smoke staggered him with one punch, grabbed him by

the neck and the back-flap and threw him down the stairs of the two story ranch house.

"Your approach to law and order is quite novel, to say the least," Mills observed.

"It gets their attention," Smoke told him, as they walked down the stairs to stand over a dazed and befuddled Luttie.

Smoke tossed Don King's personal effects to the floor. "Those belong to one of your hands. He tried to kill me last night. Somebody named Jesse shot him after I did. Get Jesse out here and do it now."

"No one named Jesse works for me," Luttie muttered, crawling to his bare feet.

Smoke drew, cocked and fired so fast it was a blur. He put a slug between Luttie's bare feet.

"Yeeeyow!" the man hollered and danced, as the splinters dug into his feet.

"I said get Jesse here," Smoke said.

"Jesus Christ!" Luttie bellered. "Jake, go get Jesse over here." He glared at Smoke. "I hate you!"

"I'm all broken up about it. Aren't you going to be neighborly and offer us some coffee?"

"Hell with you!"

"Disgusting lack of hospitality," Mills said.

"Hell with you, too," Luttie told him.

The men stood and stared at each other for a moment.

The foreman, Jake, reentered the house. "Jesse didn't come back last night. His bunk ain't been slept in."

"We have a description of him," Mills said. "I'll get a federal warrant issued for his arrest, charging him with murder and attempted murder of a law officer."

"Now both of you get out of my house!" Luttie yelled.

Smoke looked at the man's soiled long-handles. "You need to do something about your personal hygiene, Luttie."

"Get out of here!" the man screamed.

"What do you want done with the remains of poor Don King?" Smoke asked.

"Bury him!" Luttie yelled. "In the ground."

"He didn't have but two dollars on him," Mills said. "A good box costs far more than that. I personally would suggest one lined with a subtle shade of cloth, perhaps with a soft pillow on which to lay his poor dead head. A simple service will suffice, with the minister reading from the . . ."

"Shut up!" Luttie roared. "Goddamnit! I don't care if you read from a tobacco sack. Just get out of my house and put the man in the ground. Send me the bill."

"You're a true lover of your fellow man, Luttie," Smoke said, trying to keep a straight face. It was hard to do: the buttons on Luttie's back flap had torn loose, and he was trying to hold it up with one hand.

"I'm sure the service will be tomorrow," Mills said, continuing to play the game with Smoke. "Shall I tell everyone you'll be in attendance?"

Luttie started jumping up and down like a great ape in a cage. "GetoutGetoutGetoutGetout!" he screamed.

"I think we have overstayed our welcome," Smoke said. "Do you agree, Marshal?"

"Quite. Shall we take our leave?"

"Oh, let's do!"

Luttie was screaming obscenities at them as they rode away. Both breathed a little easier when they were out of rifle shot.

"Luttie, them two ain't got a lick of sense!" Jake said, when he had calmed Luttie down. "And a crazy man's dangerous!"

That set Luttie off again, jumping around and hollering.

"I think he needs a good dose of salts," a hardcase suggested. "Maybe his plumbin's all plugged up?"

*   *   *

"For a man that don't believe in going to the extreme with law and order," Smoke said, "you sure can jump right in there and help stick the needle to suspects."

"Oh, I think a bit of agitation is good for the soul. The man is unbalanced. You realize that?"

"Uh-huh. And now I hope you're not going to tell me that because he's about half nuts he shouldn't be shot if he drags iron on someone."

"There is some debate on that, I will admit. But a dangerous person is dangerous whether he's normal or insane. Besides, there are degrees of insanity. Luttie Charles is not a drooling idiot confined to a rocking chair. He simply lost control back there for a moment. He's a very cunning man." He chuckled. "Wouldn't you lose control if someone grabbed you by the ankle and jerked you out of a sound sleep, then knocked you down and threw you down the stairs?"

Smoke smiled. "I might at that." He shook his head. "That was sure some sight."

Laughing, the men put their horses into an easy canter and headed back to town. Smoke noticed that Mills had stopped bobbing up and down like a cork in the water and was riding more and more like a Westerner.

The next several days were long and boring. Providing Jake had been telling the truth back at the ranch house, Jesse had left the country.

"If that's the case," Mills observed, "it's probably for fear that Luttie would shoot him because he and that other wretch failed to kill you."

Later on that day, shortly after the stage had run, Mills came to the marshal's office. "This is it," he said, smiling and waving a piece of paper. He sat down. "It seems that Lee Slater—and Slater is his Christian name—was born in Oklahoma. He left their farm when he was about fifteen, after raping and killing a neighbor girl. He had a younger brother that disappeared shortly after robbing a stagecoach and making off with a strongbox filled with thousands of dollars. The boys were named Lee and Luther" Mills smiled again. "Luther's middle name was Charles."

"It's good enough for me, but I doubt a jury would convict on it."

"Nor do I. My superiors have given me orders to stay out here until Lee Slater and his band of thugs are contained." He sighed. "At the rate I'm going, I may as well move my belongings out here and transfer my bank account."

"Oh," Smoke said, pouring them both coffee. "It's not that bad. I tell you what I'll bet you: you stay out here a few more months, Mills, and this country will grab you. Then you won't want to leave."

"I'm afraid you may be right. Do you have any sort of plan, Smoke? I seem to be fresh out."

The gunfighter shook his head. "No, I don't, Mills. It seems to me—and I'm no professional lawman—that all we can do is wait for something to break, then jump on it like a hound on a bone."

Mills had noticed that Smoke had adopted a small cur dog he'd found wandering the town, eating scraps and having mean little boys throw rocks at it. After a lecture from Smoke Jensen about being cruel to animals, Mills was of the opinion the boys might well grow up to be vegetarians. Smoke had been rather stern.

Smoke had bathed the little dog and fixed it a bed in the office. The dog now lay in Smoke's lap, contented as Smoke gently petted it.

"You're a strange man, Smoke," Mills had to say. "You don't appear to care one whit about the life of a person gone wrong, yet you love animals."

"Animals can't help being what they are, Mills," Smoke

said with a gentle smile. "We humans can. We have the ability to think and reason. I don't believe animals do; at least not to any degree. We don't have to rob and steal and lie and cheat and murder. That's why God gave us a brain. And I don't have any use for people who refuse to use that brain and instead turn to a life of crime. You read the Bible, Mills?"

"Certainly. But what has the Bible got to do with animals?"

"A lot. I think animals go to Heaven."

"Oh, come now!" Mills gently scoffed.

"Sure. And our Bible is not the only Good Book that talks of that. Our Bible says in Ecclesiates: 'For the fate of the sons of men and the fate of beasts is the same; as one dies, so dies the other. They all have the same breath, and man has no advantage over the beasts; for all is vanity.' Paul preached about it, too. And my wife, who is a lot more religious than me, says that John Wesley came right out and outlined what he thought animals would experience in Heaven. John Calvin also admitted that he thought animals were to be renewed."

Mills shook his head. "You never cease to baffle me, Smoke. You're a . . . walking contradiction. You mentioned some other Good Book. What are you talking about?"

"The Koran. You haven't read it?"

"Good God, no! And you have?"

"Yes. Sally ordered a copy for me. I found it very interesting."

Mills studied the man for a moment. Before him was the West's most notorious gunfighter—no, Jensen wasn't notorious; "famous" was a better word—and the man was calmly discussing the world's religions. And sounding as if he did indeed know what he was talking about.

"You think you'll go to Heaven, Smoke?" Mills asked gently.

"I don't know. God loved His warriors. I do know that. But I like to think that maybe there is a middle ground for men like me."

"Like Valhalla?"

"Yes."

"Another personal question, Smoke?"

"Sure."

"How many men have you killed?"

"I honestly don't know, Mills. Over a hundred, surely, and possibly two hundred. I've got a lot of blood on my hands, I won't deny that. Jesse James gave me my first pistol, way back during the war, when I was just a kid in Missouri. A Navy .36, it was. I carried that old pistol for a long time. And put some men in the ground with it."

"What happened to it?"

"I think it's in a trunk up at the ranch house."

"You have children, Smoke?"

"Oh, yes. They're in France with their grandparents, traveling and getting an education. Baby Arthur had to go for medical treatment. Their mother couldn't go because she gets deadly ill on ship."

"Outlaws killed your first wife, didn't they?"

"Yes. And smothered my baby son in the cradle while they were raping Nicole."

Mills knew the story. It was legend. At first he thought it was all a big lie. Now he knew it was all true. How a young Smoke Jensen tracked them down and killed them all. Castrated one of them and cauterized the terrible wound with a white hot running iron.

Frontier justice, Mills concluded, doesn't leave any room for gray areas. It's all black and white and very final.

"I found Sally about a year later," Smoke said. "We married and have been together and very happy since then. You married, Mills?"

The U.S. Marshal shook his head. "No. I haven't found

the right woman yet, I suppose." He smiled, rather sadly, Smoke thought. "But I'm still looking."

"I hope you find you a good woman, Mills. There's one out there. Just keep looking."

One of Mills' men, Winston, stuck his head in the office door. "About half a dozen men riding in, Mills. They look like thugs to me."

Smoke smiled. Probably half the men in the West looked like thugs. He put the little dog in its bed and walked to the window. Winston had been correct in his assessment of the riders.

Deke Carey and Dirty Jackson were among the six men. Smoke had seen pictures of Deke, and he'd had a run-in with Dirty some years back, when both had been much younger.

"You know them?" Mills asked.

"I know them."

Mills watched as Smoke slipped the leather thongs off the hammers of his .44s. "It's come to that?"

"It's come to that." Smoke stepped out on the boardwalk.

6

Dirty cut his eyes as the six outlaws rode slowly past the marshal's office. His smile was savage.

"We'll arrest them," Mills said.

"On what charge? There aren't any warrants on them that I'm aware of."

"Then we have no right to interfere with their freedom of travel."

Smoke chuckled at that. "Deke there, he's a back shooter, a thief, and a child molester. Dirty has done it all: cold-blooded murder, rape, robbery, torture, kidnapping. I told him years ago that if I ever laid eyes on him again, I'd kill him. And that is exactly what I intend to do."

"But you said there are no warrants on them!"

"None in Colorado. But I've been holding one just for him for years."

"Where is it?"

Smoke patted the butt of a .44. "Right here in Mr. Colt. Now, Mills, you and I have become friends over the past week or so. But this is personal between Dirty and me. He killed a little girl in Nevada some years back. He bragged about doing it and then left town just ahead of the posse. He's fixing to come to trial over that killing. Right shortly."

"But . . ."

"Mills, lead, follow, or get the hell out of my way."

Smoke stepped off the boardwalk just as the outlaws were entering the saloon. Seconds later the saloon emptied of locals.

Smoke pushed open the batwings and stepped inside, Mills right behind him. Smoke heard Dirty asking for a room for the night.

"Not in this town, Dirty," Smoke called out. "The only room you're going to get is a pine box. And if there isn't enough coins in your pocket to buy a box, we'll roll you up in your blankets and plant you that way."

Mills gasped at the sheer audacity of Smoke.

Dirty turned and faced Jensen. The man was big and dirty and mean-looking. He wore one gun tied down and had another six-shooter shoved behind his belt. "You got no call to talk to me like that, Jensen."

"You ever ridden back to Nevada to put flowers on the grave of that little girl you killed, Dirty?"

Dirty flushed under the beard and the dirt on his face. "I was drunk when that happened, Jensen. Man can't be held responsible for what he does when he's drunk."

"Yeah," Smoke said sourly. "The courts will probably hold that to be true one of these days. But 'one of these days' don't count right now."

Mills grunted softly.

"Give him a drink," Smoke told the barkeep. "On me. Enjoy it, Dirty. It's gonna be your last one."

Deke Carey moved away from the bar to get a better angle at Smoke.

"Stand still, Deke," Smoke told him. "You move again and I'll put lead in you."

Deke froze to the floor, both hands in plain sight. "You think you can take us all, Jensen?"

"Yes."

Mills had moved to one side, one thumb hooked over his belt buckle. Smoke had noticed several days before that the federal marshal carried a hideout gun shoved behind his belt, under his jacket.

"Who's your funny-lookin' friend, Jensen?" another of the six asked.

"I am United States Marshal Walsdorf," Mills informed him.

"Well, la-tee-da," a young punk with both guns tied down said with a simper. "A U-nited States Marshal. Heavens!" He put a hand to his forehead and leaned up against the bar. "I'm so fearful I think I might swoon."

Mills was across the room before the punk could stand up straight. Mills hit the smart-mouthed punk with a hard right fist that knocked him sprawling. He jerked him up, popped him again, and threw him across the room. The punk landed against the cold pot-bellied stove. The stove fell over, the stovepipe broke loose from the flue collar, and the two-bit young gunny was covered with soot.

"Show some respect for the badge, if not for me," Mills said.

"I don't like your damn attitude!" another gunny said. "I think I'll just take that badge and shove . . ."

The only thing that got shoved was Mills' fist, smack into the gunny's mouth. Mills hit him two more times, and the man slumped to the floor, bleeding from nose and mouth and momentarily out of it.

Mills swept back his coat, put his hand on the butt of his short-barreled Peacemaker .45 and thundered, "I will have law and order, gentlemen!"

"Halp!" the soot-covered punk yelled. "I cain't see nothin'. Halp!"

"Let's take 'em, Greeny!" Dirty said.

But Smoke was already moving. He reached Dirty before the man could drag iron and loosened some of Dirty's teeth with a short, hard right.

Greeny swung at Mills and almost fell down as Mills ducked the punch. Mills planted his lace-up boots and decked the outlaw.

Smoke jabbed a left fist into Deke's face three times, the jabs jarring the man's head back and bringing a bright smear of blood to his mouth. He followed the jabs with a right cross that knocked Deke to the floor.

"By the Lord!" Mills shouted. "This is exhilarating." He just got the words out of his mouth when the punk hit him on top of the head with the stovepipe and knocked him spinning across the room.

Smoke splintered a chair across the punk's teeth, the hardwood knocking the kid up against a wall.

The barkeep climbed up on the bar and jumped onto Deke's back just as the man was getting to his boots. Deke threw the smaller man off and came in swinging at Smoke.

Bad mistake on Deke's part.

Smoke hit him with a left-right combination that glazed the man's bloodshot eyes and backed him up against the bar. Smoke hit him twice in the stomach and that did it for Deke. He kissed the floor and began puking.

Dirty hit Smoke a sneak punch that jarred Smoke and knocked him around. Smoke recovered and the men stood toe to toe and slugged it out for a full minute.

Mills was smashing Greeny's face with short, hard, brutal blows that brought a spray of blood each time his big fists impacted with the outlaw's face.

The soot-covered kid climbed to his boots and decided to take on the barkeep.

Bad mistake on the kid's part.

The barkeep had retreated to the bar and pulled out a truncheon, which he promptly and with much enthusiasm laid on top of the punk's head. The punk's eyes crossed, he sighed once, and hit the floor, out cold.

Dirty backed up and with Smoke's hands still balled into fists, grinned at him and went for his gun.

Smoke kicked the man in the groin, and Dirty doubled over, coughing and gagging. Smoke stepped forward and kicked the murderer in the face with the toe of his boot. Dirty's teeth bounced around the floor. He screamed and rolled away, blood dripping from his ruined mouth.

Deke grabbed for his guns, and Smoke shot him twice in the belly, the second hole just an inch above the first. Deke tried to lift his pistol, and Smoke fired a third time, the slug hitting the man in the center of the forehead.

Dirty rolled to his boots and faced Smoke, a gun in each hand, his face a bloody mask of hate.

Smoke had pulled both .44s and started them thundering. He was cocking and firing so fast it seemed a never-ending deadly cadence of thunder. Puffs of dust rose from Dirty's jacket each time a .44 slug slammed into his body. Dirty clung to the edge of the bar, his guns fallen to the floor out of numbed fingers.

"Jesus!" the barkeep said. "What's the matter with him? Why don't he say something?"

"Because he's dead," Smoke said.

Dirty Jackson fell on his face.

Greeny was moaning and crawling around on the floor. The kid was beginning to show some signs of life. The other two had wisely decided to stay on the floor with their hands in plain sight.

"You others, get up!" Smoke told the two outlaws, wide-eyed and on the floor. "And haul the kid and that jerk over there to their boots."

Greeny and the punk were jerked up. "The punk goes to jail," Smoke said. "The others get chained to that tree by the side of the office."

"Hey, that ain't right!" Greeny said. "What happens if it rains?"

"We give you a bar of soap."

"Damn!" Albert said, looking at his boss. "How come we miss all the fun, Mills?"

Mills was dabbing horse liniment on yesterday's jaw bruise and ignored the question.

"You know, Smoke," Hugh said. "You really can't keep those men chained up to that tree."

"Why?" Smoke asked, scratching the little dog behind the ears.

"Because they're human beings and as such, have basic rights accorded them by the Constitution."

Mills smiled. He'd already gone over that with Smoke. He would have gotten better results by conversing with a mule.

"Greeny didn't think much of the rights of those people he killed up in Canada, Hugh. Lebert didn't give a damn for the rights of those women he kidnapped and raped. Augie didn't have anybody's rights in mind when he tortured a man to death." Smoke held up several wire replies. "It's all right there. Deputies will be coming for Lebert and Augie. Royal Canadian Mounted Police will be here for Greeny. And I'm going to hang the punk back yonder in the cell."

"I ain't done nothin'!" the kid squalled. "You ain't gonna hang me!"

"Oh, yes, I am, kid. I say you were the one who killed that poor man back up the trail. I say you was the one who raped and killed those poor little girls. And that's what I got you charged with. You're gonna hang, punk."

Winston started to protest. Smoke held up his hand. The cell area was behind and to the right of the main office, and the kid could not see what was going on, only hear exactly how Smoke had planned it.

"Ever seen a hanging, kid?" Smoke called.

"No!"

"It's a sight to behold, boy. Sometimes the neck don't break, and the victim just dangles there while he chokes to death. Eyes bug out, tongue pooches out and turns black . . ."

"Shut up, damn you!"

". . . Fellow just twists there in the breeze. Sometimes it takes five minutes for him to die . . ."

"Damn you, shut up!" the kid screamed.

"Awful ugly sight to see. Plumb disgusting. And smelly, too. Victim usually loses all control of himself . . ."

The kid rattled the barred door. "Let me out of here!" he yelled.

". . . Terrible sight to see. Just awful. Sometimes they put a hood on the victim—I'll be sure and request one for you—and when they take that hood off—once the man's dead—his face is all swole up and black as a piece of coal."

"Jensen?" the kid called, in a voice choked with tears.

"What do you want, kid?"

"I'll make a deal with you."

Smoke winked at Mills and the others. "What kind of a deal, kid?"

"I know lots of things."

"What things?"

"We got to deal first."

"You don't have much of a position to deal from, boy. Your trial is coming up in a couple of days. The jury's already picked. And they're eager to convict. Folks around here haven't seen a good hanging in a year or more. Gonna be dinner on the grounds on the day you swing. Did you hear that hammering a while ago?"

"Yeah." The kid blew his nose on a dirty rag. "What was all that racket?"

"Fellows building a gallows, boy. That's where you're going to swing."

"I told you I'd deal!" His voice was very shaky.

"Start dealing, boy. You don't have long."

"Don't let Greeny and Lebert and Augie know nothin' about this, Marshal."

"You have my word on that."

"I'm ready when you are."

Smoke looked at Mills. "He's all yours, Mills. You wanted it legal, you got it legal." He smiled. "This time."

"Needless to say, we won't tell the kid that hammering and sawing was a man building a new outhouse."

"He might not see the humor in it."

"Get your pad and pen, Winston," Mills said. "Let's see what the kid has to say."

In exchange for escaping the hangman's noose and that short drop that culminated in an abrupt and fatal halt, the kid—his name was Walter Parsons—had quite a lot to say. He said he didn't know nothin' about Lee Slater and Luttie Charles bein' related, but they was close friends . . . or so Lee had said. But the gang was hidin' out on Seven Slash range. East of the ranch house and south of the Alamosa River. Wild country. They was plannin' to rob the miners and the stages carryin' gold and silver and Luttie was goin' to handle the gettin' rid of the boodle end of it.

How many in the gang?

The kid reckoned they was about fifty or sixty. He didn't rightly know since they wasn't camped all together. But it was a big gang.

How many people had the kid robbed and raped and murdered?

Bunches. Used to be fun, but now it was sort of borin'. All them people did was blubber and slobber and beg and cry and carry on somethin' awful. It was a relief just to shoot them in the head to shut them up.

"Disgusting!" Mills said, tossing the signed confession onto Smoke's desk. "I have never in my life heard of such depravity as that which came out of Parsons' mouth."

"You relaxing your stand on hanging now, Mills?" Smoke asked.

He received a dirty look, but Mills chose not to respond to the question.

"What are you doing to do with the kid?"

Mills shook his head. "I don't know. I can't allow the return of that vicious little thug back to a free society. That would be a grave injustice. The judge is going to have to decide that issue."

"He's never going to change."

"I know that," Mills said. "It's a dreadful time we live in, Smoke."

"It's going to get worse, Mills. Count on it. Now, then, what about Luttie?"

"We can't move against him on just the word of a common hoodlum. We've got to have some proof that he is, indeed, a part of this conspiracy. How about Greeny and Lebert and Augie? Have they agreed to talk?"

"You have to be kidding. Those are hardened criminals. They'll go to the grave with their mouths closed. They're not going to assist the hangman in their own executions."

"When will the deputies and the Royal Canadian Mounted Police come for them?"

"They said as soon as possible. Probably in a week or so."

"I've got to move the kid out of here and up to Sheriff Silva's jail. For safekeeping."

"All right. Why not do that now and as soon as the kid is gone, I'll pull those three scumbags in from the tree?"

"I would hate for a supervisor to ride by and see them chained out there," Winston said.

Smoke shook his head. "I'll be sure to take them some tea and cookies the first chance I get."

At Smoke's insistence Mills sent four of his men out early the next morning, taking the kid to the county seat and to a better and more secure jail. They would be gone at least three days and possibly four.

Smoke took down all the sawed-off double-barreled shotguns from the rack and passed them around. "Clean them up, boys, and load them up. Don't ever be too far away from one."

"Are you expecting trouble?" Mills asked. "From whom and why?"

"Yes, I'm expecting trouble. From whom? Either Lee Slater or his brother . . ."

"His assumed brother," Mills corrected. "Yes. I see. They could not want the three we have here talking and implicating either of them. Now I see why you insisted on sending more men than I thought necessary to the county seat with Parsons. I thank you for your insistence, Smoke. Parsons would be the more likely of the four to crack—as he did."

Smoke nodded his agreement as he loaded up the sawed-off with buckshot.

Winston hefted the shotgun shells in his hands. "These are heavy, too heavy for factory loads."

"I had the gunsmith across the street load them for me. They're filled with broken nails and ball-bearings and whatever else he had on hand." He looked first at Mills, then at Winston and Moss. "Any of you ever shot a man with a Greener?"

They shook their heads.

"Close in they'll cut a man in two. Makes a real mess.

Fastest man in the world won't buck the odds of a sawed-off pointed at his belly."

"You've shot men with these types of weapons?" Moss asked.

"I've shot men with muzzle-loaders, cap and ball, Sharps .52, Navy .36, and Colt and Remington and Starr .44s and .45s. I've shot them with a Remington .41 over and under. I've used knives, tomahawks and chopping axes more than a time or two. If somebody was trying to kill me or mine, I'd drop him with a hot horseshoe if that was all I could find at the moment. Gentlemen, I just have to ask a question. You all have sidestepped it before, but level with me this time. Why in the hell did your superiors send you men out here?"

Mills cleared his throat and looked uncomfortable, and both Winston and Moss blushed.

Smoke waited.

"Truth time," Winston muttered.

"Yes," Mills said. "Quite. Smoke, we are all new to the West, and to its customs. Tenderfeet, as I've read. We've worked the cities and smaller Eastern towns, but never west of the Mississippi. The United States Marshal's office is being up-graded in manpower, and, well, while we are not amateurs in this business, we, ah . . ."

Smoke held up a hand. "Let me finish it: you were sent out here to get bloodied?"

"That, ah, is a reasonably accurate assessment, yes."

"Well, you might get that chance sooner than you think. Here comes Luttie with his whole damn crew!"

7

"Maybe they're coming in to put flowers on Don's grave?" Winston said.

Smoke turned to look at him. The man had a twinkle in his eye. Mills and Moss were both smiling. The U.S. Marshals were new to the West, and perhaps had not yet been bloodied in killing combat, but they had plenty of sand and gravel in them, and a sense of humor.

"I'm sure," Smoke said, picking up the sawed-off shotgun. "Shall we step outside and greet the gentlemen?"

Luttie and Jake rode at the head of the column, and they both gave Smoke and the federal marshals curt nods, then turned toward the hitch rails at the saloon. They dismounted, looped the reins and walked into the barroom.

"I don't think they liked the sight of these shotguns," Winston said.

"I'm sure they didn't," Smoke said. He sat down on the bench in front of the office. Mills sat down beside him, Moss and Winston stood nearby.

"I wonder what they're up to," Moss said.

"A show of force?" Mills questioned. "If so, what is the purpose? We rode right up into their lair the other day. They must know that we're not going to be intimidated."

"I don't know whether any of them is that smart," Smoke replied. "If I had to take a guess, I'd guess that this move is a diversion of some sorts."

Mills was thoughtful for a moment. "Yes. I agree. Luttie and his Seven Slash bunch keep our attention here, while the Slater gang strikes somewhere in the county. But where?"

"Nowhere close, you can bet on that. Around Silver Mountain, maybe." He shook his head. "And it could be that Slater's gang is going to hit the marshals escorting the kid . . . maybe to shut the kid's mouth. Or they're coming in here to try to break their friends out of jail."

"If that bunch hits my men in force, my people won't have a chance," Mills said softly.

"I just hope I've impressed upon your people to shoot first and ask questions later," Smoke said.

"You know they won't do that."

"Then if Slater and his bunch hits them, they're at best wounded and at worst dead meat, Mills. I tried to impress upon you all that this is the West. I don't seem to be a very good teacher."

He stood up and stepped off the boardwalk. Mills' voice stopped him. "Where are you going?"

"It's a warm day. A mug of cool beer would taste good right about now."

"Step right into the lion's den, huh?"

"Might as well. We did pretty well in there the last time, didn't we?"

Mills smiled. "I should be ashamed of myself for saying this, but we damn sure did!"

"We miss all the fun," Winston said glumly.

"Don't count on that continuing," Smoke told him, as they stepped up to the batwings of the saloon. "Once inside,

Mills and I will stay together. Moss, take the right end of the bar. Winston, you take the left. Don't turn your back completely on these ol' boys. We'll see how smart Luttie is. If he tries to brace us, we'll put what's left of the bunch in jail and keep them there."

"What will we do with the rest of them?" Moss asked innocently.

Smoke looked at him. "Somebody will bury them."

He pushed open the doors and stepped inside, walking to the bar, the others right behind him.

Luttie and his crew had spread out all over the table area of the saloon, and that told Smoke a lot. None of it good.

"Setup," Mills mumbled.

"Yeah." Smoke returned the whisper. "Glad you picked up on it."

"What are you two lovebirds a-whisperin' about?" a Seven Slash hand yelled.

"You reckon they're sweet on each other, Paul?" another said with a laugh.

"That'd be a sight to see, wouldn't it—them a-smoochin'."

"Maybe we ought to see if they'd give us an advance showin'?"

"Now, that there's a right good idea," another said.

"Now, boys," Luttie said, a strange smile on his lips. "You know I can't allow nothin' like that to take place. Them fellows is lawmen. They's to be respected. Besides, that's the famous Smoke Jensen yonder. He's supposed to be the fastest gun in all the West. You boys wouldn't want to brace the likes of him, now, would you?"

His crew—and the table area filled with them—all burst out laughing.

"I won't have no more of this, now, boys," Luttie said. "Although I'm not too sure about me givin' you orders when you're on your own time. Might be some law agin that. What do you say about it, Mr. Fancy-Pants U.S. Marshal?"

"I would say that you don't have any authority to give orders when your hirelings are off the job," he said stiffly.

"Hireling?" a cowboy said. "Ain't it a fancy title, though?"

"Not really," Mills told him, a tight smile on his lips. "It means anyone who will follow another's orders for money—such as a thug or a mercenary."

Smoke was half turned, his left side facing the crowded table area. "When he gets up, Mills," he whispered, his lips just barely moving, "kill him."

Mills shook his head minutely. "I can't do that, Smoke."

The cowboy pushed back his chair. "Are you callin' me a thug, Whistle-Britches?"

"Get ready," Smoke whispered. "Cock that Greener, Mills."

"Actually, no." Mills raised his voice. "I was merely explaining to you the dictionary definition of a hireling. If you take exception to my remark, then you must have a low opinion of yourself."

"Huh?" the cowboy said.

"Charlie," another hand said. "I think he done insulted you. But I ain't real sure."

Luttie and Jake were staying out of it. Luttie had voiced his objections about his hands' needling any further, so in a court of law, he would be clear of any wrongdoing. But courts of law didn't impress Smoke Jensen. Six-gun action was much more to his liking.

"That remark of mine would only be taken as a blot on one's escutcheon if the party to whom it was directed was in actuality, a thug or mercenary." Mills further confused the cowboy and most of his buddies, including his boss and the foreman.

"What'd he say?" Jake whispered to Luttie.

"Hell, don't ask me. Sounded dirty."

"Gawddam, boy!" another Seven Slash hand said. "Cain't you talk English?"

"I was," Mills responded.

"A blot on one's escutcheon comes from medieval times," a man said from a corner table. Smoke cut his eyes. The man wore a dark suit with a white shirt and string tie. Smoke had seen him get off the stage earlier. "An escutcheon is a shield, upon which a coat of arms was painted. In other words, it means a stain on one's honor."

"Who the hell are you?" Charlie demanded.

"No one who would associate with the likes of you," the stranger said.

"Damn, Charlie," a hand said. "I think the stranger done insulted you, too."

"Now, look here," Charlie said. "I'm gettin' tarred of being in-sulted."

"You could always leave." Smoke offered him an option.

"And you could always shut your trap," Charlie told him.

"I'm right here, Charlie," Smoke told him. "Any time you think you have the *cojones* to brace me without all your buddies to back you up."

Nice way of making him stand alone whether he fishes or cuts bait, Moss thought. *I'll keep that in mind.*

The cowboy looked hard at Smoke and then sat down without another word.

"You just saved your own life, cowboy," the stranger said, rifling a deck of cards.

Charlie mumbled something and concentrated on his beer.

It isn't going to work, Luttie thought, staring at Smoke. The man is just too damn sure of himself and has the reputation to back it up. He's . . . Luttie couldn't think of the word, right off.

"Intimidating" was what he was searching for.

And who in the devil was that stranger sitting over there? He didn't think Jensen knew who he was either.

Smoke could sense the steam going out of the hardcases seated around the saloon. Four double-barreled Greeners at this distance would take out about half the crowd, inflicting horrible wounds on those they didn't kill outright. He'd seen men soak up five .44-caliber slugs and still stay on their boots and keep on coming. He had never seen anybody take a close up shotgun blast and keep going.

Smoke watched as Luttie and Jake exchanged glances. Both men knew that whatever momentum they might have had was gone.

"Drink your drinks, play cards, do some tobacco buying or whatever," Smoke told them. "First one of you that makes trouble, I either put in jail or kill. Let's go, boys."

Before he could leave the bar, a young man jumped to his boots. "They call me Sandy!" he yelled. "And I say without that shotgun, you ain't nothin', Jensen."

"Don't be a fool, lad," the stranger said. "You don't have a prayer. Sit down and shut up and live."

"You don't show me nothin' either, mister!" Sandy said.

"Don't crowd me, lad," the stranger said. "I came into town to do some gambling and some relaxing on my way to California. I have no quarrel with you. So don't crowd me."

"Stand up, you funny-talkin' dude!" Sandy yelled.

Smoke placed the man then. The accent had been worrying him. Earl Sutcliffe. And the Earl was not a first name. He really was an earl over in England. At least he had been until he killed a man after a game of chance (the man had been cheating); the man had been a duke, which was higher than an earl, and a man of considerable power. A murder warrant had been issued for Sutcliffe, and he had fled to America. Here he had made a name for himself as a very good and very honest gambler . . . and one hell of a gunfighter.

"That's Earl Sutcliffe, Sandy," Smoke said. "Sit down and finish your beer, and there'll be no hard feelings."

Earl Sutcliffe! Luttie thought. Now what in the hell was he doing in this jerkwater town?

"Stand up, Sutcliffe!" Sandy yelled the words that would start his dying on this day.

"Here now!" Mills said. "You men stop this immediately."

"Shut up," Smoke told him. "This is none of your affair."

Mills gave him a dirty look. But he closed his mouth.

"I said stand up!" Sandy yelled.

Earl put down the deck of cards and pushed back from the table. He slowly stood up, brushing back his coat on the right side.

"Primitive rites of manhood," Mills said in a whisper.

"Young man," Earl said. "I do not wish to kill you."

"You kill me?" Sandy snorted the words. "Dude, you the one that's gonna die."

"I don't think so. But I suppose stranger things have happened." Without taking his eyes off of Sandy, Earl spoke to Luttie. "You are his employer. You could order him to stop this madness."

"Sorry, Earl. The kid's on his own time today. What's the matter, you afraid of him?"

Earl smiled. "One more time, lad: give this up."

Sandy smiled, sure of himself, his youthfulness overriding caution. The young think of death only as something that happens to someone else, never themselves. "Any time you're ready," he told the Englishman.

Sutcliffe shot him. The draw was as fast as a striking rattler. The kid never had a chance to clear leather. The slug took him high in the chest, driving through a lung and slamming him back, sitting him back down in the chair he should have stayed in . . . with his mouth closed.

He opened his mouth and blood stained his lips as he struggled to speak. "You! . . ." he managed to gasp.

"Sorry, lad," Earl said, holstering his six-gun. "I tried to tell you."

"Tell me! . . ." Sandy said.

"It's too late now." Earl's words were softly offered.

"I'm cold," Sandy said.

Mills shook his head as he watched the young man hover

between life and death, with death racing to embrace him, rudely shoving life aside.

Luttie's hands sat silent, occasionally letting their eyes shift to the muzzles of those deadly sawed-off shotguns, all four of them pointed in their direction. To a man they wanted blood-revenge, but to a man they all knew that this was not the time or the place.

"I'll be damned!" Sandy suddenly blurted. "Would you just look at that!"

"What are you seein'?" Charlie asked him, his words just above a whisper.

"You hear that?" the kid said, as blood dripped from his mouth onto his shirt front.

"What are you hearin'?" Charlie asked him.

Sandy's head lolled to one side, and he closed his eyes.

"Nothing now," Mills said. "He just died."

The Seven Slash men rode out shortly after Sandy died. They took the body with them, to be buried on Seven Slash range.

"They'll be back," Smoke said. "Tomorrow, next week, next month. But they'll be back. And when they come back, they'll do their damnest to tear this town apart."

"I concur," Mills said.

"That was pushed on me," Earl said. He had sat back down and was shuffling a deck of cards. "I really did not want to kill the lad."

"I know it," Smoke told him. "I've had a hundred pushed on me."

"What's going on in this town?" the Englishman asked. "I stopped here because it seemed so peaceful."

Smoke had the barkeep draw him a mug of beer and carried it over to Earl's table, pulling out a chair and sitting down. "How'd you like to be a deputy sheriff of this county?"

Earl looked startled. "I beg your pardon?"

Smoke smiled and Mills laughed out loud.

"If you've got some time to spare, I'm authorized to pay you fifty dollars a month as a deputy."

"Fifty dollars a month?" Earl said, a smile not only on his lips but also reaching his eyes. "My, how could I possibly refuse such a generous offer?"

"There is a bedroom in the back of the jail," Smoke said. "And you can take your meals over at Bonnie's Cafe. Providing the cook isn't drunk."

"Oh, I say, now. And bed and board is included too. I suppose I could spare a couple of weeks to lend a hand in the keeping of law and order."

"We'll be facing anywhere from fifty to seventy-five hardcases, Earl," Smoke felt obliged to tell the man. "Maybe more than that."

Earl arched one eyebrow. "This sounds intriguing. You have certainly piqued my curiosity, Mr. Jensen."

"Smoke."

"Very well . . . Smoke it is. Let's take a stroll over to the livery and choose a mount for me. I'm very picky when it comes to horseflesh."

"Then you'll take the job?"

"But of course!"

Mills shook his head. He wondered how many warrants were out on Earl Sutcliffe. This was certainly an odd way to maintain law and order. Quite novel. He would have to do a paper on this and perhaps submit it to a New York newspaper for publication. The West certainly was a strange place, he concluded. He'd never seen any place quite like it.

The bartender was throwing sawdust on the pool of blood on the floor by the chair where Sandy had died as the men walked out the batwings.

8

Earl Sutcliffe looked at the star pinned to his shirt and chuckled.

"You find something amusing about being on the side of law and order?" Mills asked.

"Oh, I've always been on the side of law and order," the Englishman replied. "Providing it is good, fair, and just law and order."

"And in England? . . ." Mills left that open.

"In my case justice did not prevail."

"What can I say? It happens here, too."

Earl patted the butt of his six-gun. "It will never again happen to me."

"That isn't justice."

Earl smiled. "Oh, that depends entirely upon who is giving and who is receiving, doesn't it?"

"How did? . . . I mean . . ." Mills didn't know exactly how to phrase the question.

"How did an English nobleman become a gunfighter of

dubious reputation in the wild American West?" Earl smiled at the U.S. Marshal.

"Thank you, yes."

"I have always been good with cards, and lucky. I soon realized that if I was going to earn my living as a gambler I had better learn to be more than proficient with a firearm. There are people who, when someone is winning, will always cry cheat."

"And you don't cheat?"

"No. That is not to say I don't know how, because I certainly do. But I don't have to cheat to win. And I don't win all the time. Just enough of the time so I earn a nice income."

"And this?" Mills waved his hand at the town.

"Why am I doing it? Why don't we just say that there is as much Robin Hood in me as there is in Smoke Jensen? Neither one of us particularly cares for the rich who use their power to remain above the law."

"I can understand your feelings on the subject. But I'm not aware of any rich person who ever wronged Smoke. Besides, Smoke is a wealthy man in his own right."

Earl laughed. "Oh, so am I, Mr. Walsdorf. My home in England has forty-five rooms. My inheritance was enormous. But what does that have to do with justice?"

Mills walked away, muttering to himself.

Smoke had been listening from a doorway and stepped out to stand by the Englishman. "He's a good man, Earl. And damn tough, too. He's just hooked on Eastern law enforcement. Or, most probably, what Eastern lawyers are teaching."

"And it's spreading, Smoke. It'll be another ten years or so before it really makes an impact out here. But it's coming."

Smoke grimaced. "First time a man gives me an order telling me I can't protect what is mine with a gun, he better get ready for a showdown."

"It's coming."

Smoke shook his head and changed the subject. "Mills is no spring chicken. He's been with the Marshal's Service since getting out of college. I can't understand why he hasn't had some of those ideas of his kicked out of his head."

"He's not been a field man for very long, I should imagine. And that is perhaps where the promotions are."

"You may be right. Well, let's get some supper and talk over some options."

"Why don't we just locate the outlaws and go in shooting?" Earl suggested.

Smoke chuckled. "A man after my own heart. I suggested that to Mills. He says that is not the proper way to go about bringing men to justice."

Earl gave Smoke a quick, bemused glance. "The man does have a lot to learn, doesn't he?"

Smoke nodded his head in agreement. "I just hope he stays alive long enough to learn it."

"I came as soon as I heard about this terrible act of violence against you, Sally," the man said.

"Thank you, Larry," Sally Jensen said. She was sitting in the parlor in a rocker, her arm in a sling.

The preacher's wife, Bountiful, was sitting in the next room, but well within earshot. It just wasn't proper for a woman, especially a married woman, to receive a man alone. Besides, Bountiful didn't trust this slick-haired New York City man, all duded up and smelling of bay rum and the like. He had something up his sleeve and she would bet on that.

Sally looked at Lawrence Tibbson and wondered what in the world he was doing out here in Colorado. She hadn't seen him in several years. And she'd been with her mother then, shopping in the city. She had allowed Larry to escort her to a few functions in college, very few, but he had never—

by any stretch of the imagination—been her beau. Although he would have liked to be.

"All your old college chums are very worried about you, Sally," Larry said.

"Worried about me?" Sally asked. "Why, for heaven's sake?"

"Well, my word, Sally! You've been shot! Living out here in this wild, lawless, godforsaken place. And . . ." He shook his head.

"And what, Larry?"

He pursed his lips and shook his head. "Nothing, Sally."

"Larry," she said coyly, and batted her eyes at him. That used to do it in college.

It did it this time, too. He sighed and said, "Sally, the word is that . . . well, how to say this?"

"Just come right out and say it, Larry. That's the way out here."

"The day of the Wild West is over, Sally. It's finished, or soon will be. Despite the play and all the articles and penny dreadfuls written about Smoke, the people back East are beginning to look upon him as a cold-blooded killer. And you are being dragged in the dirt as well."

It didn't come as any surprise to Sally. She'd already heard from some of her old college friends. There was a not-so-subtle movement on in some quarters back East to discredit Smoke, and mark him as a mad-dog killer without conscience. Some were even calling for a federal investigation of him, including sending some United States Marshals out West. She didn't know whether anything had come of that suggestion.

"Go on, Larry."

"I know your parents are abroad, and plan to stay for some time, but your brother Jordan is very upset about all this awful talk about you."

"Pure flapdoodle, Larry. That's all it is."

Bountiful listened for another five minutes, and then with a frown on her face she walked silently to the doorway and stepped outside. She waved at a hand coiling a rope by the corral.

"Yes, madam?" he said, after running over to the house.

"Ride!" she told him. "Get into town, find Monte, and find out where Smoke is. Get word to him." She told him what she had overheard.

The hand threw the rope down, his face tight with anger. "I'll go in there and stomp that varmint right now!"

"No!" Bountiful told him. "Finding Smoke is more important. He might be in danger of being taken back East to stand trial in some federal court. There are U.S. Marshals after him. They might already be with him, and he doesn't know they're to arrest him."

The hand nodded his head. "You watch that skunk in yonder, Miss Bountiful. He's just too slick for my likin'."

"I'll watch him for me and Sally. You ride."

"I'm gone!"

She stepped back into the house in time to hear Sally ask, "Larry, exactly why did you come all the way out here from the city?"

"Why . . . to take you back where you belong, Sally."

"I beg your pardon?" Sally's words were filled with astonishment.

"Sally, this is still a wild and savage land. You don't belong out here. There is no culture, nothing that even resembles refinement . . . the nicer things in life. I have come to ask you to leave this place and return to the city. Not necessarily to be with me, although that is my highest aspiration. Sally, I believe once there, out of this horrible place, you will see things in a much different light and . . ."

Sally held up a hand. "That's enough, Larry! Actually, that is far too much. If my husband were here, he'd throw you out of the house for saying such things." Actually, what Smoke would probably do is shoot you! But she kept that thought to herself. "Larry, you must be insane to suggest such things."

"I have only your best interests at heart, Sally."

"I appreciate that, Larry. Now listen to me. I am a married woman with children. I love my husband very much, and I am quite happy here on the Sugarloaf . . ."

"The what?"

"The Sugarloaf—that is the name of our ranch, Larry. And I intend to stay here until I die, and be buried here. Is that understood?"

"Sally, haven't you understood a word I've said? What are you going to do when your husband is sentenced to prison?"

"Prison? What are you talking about, Larry?"

"A federal judge is right now contemplating issuing federal warrants for Smoke's arrest. All the wild men of the West are dead or dying, Sally. Most of the famed gunfighters and outlaws have met their just due. Very learned men in the field of crime have met and concluded that violence begets violence and also that the poor criminal has been greatly misunderstood. They have urged President Arthur to abolish capital punishment and to set up programs to reeducate inmates and ban the carrying of guns nationwide . . ."

Sally started laughing. She laughed until tears momentarily blinded her. She wiped them away just about the time Bountiful stopped laughing in the next room.

"I fail to see anything amusing about this, Sally," Larry said stiffly.

"It's going to be far less amusing when somebody tells my husband he can't carry a gun, Larry. What nut came up with the idea that the poor criminal has been misunderstood?"

"I would hardly call Dr. Woodward a nut, Sally."

"Dr. Woodward?"

"Yes. He has just returned from Europe where he studied

with some of the greatest doctors in the world, whose specialties include the mind . . ."

"Psychiatrists."

"Why, yes, that's right. I . . "

"Get out of here, Larry. Leave. Now. Go on back to the city and don't come West again. This is no place for you. And don't ever again suggest I leave my husband. Now, go, Larry."

When Larry had driven off in his rented buggy, Bountiful came into the room. "You heard?" Sally asked.

"Yes. I sent a hand into town to tell Monte. He'll get word to Smoke. Do you suppose there is anything to what he said, Sally?"

"Yes. I'm afraid there is." She shook her head. "The poor misunderstood criminal. What is this world coming to?"

Earl Sutcliffe was doing his best not to yawn as Mills droned on. "And in conclusion," Mills said, "it is the belief of many knowledgeable people that the criminal should not be treated nearly so harshly as we have done in the past. The criminal is literally pushed into a life of crime due to peer pressure and his social and/or economic station in life."

"Incredible," Earl said.

"Yes, isn't it? You see, Dr. Woodward has found that in many cases, say, a boy from the wrong side of the tracks falls in love with the daughter of a rich man . . . of course the two worlds can never meet. That traumatizes the young man and leaves him feeling rejected and disillusioned and angry. If he then goes out and robs or kills, it isn't really his fault."

Earl sighed. "Mills, do you really believe that nonsense?"

"Nonsense, sir?"

"Yes. Nonsense. Because that is what it is. Most people who grow up in poverty don't turn into murderers. Most do their best to work their way out of a bad economic situation.

Your Dr. Woodward is simply trying to cover up for a group of very sorry, worthless, no-good people who want something for nothing and will go to any lengths to get it. And the only length they deserve is the number of feet in a hangman's rope. Good day, sir." He rose from the bench and walked into Smoke's office.

Smoke smiled at him. "Did Mills make a convert out of you, Earl?"

"Not hardly. The man is well educated but totally out of touch with reality." He looked up at the rumble of a stagecoach pulling into town.

Both men watched as Mills was handed a small packet of mail by the driver. The man sat down on the bench and read, occasionally looking across the street at Smoke's office, a startled expression on his face.

"It concerns one of us," Earl opined.

"Any warrants out on you?"

"None that I am aware of. You?"

"I don't think so. However, anything is possible. I've been hearing rumors that are coming from back East. Somebody back there doesn't like me very much."

"So it's true, then," Earl muttered.

"You've heard them?"

"Yes. I was in St. Louis just a few months ago. I spoke with a man from Chicago who asked if I knew you. I told him only by reputation. He had heard that some federal judge back East was pushing to have some warrants reissued on you. Something about a shooting that happened years ago. Over in Idaho."

"Damn!" Smoke swore. "That was back in '73. I wasn't much more than a kid when I helped destroy the town of Bury and killed Richards, Potter, and Stratton. They were the men who helped kill my brother and my father, and who hired the men who raped and killed my first wife and killed our baby son."

Earl grunted. "Then they certainly deserved killing. Tell me, those three you mentioned—did either of them have any relative or family friend in a position of power back East?"

"Not that I know of. But it could be. But there were no warrants issued from that shooting. I'm certain of that. And I know damn well I left those men dead."

"Well, somebody has an axe to grind with you. And from the look on Mills' face, he isn't too happy with the letters he just received. Want a wager as to the identity of the party mentioned in those missives?"

"No bet. But he's a pretty straightforward type of fellow. If they're about me, he'll tell me."

They watched as Mills showed the documents to Winston and Moss. The men read the letters and shook their heads. Mills folded the letters and tucked them in an inside pocket of his jacket. The three of them then walked across the street and entered the office.

Mills came right to the point. "Smoke, we need to talk."

"You look like you just swallowed a green persimmon, Mills. What's the matter?"

"It isn't good news, Smoke." He poured a cup of coffee and sat down. "A federal judge in Washington is just about to put his signature to warrants. They're murder warrants, Smoke. On you. Three of them."

"The names of the men I'm supposed to have killed?"

"Potter, Richards, and Stratton."

"I killed them, for a fact. Over in Idaho, years ago. But it was a stand-up and fair fight. Me against the three of them."

"Tell me about it, Smoke."

Smoke's mind went spinning back through the long years.

"All right, you bastards!" Smoke yelled to Richards, Potter, and Stratton. "Holster your guns and step out into the street, if you've got the nerve."

The sharp odor of sweat was all mingled with the smell of blood and gun smoke, filling the summer air as four men stepped out into the bloody, dusty street. All around the old town were the sprawled bodies of gun hands that had been on the payroll of the three men. They had taken on Smoke Jensen. They had died. Nineteen men had tried to kill Smoke in the ruin of an old ghost town out from Bury. Only three of them were still standing.

Richards, Potter, and Stratton stood at one end of the block. A tall bloody figure stood at the other. All their guns were in leather.

"You son of a bitch!" Stratton screamed, his voice as high-pitched as a hysterical woman's. "You've ruined it all!" He clawed at his .44.

Smoke drew and fired before Stratton could clear leather. The man fell back on his butt, a startled expression on his face. He closed his eyes and toppled over.

Potter grabbed for his gun. Smoke shot him twice in the chest and holstered his gun before the man had stopped twitching in the dust.

Richards had not moved. He stood with a faint smile on his lips, staring at Smoke.

"You ready to die, Richards?" Smoke called.

"As ready as any man ever is," Richards replied. There was no sign of fear in his voice. His hands were steady by the butts of his guns. "Your sister, Janey, gone?"

"Yep. She took your money and hauled her ashes out."

"Trash, that's what she is."

"You'll get no argument from me on that."

"It's been a long run, hasn't it, Jensen?"

"It's just about over."

"What happens to all our holdings around here?"

"I don't care what happens to the mines. The miners can have them. I'm giving all your stock to the decent, honest punchers and homesteaders."

A puzzled look spread over Richards' face. "I don't understand. You did . . . all this!" He waved a hand. "For nothing?"

Someone moaned, the sound painfully inching up the street.

"I did it for my pa, my brother, my wife, and my baby son."

"It won't bring them back."

"I know."

"Good God Almighty. I wish I had never heard the name Jensen."

"You won't ever hear it again, Richards. Not after this day."

Richards smiled and drew. He was snake-quick, but hurried his shot, the slug digging up dirt at Smoke's boots.

Smoke shot the man in the shoulder, spinning him around. Richards grabbed for his left-hand gun, and Smoke fired again, the slug taking the man in the chest. Richards cursed Smoke and tried to lift his Colt. He managed to cock it before Smoke's third shot took him in the belly and knocked him down to the dirt. He pulled the trigger, blowing dust into his face and eyes. He tried to crawl to his knees but succeeded only in rolling over onto his back, staring at the blue of the sky.

Smoke walked up to the man.

Richards opened his mouth to speak. He tasted blood on his tongue. The light began to fade around him. "You'll . . . you'll meet . . ."

Smoke never found out who he was supposed to meet. Richards' head lolled to one side, and he died.

Smoke holstered his guns and walked away.

"His brother," Mills said. "Has to be. The judge's name is Richards."

"Well, then, he's just as sorry as his damn brother was,"

Smoke said. "And I'll tell you this, Mills: no man will ever put handcuffs on me. No man."

"Smoke . . ."

"No man, Mills. That was a fair fight, and Judge Richards can go right straight to hell and take his warrants with him."

Mills wore a crestfallen expression. "What if I'm ordered to arrest you?"

"Tell them you can't find me. Ignore it. Quit your job. But don't try to put cuffs on me. The warrants are bogus, Mills. It's a made-up charge. There were dozens of people who witnessed that fight from the hillsides around the town. Don't force my hand, Mills. It's not worth your life, or any other lawman's life."

"You'd draw on me, Smoke?" the U.S. Marshal asked in a soft tone.

"If you forced me to do it. Lord knows I don't want to drag iron against you, or any lawman, for that matter. But I won't be arrested for something I didn't do."

"Smoke, the Marshal's Service knows you're here! If Judge Richards signs those warrants, I will have no choice but to place you under arrest."

"We all have choices, Mills. We all come to crossroads sometime in our lives. Many times the legal road is not the right road."

Mills looked at Earl Sutcliffe. "And you, sir?"

"I stand by Smoke. I've talked to too many people who were at that fight in the ghost town. It was exactly as Smoke called it. I can have a dozen of the West's most famed gunslicks in here in a week . . . all to stand by Smoke Jensen. If you want a bloodbath, just try to arrest Jensen."

Mills shook his head. "I don't know what to do," he admitted. He and his men left the office.

"Goddamn a bunch of political appointees," Earl swore, which was something he did rarely. "Your government is becoming like the one I left across the waters: out of control."

"Can you imagine what it will be like a hundred years from now?" Smoke asked, sitting down and picking up the little puppy from its bed by his desk.

Earl grimaced "That, my friend, is something that boggles the mind. But let's concentrate on the present. What are you going to do if the judge signs those warrants?"

"I damn sure won't be placed under arrest." Smoke took paper from his desk and dabbed pen into the ink well. "I'll write a friend of mine up in Denver. He's a federal judge. I'll ask him to look into the matter. I'll ask him to block those warrants until a complete investigation is done into the matter. I'll take the legal course until the road ends."

Earl did not have to ask what Smoke would do once, or if, that legal road came to a blockade. He knew only that if any man tried to arrest Smoke Jensen for something he was innocent of, the streets would run red with blood. And Earl Sutcliffe knew this, too: he would do the same thing.

There comes a time when legal proceedings come into direct conflict with a law-abiding person's basic human rights.

And this was damn sure one of those times.

Earl walked outside, leaving Smoke's pen-scratching behind him. He looked up and down the wide street of the tiny village. "Don't send good men in here to do a bad thing," he muttered. "Because if you do, you'll force another good man to turn bad. And I'll be standing by his side," he concluded.

9

The stagecoach ran and Smoke had mail. He tore open the letter and quickly scanned the contents. Sheriff Monte Carson of Big Rock wrote that he now had flyers from the United States government proclaiming Smoke Jensen to be an outlaw and a murderer. There was a ten-thousand-dollar price on his head. Events were moving very fast, and he advised Smoke to haul his ashes out of there until this matter could be resolved.

Smoke showed the letter to Earl.

"I'll go with you," the Englishman said.

Smoke nixed that. "I'd appreciate it if you'd stay on here as marshal and deputy sheriff. Mills is going to need help with the outlaws."

The man met his eyes. "The system is turning against you, yet you still have law and order in your heart. I don't know that I could feel so magnanimous toward such a system."

"Without some form of law, the country would revert to anarchy, Earl. I'll head for the high country and wait until things straighten out. I've got some good people working in my behalf."

"I'll go purchase a few things for you at the store and arrange for a packhorse. I'll have things ready to go in an hour. Did Mills receive any mail this run?"

Smoke smiled and handed Earl a letter from the U.S. Marshal's office in Washington, D.C. "I told the driver I'd see that Mills got this. Next time the stage runs, give this to him."

Earl chuckled. "I don't believe that delay will disappoint Mr. Walsdorf one bit."

Smoke grinned. "I may be on the run, but I'm going to see if I can't harass Luttie Charles and the Slater gang while I'm dodging the law."

"One-man wrecking crew?"

"I've done it before."

"You'll stay in this area?"

"Oh yes. I'll check back with you from time to time. If the town fills with U.S. Marshals, tie a piece of black cloth on the bridge railing north of town. I'll be warned then."

"Will do."

"Take care of my little dog for me, will you, Earl?"

"I certainly shall."

"I anticipated this, so I moved my gear out of the hotel yesterday and stowed it in the shed out back."

"I'll go get you provisioned."

Smoke sat down behind the desk and cleaned his .44s and his rifle. He filled a pouch full of shotgun shells and cleaned a Greener. He put on a fresh pot of coffee to boil and then went out back to the shed. There he checked on the bag of dynamite he'd bought along the trail coming here and carefully inspected his fuses and caps, then replaced them in a waterproof pouch and rewrapped the bag in canvas.

He checked his clothing in his saddlebags and found they had not been disturbed; the same with his bedroll and ground sheet. He went back into the office and picked up the little dog, petting it.

"You behave yourself now," he said softly. "Mind Earl. You hear?"

The little dog wriggled and squirmed and licked his hand, and Smoke smiled at its antics.

Earl opened the door. "You're all set," he said. "The food should last five or six days if you're careful. I put half a dozen boxes of .44s in the pack for you."

"I'll pull out now, then. Leave the back way. Take care of yourself, Earl."

The Englishman winked at him. "You take care of yourself, friend. I told the liveryman to get lost for a few minutes. You should have no trouble."

Smoke slipped out the back, picked up his gear from the shed, and made his way to the livery stable. Buck was about ready to kick in the walls of his stall. He was a horse that liked to ramble, and he'd been confined to a stall for just too damn long. He tried to step on Smoke's foot, and when that failed, tried to bite him.

"Settle down, damn it," Smoke told him, smoothing out the blanket and tossing the saddle on him, cinching it down. For once, Buck didn't try to puff up on him. Smoke stowed his gear on the packhorse, one of the strongest and best-looking pack animals he'd ever seen, and led both horses out the back. He swung into the saddle and looked back at the town.

"You better hunt you a hole, Judge Richards," he said softly. " 'Cause when this is over, I'm coming after you and I'm going to stomp your guts into a greasy puddle. And that's a promise, you damn shyster."

He touched his spurs to Buck's sides, and they moved out, heading into the wild country of southern Colorado.

Smoke made his first night's camp just off the Continental Divide Trail. As was his custom, he cooked his supper over a hat-sized fire, then erased all signs of it and moved several miles before bedding down for the night. It was a cold camp, but a safe one.

Up before dawn, he walked the area several times, stopping often to listen. The horses were relaxed, and Buck was better than a watchdog. Satisfied that he was alone, Smoke built a small fire against a rock wall and cooked his breakfast of bacon and potatoes and boiled his coffee.

After eating, he washed his dishes, packed them, and sat back down for a cigarette and some ruminating.

First of all, he wanted to find the Slater gang and start his little war with them. He could not get the picture of that man and woman and the girls he'd found along the trail out of his mind. Men who would do something like that were not to be considered human beings, and it would be very unfair to call them animals. Animals didn't do things like that. Animals killed for a reason, not for sport and fun. He had promised the dying woman that her grief and pain would be avenged. And Smoke always kept his promises.

He picketed the pack animal in the deep woods, near plenty of water and graze, and saddled Buck. "You ready to go headhunting, boy?"

Buck swung his big head and looked at Smoke through mean eyes. Buck was anything but a gentle animal. Smoke could handle him, and the horse had never harmed a child. But with adults whom he disliked, and that was most of them, the animal could be vicious.

"I thought so," Smoke said, and swung into the saddle.

He climbed higher, staying in the thickest timber and brush he could find and letting Buck pick his way. Coming to a halt on a ridge that offered a spectacular view for miles around in all directions, Smoke dismounted and took field glasses from his saddlebags and began carefully scanning the area.

His sweep of the area paid off after only a few minutes.

He knew where the mining camps were, and where the few homesteaders lived—this was not a country for much farming other than small gardens—and discounted them. With a smile on his lips, he put his binoculars back into the saddlebags and mounted up.

He figured it was time to be sociable and do some calling on folks.

Two hours later, he picketed Buck and hung his spurs on the saddle horn. Taking his rifle, he began making his way through the timber, carefully and silently working his way closer to what he figured was an outlaw camp. He bellied down in thick underbrush when he got within earshot of the mangy-looking bunch of hardcases.

"I'm a-gittin' tarred of this sittin' around doin' nothin'," a big, ugly-looking man said. "I say we go find us some homesteaders with kids and have our way with the girls."

"Nice young tender girlies," another man said with a nasty grin. "I like to hear 'em squall." He pulled at his crotch. "I like to whup up on 'em, too. I like it when they fight."

"Maybe we could find us a man to use as target practice," another mused aloud. "Kill 'im slow. That's good fun."

"Slater says we got to wait," yet another outlaw said. "They gonna be shippin' out gold and silver in a few days, and we wait until then."

"Let's hit the town," a man suggested, leaning over and pouring a tin cup full of coffee from a big pot. "We're runnin' out of grub and besides, they's wimmin in that little town. I seen me a big fat one. I like fat wimmin. More to whup up on when they's fat."

Smoke shot him in the belly.

The gut-shot outlaw screamed and threw the coffeepot, the contents splashing into another man's face. The scalded punk howled in pain and rolled on the ground, both hands covering his burned face.

The gunny who liked to rape little girls jumped to his

boots, his hands filled with six-shooters. He looked wildly around him. Smoke took careful aim and shot a knee out from under the man, the .44 slug breaking the knee.

The man folded up and lay screaming on the ground, his broken knee bent awkwardly. He would be out of action for a long time.

Smoke lined up a punk who'd grabbed up a rifle and put a round in the center of his chest. The man dropped like a rag doll and did not move. He had fallen into the campfire, and his clothing ignited in seconds. The stench of burning flesh began to foul the morning coolness.

Smoke shifted positions as the outlaws fell into cover and began slinging lead in his direction. He rolled for several yards and then belly-crawled a dozen more yards, coming up behind a huge old fallen log.

"Somebody pull Daily outta that far!" a man yelled. "He's a stinkin' up ever'thang."

"You pull him out," another suggested.

"You go to hell!" the first man told him. "I ramrod this outfit, and you do what I tell you to do."

The second man told the ramrodder where he could ram his orders. Bluntly.

Smoke waited, his Winchester .44 ready. He caught a glimpse of a checkered shirt and lined it up. It was a man's arm. Smoke waited, let out some breath, took up the slack on the trigger and let the rifle fire. The man screamed and rolled on the ground, the bullet-shattered arm hanging painfully and uselessly. The .44 slug had hit the man's elbow. Another out of action.

A smile of grim satisfaction on his lips, Smoke began working his way back, not wanting to risk any further shots. If he waited much longer, the hunter would soon become the hunted.

Back with Buck, he stepped into the saddle and took off in search of a hole.

* * *

"Damn it, Earl!" Mills hollered, waving the letter. "This is tampering with the mail. That's against the law."

"I didn't tamper with anything," the Englishman said. "The driver handed Smoke the mail, and Smoke told me to give this to you. I gave it to you."

"You assisted him in getting away!"

"As far as I knew, he was a free man. He could leave anytime he chose." He shrugged. "He chose to leave."

Mills stomped out of the office. The men who had escorted the prisoner up to the county seat had returned. Mills started hollering for them to saddle up, they had to find and arrest Smoke Jensen.

The marshals all looked at one another. Going after outlaws was one thing. Tangling with Smoke Jensen was quite another matter.

A trio of deputy sheriffs, come to fetch one of the prisoners in jail, exchanged glances. One asked, "You boys are gonna go do what?"

"We're going to arrest Smoke Jensen," Albert said glumly.

"What the devil for?" a deputy asked.

"Federal warrants," Mills told him, walking up to the group standing on the boardwalk in front of the saloon. "The prisoners can remain in jail. By the powers vested in me by the United States government, I am hereby deputizing you men as deputy U.S. Marshals. You will accompany us in the pursuit and arrest of Smoke Jensen."

"You can go right straight to hell, too," a deputy told him. "I ain't got nothing against Smoke Jensen."

"Me, neither," another said.

The third deputy turned and started toward the alley.

"Where are you going?" Mills demanded.

"To the outhouse," the man called over his shoulder. "And as full of it as you are, you best do the same."

"You men do not seem to understand the gravity of this situation!"

"I understand this," a deputy told him. "You go after Smoke Jensen, you're gonna come back —if you come back at all— across your saddle."

"Yeah," the second deputy said. "If I was you, I'd sit on that warrant for a time. Smoke is a respected rancher of some wealth. I'll wager that warrant ain't worth the paper it's written on. Besides, do you know what you'd get if you crossed a grizzly bear and a puma and a rattlesnake and a timber wolf and some monster outta Hell?"

"I have not the vaguest idea."

"You'd get Smoke Jensen. You best leave him alone. That ol' boy was born with the bark on and was raised up by mountain men and Injuns. They's tribes all over the West sing songs about how feeroocious Jensen is. 'Sides, you ever heard of gunslingers name of Charlie Starr, Monte Carson, Louis Longmont, Johnny North, Cotton Pickens, and the like?"

"Of course I've heard of them! What's that got to do with anything?"

"Man, how'd you like to see them ol' boys and thirty more just as randy come a-foggin' in here, reins in their teeth and hands full of Colts, all of 'em mad at you?"

"That . . . would not be a pleasant sight," Mills admitted.

"Pleasant sight! You couldn't see nothin' like it this side of Hell! Now you just pull in your horns and give that warrant time to rest, Mr. U.S. Marshal. Things will work out. You keep your nose out of Smoke Jensen's business. That way, you'll stay alive."

"I have a job to do, sir!"

"So do we," the deputy said. "But sometimes you got to let common sense take over. Smoke's killed a lot of sorry ol' boys in his time, but he ain't no back-shootin' murderer. All them he put in the ground was either stand-up fair fights—

and usually he's facin' two or three at a time—or punks that was after him and he waylaid 'em to shorten the odds. You think about that warrant, mister. You think a long time about it. The longer you think, the longer you got to live."

The deputies collected their prisoner and pulled out that afternoon. The RCMP were due in town within the next several days. Mills looked at Earl, who was looking at him.

"You'll stay to sign the papers and give the prisoner to the Canadians?"

"Uh-huh. Where are you going?"

"I have a man to arrest."

"You best use pen and paper in the office, then," Earl said solemnly.

"To do what, sir?" Mills asked.

"To leave me the name of your next of kin."

Foolishly, the outlaws in the camp Smoke attacked came after him. He led them on a goose hunt in the mountains and then tired of the game. He dismounted and took his rifle from the boot, then selected a position on a ridge where he could effectively cover his back trail.

The gang came in a rush, whipping their lathered and tired horses. Smoke emptied two saddles, and the others retreated down the slope, for the moment out of range. Smoke nibbled on a cold biscuit, took a sip of water, and waited. The old mountain man Preacher had taught him many things as a boy, one of which was patience.

After several moments, a man shouted out, "Who you be up yonder?"

"An avenging angel!" Smoke returned the shout, then shifted positions.

He could not hear the reply, if any, but he was certain the mutterings among the scum were highly profane.

"What's your beef with us?" someone finally shouted.

Smoke shifted his eyes, sensing that conversation on the part of the outlaws would be nothing more than a cover for someone trying to slip around and flank him.

But he had not chosen his position without an eye for detail. To his left lay a sheer rock face. To his right, a clear field of fire, virtually without cover for anyone except a very skilled Indian warrior. The outlaws would have to come at him from the front.

"You deef up there?"

Smoke offered no reply. A few shots were fired at him, but they fell far short of his position. It was an impasse, but one that Smoke knew he would win simply because he had more patience than the outlaws. The men he had shot lay sprawled on the trail. One he had shot dead, the other had died only moments before, gut-shot and dying hard, calling out for God to help him. The same God the girls he had helped rape and torture had called out to, no doubt.

Smoke watched as the men broke cover and ran for their horses. He waited and watched as they rode back down the trail. Smoke slipped back to Buck, booted his rifle, and took off. He would hit another outlaw camp that evening. He liked the night. He was very good in the night. The Orientals had a word for it that Smoke had read in a book Sally had bought for him. Ninja.

He liked that.

"That dude is still at the hotel, ma'am," a hand reported to Sally. "He's gonna get his ashes hauled if he don't stop with the bad mouth against Smoke."

"He'd just sue you," Sally told him.

"One of them," the hand said disgustedly.

"I'm afraid so. What's he saying about my husband?"

"That Smoke has turned cold-blooded killer. That he enjoys killin'. That he's crazy. Monte is gonna have to put him in jail for his own protection if this keeps up."

Sally nodded her head. "I wired friends back East to check into whether there is any connection between Judge Richards and Larry. They could find none—at least on the surface. I don't believe there is any connection. Larry is just meddling, hoping to discredit Smoke in my eyes."

"You want me to conk him on the head and toss him in an eastbound freight wagon, ma'am?"

Sally laughed. "No, Jim. But I'm not going to ask anyone to protect him either. Larry is, I'm afraid, going to learn a hard lesson about the West and its people."

"He's liable to end up in a pine box, ma'am."

"Yes," she agreed. "There is always that possibility. But he's a man grown, and has to take responsibility for his words and deeds. I warned him of the consequences if he persisted in spreading vile gossip about my husband. We'll just let the chips fall, Jim."

"It won't be long, ma'am. Somebody's gonna tell that greenhorn lawyer to check, bet or fold pretty darn quick." He put his hat back on his head. "And, ma'am . . . it's likely to be me that does it."

Sally watched the hand walk back to the bunkhouse. She knew that the West was, in many respects, a very tolerant place. A person's past was their business. A handshake was a deal sealed. A person gave their word, it was binding. And if you bad-mouthed somebody, you had damn well better be prepared to back it up with guns or fists. It was the code, and the code was unwritten law in the West.

"Larry," she muttered, "you're heading for a stomping if you don't close that mouth."

10

"That's it, mister!" a cowboy said to Larry. "I've had it with your flappin' mouth. Now shut the damn thing and shut it now!"

Larry turned in his chair and stared at the man. The others in the cafe fell silent. For days the citizens in and around Big Rock had put up with the Easterner's bad-mouthing of Smoke Jensen. Most of them felt it was just the man's ignorance and let it slide. But it was getting wearing . . . very wearing. The cowboy from Johnny North's ranch was one of those Smoke had befriended, and he had had quite enough of Larry's mouth.

"I beg your pardon, sir?" Larry questioned, removing his napkin from his shirtfront and laying it on the table.

"I said for you to close that flappin' trap of yours," the cowboy said. "Smoke ain't here to defend himself agin your lyin' mouth. And I for one have had enough of it." He pushed back his chair and stood up, walking to Larry's table.

"Sir," Larry said, "I have a right to an opinion. That is a basic right. One only has to look at Jensen's record of brutality and callousness to see that the man has no regard for law and order and the rights of others. I . . ."

The cowboy slapped him out of the chair. Larry's butt bounced on the floor. He stared up at the man, his mouth bloody from the callused hand of the cowboy. His eyes were wide from shock.

Larry looked over at the sheriff. Monte Carson was recovering from his wounds, his left arm still in a sling where the .45 slug had busted his forearm. He stared at Larry with decidedly unfriendly eyes.

"Do something!" Larry hollered.

"What do you want me to do?" Monte questioned.

"This brute assaulted me!" Larry yelled, crawling to his knees and grabbing the back of a chair for support. "I want him placed under arrest."

"You're under arrest, Clint," Monte said, sugaring his coffee.

"The fine for disturbing the peace is two dollars," Judge Proctor said, carefully cutting the slice of beef on his lunch plate.

Twenty silver dollars hit the floor from the pockets of patrons seated around the cafe.

Willow Brook, wife of the town's only lawyer, Hunt, counted the money on the floor. "I think that means you can break the law a few more times, Clint," she said.

"What?" Larry screamed. "What kind of justice is this?"

"Western kind," Clint said, and jerked the man up by his shirt.

"Unhand me, you heathen!" Larry yelled.

Clint did just that. He tossed Larry out the front door, and the man landed in a horse trough.

"And don't come back in here!" the cafe owner yelled, once Larry had bubbled to the surface. "You are now officially barred from dinin' in my establishment."

"The cuisine was terrible anyway!" Larry yelled.

"I ain't never served nothin' like that in my life!" the cook screamed from the back.

"Ignorant oaf!" Larry said, stepping out of the horse trough with as much dignity as he could muster under the circumstances. "I'm going to sue everybody in that establishment!" He pointed at the cafe.

Monte walked to the door. "Get off the street, or I'll put you in jail for attempting to incite a riot," he told Larry.

"You'll put me in jail!" Larry shouted. He shook his finger at the sheriff. "You've not heard the last of this, sir," he warned. "I am an attorney of some reputation. I can assure you all that the consequences will be dire. I . . ."

"You got nine more chances, Clint," Monte said.

The cowboy stepped out onto the shaded boardwalk, and Larry took off running toward the Majestic Hotel. His shoes squished with every step. His ears were flame-red from the laughter he was leaving behind him.

Mills Walsdorf led his men some twelve miles out of town and halted the parade.

"What's up, Mills?" Moss asked.

"We make camp here."

"Lot of daylight left." Winston pointed out the obvious.

"We have to make plans," Mills told them, swinging down from the saddle. "And that might take several days. Perhaps even a week or more. We can't just go riding willy-nilly after Smoke Jensen."

The U.S. Marshals looked at each other and smiled. Harold said, "I wondered why you bought so many provisions."

"We must always be prepared. We're on our own now, men. No one back in town knows where we are. I told Earl we were heading east."

"But we rode north!" Sharp said.

"Precisely."

"I'll gather some firewood," Winston said, turning his head to hide his smile.

"We'll all gather wood," Mills said. "Since we're going to be here for some time."

Smoke saw to his horses' needs first, rubbing them down carefully and picketing them near graze and water. He then ate a cold and early supper. He slipped off his boots and stuck his feet into moccasins that had been made especially for him. They were Apache moccasins, with high leggings that would prevent his trousers from catching on low branches or underbrush. He blackened his face with dirt and tied a dark bandanna around his forehead. He checked his guns and his knife, then picked up his rifle and slung it over his shoulder.

He knew where another of Slater's camps was, having checked the area carefully with his field glasses, spotting the smoke and mentally marking the location. This coming night was going to turn deadly for some of the outlaws.

Smoke was moving long before twilight placed its dusky hand upon the high country. He was dressed in clothing that would blend with the night and the terrain, and there was nothing on him that would rattle or clank. Moonlight, when it came up, might reflect off the brass of his .44 rounds in his ammo belt, but that was the only thing unnatural about him in the gathering gloom. He slipped through the timber and brush like a wraith.

The outlaws were a careless bunch. Smoke spotted their campfires long before he caught sight of any human movement. When he was within hailing distance of them, he squatted down and became as one with the brush. He moved only his eyes as he studied the encampment.

He concluded that Slater had split his people up into at least three bunches. Maybe four since he wasn't sure of the size of the gang. This gang of trash and thugs numbered about fifteen. They were all heavily armed, their weapons looking well used but well cared for.

Smoke moved closer, to better listen.

The outlaws were bitching about the inactivity and the lack of women and whiskey. They bragged about the men and women they had killed and raped and tortured. Smoke's face tightened in silent rage as the men laughed about the two little girls they'd had back up the trail.

Smoke knew which two girls they were talking about.

He'd buried them both.

He watched one man leave the bonfire-lighted area and move toward the dark timber, toward where Smoke squatted, waiting to strike. The man was removing his galluses as he walked to find a spot to relieve himself.

He was taking his last walk.

Smoke wiped his bloody blade clean on the dead man's shirt and shifted positions after rolling the body under some brush. He moved right to the edge of the encampment, very close to where an outlaw lay on his dirty blankets, his head on a knapsack probably filled with his possibles.

Smoke edged closer and looked with disgust at what was tied to the man's saddle. A human scalp. Blonde hair. Long blond hair. He knew where that came from, too. One of the little girls he'd buried.

Smoke cut the man's throat with a movement as furtive as a ghost and as fast and as deadly as a viper. He eased the man's head down until his chin was resting on his chest. With the bloody knife in his hand, Smoke backed away, again shifting positions, working his way around to the other side of the camp. He paused along the way to wipe his blade clean on some grass.

"Hey, Frank!" one outlaw yelled. "Did you get lost out in them woods?"

Frank lay as silent as the woods.

"Frank?" The call was repeated several times by half a dozen of the thugs.

The outlaws looked at one another, suspicion and a touch of fear entering their eyes.

"Dolp ain't moved none," one outlaw observed, looking at the man with his head on his chest.

"All that hollerin' would have been shore to wake him up," another remarked.

"Well, he ain't moved. Somebody go over yonder and kick him a time or two."

A man walked over to Dolp and nudged him with the toe of his boot. Dolp's head lolled to one side and he fell over, the movement exposing the horrible wound on his neck.

Smoke eared back the hammer on his Winchester.

The outlaw screamed, "His throat's been cut." Smoke shot him, the .44 slug severing his spine. The man slumped to the ground in a boneless heap.

The camp erupted in a mass of yelling, running men, all grabbing for their weapons and firing in every conceivable direction, hitting nothing but air.

Smoke shot one in the belly, doubling him over, and dotted another's left eye with lead. He decided it was time to haul out of there; he'd pushed his luck and skill far enough.

He left behind him a camp filled with frightened and confused outlaws. They were still shooting at shadows and hitting no more than that. However, Smoke thought, if he was lucky, two or three of them might shoot one of their own.

"They had a bad home environment," he muttered, as he silently made his way back toward his horses. "I'm going to have to remember to tell Sally about this new excuse for becoming a criminal. She probably could use a good laugh."

An hour later he rolled up in his blankets and was asleep in two minutes. He did not worry about the outlaws finding his camp. They were probably still trying to figure out what had hit them on what they considered to be home ground. And had they been more careful, it would have been safe ground. It was rugged country; no country for a tenderfoot. And a man could easily live off the land—there were bear, deer, elk, and plenty of streams in which to fish. But an outlaw wasn't going to do anything like that; they were too damn lazy and sorry. If they couldn't steal it, they didn't want it.

Smoke woke up to the sounds of a jaybird fussing at him, telling him it was a pretty day and to stop all that lollygagging around in the bed. As was his custom, Smoke did not move for a moment, letting his eyes sweep the terrain around him for trouble. He spotted nothing to indicate trouble. Birds were singing, and the squirrels were jumping and dancing from limb to limb. He rolled out of his blankets and pulled on his boots, put his hat on his head, and slung his guns around his waist.

He chanced a very small fire to boil his coffee. When the coffee was ready, he put out the fire and contented himself with a cold breakfast of bread and some berries he'd picked from nearby bushes.

By now, he figured, riders would have gone out from the camps he'd attacked, and Lee Slater, if he was not a stupid man, and Smoke didn't think he was—just a no-good, sorry excuse for a human being—would be pulling in his people, massing them for some planning. That was fine. Smoke figured he'd done enough head-hunting in this area. Today he would begin his ride over to the Seven Slash range and see what mischief he could get into there.

He pondered his future as he sipped his coffee. It would be at least another day or two before his friend, the federal judge up in Denver, received his letter. Another day or two before whatever action he took—if any, and that was something Smoke had to consider—went into effect.

But a much more dangerous aspect of his situation had to be taken into consideration: bounty hunters. As soon as word hit the country that a reward was out for Smoke Jensen—and Judge Richards probably made it dead or alive—the country would be swarming with bounty hunters and those looking for a reputation as the man who killed Smoke Jensen.

Well, he thought, I've done this before, so it's nothing new to me. I'll just have to ride with my guns loose and my eyes missing nothing.

He broke camp, saddled up, and headed for Seven Slash range.

"Had to be Jensen," Lee Slater said to some of his men. "Nobody else would be that stupid . . ."

It never occurred to Lee that stupid had nothing to do with it. "Skilled" was the word he should have used in describing Smoke's attack on his camps.

". . . He's got to be tooken out. And tooken out damn quick. He could screw up the whole plan."

"What plan?" a gunny who called himself Tap demanded. "All we been doin' for days is sittin' around on our butts. If somethin' don't happen pretty damn quick, I'm pullin' out for greener pastures."

Zack nodded his head in agreement. "I'm with Tap. We got money in our pockets and no place to spend it. They's thousands of dollars worth of gold and silver in this area, and we ain't doin' a damn thing about takin' it. I'm tarred of sittin' around. Let's get into action, Lee."

Lee knew he could not hold his men back much longer. Not and keep his gang together. And he knew he had to do that because there was strength in numbers. Luttie was moving too slow to suit Lee. He couldn't understand why his brother was dragging his boots. He needed to see Luttie, but it was risky leaving the mountains just for a visit.

"Couple more days, Zack," the outlaw leader said. "I promise you."

The men all looked up at the sound of a rider coming into camp. "I got news!" the rider yelled. He swung down and poured himself a cup of coffee, then walked over to Lee, waving the other men close in.

"Well?" Lee demanded. "What news?"

"Lemme drink some coffee, man!" the outlaw said. "Catch my breath. I been ridin' all night to get here." He drained his cup and tossed the dredges. "A federal judge back East done put out warrants on Smoke Jensen. Murder warrants from that shootin' over to Idaho some years back. Three warrants. The re-ward money totals over thirty thousand dollars to the man who brings him in—dead or alive."

"Well, now," Lee said, sitting down on a log. "Ain't that something? What's Jensen doin' about this sicheation?"

"He's on the run. Somewhere betwix here and the border."

Lee brought the man up to date on the attacks of the previous night.

"Thirty thousand dollars," outlaw Boots Pierson whispered. "That's a fortune. A man could live real good for a long time with that money."

"They's more news," the man who brought the word said, pouring himself more coffee. "The word is out, and bounty hunters from all over is comin' in. If we're gonna do something about Jensen, we damn well better get movin' 'fore all them other hardcases come a-lookin'.'"

"That there's a puredee fact," Tom Post said.

Lee looked at his men, knowing that any plans he might have had were now gone with the wind. All his men were thinking about was that thirty-thousand-dollar reward and the reputation that went with being the man who brung in Smoke Jensen belly down across a saddle.

The camp of crud and no-goods broke up into small groups, all talking at once about what all that reward money could buy them. Women, whiskey, and gambling, for the most part.

"All right, all right!" Lee finally managed to shout the camp silent. "Let's plan. Now for sure we can't go after him in a bunch. He'd see and hear us coming miles away. So let's split up into groups of six. That'd be damn near ten groups workin' the mountains. Y'all talk it over and form up with men you wanna ride with. Then we'll settle down and go over what group is gonna cover what area."

The men split up into groups of six and seven, each group made up of men who had known each other for a long time, or who knew each other's reputation.

Lee had started out with a small army of crud, over seventy-five men. He was now down to nine groups of six each. Fifty-six men. He thought about that for a minute. Fifty-four men. Whatever!

Lee found him a stump of pencil and sat down, scribbling on a dirty envelope. Four were either in jail or being transported back to states that had warrants on them. Jensen had killed two on the trail coming into town. A half dozen had left the gang after the raid against Big Rock. That meant that Jensen had killed about ten the previous night . . . give or take two or three. The man was a devil, for a fact, but he was still only one man. They would find him, and they would kill him.

Lee waved his group over to him. To his mind, he had chosen well the five men who would ride with him. They were all vicious killers. Curt Holt, Ed Malone, Boots Pierson, Harry Jennings, and Blackjack Simpson.

The young punks had banded together, as Lee had figured they would, with the punk kid Pecos their leader. All the other groups were electing leaders. Curly Rogers was bossing one group, Al Martine another. Whit was fronting another group and Ray yet another. The last two were being led by Crocker and Graham.

Personally, Lee didn't give a damn which group got Smoke Jensen, just as long as somebody got him. Not that he didn't think thirty thousand was a lot of money. It was. But there was a lot more than that to be had in these mountains once Jensen was out of the way.

Lee stood up and hitched at his gun belt. "Let's ride, boys. We got us a legend to kill."

11

But legends oftentimes grow out of fact. And Smoke Jensen was not an easy man to kill. There had been many over the long and bloody years who had thought that fact not to be true. Somebody had buried them all.

Smoke rode the big buckskin through the windy and lonely high country, once again a man with a price on his head. But this time, the price came from a corrupt judge. And Smoke would deal with him when this little matter in the mountains was settled. He didn't know just how he would deal with him, but deal with him he damn sure would.

Smoke sat the saddle like a man born to it. His back was straight and his eyes constantly moving, scanning the terrain ahead of him and on both sides.

He stopped to rest on a bluff high above the road that led to the little village, and he was not surprised to see wagon after wagon heading for the town. There were wagons and buggies of all descriptions and men on horseback, all heading for the town. It wasn't gold or silver that drew them there—although that was a part of it. It was the news that Smoke Jensen was a wanted man.

Smoke rested his horses and squatted down, his field glasses in his big hands, and studied the passing parade unfolding far below him.

He grunted as he picked out two of the West's most notorious bounty hunters. Ace Reilly and Big Bob Masters. They were riding together.

There was Lilly LaFevere in her fancy buggy, with several wagonloads of ladies of the evening right behind her. He saw several well-known gamblers that he was on speaking terms with.

Then he laughed aloud. There was Louis Longmont, riding a beautiful high-stepping black, with a wagon pulled by four big mules right behind him, driven by his personal valet and cook . . . he wondered if it was still Andre. Louis Longmont, a millionaire professional gambler who owned a casino in Monte Carlo, who owned banks and railroads and entire blocks of cities, and who was one of the most feared gunfighters in all the world. In the wagon would be jars of caviar, cases of fine French wines, and plenty of Louis' favorite scotch whiskey, Glenlivet.

Smoke felt a lump knot up in his throat as he scanned the road below. There was Cotton Pickens from up in Puma County, Wyoming. Their paths had crossed a time or two, when Smoke had pulled Cotton out of a couple of bad spots. Now he'd come to help out Smoke.

"Well, I'll just be damned!" Smoke whispered, as he focused his glasses on Johnny North, who had a ranch about twenty miles from Smoke and Sally's Sugarloaf. Johnny had married the Widow Colby and hung up his six-shooters years back. Now he had cleaned them up, oiled the leather, and strapped them on and was coming to help his neighbor.

"My God!" Smoke said, as his eyes touched upon a man with gray shoulder-length hair. "I was told you were dead!"

He was looking at the legendary Charlie Starr.

Smoke chuckled. "Going to get real interesting around the town very soon," he muttered. "Real interesting."

Smoke leaned back against a huge boulder and rolled a cigarette, lighting up. If he was right in his thinking, Lee Slater was probably right now splitting up his gang into small groups and starting a concentrated search for their prey . . . that being Smoke Jensen. Smoke smiled. He hoped Lee would do that. Small groups were easier to handle.

He smoked his cigarette and carefully extinguished it. He took his field glasses and once more studied the increasing traffic on the road below.

The town was going to boom for a time. The stage line would put on more stages and roll them in and out at least once a day from north and south, and maybe more than that.

"Well, now," Smoke said, as he picked out Dan Diamond, another bounty hunter. The man riding with him was familiar, but it took Smoke a minute or so to put a name on the face. Nap Jacobs. Nap was a thoroughly bad man. Fast with a gun and seemingly without a nerve or a scruple in his entire body. And he didn't like Smoke at all. And there was Morris Pattin, another bounty hunter who hated Smoke Jensen.

Smoke tightened the cinch on Buck and put the pack back on the pack animal. "Time to go, boys. I'm going to find you both a nice little box canyon, with good graze and water, and let you both rest for a time. Then I'm going to lay out some ambushes."

"Good to see you again, Earl!" Louis said, stepping up on the boardwalk and shaking hands with the Englishman.

"By the Lord! It's grand to see you, Louis. It's going to get rather interesting around this little village before very long. Who are your friends?"

"Johnny North, a neighbor of Smoke Jensen's. Cotton Pickens, a rancher from up Wyoming way, and this, Earl, is Charlie Starr."

"I am awed and humbled, sir," Earl said, with genuine emotion in his voice. "You rank among the few men who have become a legend in your own time."

"Thank you, sir," Charlie replied, shaking hands with the gambler/gunfighter. "I may take it that you are a friend of Smoke Jensen?"

"You may. Let's go into my office, and I'll bring you up to date on Smoke's troubles."

Larry Tibbson had taken the first stage out of Big Rock, heading down to where Smoke was hiding out. He kept a very low profile and kept his big mouth shut concerning his opinions of Smoke Jensen. He decided that since the town was growing so quickly—he didn't have sense enough to know what was causing the rapid growth, nor that it would very likely bust as quickly as it boomed—he would hang out his shingle in the newly named town of Rio. Everybody needed the services of a good attorney from time to time, and this looked like the ideal spot to make some quick money.

But my word! Larry thought, stepping off the stage, it was so rowdy here. All these rough-looking fellows carrying guns and knives right out in the open. Shocking! He had never seen anything like it. And their boorish behavior was offensive to someone of Larry's gentle sensibilities. All the more reason to stay, he thought. Bring some refinement to the savages.

He managed to get the last room available in the hotel— and he did that by paying five times the usual going rate.

"Them sheets ain't been slept on but three times," the man told him, in protest over Larry's demand for clean sheets. "The last feller used 'em didn't appear to have no fleas."

"Change the sheets!"

"All right, all right," the newly hired room clerk grumbled.

Larry turned to the stairs and was stopped in his tracks at the sight of Louis Longmont dismounting and shaking hands with what appeared to be a constable of some sort. It was hard to tell in this barbaric setting, since lawmen, for the most part, did not wear uniforms denoting their profession, as was the case in more civilized parts of the nation.

Louis Longmont . . . here? Larry walked to the window of the saloon and looked out, seeing the six-guns belted around the millionaire's waist. So the rumors were true after all, Larry mused. The man was an adventurer. But was he here to hunt down Smoke Jensen, or to aid the gunfighter?

And who was that long-haired, grizzled-looking older man shaking hands with the constable? Obviously some sort of gunfighter, but it was hard to tell, since all those gathered around the constable wore two guns, tied down. It was so confusing out here.

With a sigh, Larry turned to climb the stairs. He angled over and spoke to the room clerk, whose small station was at the end of the bar.

"Do you have inside facilities?" Larry inquired.

"Huh?"

"Water closets inside."

"Hell, no!"

Larry shook his head and headed for the room.

"You forgot your bags," the room clerk called.

"Carry them up for me."

"Tote your own damn bags, mister!"

Larry climbed the stairs, sweating under the load of his trunk. All in all, he thought, the West just had to be the most barbaric and inhospitable place he had ever traveled.

*   *   *

"How many men in Slater's bunch?" Johnny asked.

Earl spread his hands. "Fifty to seventy-five are the numbers I keep hearing."

"Smoke's a tough ol' boy," Charlie Starr said. "But he's not indestructible. He's gonna need some help with this one. Come the morning I'll provision up and head out for the lonesome. Louis, I think you and Johnny and Cotton ought to stay close to here. This town's a-fixin' to bust wide open and Earl, here, is gonna need some help keepin' order. 'Sides, Smoke needs all the friendly ears he can use right here."

"I agree," Louis said. "Sooner or later, Smoke is going to tire of the mountains and come into town, and to hell with the U.S. Marshals. We need to be here to back him up."

Johnny had left Big Rock before Larry Tibbson started with all his mouth, so all he knew about the Eastern lawyer was that he'd come trying to spark a married woman, Sally, and that was a stupid thing to do. If Smoke had been home, the lawyer would be cold in the ground with the worms playing the dipsy-doodle around his sewed-together lips. Which was about the only way anybody could get a lawyer to shut up.

Someone had set up a portable saw mill and was already backed up with orders for lumber. The sounds of sawing and hammering and nailing and cussing overrode any other sound in the town. With Earl Sutcliffe as the marshal, few dared to fire a pistol, even for fun. And the whole town knew within minutes of their arrival that Cotton Pickens, Johnny North, Charlie Starr, and Louis Longmont were on the side of the law with Earl Sutcliffe. That knowledge smoothed out just a whole bunch of otherwise sharp and explosive tempers. It would take a puredee damn fool to go up against those five.

"Now," Earl said, "we have to see about rooms for you gentlemen."

Louis shook his head. "No need. Andre is hiring people

now to erect my saloon and gambling hall. We'll have board floors and wooden sides, but a canvas top. I'll have the workmen build an addition to the saloon for us. Until then, we'll sleep out under God's blanket."

"I'm gonna start puttin' my provisions together," Charlie said. "I get it done soon enough, I just might take off while there's a few hours of daylight left."

"Get whatever you need and charge it, Charlie," Earl told him. "Your money is no good in this town."

Charlie looked at the man. "I ain't no broke saddle bum, Earl."

"Of course you're not," Louis said with a smile. "If you wish, you can settle up when you return from the mountains."

"I just might do that. See you boys." The old gunfighter left the office.

"Whew!" Johnny said. "That, fellers, is one randy ol' puma."

"I concur," Louis said. "Have you ever seen him in action, Earl?"

"No, never."

"Awesome. He's a little slower than he used to be, I would imagine. But still one of the fastest guns around. And he never misses."

"I would like to get word to Smoke that you are here," Earl said. "But I haven't the foggiest where he might be."

Louis shrugged his shoulders. "Knowing Smoke as I do, he probably already knows. Although how he manages to learn those things mystifies me."

"Indians say that eagles come tell him," Cotton said.

"I've heard that, too," Johnny said.

"If he knows you gentlemen are here," Earl said drily, "it is probably because he squatted on a mountain and watched the road below through field glasses."

"I like the eagle story better," Louis said, and the men burst out laughing.

A bounty hunter they called Slim Williams wasn't laughing. He had left the road miles from the newly named town of Rio and headed into the high country. He'd come upon tracks: a man riding and a packhorse behind.

He found where the man had stopped and dismounted for a drink of water at a rushing mountain stream. A big man, judging by his boot tracks. And Smoke Jensen was a big man.

Then he lost the trail. Slim wandered around for a hour and never could pick it back up. He had sat his horse for a time, smoking a cigarette and thinking things through. His eyes caught movement in the timber, about a hundred yards away. Then the man—and he was sure it was a man—was gone.

"What the hell?" Slim said. He rode his tired horse over to the spot where he'd seen the movement and dismounted. There were tracks, and the print was about the same size as those he'd seen back at that little crick. But this man was wearing moccasins. And it hadn't been no Injun neither. Slim was sure of that. This man seemed to have some sort of black bandanna tied around his head and his hair had been cut short.

He walked back to where he'd left his horse reined. The damn horse was gone!

"Shotgun!" Slim called. "Come on, Shotgun. Come to Slim, boy."

Silence greeted him from the high country timber.

Slim began to worry. He could make it back to the road; he wasn't worried about that. But all his possessions were in the saddlebags or tied in his bedroll.

"Shotgun! Now come on, boy. Come to ol' Slim, Shotgun."

Slim spun around, a Colt leaping into his hand as the

voice came out of the timber. "Shotgun was tired. He needed a rest."

"Who the hell are you, mister? You gimmie back my damn horse, you thief!"

"A back-shooting murderer calling me a thief." The voice laughed. "That's very funny."

Slim cussed him.

Smoke said, "You looking for Smoke Jensen?"

"That ain't none of your concern, mister."

"I can lead you to him."

"Oh, yeah?"

"Yeah. I get half the reward money, though."

"You go suck an egg, mister." Slim thought for a moment. "Tell you what I'll do, mister. You step out so's I can see you, and we'll talk."

"You put that gun up, and I'll do that." The voice was closer, and coming from a different location each time.

Damn, Slim thought. The man moves like a ghost. And I know that voice from somewheres. "Deal." Slim holstered his gun, thinking that if the man was planning to kill him, he'd have done so already.

"Turn around." The voice came from behind him.

Slim turned, and felt his stomach do a slow rollover. He was facing Smoke Jensen. "Hello, Smoke. It's been a long time. Years."

"You should have stayed home, Slim," Smoke told him.

"Man's got to make a livin', Smoke."

"You know damn well those warrants out on me are bogus. You're a man-hunter, Slim. Out for the money. I got no use for scum like you."

"You ain't got no call to talk to me like that, Smoke. This ain't nothin' personal 'tween us. You've kilt more'un your share of men. You ain't no better than I am."

"We'll let God be the judge of that, Slim. You came looking for me, now you've found me. Make your play."

Slim began to sweat. He hadn't planned on this. He'd planned on back-shootin' Smoke. His tongue snaked out to wet dry lips. "We can deal, Jensen. I can just ride on out of here and not look back."

"That's the same deal you made with the breed, Cloud walker. Then you shot him in the back, all the time knowing he was an innocent man."

"Hell, Smoke, he was a damn Injun!"

"He was an innocent man. I've stayed with Crows and Utes and Sioux and Cheyenne. I have a lot of good Indian friends. It doesn't make any difference to me if a man is red, white, Negro, or Oriental."

"Don't preach to me, Jensen!" Slim got his dander up. "I don't need no goddamn gunslick sermonizin' to me."

"Draw, Slim!"

Slim grabbed for iron. Smoke's .44 slug caught him dead center in his chest and knocked him back against a tree. He finally managed to pull iron, and Smoke's second shot tore into his belly.

Slim screamed as the .44 slug ripped through his innards like a white-hot branding iron. His .44 dropped from dying fingers. He slumped to the cool ground.

"You gonna bury me proper, ain't you, Jensen?" He gasped the question.

"I'll toss some branches and rocks over you, Slim. I don't have a shovel."

"I hate you, Jensen!"

"I don't understand that, Slim. What did I ever do to you to cause you to hate me?"

"Jist . . . bein' . . . you!" Slim closed his eyes and died.

Smoke went through Slim's pockets before he piled branches and rocks over the body to discourage smaller animals, all the while knowing that a bear could, and probably would, rip it apart in seconds. He would give the money to some needy family. There was no indication that Slim had a family. Smoke shoved one of Slim's .44s behind his gun belt and kept the other one in leather, hanging on his saddle horn. He inspected the late Slim's Winchester .44-40. It was in excellent condition and this one had an extra rear sight, located several inches behind the hammer, for greater accuracy. He found three boxes of .44-40s in the saddlebags. Slim also had a nice poke of food: some bacon and bread and biscuits and three cans of beans that would come in handy on the trail.

Smoke hesitated, then carved Slim's name on the tree that towered over the man. He put the date below the name and mounted up and pulled out, knowing that shots carry far in the high thin air of the lonesome.

He stopped once, looking back at Slim Williams' final resting place. "You should have picked another line of work, Slim. That's about the best I can say for you. God's gonna have the final word anyway."

12

"Them was shots," Crocker said. "Come from over yonder." He pointed. "Let's go!"

"That's Horton's assigned area," Graham said.

"Hell with Horton." Crocker blew away the myth about honor among thieves. "Don't you want that money? Man, that's five thousand apiece if we cut it up."

"What'd you mean, if we cut it up?" Causey asked.

"All right, when we cut it up. Does that make you feel better?"

"Let's ride!" Woody said. "Damn all this jibber-jabber. Smoke'll be in the next county 'fore we get done talkin'."

They found where Smoke had carved Slim's date of death in the tree.

"Knowed him," Dale said. "He was good with a gun."

"Not good enough." Haynes summed it up. "Let's drag him out and go through his pockets."

The men tore away the rocks and branches and searched the stiffening form of Slim. They found nothing of value.

Woody did take the man's boots, putting them on and throwing his worn-out boots by the body. They left Slim sprawled on the ground, one big toe sticking out of the hole in his dirty sock.

A bear came lumbering out of the timber and sniffed the dead man. He dragged Slim off a few hundred yards and covered him up with branches. When Slim ripened some he would be back for a meal.

"Hey, old man!" the young man called out to Charlie Starr, as Charlie sipped his whiskey prior to hitting the saddle for the high lonesome.

Charlie ignored him.

"I'm talkin' to you, old shaggy-haired thing you!"

Most of the men in the crowded saloon were chance-takers and gamblers and gun hands and bounty hunters. None of them knew the gray-haired man with the tied-down guns, the wooden handles worn smooth, but they could sense danger all around him.

Charlie took a small sip of his whiskey—holding the glass in his left hand—and decided to wait it out. He'd been around for a long time, and knew there was a chance—albeit a small one—that he could avoid having to deal with this young smart-mouth. Maybe his friends would sit him down. Maybe.

"Damn!" the young gunslick yelled. "His hair's so shaggy it's blockin' his ears. Maybe we ought to give him a haircut."

We! Charlie thought. More than one. But maybe his friends will stay out of it. Maybe.

"Bobby . . ." a young man said, pulling at the young smart-mouth's arm.

"Shut up!" Bobby said. "You don't have the balls for this, stay out of it."

Charlie sipped his drink. The whiskey tasted good after the dust of the road. He'd been a hard-drinkin' man in his younger days. Now he enjoyed just an occasional drink, liked to linger over it. In peace. Young Bobby was pushing. Hard. Just a few more words and he would step over the line. Charlie hoped the young man would just sit down and shut up.

"Goddamn mangy old fart!" Bobby yelled. "You wear them two guns like you think you're hot stuff. Turn around and prove it!"

There it was, Charlie thought. He would have liked to just finish his drink and walk out the door. But the code demanded that he do otherwise.

No, Charlie corrected that. It wasn't just the code. It was much more than that. It came with manhood. It was part of maintaining one's self-respect. It . . .

Larry Tibbson walked down the rickety stairs and stepped into the barroom.

. . . was just something that a man had to do. Right or wrong, and Charlie had thoughts about that, it just had to be.

"I called for hot water!" Larry said.

"Shut up and git out of the way," the bartender told him.

"You goddamn old turd!" Bobby hollered. "Turn around and face me."

"What on earth is taking place here?" Larry asked, looking around him. "And where is my hot water? I want to take a bath."

The barkeep reached over the bar and pulled Larry to the far end of the long bar. "Shet your trap, boy," he told Larry. "Lead's a-fixin' to fly."

Charlie finished his drink and slowly set the glass on the bar. He turned around, his hands by his sides. "Go home, boy," he told Bobby. "I ain't lookin' for trouble."

"Well, you got it!" Bobby told him.

"Why?" Charlie asked. "I don't know you. I never seen you before in my life. Why me?"

" 'Cause I think you maybe believe you're a gun hawk, that's why."

"Son, I was handlin' guns years before you were born. Now, why don't you just sit down and finish yur drink, and I'll just walk out the bats?"

"Yellow!" Bobby sneered at him. "The old man's yellow. He's afraid of Bobby Jones."

Charlie smiled. "I never heard of you, Bobby. Are you lookin' for a reputation? Is that it?"

"I got a rep!"

"I ain't never seen none of your graveyards, boy."

"You just ain't looked in the right place. As far as that goes, where's your graveyards?"

"All over the land, son. From Canada to Mexico. From Missouri to California."

"You say!"

"That's right, son. I say."

Earl Sutcliffe pushed open the batwings and stood there, sizing up the situation. "What's the trouble here?"

"Stay out of this, Marshal," Bobby said. "This is between me and this old goat here."

"You know who that old goat is?" Earl asked.

"Don't make no difference to me. I don't like this old coot's looks, and I told him so. He's afraid of me."

Earl laughed. "Boy, that man is not afraid of anything. That's Charlie Starr."

Bobby looked like a horse just kicked him in the belly. His face turned white and sweat popped out on his forehead. But he had made his bed—or in this case, dug his grave—and now he would be forced to lie in it. Unless he backed down.

"Give it up, son," Earl told him. "Sit down and live."

Bobby's hands hovered over the pearl handles of his brand new matching .45s. Those raggedly-looking guns of

Charlie's looked to Bobby like they was so old they probably wouldn't even fire. Looked like they'd been converted from cap and ball to handle brass cartridges.

Bobby stepped down into the damp, chilly grave he'd just dug for himself. "You're yellow, old man!" he shouted. Charlie Starr's done turned yellow. You're standin' on your reputation, and I'm gonna be the man who jerks it out from under you."

Charlie straightened up, his mouth tight and his face grim. Earl knew it was nearly over. A man can only take so much, and Charlie had given the young punk more than ample opportunity to back down. "Enough talk," Charlie said. "Make your play, you stupid little snot."

"Here now!" Larry said. "This has gone entirely too far. You there," he said to Charlie. "You stop picking on that boy."

"Shut up," Earl told him.

Louis Longmont, Johnny North, and Cotton Pickens had walked into the saloon, standing on either side of Earl. "Fifty dollars says the kid never clears leather." Louis offered up a wager.

"You're on," a young man at the table where Bobby should have stayed seated said. "That there's Bobby Jones. He's faster than Smoke Jensen."

"He couldn't lick Smoke's boots," Charlie said.

"What!" Bobby screamed. "Draw, you old fart!"

"After you, boy," Charlie told him. "I don't ever want it said that I took advantage of a young punk."

"I ain't no punk!"

"Then show that you're a man by sittin' down and lettin' me buy you a drink. That's my final offer, son."

"You mean, that's your final statement. 'Cause I'm gonna kill you, Starr."

"That's it," Louis muttered. He knew, as did everyone else

in the bar, that those words, once spoken, were justification to kill.

Charlie shot him. His draw was so smooth, so practiced, so fast, so professional, that it was a blur to witness. Flame shot out the muzzle of his old long-barreled .44. Gray smoke belched forth, obscuring vision. Bobby was jarred back as the slug ripped his belly and wandered around his guts, leaving a path of pain wherever it traveled.

He imagined himself jacking the hammer back on his .45 and pulling the trigger. He actually did just that. But his guns were still in leather. He leaned against a support post and finally dragged iron.

Charlie let him cock his .45 before he put another slug in the punk's guts. Bobby yelled and slumped toward the floor, sliding down the post and sitting down heavily. He pulled the trigger and blew off several of his own toes. He screamed in pain and tried to lift the .45. It was just too heavy.

The .45 clattered to the littered floor.

"By God," one of Bobby's friends declared. "That'll not go unavenged." He stood up, a pistol in his hand.

Charlie drilled him in the brisket and doubled the young man over like the closing of a fan. The young man fell, landing on Bobby.

Bobby screamed in pain.

"You still owe me fifty dollars," Louis reminded the gut-shot punk who'd wanted revenge for Bobby.

"Help me!" the second punk bellered. "Oh, Lordy, Lordy, my belly's on fire."

"My God!" Larry yelled. "Somebody get a doctor and call the police."

He was ignored.

Bobby's other friends sat quite still at the table, their faces a sickly shade of green.

"Gimme a drink and one of them eggs over yonder,"

Charlie told the bartender. "Shootin' always makes me hungry."

"You barbarian!" Larry yelled at him.

Charlie noticed the man wasn't wearing a gun, so he did the next best thing. He walked over to him and slapped Larry across the mouth, knocking him down.

"I'll sue you!" Larry hollered.

Bobby broke wind and died.

His friend yelled, "Help me!"

Charlie punched out his empties, loaded up full, holstered his gun, and began peeling the egg.

"Somebody run fetch that new undertaker feller that just set up business down the street," the barkeep suggested. "I wanna see that shiny black hearse and them fancy-steppin' horses."

"You're all mad!" Larry said, getting to his shoes. "Somebody get a doctor for that poor boy."

"Ain't no doctor," a man told him. "Go get the barber."

"The barber!" Larry exclaimed in horror.

"There's a Ute medicine man down on the La Jara. But that young pup'll done be swelled up and stinkin' something awful time he gets here. That old Ute's pretty good, but I ain't never heard of him raisin' the dead."

"Halp!" the second punk yelled.

His voice was getting weaker.

"Won't be long now," Earl said, bending over the gut-shot young man. "Where's your next of kin, lad?"

"I don't wanna die!"

"Then you should have chosen your companions with a bit more care. Next of kin?"

"I got a sister up in Denver. But she threw me out a couple of years ago."

The batwings flapped open, and a man dressed all in black stood in the space. "I heard shooting!"

"My, but your hearing is quite keen," Earl commented drily.

"I am the Reverend Silas Muckelmort. A minister of the gospel. I have come to this town to bring the word of God to the sinners who lust for blood money. Has that young man passed?" He pointed to Bobby.

"Cold as a hammer," Cotton told him.

"Then it is my duty to tend to his needs," the Reverend Silas Muckelmort said.

"You keep your shit-snatchers off my body!" a small man dressed in a dark suit said, stepping into the barroom. "I'm the undertaker in town."

"His spiritual needs, you jackass!" Silas thundered.

"Pass the salt and pepper," Charlie told the barkeep. "I can't eat an egg without salt and pepper."

Smoke holed up in the most inhospitable place he could find, very near the timber line, knowing the outlaws would, most likely, find the most comfortable spot they could to bed down for the night. He had already found a spot he would use to leave his horses, in an area so remote it would be pure chance if anyone stumbled upon them. Tomorrow he would ride there and leave them, packing on his back what he felt he would need in his fight against the bounty hunters and the Lee Slater gang.

Smoke rolled up in his blankets and went to sleep. The next several days were going to be busy ones.

He was up and riding before dawn, having committed to memory the trail to the cul-de-sac where he would leave the horses. He was there by midmorning. He transplanted several bushes over to the small opening and carefully watered them. To get to the opening, he had to ride behind a thick stand of timber, then angle around a huge boulder, and finally take a left into the lush little valley of about ten acres with a small pool next to a sheer rock wall. The grass was belly high in places; ample feed for the horses for some time. If he did not return, they could easily find their way out.

Smoke put together a pack whose weight would have staggered the average man. He picked it up with his left hand.

He sat for a time eating a cold . . . what was it Sally called a mid-morning meal? Brunch, yeah, that was it . . . and wishing he had a potful of hot, strong, black coffee. But he couldn't chance that. He would hike a few miles and then have a hot dinner—lunch, Sally called it—and drink a whole pot of strong cowboy coffee. He wanted the scum and crud to see that smoke. He wanted them to come right to that spot. By the time they got there, he would have a few surprises laid out for them.

He walked over and spoke with Buck for a few moments. Rubbing his muzzle and talking gently to the big horse. Buck seemed to understand, but then, everybody thinks that of their pets and their riding horses. Shotgun, the pack animal, and Buck watched Smoke pick up his heavy pack and leave. When he was out of sight, they returned to their grazing.

Smoke hiked what he figured was about three miles through wild and rugged country, then stopped and built a small, nearly smokeless fire for his coffee and bacon and beans. While his meal was cooking and the coffee boiling, he whittled on some short stakes, sharpening one end to a needle point. After eating, he cleaned plate and skillet and spoon and packed them away. Then he went to work making the campsite look semi-permanent and laying out some rather nasty pitfalls for the bounty hunters and outlaws.

That done, he tossed some logs on the fire and slipped back into the timber where he'd hidden his pack. He waited.

Curly Rogers and his pack of hyenas were the first to arrive.

Smoke was back in the timber with the .44-40, waiting and watching.

The outlaws didn't come busting in. They lay back and looked the situation over for a time. They saw the lean-to Smoke had built, and what appeared to be a man sleeping under a blanket, protected by the overlaid boughs.

"It might not be Jensen," Taylor said.

"So what?" Thumbs Morton said. "It wouldn't be the first time someone got shot by accident."

"I don't like it," Curly said. "It just looks too damn pat to suit me."

"Maybe Slim got lead into him?" Bell suggested. "He may be hard hit and holed up."

Curly thought about that for a moment. "Maybe. Yeah. That must be it. Lake, you think you can Injun up yonder for a closer look?"

"Shore. But why don't we just shoot him from here?"

"A shot'd bring everybody foggin'. Then we'd probably have to fight some of the others over Jensen's carcass. A knife don't make no noise."

Lake grinned and pulled out a long-bladed knife. "I'll just slip this 'tween his ribs."

As Lake stepped out with the knife in his hand, Smoke tugged on the rope he'd attached to the sticks under the blankets. What the outlaws thought to be a sleeping or wounded Smoke Jensen moved and Lake froze, then jumped back into the timber.

"This ain't a-gonna work," Curly said. "We got to shoot him, I reckon. One shot might not attract no attention. Bud, use your rifle and put one shot in him. This close, one round'll kill him sure."

Bud lined up the form in the sights and squeezed the trigger. Smoke tugged on the rope, and the stick man rose off the ground a few inches, then fell back.

"We got him!" Bell yelled, jumping up. "We kilt Smoke Jensen. The money's our'n!"

The men raced toward the small clearing, guns drawn and yelling.

Taylor yelled as the ground seemed to open up under his boots. He fell about eighteen inches into a pit, two sharpened stakes tearing into the calves of his legs. He screamed in pain, unable to free himself from the sharpened stakes.

Bell tripped a piece of rawhide two inches off the ground and a tied-back, fresh and springy limb sprang forward. The limb whacked the man on the side of his head, tearing off one ear and knocking the man unconscious.

"What the hell!" Curly yelled.

Smoke fired from concealment, the .44-40 slug taking Lake in the right side and exiting out his left side. He was dying as he hit the ground.

"It's a trap!" Curly screamed, and ran for the timber. He ran right over Bell in his haste to get the hell into cover.

Smoke lined up Bud and fired just as the man turned, the slug hitting the man in the ass, the lead punching into his left buttock and blowing out his right, taking a sizeable chunk of meat with it.

Bud fell screaming and rolled on the ground, throwing himself into cover.

Thumbs Morton jerked up Bell just as the man was crawling to his knees, blood pouring from where his ear had once been, and dragged him into cover just as Smoke fired again, the slug hitting a tree and blowing splinters in Thumbs' face, stinging and bringing blood.

"Let's get gone from here!" Curly yelled.

"What about Taylor?" Thumbs asked, pulling splinters and wiping blood from his face.

"Hell with him."

With Curly supporting the ass-shot Bud, and Thumbs helping Bell, the outlaws made it back to their horses and took off at a gallop, Bud shrieking in pain as the saddle abused his shot-up butt.

Smoke lay in the timber and listened to the outlaws beat their retreat, then stepped out into his camp. He looked at Lake. The outlaw was dead. Smoke took his ammo belt and tossed his guns into the brush. He walked over to Taylor, who had passed out from the pain in his ruined legs. He took his ammunition, tossed his guns into the brush, and then jerked the stakes out of the man's legs. The man moaned in unconsciousness.

Smoke found the horses of the men, took the food from the saddlebags, and led one animal back to the campsite. He poured a canteen full of water on Taylor. The man moaned and opened his eyes.

"Ride," Smoke told him. "If I ever see you again, I'll kill you."

"I cain't get up on no horse," Taylor sobbed. "My legs is ruint."

Smoke jacked back the hammer on his .44. "Then I guess I'd better put you out of your misery."

Taylor screamed in fear and crawled to his horse, pulling himself up by clinging to the stirrup and the fender of the saddle. He managed to get in the saddle after several tries. His face was white with pain. He looked down at Smoke.

"You ain't no decent human bein'. What you're doin' to me ain't right. I need a doctor. You a devil, Jensen!"

"Then you pass that word, pus-bag. You make damn sure all your scummy buddies know I don't play by the rules. Now ride, you bastard, before I change my mind and kill you!"

Taylor was gone in a gallop.

Smoke shoved Lake's body over the side of the small plateau and began throwing dirt over the fire, making certain it was out. Then he sat down, rolled a cigarette, and had a cup of coffee.

All in all, he concluded, it had been a very productive morning.

13

The townspeople all turned out for the funeral parade that morning. Bobby had had enough money on him to have a fine funeral, complete with some wailers Reverend Muckelmort had hired. He'd found someone with a bass drum and a fellow who played the trumpet. It was a sight to see, what with the thumping of the bass drum and the tootin' on the trumpet.

Muckelmort was something of a windbag. By the time he'd finished with his lengthy graveside harangue, nobody was left but the wailers—they were paid to stay—everybody else had retired to the saloon.

Nobody knew the second punk's name, and he'd only had ten dollars on him, so he was wrapped in a blanket and stuck in an unmarked hole. Two dollars went to the grave digger, two dollars for the blanket, two dollars for the preacher, and the remaining four bucks went to buy drinks after the service. Somebody recalled that four of them had ridden into town together. But the other two had split just after the shooting. One of them was heard to say that milkin' cows wasn't all that bad after all. He was headin' back to the farm.

The RCMP had ridden in and collected the last prisoner, and the jail was empty.

When the morning stage rolled in, it was filled with reporters, all from back East. "Be another stage in this afternoon," the driver told Earl. "We're gonna be runnin' two a day while this lasts. We must have passed five hundred people on the road, all headin' this way."

Sheriff Silva rode in, looked around, cussed, and then commented to Earl that he reckoned he'd better hire some more deputies. Fifteen minutes later, he swore in Louis, Johnny, and Cotton. Louis asked him if he'd received warrants for Smoke's arrest.

"I tossed 'em in the trash can," the sheriff said. "There ain't no lawman out here gonna try to arrest Smoke Jensen. Not none that has a lick of sense. I know all about that shootin' in Idaho years ago. It was a fair fight, if you wanna call Smoke bein' outnumbered twenty to one fair. Those warrants are bogus."

A miner riding into town loping his mule as hard as he could cut off the conversation. He pulled up short at the sight of all the activity. When he'd been here last month there hadn't been more than seventy-five people in the whole damn town. Now it looked to him like there was more than a thousand.

With a confused look on his face, he tried to kick the mule into movement. But the mule was smarter than the rider. When a mule is tired or is loaded too heavily, it just won't move and no amount of cussing or kicking or threatening will make it move. The miner slid out of the saddle and ran up to Sheriff Silva and the other deputies.

The mule sat down in the street.

"Big shootin' about ten miles out of town, Sheriff," the miner said, pointing. "I don't know if they was outlaws or bounty hunters—one and the same if you ask me. But anyway, the man who stopped by my tent for bandages and sich had one ear tore slap off. He said another man dropped into a pit of some sort that had sharpened stakes in it; run through both his legs. Terrible sight to see, he said. Another feller was shot dead and another was shot plumb through his ass—both sides!"

"Stay out of the mountains," the sheriff told the man. "And tell other miners to do the same. That's the Lee Slater gang—and some bounty hunters—chasing a man. It looks like some of them caught up with him."

"All them fellers chasin' after just one man? Good Lord, who are they after?"

"Smoke Jensen."

"Smoke Jensen!" the miner hollered. "Then they all must be nuts! I'd sooner run up on a pack of grizzly bears than tangle with him."

"I think they're beginning to discover that," Earl remarked. "But I'll wager they'll press on because they have no choice in the matter. They have to get Smoke out of the way."

The miner wandered off, muttering about crazy people. He tried to get his mule up off his butt, but the mule just brayed at him, telling him in no uncertain terms to get lost. He was tired, he was going to rest, so beat it.

"Has Luttie and his crew been back into town?" Sheriff Silva asked.

"No. Not in days."

The sheriff lit a cigar and said, "Main reason I rode down here was to tell you that Luttie's hirin' fightin' men. Payin' top wages. Whole passel of them rode through my town. Me and the boys sent them packin'. One-Eyed Jake and that Mexican gunslinger, Carbone, was among the bunch."

"I know them both," Johnny said. "They're top guns. Did you recognize any of the others?"

"Yeah. Nick Johnson, the twins, the Karl Brothers—Rod and Randy, and Rich Coleman."

"That's a whole army right there," Cotton said, hitching at his gun belt. "Earl's told us something about this Luttie Charles. About his bein' the brother to Lee Slater. About how it's a good bet that he's tied up in all this. Ain't they enough evidence to move against him and shut him down?"

"Not . . . quite," Silva said with a sigh. "I received a wire from the governor this morning. Early this morning. He's not happy with all the press we're getting. He's afraid this town is going to blow wide open, and personally I think there is a good chance of that happening. There's a federal judge in Denver working very hard to overturn those warrants against Smoke, but that's going to take time. The governor said Smoke was on his own in this. I wired him back and told him that Jensen was one of my deputies, and he damn sure was not alone in this. Whatever he was doing up in the mountains comes under the business of keeping the law and order. I expect by the time I get back, I'll have several replies on my desk." Silva smiled. "They should make for interestin' readin'."

"Reading between the lines, Sheriff," Johnny said. "Smoke's on his own in the mountains, except for Charlie—and you want us to stay in Rio, right?"

"I'd appreciate it, boys. If the governor has to send the state militia in here, that's gonna make him very unhappy."

"Then here we'll stay, Sheriff," Louis assured the man. "Do you think Luttie has plans to attack the town, strip it bare, and leave this part of the country?"

"It's a possibility that I've considered. At first I think his plan was to hit the miners and the stages carrying gold and silver out. Maybe he might still do that. But I think now that Jensen has his brother's men out looking for him, he just might turn his back on Lee and use the men he has to wipe this town clean."

"Brotherly love doesn't run very deep in that family, does it?" Earl said softly.

Silva shrugged. "That's just a guess on my part. Who the hell really knows what Lee and Luttie will do?"

The men fell silent in the noisy, busy town, their eyes on the mountains that loomed around them. All of them had one overriding thought: Could Smoke pull this off?

Charlie Starr watched with some amusement in his hard eyes as Curly's group tried to treat the wounded. He had left his horse and walked to within fifty yards of the outlaw band's camp, casually leaning up against a tree at the edge of the clearing.

Bud was lying on his stomach, his britches down around his boots, his bare butt shinin' in the sunlight, while Thumbs Morton poured alcohol on the bullet holes. That set Bud off, jerking and squalling.

One side of Thumb's face was swollen and red-looking.

Bell Harrison had a bloody bandage wrapped around his head, and Taylor's legs, from the knees down, were wrapped in dirty, bloody bandages.

"I'm a-gonna kill that son of a bitch!" Bell said, considerable heat in his voice. "Torture him. Make it last. Burn him. I'll start with his feet in a fire and work up. I hate Smoke Jensen."

Charlie grinned. Smoke had really done a job on this bunch of no-goods.

"My legs is real hot, boys," Taylor said with a moan. "I'm burnin' up. I think Jensen put something on them stake points. Poison, maybe."

Probably so, Charlie thought. He probably found him some bear shit and smeared the points with it. Or he might have used some poisonous plant leaves. Ol' Preacher taught him every mean and dirty trick in the book when it came to survival. You boys done grabbed hold of a grizzly bear's tail when you decided to take on Smoke Jensen.

"I can't do no more for you, Bud," Thumbs said.

"I hate Smoke Jensen!" Bell said.

Charlie worked his way around the clearing until he had reached a spot about twenty yards from the bitching and moaning group of deadbeats. He pulled both .44s from leather and jacked the hammers back.

"What the hell was that?" Curly said, grabbing up a rifle and looking all around him.

"I didn't hear nothin'," Taylor said.

"I wonder if Jensen give Lake a decent buryin'?" Thumbs said.

"About the same as I'm gonna give you," Charlie said, and stepped out and started shooting.

Curly recognized the man at once. Charlie Starr! He jumped away from the group and headed for the horses, none of whom had been unsaddled. Curly wanted no part of Charlie Starr. Smoke Jensen was bad enough, but combine him with Charlie, and that was just too much.

Curly left his fearless little group to fight it out by themselves.

Charlie's first slug knocked Bell sprawling, his right arm hanging broken and useless by his side. Thumbs Morton was hit in the right side, the bullet shattering a rib and angling off to tear through a kidney. He lifted his six-gun, a curse forming on his lips, and got off one round, which missed.

Charlie didn't miss. He didn't even flinch as the slug from Thumbs' gun tore bark from a nearby tree. He leveled his long-barreled .44 and shot Thumbs in the belly, knocking the man down, hard-hit and dying.

Bell struggled to his boots and lifted his left-hand gun. Charlie perforated the man's belly, and Bell would never again have to worry about indigestion or how to keep his hat on his head with only one ear. Now all he had to worry about was facing God.

Charlie stepped back into the timber and was gone, leaving Bud and Taylor alive in the middle of carnage. He'd seen Curly Rogers hightail it out. Charlie knew Curly from way back. Knew him for the coward and the bully he was. Let him go; they would meet up again.

Charlie walked swiftly back to his horse, reloading as he went. He swung into the saddle, and was gone, a warrior's smile on his lips.

"Oh, my God!" Taylor yelled, the pain in his legs fierce. "What are we gonna do, Bud?"

Bud couldn't even stand up. His britches and his galluses were all tangled up around his boots. "Oh, Lord, I don't know!" Bud wailed. "I wish I'd never heard of Smoke Jensen. I wish I'd never left the farm."

"I think I'm gonna die, Bud. My legs is swellin' something awful."

"Hell with your legs. My ass hurts," Bud moaned.

Several of the groups had returned to base camp as night grew near. They all gathered around as Lee Slater listened to Curly's babblings, a disgusted look on his ugly face. He finally had enough and waved Curly silent. "Goddamnit, boys!" he yelled. "Smoke's jist one man. You're lettin' him buffalo you all."

"What about Bud and Taylor?" Horton asked.

"What about them?" Lee demanded. "Hell, they know the way back to base. We've all been shot before and managed to stay on a horse. If they got so much baby in them they can't ride through a little pain, we don't need them."

The young punks, Pecos, Miller, Hudson, Concho, Bull, and Jeff, all nodded their agreement and hitched at their gun belts. None of them had ever been shot so they really didn't know what they were agreeing to. It just seemed like it was the manly thing to do.

"We put out guards this night," Lee said. "There'll be no more of Jensen slippin' up on us."

Miles away, Smoke had no intention of slipping up on anything that night, except sleep. Let the outlaws sweat it out and get tired and nervous. He would fix a good meal and rest.

Charlie had found him a nice comfortable little hidey-hole and was boiling his coffee and frying his bacon. He would get a good night's sleep and start out before dawn the next morning.

Back in Rio, a half dozen more rowdies had ridden in, on their way to the Seven Slash Ranch. They reined up in front of the saloon and swung down from the saddle, trail weary from a long day's ride. A whiskey would taste good.

"Keep movin', boys," the voice from behind them said.

They turned, and what they saw chilled them right down to their dirty socks. Louis Longmont, Cotton Pickens, Johnny North, and Earl Sutcliffe stood in the now quieted street, all of them with sawed-off shotguns in their hands. To a man they kept their hands very still.

"We just wanted to buy a drink of whiskey, Earl," John Seale said.

"You won't buy it here. None of you. Ride on to the Seven Slash if you want a drink."

"How'd you know? . . ." Mason Wright cut that off in mid-sentence. But it was too late; he'd tipped his hand and he knew it.

The others gave him dirty looks.

"Pack it in, Louis," Frankie Deevers said, looking at the millionaire gambler. "If you don't, you're gonna lose this pot. Believe me."

Louis smiled. "And who says life is not a game of chance, eh, Frankie?"

"Put them Greeners down, and we'll take you all right here and right now," a gunny snarled at Louis.

"Now, now, Willis," Louis said. "You know how talking strains your brain."

Larry chose that time to step out of the saloon/hotel for a breath of fresh air. The beery, sweaty odor from those unwashed cretins in the bar had drifted up to his room and was making him nauseated. But Larry was wising up to the West and after giving the group in the street a quick look, he moved down the boardwalk, well out of the way.

"Longmont," Willis said. "I ain't never liked you. You got a smart damn mouth hooked to your face. I've always heard how bad you was, but I'm from Missouri, and I gotta be showed. So why don't you just show me?"

Louis lowered the shotgun and leaned it against a water trough. He swept back his coat and said, "Any time you're ready, Willis."

Johnny, Earl, and Cotton backed off, still holding the express guns up and pointed at the gunnies.

"You can take him, Willis," Frankie said. "He's all showboat; that's all he is."

"A hundred dollars says he can't." Louis smiled the words.

"You got a bet, gambler!"

Willis made his play. Louis shot him just as the man cleared leather, the slug knocking him back on the steps leading up to the boardwalk. Willis lifted his gun and Louis plugged him again. Bright crimson dotted his dirty white shirt.

"You dirty son!" Willis gasped, still trying to jack back the hammer of his .45.

His friends desperately wanted to get into the fray, but the muzzles of those sawed-offs were just too formidable to breach.

"I can still do it!" Willis said, his blood staining his lips. He cocked his .45 and lifted it.

Louis shot him a third time, this time placing his shot with care. A blue-black hole appeared in the center of Willis' head. He died with his mouth and his eyes wide open.

"You owe me a hundred dollars," Louis said, looking at Frankie.

"I'll pay you," Frankie said through tight lips.

A young gunny who had ridden in with the hardcases and had not been recognized by any of the lawmen asked, "Is Jensen faster than you?"

"Oh, yes," Louis told him. "Smoke Jensen is the fastest man alive."

The young gunny took off his gun belt and looped it on the saddle horn. "If it's all right with you boys, I'll just have me one drink to cut the dust, a bite to eat at that cafe over yonder, and then I'll ride out of town. Not in the direction of the Seven Slash."

"You yellow pup!" Mason Wright told him. "I knowed you didn't have no good sand bottom to you."

"Shut up, Mason," Earl said. "The boy is showing uncommonly good sense." He looked at the young man. "Go have your drink and something to eat."

"Thank you kindly, sir." The rider walked up the steps and entered the barroom, the batwings slapping the air behind him.

Louis walked to Frankie. "A hundred dollars, Frankie. Greenbacks or gold."

Frankie paid him. "Your day's comin', Louis. You just remember that."

"If it comes from the likes of you, Frankie, it'll come from the back." Frankie flushed deeply. "Because you don't have the courage to face me eye to eye, with knife or gun or even fists, for that matter." Louis was a highly skilled boxer, and Frankie knew it.

"We'll see, Louis. We'll see."

"How about now, Frankie?" The gambler laid down the challenge. "You want to bet your life?"

"Let's go, Frankie," Mason urged him. "We can deal with this bunch later."

Incredible! Larry thought. The man is a millionaire and is risking his life in a dirty street of a backwater town. I do not understand these men and their loyalty to someone of Smoke Jensen's dubious character.

The gunhands rode out of town, leaving Willis' body still sprawled on the steps of the saloon. Muckelmort and the undertaker came running over, squabbling at each other.

"Get a good night's rest, Smoke," Johnny North muttered, looking at the darkening shapes of the mountains all around the little town. "There's gonna be hell to pay in the morning, I'm thinkin'."

14

The body of Willis was toted off—Muckelmort and the undertaker would go through his pockets to determine the elaborateness of the funeral—and the town began once more coming back to life as darkness settled in. The saloon was doing more business than it could handle, and the owner actually wished the other saloons would hurry up and get their board floors down and the canvas sides and roof up to take some of the pressure off his place.

Louis volunteered to take the first shift, and the others went to bed early—they each would do a four-hour shift.

In the mountains, the outlaws slept fitfully, not knowing when or even if Smoke Jensen or that old warhorse Charlie Starr would strike.

Charlie and Smoke, camped miles apart, slept well and awakened refreshed. They rolled their ground sheets and bedding, boiled their coffee and fried their bacon, then checked their guns and made ready for another day.

The members of Lee Slater's gang, their size now cut by three more, were quiet as they fixed their breakfast and drank their coffee. Taylor and Bud had ridden in during the early evening, and Taylor's condition had both depressed and angered the outlaws. His legs were swollen badly, and the man had slipped into a coma as blood poisoning was rapidly taking his life.

"That there's the most horriblest-lookin' thing I ever did see," Woody commented, looking at Taylor. "Smoke Jensen don't fight fair a-tall."

"My ass hurts!" Bud squalled.

"Pour some more horse liniment on it," Lee told a man.

Bud really took to squalling when the horse medicine hit the raw wounds. Everyone was glad when he passed out from the pain and the hollering stopped.

The men mounted up and pulled out, a silent and sullen group of no-goods.

"How long do we intend to remain here?" Albert asked Mills, over breakfast.

"Until we come up with a plan to capture Smoke Jensen," the senior U.S. Marshal said. "Anybody got one?"

No one did.

"Pass the beans," Mills said.

Back in Washington, D.C., the chief of the U.S. Marshal's Service looked across his desk at a group of senators. The senators were very unhappy.

"Smoke Jensen is a national hero," one senator said. "He's had books and plays written about him. School children worship him, and women around the nation love him for the family man he is. The telegrams I'm receiving from people tell me they don't believe these murder warrants are valid. I want your opinion on this matter, and I want it right now."

Without hesitation, the man said, "I don't believe the

charges would stick for a minute in a court of law. But a federal judge signed them, and we have to serve them." He smiled. "But the information I'm receiving indicates that our people out West are not at all eager to arrest Smoke Jensen." He lifted a wire from Mills Walsdorf. "They have, shall we say, dropped out of sight for a time."

"Then the Marshal's Service is out of the picture?" another senator questioned.

"For all intents and purposes, yes."

The senator lifted a local newspaper. "What about these hundreds of bounty hunters chasing Jensen?"

The marshal shook his head. "You know how that rag tends to blow things all out of proportion. The reporter they sent out there to cover this story wouldn't know a bounty hunter from a cigar store Indian. He's never been west of the Mississippi River in his entire life . . . until now."

Another senator lifted a New York City newspaper and started to speak. The marshal waved him silent. "That paper is even worse. Smoke Jensen is probably up against a hundred people . . ."

"A hundred?" a senator yelled. "But he's just one man."

The marshal smiled. "You ever seen Smoke Jensen, sir?"

"No, I have not."

"I have. One time about ten years ago when I was working out West. Three men jumped him in a bar in Colorado. When the dust settled, two of those men were dead and the third was dying. Smoke was leaning up against the bar, both hands filled with .44s. He holstered his guns, drank his beer, fixed him a sandwich, and went across the street to his hotel room for a night's sleep. I'm not saying he can pull this thing off and come out of it without taking some lead, but if anyone can do it, Smoke Jensen can. I can wish him well. But other than that, my hands are tied until some other federal judge overrides those warrants."

"Judge Richards has left town on a vacation," a senator said. "He'll be back in two weeks, so his office told me."

"He'd better stay gone," the marshal said. " 'Cause when Smoke comes down from those mountains, I got me a hunch he's Washington bound with a killin' on his mind."

"Well, now!" another senator puffed up. "We certainly can't allow that."

The marshal smiled. "You gonna be the one to tell Jensen that, sir?"

The senator looked as though he wished the chair would swallow him up.

Smoke released his hold, and the thick springy branch struck its target with several hundred pounds of impacting force. The outlaw was knocked from the saddle, his nose flattened and his jaw busted. He hit the ground and did not move. Smoke led the horse into the timber, took the food packets from the saddlebags, and then stripped saddle and bridle from the animal and turned it loose.

Smoke faded back into the heavy timber at the sounds of approaching horses.

"Good God!" a man's voice drifted through the brush and timber. "Look at Dewey, would you?"

"What the hell hit him?" another asked. "His entar face is smashed in."

"Where's his horse?" another asked. "We got to get him to a doctor."

"Doctor?" yet another questioned. "Hell, there ain't a doctor within fifty miles of here. See if you can get him awake and find out what happened. Damn, his face is ruint!"

"I bet it was that damn Jensen," an unshaven and smelly outlaw said. "We get our hands on him, let's see how long we can keep him alive."

"Yeah," another agreed. "We'll skin him alive."

Smoke shot the one who favored skinning slap out of the saddle, putting a .44-40 slug into his chest and twisting him around. The man fell and the frightened horse took off, dragging the dying outlaw along the rocks in the game trail.

"Get into cover!" Horton yelled, just as Smoke fired again.

Horton was turning in the saddle, and the bullet missed him, striking a horse in the head and killing it instantly. The animal dropped, pinning its rider.

"My leg!" the rider screamed. "It's busted. Oh, God, somebody help me."

Gooden ran to help his buddy, and Smoke drilled him, the slug smashing into the man's side and turning him around like a spinning top. Gooden fell on top of the dead horse, and Cates screamed as the added weight shot pain through his shattered leg.

Horton and Max put the spurs to their horses and got the hell out of there, leaving their dead and wounded behind. Smoke slipped back into the timber.

The screaming and calling out for help from Gooden and Cates were soon lost in the ravines and deep timber of the lonesome. Dewey lay on the trail, still unconscious.

Smoke seemed to vanish. But even as he made his way through the thick brush and timber, he knew he had been very lucky so far. He fully understood that there was no way he was going to fight a hundred of the enemy without taking lead at some point of the chase and hunt.

He just didn't know when.

Lee and his bunch muscled the dead horse off Cates and to a man grimaced at the sight of his broken and mangled leg.

"We got to set and splint it," Curly said. "Anybody got any whiskey?"

A bottle was handed to him. Curly gave the bottle to Cates. "Get drunk, Cates. 'Cause this is gonna hurt."

Cates screamed until he passed out from the pain.

Gooden was not hurt bad, just painfully, the slug passing through and exiting out the fleshy part of his side. Dewey's face was a torn, mangled mess. He was missing teeth, both eyes were swollen shut and blackened with bruises, and his nose and jaw were shattered.

"We got to get 'em, boss," Boots said. "Both Jensen and that old coot, Charlie Starr. This is gettin' personal with me now. Me and Neal go way back together."

"What you got in mind? I'm damn shore open to suggestions."

"I go in after him on foot. Hell, he can hear horses comin' in from a long ways off. My daddy was a trapper and a hunter up in Northwest Territories. I can Injun with the best of them."

Lee shook his head. "I like the idea, but two would be better than one. You might get him in a cross fire."

"I'll go with him," Harry Jennings volunteered. "I'd like to skin that damn Jensen alive."

Both Jennings and Boots were old hands in the timber, and they carried moccasins in their saddlebags. They left behind boots and spurs, took two days' provisions, and struck out, following the very faint trail that almost anyone leaves in the brush: bent-down blades of grass, a broken twig or lower limb from a scrub tree, a heel print in damp earth.

"He ain't that far ahead of us," Boots whispered, after having lost the trail at mid-morning and then picking it up a few minutes later. Boots was a thieving, murdering no-account through and through, but he was just about as good a trailsman as Smoke. "Grass hadn't started springin' back yet. No talkin' from now on—he's close. Real close. Come on."

Smoke had watched his back trail. He had felt in the back of his mind that sooner or later somebody would try him on foot. Leaving his pack on the ground in some brush, he climbed a tall tree and began scanning his back trail with his field glasses. On his second sweep he caught the two men as they skirted a small meadow, staying near the timber.

Smoke backtracked and left a trail, not a too obvious one, for that would be a dead giveaway, but a trail a skilled woodsman would pick up. He had a hunch those two men behind him were very good in the woods, for he hadn't been leaving much of a trail for anyone to follow.

Back at a narrow point in the game trail, he quickly rigged a swing trap, using a young sapling about as big around as his wrist. The shadowy brush-covered bend in the trail should keep even the most skilled eyes from seeing the piece of dirt-rubbed rawhide he'd placed as the trip.

Smoke carefully backed off about twenty yards and bellied down against the cool earth under some foliage and took a sip of water from his canteen. Tell the truth, he was grateful for the time to rest.

"Pssttt!" He heard the call from one of the men.

He could not yet see them, but they were very near.

Stay on the trail, boys, he silently wished. Just stay on the trail. Do that, and I'll soon have just one to contend with.

Jennings eased forward, his smile savage as he saw the just crushed foliage on the trail. He touched it; it was very fresh. Smoke Jensen was only minutes ahead of them. Just minutes away from being dead meat, and Jennings and Boots would be thousands of dollars richer.

His left boot stepped over the trip; the right toe of his boot snagged it. Jennings experienced a savage blow in his belly, just below the V of the rib cage. Then the pain hit him. The most hideous pain he had ever experienced in his life. He forced his eyes to look down. He screamed at the sight.

A stake had been rawhided to the sapling. He had tripped a wire or something that had released the booby trap. The stake was now buried in his belly, his blood gushing out.

"Jesus God!" Boots whispered as he crept around the dark trail and saw what Smoke Jensen had done.

"Oh, my Lord!" Jennings wailed. "I cain't stand the pain. Shoot me, Boots. Shoot me!"

"Yeah," Smoke's voice came out of the thick vegetation beside the trail. "Shoot him, Boots."

"You son of a bitch!" Boots yelled, dropping to his knees on the old trail. "You ain't no decent human bein'. This ain't fightin' fair a-tall."

Smoke laughed at the protestations of the outlaw/murderer/rapist. His laughter was taunting.

Jennings' screaming was a frightful thing to hear. He stood in the center of the game trail, afraid to move, both hands clutching the bloody end of the stake.

Smoke tossed a stick to his right. As soon as the stick hit the ground, Boots's rifle barked three times, as fast as he could work the lever.

Smoke laughed at his efforts.

Boots cussed Smoke. Called him every ugly and profane and insulting name he could think of, anything to draw the man out where he could get a clear shot at him.

Nothing worked.

"You ain't got no right to do this!" Boots yelled. "This ain't the way it's supposed to be."

"Jesus Christ, Boots," Jennings moaned. "You got to help me. I cain't stand no more of this."

Boots thought hard for a moment. He knew there was nothing he could do for Jennings. He was dying before his eyes. Not even a doctor right now could save him. Blood was dripping from Jennings' lips; that told Boots the stake had rammed right through the man's stomach. The point of the stake was sticking out the man's back.

Jennings died before Boots' eyes. The man's legs were spread wide, and both hands held on to the end of the stake. The thick sapling kept him in an upright position.

Boots didn't know what the hell to do. He knew that Smoke was over yonder, just ahead and to his right . . . at least the last time he'd laughed he was. But the way the man moved, hell, he might be anywhere by now.

Boots got down on his belly and started crawling away from the bloody scene. He was scared; he wasn't ashamed to admit it. A thrown stick landed just a few inches from his nose, and Boots almost crapped his long-handles.

"Wrong way, Bootsie," Smoke called.

"Stand up and fight me like a man, goddamn you!" Boots yelled. "Give me a chance."

"The same kind of chance you gave those little girls you raped and tortured and scalped and killed, Bootsie?"

"I didn't scalp nobody! That was Dolp what done that. And you done kilt him."

"I'm going to kill you, too, Bootsie."

"I surrender!" Boots shouted. "I give up. You got to take me in for a trial. That's the legal way."

"I'm a wanted man, Bootsie," Smoke said with a chuckle. "I've got murder warrants out on me. That's why you boys are chasing me. To collect those thousands of dollars. Now how in the hell can you surrender to me?"

Boots silently cursed. Didn't do no good to cuss out loud. Jensen wasn't gonna be rattled by that. Boots knew he was caught between a rock and a hard place. He could shuck his guns and stand up, his hands in the air. But as sure as he done that, Jensen would probably gut-shoot him. He knew how Jensen felt about criminals.

He was a thug and a punk and a lot of other sorry-assed things—he knew that, wasn't no point in makin' excuses for what he'd done—but Boots was a realist, too. He knew damn well he was a dead man any way it went. "I'm a-gonna stand up, Jensen," he called. "My rifle's on the ground. My gun's in leather. We'll fight this out man to man. I'll . . ."

He screamed in fright as a hard hand closed around one ankle and jerked just as he was standing up. Boots hit the ground, belly-down, knocking the breath from him. Something with the strength of a bear flipped him over and tore the gun belt from his waist. He watched belt and guns go sailing into the woods.

He looked up into the cold brown eyes of Smoke Jensen. God, the man was big.

"Get up," Smoke told him.

Boots crawled to his moccasins and watched as Smoke smiled at him and lifted his hands, clenching them into big leather-gloved fists. Boots grinned. Bare-knuckle, stomp and kick fighting was something he liked. He might have a chance after all.

"Okay, Jensen. Now you're playin' my game. I'm a-gonna stomp you into a greasy puddle."

Smoke hit him flush in the mouth and knocked him up against the bloody body of Jennings. Boots recoiled in horror and lunged at Smoke, both fists flailing the air.

Smoke hit him with a combination left and right that staggered the outlaw and pulped his already split lips. Boots shook his head and tried to clear it. But Smoke pressed him hard, not giving him a chance to do anything except try his best to cover up.

Boots held his fists in front of his face. Smoke hammered at his belly with sledgehammer blows. Boots felt ribs crack and knew that Jensen was going to beat him to death. He tried to run. Smoke grabbed him by his dirty shirt collar and threw him back onto the trail.

"Get up and fight, you yellow bastard," Smoke told him.

Boots crawled to his feet, wondering if Smoke was going to kick him. That's what he would have done if it had been Jensen on the ground. He started to raise his fists, and Smoke drove a right through his guard and flattened his nose. Blood and snot flew from his busted snout, and Boots backed up against a tree as his eyes watered and his vision turned misty.

He heard Smoke say, "This is for those little girls back on

the trail, Boots. For that poor woman and that man you sorry lumps of shit used for target practice."

Pain exploded in wild bursts in Boots' chest and belly and sides as Jensen pounded him unmercifully. Ribs popped and splintered like toothpicks. The last thing Boots would remember for a while was those terrible cold eyes of Smoke Jensen.

He knew then why people called him the Last Mountain Man.

15

Al Martine and his bunch came upon Jennings and Boots in the midafternoon. Several of the outlaws lost their lunch when they found them.

Boots screamed hideously when the outlaws tried to move him.

"Jensen busted all his ribs," Al said, a coldness touching his guts. "Them ribs is probably splintered into his innards." He looked down at Boots. "There ain't nothin' we can do for you, Boots."

"Shoot me," Boots whispered.

Al just looked at him. "We'll get Jensen for you, Boots. That's a promise." Boots whispered something. "I can't hear you, Boots. What'd you say?"

"Give it up," Boots said through his pain. "Leave the gang. Leave the mountains. Go to farmin', or something. If you're gonna outlaw, git a thousand miles away from Jensen. He's a devil. Leave him alone."

"You don't mean that?" Zack said. "That's just your pain talkin'."

"Don't you want revenge?" Lopez asked.

Boots grinned, a bloody curving of the lips. "Hell, boys. That ain't gonna do me no good. I'm dead." And he died.

Since none of them had shovels, they wrapped Boots Pierson and Harry Jennings in their blankets and covered them with branches. None of them had a Bible either. The outlaws just stood around and looked at each other for a time. The gang of young punks rode up just as the last branch was put on the pile.

"Taylor's dead," Pecos announced. "Blood poisonin' kilt him, I reckon."

"This ain't workin' out like we planned, Al," Crown said. "This was supposed to be an easy hunt. Ever' day we're losin' two, three men to Jensen or Charlie Starr. Another week and there ain't gonna be none of us left."

"Yeah," Lopez said. "And Jensen could be Injunin' up on us right now."

All of them quickly found their mounts and hauled out of there. They rode until they came upon Ray's group and brought them up to date.

"A stake through his belly?" Keno said, his voice filled with horror. He shuddered. "Jesus, man, that ain't no fair way to fight no fight."

Concho said, "Jensen ain't playin' by no rule book."

"Did we ever?" Pedro asked softly in an accented voice. "Unlike the rules set forth in law books and courts of formal law, Jensen is giving us what we have given so many other people over the years. The way I see it, there is only two things we can do: continue the hunt until we kill Jensen or he kills us, or turn tail and run away."

"I ain't runnin' from Jensen," the young punk Concho said, swelling out his chest. "I think I can take him in a stand-up shoot-out."

"You are a fool," Lopez told him bluntly. "I have seen

Jensen work. He is smooth, my young friend, and very, very quick. His draw is a blur that the eyes cannot catch."

"I'm faster," Concho said.

Lopez shook his head and said no more. Let the young punk find out for himself, he thought. When he challenges Smoke Jensen, he will have a few seconds of life left him to ponder his mistakes as the gunsmoke clears, and he rides to Hell.

"It'll be dark in a few hours," Al said, looking up at the sky. "And it's gonna rain. Let's get back to the base camp and tell Lee what happened."

Smoke sat in his lean-to and drank his coffee and ate his early supper. He felt that outlaws being what they were, he would be reasonably safe from search in the cold, pouring rain. They would be too busy staying dry to look for him.

But he still carefully put out his fire before he rolled up in his blankets and closed his eyes.

Since Mills and his marshals were going to stay a spell where they were, they made their camp a secure and snug one, using canvas and limbs. The quarters were close together, with a cooking area just in front, easily accessible to all.

"This should bring the killing to a halt for a time," Mills said, looking out at the driving rain. "Maybe" he added. "I don't approve of what Smoke is doing, but I understand why he's doing it."

"There is a strange code out here," Albert said. "One that I'm sure our fathers swore to—at least to some degree."

"Or swore at," Sharp said.

"Probably a little of both." Harold poured a cup of coffee and stared out at the silver-streaked gloom of late afternoon.

"Even after all this is said and done," Winston said, "we're still going to have to enforce the law once the warrants you requested on all those outlaws arrive."

"Yes," Mills said. "The San Francisco office is supposed to be getting them to Denver by train, then stagecoach to Rio. I requested them to be posted to the local marshal's office. I'll ride into town in a few days and check. By that time, I hope all this . . . nonsense concerning Smoke will be over."

The deputy U.S. Marshals looked at each other. They hoped the same thing. None of them wanted to confront Smoke Jensen with an arrest warrant. None of them knew if they would even try to do that. Aside from the fact that he was the most famous gunslinger in the West, they all genuinely liked the man.

Most of the miners within a forty-mile radius of the fight had left the mountains and descended on Rio. They didn't want to be caught up in the middle when the lead started flying. As it was, many of them had been close enough to hear the shots from Smoke's and Charlie's guns. And from the guns of the outlaws.

Made a man plumb edgy.

Louis' saloon and gambling hall had been erected—due in no small part to the fact that Louis paid three times what others did for workmen. A smaller building had been built in the rear; this housed the kitchen, living quarters, and a privy attached to the building for maximum comfort and privacy. Cotton was on duty on the streets, and Louis and Johnny sat in the rear of the big wood and canvas saloon and talked in as low tones as the drumming of the rain overhead would permit. Earl was out of town.

"You heard that miner over yonder, Louis," Johnny said, cutting his eyes to a miner who had just come into town and was now sucking on a mug of beer. "What'd you think?"

"As near as I can figure—discounting the inevitable exaggeration—Smoke and Charlie have killed seven or eight of Slater's gang, and a couple of bounty hunters. This storm will probably blow out of here sometime tonight—it's raining too hard to keep this up long—so the hunt will resume tomorrow. Slater has to be getting frustrated, and frustration leads to desperate and careless acts. Smoke is fighting several fronts, and using varying tactics, including guerrilla warfare. Guerrilla warfare is a nasty business. It's demoralizing for those on the receiving end of it. Slater's people and the bounty hunters will be shooting at shadows from now on. And it's going to be just as dangerous in those mountains for Smoke and Charlie as it is for the outlaws and bounty hunters. Smoke will take some lead in this fight, my friend. I don't see how he can avoid it, and I would imagine he has already mentally prepared himself for it."

Johnny listened to the rain beat against the canvas for a moment. "Seems like trouble has been on Smoke's back trail nearabouts all his life. Ever since I've known him—and years before that—all Smoke wanted was to be left alone to run his ranch, love his wife and kids, and live in peace. He changed his name and hung up his guns for several years, but no man should have to do that. That just isn't right. He never wanted the reputation of gunfighter. Never got a dime out of any of them penny dreadful books or plays about him. He didn't want the money. But he's a man that won't take no pushin'. Man pushes Smoke, Smoke'll push back twice as hard as he got. Them mountains best be cleaned good by this rain, 'cause come the mornin', they're gonna run red with outlaw blood."

The terrible storm raged over the mountains and then trekked east. Before dawn, Smoke was wide awake and looking at a star-filled sky. It was still dark when he broke camp, picked up his heavy pack, and headed down out of the high lonesome to face the ever-growing numbers of bounty hunters and the Lee Slater gang.

"Come on, boys," he muttered to the chattering squirrels and the singing birds. "Let's get this over with. I want to get back to Sally and the Sugarloaf."

A rifle cracked and bark stung the side of his face. Smoke hit the ground, struggled out of his pack, and wormed his way forward, the .44-40 cradled in his arms.

"I seen him go down!" a man yelled.

"Down is one thing," another voice was added. "Out is another. Jensen's hard to kill."

"Move out," a third voice ordered. "But watch it. He's tricky as a snake."

Three men, Smoke thought. Bounty hunters or outlaws? He didn't know. He didn't really care. Man comes after another man for no valid reason, that first man better be ready to understand that death is walking right along beside him.

"Where is the bastard?" the shout echoed through the lushness of timber.

Smoke saw a flash of color from a red-and-white-checkered shirt, and put a .44-40 slug in it. The man screamed and went down, kicking and clawing. Lead sang around Smoke's position, whining and howling as fast as the hunters could work the levers on their rifles. Smoke stayed low, and the lead sailed harmlessly over his head.

"Oh God!" the wounded man moaned. "My shoulder's broke. I can't move my arm."

Smoke watched as a hand reached up and shook a bush, trying to draw his fire. He waited. The hand reached up again and exposed a forearm. Smoke shattered the arm. The man screamed in pain. Smoke fired again, and the man's screaming choked down to silence.

"Back off, John," a voice called. "He's got the upper hand now."

"What about Ned?" a pain-filled voice called.

"Ned's luck ran out."

Ned, Smoke thought. Ned Mallory, probably. A bounty hunter from down New Mexico way. He lay still and listened to the two men back off and move through the brush. After a few minutes, he heard their horses' hooves fade away. He made his way to Ned and stood over the dead man. His first slug had broken the man's forearm; the second slug had taken him in the throat. It had not been a very pleasant way to die. But what way is?

Smoke refilled his .44 loops with the dead man's cartridges and left him where he lay. He was not being unnecessarily callous; this was war, and war is not nice any way one chooses to cut it up.

He figured the shots would draw a crowd, and he headed away from that location, but every direction he walked, he saw riders coming before they saw him.

Smoke cussed under his breath. "All right," he muttered. "If this is the way it's going to be, all bets are off. I can't fight any other way."

He lifted his .44-40 and blew a man out of the saddle, the slug taking him in the center of his chest.

"Over yonder!" another man yelled, pointing, and Smoke sighted him in. The man moved just as he squeezed the trigger, and that saved his life, the slug hitting his shoulder instead of his chest. The rider managed to stay in the saddle, but he was out of this hunt, his arms dangling uselessly by his sides.

A round stung Smoke's shoulder, drawing blood, and another just missed his head. Smoke emptied another saddle, the rider pitched forward, his boot hanging in the stirrup. The horse ran off, dragging the manhunter.

Smoke slipped back into the timber and jogged for several hundred yards before he was forced to stop to catch his breath. He chose a spot where his back and his left flank would be protected and rested. He could hear the sounds of horses laboring up the grade.

"He's trapped!" a man shouted. "We got him now, boys. Let's go." He forced his tired horse up the slope, and Smoke sighted him in, squeezed the trigger, and relieved the nearly exhausted animal of its burden. The hunter bounced on the ground and then lay still.

Smoke drank some water and ate a piece of dry bread and waited. He was in a good spot and thought he saw a way out of it should it come to that. But he didn't think it would. The manhunters would soon realize that the advantage was all his—this time—and probably back off.

After a few minutes, a shout rang up the slope. "Give it up, Jensen! They's a hundred men ringin' this range. You can't get out. Come on down, and we'll take you in alive for trial."

"Sure you will," Smoke muttered.

A man deliberately ran from his cover for a short distance, exposing himself for no more than two or three seconds.

"Fool's play, boys," Smoke whispered. "You must have cut your teeth on amateurs."

He held his fire.

The manhunters began firing indiscriminately, the slugs howling around the rocks and trees. They were trying for a ricochet, not knowing that Smoke had taken that into consideration when he chose the spot to hole up. They wasted a lot of lead and hit nothing.

Another group rode in, and the men began arguing among themselves. Smoke shouted, "Why don't you boys try for the Slater gang? The mountains are full of them. There's about fifty of them, and they're all wanted by the law."

"Nickel and dime re-wards, Jensen," he was told. "You're worth a lot more."

"Look around you," Smoke verbally pointed out. "The

ground is covered with the blood of those who thought the same thing. Think about it."

The bounty hunters fell silent as some of them did just that.

Rested, Smoke took that time to slip through the rocks and make his way around his left flank. But he had to leave his heavy pack, taking with him only what he absolutely needed for survival. He packed that in his bedroll and groundsheet, tied it tight, secured it over one shoulder, and Injuned his way out of the rocks.

When he had worked his way several hundred yards above his last location, he paused and looked down. The sight did not fill him with joy. There were at least thirty men in position, grouped in a semicircle, around where the man-hunters believed him to be.

A grim smile curved his lips. He took four sticks of dynamite from his roll and planted them under four huge boulders, making each fuse slightly longer than the other. Then he lit the fuses and got the hell gone from there.

The explosives moved three of the huge boulders, sending them cascading down the mountain, picking up small boulders as they tumbled. Even from his high-up location, he could hear the screaming of the men as the boulders, large and small, crushed legs and arms and sent the man-hunters scrambling for cover.

"You opened this dance, boys," he said. "Now it's time to pay the band."

"Good God!" Cotton said, as the first of the shot-up and avalanche victims came limping and staggering back into town.

Johnny stepped out into the muddy street and halted the parade of wounded. "Where'd you boys tangle with Smoke Jensen?"

A man with a bloody bandage tied around his head said, "Just south of Del Norte Peak. They's a half a dozen men buried under the rocks. Jensen is a devil! He caved them rocks in on us deliberate."

"And I suppose you boys were just ridin' around up there takin' in all the scenery, huh?" Johnny said sarcastically.

The man didn't answer. But his eyes drifted to the badge on Johnny's chest. "You the law. I want to swear out a warrant agin Smoke Jensen."

Johnny laughed at him. "Move on, mister. There's a new doctor just hung out his sign down the street."

"You ain't much of a lawman," another bounty hunter sneered at him. "What's your name?" He spoke around a very badly swollen jaw.

"Johnny North."

The manhunter settled back in his saddle with a sigh and kept his mouth shut.

"Move on," Johnny repeated. "And don't cause any trouble in this town or you'll answer to me."

Cotton and Louis had stepped out, Louis out of his gambling house and Cotton out of the marshal's office, to stand on the boardwalk and watch the sorry-looking sight.

Cotton and Johnny joined Louis. "I count twelve in that bunch," Louis said. "Did he say there were half a dozen buried under rocks?"

"Yeah. Smoke musta started a rock slide. Earl said he took a case of dynamite with him. When's Earl gettin' back? I ain't seen him since he rode up to the county seat."

"Today, I would imagine. He said he'd be gone three days. He was going to send some wires. I don't know to whom, but I suspect they concern Smoke."

"You think he really knows the President of the U-nited States?" Cotton asked.

"Oh, he probably does." Louis smiled. "I do."

* * *

Smoke reared up from behind the man, jerked the rider off his horse, and slammed him onto the ground. He hit him three times. Three short, vicious right-hand blows that crossed the man's eyes, knocked out several teeth, and left the rider unconscious. Smoke knew the guy slightly. Name of Curt South. He was from Utah, Smoke remembered. A sometimes cowboy, sometimes bounty hunter, sometimes cattle thief, and all around jerk. He released Curt's shirt, and the man fell to the ground, on his back, unconscious. Smoke left him where he lay and swung into the saddle. The stirrups were set too short, but he didn't intend to keep the horse long.

Smoke headed across country, for the deep timber between Bennett Mountain and Silver Mountain. After a hard fifteen-minute ride, Smoke reined up and allowed the horse to blow while he inspected the bedroll and saddlebags. The blankets smelled really bad and had fleas hopping around them. He threw them away and kept the groundsheet and canvas shelter half. He found a side of bacon wrapped in heavy paper and some potatoes and half a loaf of bread that wasn't too stale. He smashed Curt's rifle against a rock and swung back into the saddle.

Minutes later, he came around a clump of trees and ran right into the outlaw Blackjack Simpson—literally running into him. The two horses collided on the narrow game trail and threw both Lee and Smoke to the ground, knocking the wind out of both of them. Blackjack came up to his knees first and tried to smash Smoke's head in with a rock. Smoke kicked him in the gut and sent the man sprawling.

Guns were forgotten as the two men stood in the narrow trail and slugged it out. Blackjack was unlike most gunmen in that he knew how to use his fists and enjoyed a good fight. He slammed a right against Smoke's head and tried to follow through with a left. Smoke grabbed the man's arm, turned, and threw him to the trail. Blackjack got to his feet, and Smoke busted his beak with a straight right that jarred the man right down to his muddy boots. The blow knocked him backward against a tree.

With the blood flowing from his broken nose, Blackjack came in, both fists swinging. Smoke hit him with a left-and-right combination that glazed the man's eyes and buckled his knees. Smoke followed through, seizing the advantage. He hammered at the man's belly with his big, work-hardened fists, the blows bringing grunts of pain from Blackjack and backing him up.

Smoke's boot struck a rock and threw him off balance. Blackjack grabbed a club from off the ground and tried to smash in Smoke's head. Smoke kicked him in the private parts, and Blackjack doubled over, gagging and puking from the boot to his groin.

Smoke grabbed up the broken limb and smacked Blackjack a good one on the side of his head. Blackjack hit the ground and didn't move.

Smoke took the man's guns and smashed them useless, then caught up with the spooked horse. He took Blackjack's .44-40 from his saddle boot and shucked out the ammo, adding that to his own supply. Then he smashed the rifle against a tree.

He knew he should kill Blackjack; the man was a murderer, rapist, bank robber, and anything else a body could name that was low-down and no-good.

But he just couldn't bring himself to shoot the man.

Trouble was, he didn't know what the hell to do with him.

"Can't do it, can you, Jensen?" Blackjack gasped out the words.

"Do what, Blackjack?" Smoke backed up and sat down on a fallen log.

"You can't shoot me, can you?"

"I'm not a murderer."

"That'll get you killed someday, Jensen." The man tried to get to his feet, and Smoke left the log and kicked him in the head.

Smoke took Blackjack's small poke of food from his saddle-bags, cut Blackjack's cinch strap and slapped the horse on the rump. He swung into his saddle and looked at the unconscious outlaw.

"I should kill you, Blackjack. But I just can't do it. If I did that, I'd be across the line and joined up with the likes of you. God forbid I should ever enjoy killing."

He rode into the timber, straight for trouble.

16

Those men who came into Rio thinking the hunt for Smoke Jensen would be no more than a lark took one last look at those manhunters who staggered out of the mountains and hauled their ashes out of the country.

With their departing, they left behind them only the hardcases of the bounty hunting profession. Men who gave no thought to a person's innocence or guilt. Men who were there only for the money.

"Amazing," Earl said, gazing at the ever-growing number of manhunters converging on the town. "The mountains are full of members of the Lee Slater gang—all with a price on their heads—and these dredges of society would willingly consort with them to get to Smoke."

"There isn't much to them," Louis agreed. "I've seen their kind all over the West. Most lawmen don't like them, and few decent members of society have anything more than contempt for them. But I suppose in some instances, they do provide a service for the common good."

"Name one," Johnny said sourly.

"I would be hard-pressed to do so," Louis admitted. He cut his eyes. "Well, now. Would you just look at this."

The men looked up the street. Luttie Charles and his crew were riding in, and his crew had swelled considerably. The men of the Seven Slash turned in toward the marshal's office, where Earl and the other "deputies" were standing on the boardwalk. The men sat their saddles and stared at the quartet.

"Loaded for bear," Cotton whispered, taking in the bulging saddlebags and bedrolls.

"Yeah," Johnny said. "I got a hunch this ain't no good news for Smoke."

"I am here to announce our intentions, gentlemen," Luttie said.

Earl stared at the man, saying nothing.

"Smoke Jensen is a wanted man, correct?" Luttie asked, his smile more a nasty smirk.

"That is, unfortunately, correct," the Englishman acknowledged.

"That being the case," Luttie said, "we have come to offer our services toward the cause of law and order."

"Like I said," Johnny whispered. "No good news for Smoke."

"We want this to be legal and aboveboard," Luttie said. "So we came to the appointed law first."

"Get to the point," Cotton said bluntly.

"We are going into the mountains to bring back the murderer Smoke Jensen," Luttie said around his smirky smile.

"Dead or alive," Jake said.

The Karl Brothers, Rod and Randy, giggled. Both of them were about four bricks shy of a load, and were men who enjoyed killing.

Johnny spat on the ground to show his contempt for the goofy pair.

Rod grinned at him. "If you wasn't wearin' that tin star, I'd call you out for that, North."

Johnny reached up, unpinned the badge, and put it in his pocket. "Then make your play, you stupid-lookin' punk."

"No!" Luttie's command was sharply given. "We have no quarrel with the law, and that's an order."

Rod relaxed and grinned at Johnny. "Some other time, North."

"I'm easy to find, goofy."

"Anything else you gentlemen need to know before we pull out?" Luttie asked.

"That about does it, I suppose," Earl told him.

"Ain't you lawmen gonna wish us luck?" One-Eyed Jake asked.

"Personally, I hope you fall off your horse and break your damn neck," Cotton told him.

"You ain't got no call to talk to me like that!" Jake protested.

"You wanna do something about it?" Cotton challenged.

"Let's ride, boys," Luttie said. "We got a killer to bring to justice."

"Maybe later," One-Eyed Jake said.

"Anytime," Cotton told him.

The Seven Slash crew and the hired guns who rode among them slopped out up the muddy street.

"Sixteen more after Smoke's hide." Johnny spoke the words bitterly. "Smoke's gonna need all the luck and skill he can muster to come out of this alive."

"How about them wires you sent, Earl?" Cotton asked.

Earl shook his head. "The Marshal's Service is out of it. But until a panel of federal judges can gather and review all the evidence against Smoke, the warrants stand."

"Damn!" Louis said.

"Quite," the Englishman said. "And Sheriff Silva said if

we went into the mountains to help Smoke, there would be warrants issued for us. He said he was sorry about that, but that was the way it had to be."

"I can understand that," Johnny said. "He's stickin' his neck out pretty far for Smoke now."

Louis looked toward the mountains. "We've all been concentrating on how Smoke is doing. I wonder how Sally is coping with all this?"

"Sally's gone!" Bountiful yelled, bringing her buggy to a dusty, sliding halt.

"What?" Sheriff Monte Carson jumped out of his chair. "What do the hands say?"

"I finally got one of them to talk. He said he took her down to the road day before yesterday, and she hailed the stage there. He said she had packed some riding britches in her trunk, along with a rifle and a pistol. She was riding the stage down to the railroad and taking a train from there. Train runs all the way through to the county seat. Lord, Lord, Monte, she's just about there by now. What are we going to do?"

Monte led her into his office and sat her down. Bountiful fanned herself vigorously. He got her a drink of water and sat down at his desk. "Nothin' we can do, Miss Bountiful. Sally's gone to stand by her man. And them damn outlaws and manhunters down yonder think they got trouble with Smoke. I feel sorry for them if they tangle with Miss Sally. You know she can shoot just like a man and has done so plenty of times. She's a crack shot with rifle and pistol. Smoke seen to that."

"I just feel terrible about this. I should have guessed something was up when I saw her oiling up that .44 the other day. But out here . . . well, we all keep guns at the ready."

"T'wasn't your fault, Miss Bountiful. She's doin' what she feels she has to do, is all." He took off his hat and wiped his forehead with a bandanna. "This situation is gettin' out of hand."

Lee Slater and his bunch came upon Blackjack just as he was getting back on his feet. The man's face was swollen from the kick he'd received from Smoke. That kick had put him out for nearly half an hour.

"Cut my cinch and smashed my guns," Blackjack mumbled. "I'm gonna kill that dirty bastard!"

"There's a lot of people been sayin' that," Ed told him. "So far the score is Jensen about fifteen and the other side zero. And we're the other side."

Someone rounded up a horse for Blackjack and loaned him a spare gun. Blackjack swung the horse's head.

"Where are you goin'!" Lee shouted.

"To kill Smoke Jensen," Blackjack snarled. "And this time I'm gonna do it."

Lee started to protest. Curt waved him silent. "Let him go. You know how he is. When he gets mad, he's crazy. Hell, we're better off without him until he cools down."

" 'Spose he gets to Jensen afore we do?" Ed asked.

"They'll be one less to share the re-ward money with," Curly said. "Blackjack ain't gonna take Jensen, 'lessen he shoots him in the back."

"Let's make some coffee," Ed suggested. "I could do me with some rest."

None among them had considered how, as wanted outlaws, they would collect any reward money should they manage to capture Smoke.

* * *

Nearly everyone on Main Street had seen the elegantly dressed lady step off the train and stroll to the hotel, a porter carrying her trunk. As soon as she signed her name, the desk clerk dispatched a boy to run and fetch the sheriff.

Sally had signed the register as "Mrs. Smoke Jensen."

Sheriff Silva was standing in the lobby, talking to several men, and he nearly swallowed his chewing tobacco when Sally walked down the stairs.

She was wearing cowboy boots and jeans—which she filled out to the point of causing the men's eyeballs to bug out—a denim shirt that fitted her quite nicely, too, and was carrying a leather jacket. She had a bandanna tied around her throat, and a low crowned, flat-brimmed hat on her head. She also wore a .44 belted around her waist and carried a short-barreled .44 carbine, a bandoleer of ammo slung around one shoulder.

"Jesus Christ, Missus Jensen!" Sheriff Silva hollered. "I mean, holy cow. What do you think you're gonna do?"

"Take a ride," Sally told him, and walked out the door.

Silva ran to catch up with her. "Now you just wait a minute, here, Missus Jensen. This ain't no fittin' country for a female to be a-traipsin' around in. Will you please slow down?"

Sally ignored that and kept right on walking at a rather brisk pace.

She turned into the general store and was uncommonly blunt with the man who owned the store. "I want provisions for five days, including food, coffee, pots and pans and eating utensils, blankets, groundsheets, and tent. And five boxes of .44s, too. Have them ready on a pack-frame in fifteen minutes. Have them loaded out back, please."

"Now you just hold up on that order, Henry," Sheriff Silva said.

"You'd better not cross me, Henry," Sally warned him, a

wicked glint in her eyes. "My name is Mrs. Smoke Jensen, and I can shoot damn near as well as my husband."

"Yes'um," Henry said. "I believe you, ma'am."

"And you"—Sally spun around to face the sheriff—"would be advised to keep your nose out of my business."

"Yes'um," Silva said glumly, and followed her to the livery.

Sally picked out a mean-eyed blue steel that bared its teeth when the man tried to put a rope around it. Sally walked out into the corral, talked to the big horse for a moment, and then led it back to the barn. She fed him a carrot and an apple she'd picked up at the store, and the horse was hers.

"That there's a stallion, ma'am!" Silva bellered. "He ain't been cut. You can't ride no stallion!"

"Get out of my way," she told him.

"It ain't decent, ma'am!"

"Shut up and take that pack animal around to the back of the store."

"Yes'um," Silva said. "Whatever you say, ma'am." While Sally was saddling up, he turned to the hostler. "Send a boy with a fast horse to Rio. Tell them deputies of mine down there that Sally Jensen is pullin' out within the hour and looks like she's plannin' on joinin' up with her husband. Tell them to do something. Anything!"

"Sheriff," the hostler said, horror in his voice. "Don't look. She's a-fixin' to ride that hoss astride!"

"Lord, have mercy! What's this world comin' to?"

"Looking for me, boys?" Smoke called.

Crocker and Graham spun around, dropping their coffee cups, and grabbing for iron.

But Smoke was not playing the gentleman's game. His hands were already filled with .44s. He began firing, firing and cocking with such speed the sounds seemed to be a continuous roll of deadly thunder. Crocker literally died on his feet, two slugs in his heart. Graham was turned completely around twice before he tumbled to the earth. He died with his eyes open, flat on his back and staring upward.

Smoke reloaded, listened for a moment, and then walked to the fire, eating the lunch and drinking the coffee the outlaws had fixed and no longer needed.

He drank the pot of coffee, kicked out the fire, and left his tired horse to roll and water and graze, throwing a saddle on a fresh horse that was tied to a picket pin. He took what was left of a chunk of stale bread, sopped out the grease in the frying pan to soften it up, and finished off his lunch.

He looked at Crocker and Graham. "Nothing personal, boys. You just took the wrong trail, that's all." He swung into the saddle and put the camp of the dead behind him. Ray's group came upon the bodies of Crocker and Graham and sat their horses for a time, looking around the silent camp.

"I'd like to think they et a good meal 'fore Jensen or that damned ol' Charlie Starr come up on them," Keno said. "But if I was to bet on it, I'd wager that Jensen kilt 'em and then sat down an' et their food." He shook his head. "We're gonna lose this fight, boys. Somebody is shore to get lead in Jensen, least the odds lean thataway, but in the end, we'll lose."

Sonny shook his head. "It just ain't possible what he's a-doin'. By rights, we should have kilt him the first day or two. This makes nearabouts ten of us he's kilt—and half a dozen or more bounty hunters—and we ain't got no clear shot at him yet. I just ain't likin' this, boys."

Jerry nodded his head in agreement. "I got me a bad feelin' in my guts about this fight. But, hell, way I see it, we ain't got no choice 'cept to go on with it."

Ray swung down from the saddle. "Let's give the boys a buryin'. Stoke up that far, McKay, make some coffee."

* * *

"We got no quarrel with you, Charlie," Luttie told the old gunfighter. "It's Jensen we're after."

Charlie had stepped out of the timber, blocking the trail. His hands were by his sides, by the butts of his guns, and his eyes were hard and unblinking. "You got a quarrel with Smoke, you got a quarrel with me. That's the way it is. So I hope you made your peace with God." He jerked iron and opened the dance.

Two of Luttie's hands went down before anyone could react to the sudden gunfire. Horses were rearing and screaming in fright; several of the riders were dumped from the saddle. Charlie shot Nick Johnson between the eyes, and he fell over against Luttie, knocking the man from the saddle and falling on top of him in the brush.

Charlie took a round in his side, flinched from the painful impact, jerked out two spare six-guns from behind his gun belt and kept on throwing lead.

A young hand who fancied himself a gunslick pulled iron and jacked the hammer back. One of Charlie's slugs caught him in the chest and knocked him to the ground. He died calling for his mother.

Charlie's left leg folded under him as a .45 hit him in the thigh. He went down rolling into the brush. Just as he got to his boots and staggered off into the timber, toward his horse, he turned and blew another of Luttie's hired guns out of the saddle. Ted Danforth took the slug in the belly and hit the ground. He died on his knees.

Charlie managed to get into the saddle and point his horse's head south, toward Rio.

"No need to chase after him, Luttie," Jake said, after the spooked and screaming horses had been settled down. "He's had it. I seen him take at least three slugs. He's dead in the saddle by now."

Luttie looked around him at the carnage. "That old bastard just jumped out and killed five of my men. I ain't believin' this!" He was rubbing the bump on his head where his noggin hit a rock. "I started out with sixteen top guns, and my people has been cut damn near a third in less than a minute and a half. Jesus Christ!"

"But now Smoke is alone up here," One-Eyed Jake pointed out.

"Wonderful," Luttie said sourly.

Blackjack reined up when he spotted the ground-reined horse. That wasn't the horse Smoke had been riding, but he could have changed horses somewhere along the way. Blackjack stepped down from the saddle and took cover behind a tree, his eyes sweeping the area in front of him. He should have been looking behind him.

Blackjack was so mad he wasn't thinking straight. His head ached where Smoke had kicked him, and his nose and mouth hurt, too. All he could think about was killing Smoke Jensen. And he didn't want to do it quick, neither. He wanted Jensen to suffer. He had plans for Smoke Jensen. Painful plans.

But a higher power had already checked off Blackjack's name in the book of life.

"You should have stayed where I left you, Blackjack," Smoke said from behind the outlaw.

Blackjack whirled around, a curse on his lips and his right hand filled with a .45. Smoke shot him twice, in the belly and the chest, as the .44 rose in recoil.

Blackjack sighed once and fell back against the tree he'd thought was giving him cover. The .45 fell from his numbed hand. "Damn you, Jensen!" he gasped.

"Sometimes the cards just don't fall right," Smoke told him.

The light was fading around Blackjack.

"Any family?" Smoke asked.

"None that would give a damn about me dyin'."

"Too bad."

"You're a . . . devil, Jensen! You musta . . . come here from somewhere's outta hell." His legs would no longer support him. He slumped to the ground.

Smoke kicked the .45 far from Blackjack's reach and walked toward his horse, reloading as he walked. Blackjack's voice stopped him.

"Yes?" he asked.

"Stay with me 'til I'm gone, Jensen—please?"

"All right," Smoke said.

Smoke walked to him, reached down, and took the .41 derringer Blackjack had slipped from behind his big silver belt buckle. Blackjack let his hand fall to his side.

"Damn you!" the outlaw moaned. "How'd you know?"

"I didn't. But people like you never change." He broke open the derringer and checked the loads. Full. He slipped the tiny gambler's backup behind his belt.

"I'll see you in hell, Jensen!"

"Maybe. I've done some things that probably qualify me for that place."

Blackjack fell over on his side. "We was all so shore about this. Fifty, sixty . . . of us. One of you. I just cain't understand it." He shuddered and grabbed the ground in his pain. "What is it that . . . makes you so damn hard to kill?"

"Maybe it's because I'm right, and you boys are wrong."

Blackjack laughed bitterly.

"You got any money you want me to give to a church or an orphanage, Blackjack?"

Blackjack sneered past bloody lips and said some pretty terrible things about churches, orphans, the public in general and Smoke in particular.

He died with a curse on his lips.

"I don't understand it either, Blackjack," Smoke said to the dead outlaw.

Smoke stripped the saddle and bridle from Blackjack's horse and turned the gelding loose. "Run free for a time, boy. You earned it."

The last mountain man walked to his horse and swung into the saddle. "Let's go meet what I was born to meet, boy," he said. "No point in prolonging this."

17

"What?" Earl almost lost his English cool.

"That's what the sheriff said," the young man told him. "Missus Sally Jensen is headin' into the mountains."

Louis took off his badge and handed it to Earl. "I hereby resign my commission," he told him. "The rest of you stay here. I've got to get into the mountains and head her off."

"Look!" a citizen said, pointing up the muddy street.

"That's Charlie!" Johnny shouted, running toward the man who appeared to be unconscious in the saddle.

"Get the doctor!" Cotton yelled, running after Johnny.

They gently took Charlie from the blood-soaked saddle and laid him down on the boardwalk. Charlie's eyes fluttered open. "I'm hard-hit, boys."

"You'll make it, you old warhoss," Johnny told him.

"I put about five or six of 'em down 'fore they plugged me," the old gunfighter said. "Seven Slash bunch."

"Don't talk, Charlie," Lilly LaFevere said, kneeling down beside him.

"Hello, baby." Charlie grinned up at her. "I ain't seen you in ten years."

"Nine," she corrected him. "We was down on the border. Now hush your mouth."

"Tired," Charlie whispered. "Awful tired."

"Take him to my quarters and put him in my bed," Lilly told the men. "Move him gentlelike. I count three bullet holes in his ornery old hide." She looked around her. "Where's that goddamn sawbones?"

"He's on the way," a citizen said. "Is that really Charlie Starr?"

"Yeah," Lilly said. "Now get the hell outta the way and give the man room to breathe."

"I'm gone," Louis said. "See you boys later."

"You got enough grub?" Cotton asked.

"They'll be food in the saddlebags of the outlaws," Louis told him. "I'll have a week's supply fifteen minutes after I hit the mountains."

He lifted the reins and was gone.

With his knife and strips of rawhide, Smoke made a pack out of two saddlebags, then carefully repacked all the supplies he'd taken from several dead men. He had a good five days' food and plenty of ammo.

He tried not to think about when his luck was going to run out.

But he knew it would, sooner or later. The odds were just too great against him.

He was only a few miles away from where he'd left his horses—as the crow flies—but he didn't want to head there, just yet. He stripped saddle and bridle from his borrowed horse and turned it loose to roll and water and graze. Then he picked up his pack and rifle and headed into the deep timber, to a place he remembered when roaming the country with old Preacher.

"You may get me, boys," he said to the sighing winds and the soaring eagles high above him. "But you'll pay a fearful price before you do."

"Scum," Louis said to the two riders.

"Huh?" one asked.

"I said you're scum," Louis repeated.

Stan and Glover had gotten separated from Noah's group. They'd been wandering around in circles when they came upon the tall, well-built man dressed all in black. Kind of a dudey lookin' fellow—except for those guns of his. They looked well used. And his coat was brushed back to give him free access to the Colts. He was just standing in the middle of the trail, smiling sort of strange-like. Now he was insulting them.

"Git out of the way, fancy-pants!" Glover told him.

"I like it here."

"Well, you about a stupid feller, then. I might decide to just run you down with this here horse. What do you think about that?"

Louis smiled. "I think your blowhole is overloading your mouth, punk."

Glover and Stan exchanged glances. It just seemed like nothin' had worked out right since they'd left the West Coast and come to Colorado. All them hayseeds and hicks out in the rural areas of the coast states knowed who the Lee Slater gang was, and they kowtowed and done what they was told. But it seemed like that ever since they'd come to Colorado, all that was happenin' was they was gettin' the crap shot out of them. And nobody seemed to be afraid of them.

"You a bounty hunter, mister?" Stan asked.

"You might say that. I hunt punks. And it looks like I found me a couple."

"I'm gettin' tarred of you in-sultin' me!" Glover popped off.

"Yeah," Stan flapped his mouth. "We're lookin' for Smoke Jensen so's we can collect the re-ward money."

"You dumb clucks," Louis said with a chuckle. "You're part of the Lee Slater gang. You're all wanted men, with bounties on your own heads. How in the devil do you think you're going to collect any reward money?"

Stan and Glover exchanged another look. That hadn't occurred to either of them.

"Uhhh . . ." Glover said.

"Well . . ." Stan said.

"Get off your horses, throw your guns in the bushes, and start walking," Louis told them.

Stan told him what he could do with his orders. Sideways.

Louis shot him. His draw was like a blur and totally unexpected. Stan pitched from the saddle, and Louis turned his gun toward Glover just as the outlaw was jerking iron. Louis waited, a slight smile on his lips, as the man cursed and jacked back the hammer.

That was as far as he got before Louis drilled him dead center in the chest, the slug knocking the outlaw out of the saddle, dead before he hit the ground. Quite unlike him, Louis twirled his six-shooter twice before dropping it back in leather.

"Punks," he said scornfully.

He went through their saddlebags and took out bacon, potatoes, bread, onions, and coffee. Fortunately, he did have with him his own coffeepot and small frying pan. The one he took from Stan's saddlebag was so coated with old grease and other odious and unidentifiable specks it was probably contagious just by touch. With a grimace of disgust, Louis tossed it into the bushes.

He stripped both horses of saddle and bridle and turned them loose, then swung back into the saddle and headed out. He did not look back at the dead outlaws lying sprawled on the trail.

It was nearing dusk when Al Martine and his bunch spotted Smoke high up near the timberline in the big lonesome.

"We got him, boys!" Al yelled, and put the spurs to his tired horse.

A rifle bullet took Al's hat off and sent it spinning away. The mountain winds caught it, and it was gone forever.

"Goddamn!" Al yelled, just as another round kicked up dirt at his horse's hooves, and the animal started bucking. It was all Al could do to stay in the saddle.

A slug smacked Zack in the shoulder and nearly knocked him from the saddle. The second shot tore off the saddle horn and smashed into Zack's upper thigh, bringing a scream of pain from the outlaw.

"He's got help!" Pedro yelled. "Let's get gone from here."

The outlaws raced for cover, with Zack flopping around in the saddle.

Smoke looked down the mountain. "Now, who in the devil is that?" he muttered.

Sally punched .44 rounds into her carbine and settled back into her well-hidden little camp in a narrow depression with the back and one side a solid rock wall.

"Who you reckon that was a-shootin' at us?" Tom Post yelled over the sounds of galloping horses.

"I don't know." Crown returned the yell. "But he's hell with a rifle, whoever he is."

Using field glasses, Sally watched them beat a hasty retreat, and then laid out cloth and cup, plate and tableware, and napkin for her early supper. Just because one was in the wilderness, surrounded by godless heathens, was no reason to forgo small amenities.

She opened a can of beans, set aside a can of peaches for dessert, and spread butter on a thick slice of bread. Before eating, she said a prayer for the continuing safety of her man.

"Hello the far!" the voice came out of the timber.

Louis edged back into the shadows and lifted his Colt. "If you're friendly, come on in."

"I reckon we're friendly," came the call. Two men stepped into the small clearing. "We're all in this together, a-huntin' that damn Smoke Jensen. Share your coffee, friend?"

"Why, certainly!" Louis called out cheerfully. "Step right on in, boys."

"Kind of you." The men stepped closer. "I'm Nick Reeves, and this is my partner, Mike Beecham."

Louis knew them both. No-goods from down near the Four Corners.

"What might your name be, mister?" Mike asked, squatting down by the small fire. "I think I know the voice, but I cain't hardly see you in them shadows."

"Louis Longmont, you cretin!"

Both men yelled, cussed, and grabbed for iron. Louis had both hands filled with .44s, and the campsite thundered with shots, the moist evening air filling with gray smoke.

Louis reloaded, then dragged the bodies away, heaving them over a small cliff. He went through their saddlebags and found more food, a goodly amount of .44 ammo, and some stinking socks and dirty long-handles. He kept the food and the ammo and turned their horses loose after relieving them of saddle and bridle. He returned to his fire and slowly ate his supper, scoured out his pan and plate, then broke camp and moved on about a mile, before bedding down for the night.

* * *

"Got more bounty hunters in the mountains than boys left in the gang," Lee Slater said glumly. He sat staring into the flames of the campfire and sucking on a bottle of rye whiskey.

His brother, Luttie, sat across the fire from him, equally morose. He took a drink from his bottle and wondered how all this was going to turn out. The shock of losing five of his men in a matter of seconds earlier that day still had not entirely left him. He wondered if his boys had managed to get enough lead in that damned ol' Charlie Starr to kill him. He doubted it.

"Twelve dead, last count," Lee said. "Six wounded. And you lost five of your boys to Starr."

"You don't have to keep reminding me," Luttie said sourly. "This wouldn't have happened if you had kept a tight rein on your boys. The dumbest damn thing you did was attackin' Big Rock and shootin' up the place. The second dumbest thing you done was shootin' Smoke Jensen's wife. And the third dumbest thing you done is torturin' and rapin' and killin' that family up north of here."

"Aw, shut up!" Lee told him.

"Don't tell me to shut up! I told you to come straight here and stay out of trouble on the way. We could have had it all, Lee. We could have taken a million dollars' worth of gold and silver from the miners and stages and banks and done been gone from this damn place. But, oh, hell no. You had to surround yourself with idiots and screw it all up."

"If he's talkin' about idiots, he must be talkin' about you boys," Lopez said to the Karl brothers.

Rod gave him a dirty look, and Randy gave him an obscene gesture.

"We got Smoke to the north of us," Curt said. "A damn good rifleman to the East of us, and it looks like Louis Longmont is to the south of us."

"And a bunch of U.S. Marshals camped at the edge of the mountains," Dale pointed out.

"Maybe it's time to haul out of here," Max suggested.

"I'll be damned!" Lee snarled at him. "Good God, people! Countin' Luttie's bunch, they's nearly fifty of us left, all told, and we're lettin' two or three people whup us. What the hell's the matter with you? No one or two people ain't never whupped fifty people. We're doin' somethin' wrong, is all. We got to study this out and find out what it is."

"Smoke Jensen and Louis Longmont ain't no average two people," Al Martine pointed out. "And that rifleman that hit us this afternoon wasn't no pilgrim, neither. Now you think about this—all of you: hittin' Rio is out the winder. They'd shoot us to pieces in ten seconds. The miners has all shut down and gone into town; they ain't diggin' no gold, and they shore ain't shippin' none. The county seat is out of the pitcher; Sheriff Silva ain't no man to fool with. So where the hell does that leave us?"

"My ass hurts!" Bud complained.

"He's up there," Ace Reilly said, his eyes looking at the timberline. Good light of morning, the air almost cold this high up.

Big Bob Masters shifted his chew from one side of his mouth to the other and spat. "Solid rock to his back," he observed. "And two hundred yards of open country ever'where else. It'd be suicide gettin' up there."

Ace lifted his canteen to take a drink, and the canteen exploded in his hand, showering him with water, bits of metal, and numbing his hand. The second shot nicked Big Bob's horse on the rump, and the animal went pitching and snorting and screaming down the slope, Big Bob yelling and hanging on and flopping in the saddle. The third shot took off part of Causey's ear, and he left the saddle, crawling behind some rocks.

"Jesus Christ!" Ace hollered, leaving the saddle and finding cover. "Where the hell is that comin' from?"

Big Bob's horse had come to a very sudden and unexpected halt, and Big Bob went flying ass over elbows out of the saddle to land against a tree. He staggered to his feet, looking wildly around him, and took a .44 slug in the belly. He sank to his knees, both hands holding his punctured belly, bellering in pain.

"He's right on top of us," Ace called to Nap. "Over there at the base of that rock face."

Smoke was hundreds of yards up the mountain, just at the timberline, looking and wondering who his new ally might be. He got his field glasses and began sweeping the area. A slow smile curved his lips.

"I married a Valkyrie, for sure," he muttered, as the long lenses made out Sally's face.

He saw riders coming hard, a lot of riders. Smoke grabbed up his .44-40 and began running down the mountain, keeping to the timber. The firing had increased as the riders dismounted and sought cover. Smoke stayed a good hundred yards above them, and so far he had not been spotted.

"Causey!" Woody yelled. "Over yonder!" He pointed. "Get on his right flank—that's exposed."

Causey jumped up, and Smoke drilled him through and through. Causey died sprawled on the still damp rocks from the misty morning in the high lonesome.

"He's up above us!" Ray yelled.

"Who the hell is that over yonder?" Noah hollered, just as Sally fired. The slug sent bits of rock into Noah's face, and he screamed as he was momentarily blinded. He stood up, and Smoke nailed him through the neck. Smoke had been aiming for his chest, but shooting downhill is tricky, even for a marksman.

Big Bob Masters was hollering and screaming, afraid to move, afraid his guts would fall out.

Smoke began dusting the area where the outlaws and bounty hunters had left their horses. The whining slugs spooked them and off they ran, reins trailing, taking food, water, and extra ammo with them.

"Goddamnit!" Woody yelled, running after them. He suddenly stopped, right out in the open, realizing what a stupid move that had been.

Smoke and Sally fired at the same time. One slug struck Woody in the side, the .44-40 hit him in the chest. Woody had no further use for a horse.

Smoke plugged Yancey in the shoulder, knocking the man down and putting him out of the fight. Yancey began crawling downhill toward the horses, staying to cover. He had but two thoughts in mind: getting in the saddle and getting the hell gone from this place.

"It's no good!" Ace yelled. "They'll pick us all off if we stay here. We got to get out of range. Start makin' your way down the slope."

The outlaws and bounty hunters began crawling back, staying to cover. Smoke and Sally held their fire, neither of them having a clear target and not wanting to waste ammo. They took that time to take a drink of water, eat a biscuit, and wait.

Haynes, Dale, and Yancey were the first to reach the horses, well out of range of the guns of Smoke and Sally.

Haynes looked up, horror in his eyes. A man dressed all in black was standing by a tree, his hands filled with Colts.

"Hello, punk!" Louis Longmont said, and opened fire.

18

The last memory Haynes had, and it would have to last him an eternity, was the guns of Louis Longmont belching fire and smoke. He died sitting on his butt, his back to a boulder. Yancey tried to lift his rifle, and Louis shot him twice in the belly. Dale turned to run, and Louis offered him no quarter. The first slug cut his spine, the second slug caught him falling and took off part of his head.

Louis reloaded his Colts, then picked up his rifle and took cover.

"We yield!" Nap Jacobs yelled.

"Not in this game," Louis called.

"Somebody come hep me!" Big Bob Masters squalled. "I cain't stand the pain!"

The pinned-down gunmen looked at each other. There were four of them left. Nap Jacobs, Ace Reilly, and two of Slater's boys, Kenny and Summers.

All knew Big Bob Masters was not long for this world. His yelling was growing weaker.

"I ain't done you no hurt, Longmont!" Ace yelled. "You got no call to horn in on this play."

"But here I am," Louis said. "Make your peace with God."

The silent dead littered the mountain battlefield. Below them, an outlaw's horse pawed the ground, the steel hoof striking rock.

"And I don't know who you is over yonder in the rocks," Nap yelled. "But I wish you'd bow out."

"I'm Mrs. Smoke Jensen!" Sally called.

"Dear God in Heaven," Ace said. 'We been took down by a damn skirt!"

"Disgustin'!" Nap said.

Kenny looked wild-eyed all around him. He was mumbling under his breath. His eyes held a touch of madness, and he was breathing hard, his chest heaving. Drool leaked from his mouth. "I'm gone," he said, and jumped up.

Three rifles barked at once, all the slugs striking true. Kenny was slammed backward, two holes in his chest and one hole in the center of his forehead.

Nap looked over at Ace. "This ain't no cakewalk, Ace. We forgot about Smoke's reputation once the battle starts."

"Yeah," Ace said, his voice low. "Once folks come after him, he don't leave nobody standin'."

"I got an idea. Listen." Nap tied a dirty bandanna around the barrel of his rifle and waved it. "I'm standin' up, people!" he shouted, taking his guns from leather and dropping them on the ground. "I walk out of here, and I'm gone from this country, and I don't come back." He looked at Ace. "You with me?"

"All the way—if they'll let us leave."

"I ain't playin', Ace. If they let us go, I'm gone far and long."

"My word on it."

"How about it, Jensen?" Nap shouted.

"It's all right with me." Smoke returned the shout. "But if I see you again, any place, anytime, and you're wearing a gun, I'll kill the both of you. That's a promise."

"Let's go," Nap said. "I always did want to see what's east of the Mississippi."

The three of them shifted locations, leaving the dead bodies behind them. They knew all those shots would soon bring other trouble hunters on the run.

Louis reached out to stroke the blue steel's head, and the stallion almost took some fingers off. Louis got his hand out of the way just in time.

"Vicious brute!" he said.

The stallion walled his eyes and showed Louis his big teeth.

"Gentle as a baby," Sally said, giving him a carrot.

The stallion took the carrot as gently as a house pet.

"We've got to get Sally out of here," Smoke said.

"I concur," Louis said. "However . . ."

"You can both go straight to hell!" She cut off Louis' words. "I didn't travel two hundred and fifty miles from the Sugarloaf to sit in some hotel room. I came to stand by my man, and that's exactly what I intend to do."

Smoke shrugged. "You were about to say, Louis? . . ."

"That it might not be possible to get Sally out of the mountains. Bounty hunters and assorted other crud and punks were still pouring into town when I left. We cut the odds down some today, but I'll wager that double that number came into the mountains."

Smoke had taken a big, tough-looking horse from the mounts that the dead would no longer need. They had all carried food in their saddlebags, so that problem, at least, was solved. They had plenty of coffee and ammo as well.

"If we could just find a place to hole up until those warrants are lifted," Smoke said wistfully. He was weary of the killing. Weary of the blood and pain and sweat and tension.

Louis shook his head. "No, my friend. That wouldn't stop most of them. The bloodlust is high and hot now. They're like hungry predators on a blood scent."

Smoke drained his coffee cup and tossed the dredges. "Let's get moving. We've got to find a place that we can defend."

"He'll make it," the young doctor said, stepping out of the room and gently closing the door behind him. "That is one tough man in there."

Charlie Starr was sleeping with the aid of some laudanum.

The doctor dropped three chunks of lead on the table. "I dug one out of his leg, one out of his side, and another was lodged in his arm. Another bullet grazed his head. He'll have a frightful headache for a time, and a hat would be uncomfortable, but he'll be flat on his back a long time before he needs a hat."

"Don't you bet on that," Lilly told him. "That's a warhoss in there in my bed." She grinned wickedly. "And it ain't the first time he's been in my bed." The doctor blushed. "I've wore him down to a frazzle a time or two myself. You got any pills you want me give him?"

"You're staying with him?"

"Night and day until I'm sure he's all right."

Earl stepped into the room. "You've got to see this, Johnny," he said. "You might never see another sight like it."

Johnny walked outside and stood with Earl and Cotton, staring at the lawyer Larry Tibbson. Larry had bought himself some cowboy clothes, from hat to boots, and was wearing two pearl-handled .45s and carrying a Winchester rifle. There was a bandoleer of ammo looped across his chest.

"He wants to be a deputy," Earl said.

"Boy," Johnny said, after he recovered from his shock at the sight. "Are you tryin' to get yourself killed?"

"I am going into the mountain to aid Miss Sally," Larry said stiffly.

"Miss Sally don't need no aid from you," Johnny bluntly told him. "Boy, if you go blundering around up in them mountains, you probably gonna get lost and eat up by a bear. That's the best way you might leave this world. The worst is gettin' taken alive by them outlaws and havin' them stick your bare feet in a fire for the fun of it."

"I am perfectly capable of taking care of myself," Larry informed him. "I'll have you know that I belong to the New York City Pistol Club, am a very good shot, and have been duck-hunting many, many times."

"That's good, Lawyer. Dandy," Cotton said. "I'm proud of your accomplishments. But have you ever faced a man who was shootin' at you? And plugged him?"

"Heavens, no!"

The men stood for fifteen minutes, begging and pleading with Larry to give up his plan. He stood firm. Finally Earl sighed. "Go get me a badge, Cotton. We'll swear him in. That might give him some edge."

"Get him killed," Cotton said. He stepped off the boardwalk and paused, looking back. "I seen Mills in town just before the stage run. Did he say anything to any of you? He looked sort of jumpy to me. Excited, I guess it was."

"No," Earl said. "I saw him. He met the stage and was gone before I could talk to him. And I wanted to tell him about Charlie."

"I wonder what he's got up his sleeve?"

"I shall endeavor to join with that stalwart group," Larry said.

"Whatever that means," Cotton said, walking off.

* * *

"Here they are," Mills said excitedly, jumping from his horse. "The warrants on the Lee Slater gang. Saddle up, men! We're riding for the deep timber."

The men broke camp quickly and were in the saddle within fifteen minutes.

"We've got a few hours of daylight left," Mills said. "We'll get in close and camp, hit the outlaws at first light."

"Ah . . . Mills, we don't know where they are," Albert pointed out.

"We'll follow the sounds of shooting." Mills spoke the words in a grim tone. "And we'll put a stop to it before it can escalate further."

The marshals exchanged glances.

"Pin your badges to your jackets," Mills ordered. "These men have got to learn to respect the law."

"And you think these badges are going to do that?" Moss asked.

"Certainly!"

"Right," Winston said, with about as much enthusiasm as a man going to his own hanging.

Larry was dismayed when he could not find a proper English riding saddle anywhere in town. But he was not discouraged. He left town armed to the teeth, sitting in a Western rig, bobbing up and down in the saddle as he had been taught. The horse wore a very curious expression on its face.

"He's gonna get killed," Cotton predicted.

"Maybe not," Earl said. "Men like that seem to lead a charmed life. But there is one thing for certain: he won't be the same man coming out as he is going in."

* * *

Not a single shot was fired in anger the rest of that day. When the news of the shoot-up on the slopes reached Lee and Luttie, they signaled their men back to camp for a pow-wow.

Even some of the bounty hunters had lost their enthusiasm for the chase.

"Has to be bad when Nap and Ace give it up," Dan Diamond opined.

"Big Bob gone," Morris Pattin said. "He was one tough son of a bitch."

Several bounty hunters—older, tougher, and wiser hands—quietly packed their gear and pulled out. In the Lee Slater group, Bud, Sack, Cates, Dewey, and Gooden rode into Rio under a white flag and turned themselves in to the sheriff's deputies. Bud had passed out in the saddle a half a dozen times from the pain in his buttocks.

"We might have to amputate," the doctor said, after winking at Johnny.

"Cut off my ass!" Bud yelled; then he really started bellering.

Smoke, Louis, and Sally worked until dark rigging their new defensive position above the timberline in the big lonesome. Smoke planted almost all of his dynamite under heavy boulders in carefully selected spots while Louis rigged deadfalls far below their position; they might not fall for them, but it would make them cautious. Then they all set about gathering up wood for a fire.

"We'll take a lot of them out," Smoke said. "But they'll eventually breach our position. Just before they do, we'll slip out through that narrow pass behind us and blow it closed. It'll take them half a day to work around this range. By that time we'll be long gone . . . hopefully," he added. "We'll have us a good hot meal this evening. They know where we are;

our trail is too easy to follow. Anyway, we've got to have a fire this high up; we'd freeze to death without it. Let's settle in and rest and eat. It's going to get busy come first light."

Larry built a fire large enough to endanger the forest. And it wasn't just for heat. Spooky out here. All sorts of strange sounds were coming out of the darkness surrounding him. Larry imagined huge bears staring at him, vicious packs of wolves, and slobbering panthers waiting to pounce and eat him if he let the flames die down.

He needn't have worried about four-legged animals. No woods' creature would come within a mile of that mini-inferno he kept feeding during the night. All in all, Larry cleared about an acre of land getting fuel for the fire. It looked like Paul Bunyan had been on a rampage.

"Who in the hell is that down yonder?" Curly asked, looking at the glowing bright spot surrounded by a sea of darkness.

"That goofy lawyer we was told about," Carbone said, returning from his stint on guard. "The one with a crush on Sally Jensen."

"Oh," the others said, and dismissed Larry without another thought.

Mills and his marshals came upon Larry just after first light. He was trying—unsuccessfully—to fry a potato in bacon grease.

"You got to peel it and cut it up first," Moss told him.

"Oh, Larry said. "I employ a cook back home. I'm not much of a hand in the kitchen."

"I never would have guessed," Mills said. "Who are you?" he asked. He'd never seen anyone try to fry a whole potato.

"I am an attorney from back East. I have come into these battle-torn mountains to offer my assistance in bringing to justice the hooligans and ruffians who are endangering Miss Sally Jensen's life."

"Sally Jensen!" the marshals all hollered. Mills said, "Are you saying that Smoke's wife has joined him?"

"Most assuredly. I am not a man of violence, but with this new development, I felt compelled to pick up arms and race to the rescue."

"Let me fix breakfast," Hugh said. "After I build another fire," he added. "I can't get within five feet of the one you got."

"Are you lost?" Winston asked.

"Oh, no." Larry smiled. "I may not be much of a cowboy—as a matter of fact, I'm not a cowboy at all—but I spent some time at sea. It would be difficult to get me lost anywhere. I take my bearings often."

"Can you use those guns?" Sharp asked.

"I've never shot a man before. But I'm quite good at target shooting. Have you ever shot a man?"

"Ah . . . no," Sharp admitted.

"Any of you?" Larry questioned.

The marshals all looked embarrassed.

"This is going to be quite an expedition we're mounting," Larry mused.

Far in the distance, the faint sounds of gunshots drifted to them.

"I think we'd better forgo breakfast," Larry said.

"Let them bang away," Smoke said. "They're far out of range and shooting uphill. All they're doing is wasting ammunition."

Louis lay behind cover and counted puffs of smoke until

he grew tired of counting. He looked at Smoke. "Over thirty down there."

"And more coming," Smoke replied, cutting his eyes to the East.

Sally was looking through field glasses. "Eleven of them. And another bunch right behind them."

"How many in the second bunch, honey?"

"They're too far off to make out yet. Now they've disappeared into the timber."

"Gathering like blowflies on a carcass," Louis said, his words filled with contempt. "Blowflies one day and maggots the next."

The three of them were in a natural rock depression with a clear field of fire in all directions except the rear. They had hauled in branches and dead logs the previous afternoon and stacked them to their rear, against the stone face. The wood would soak up slugs and would prevent any ricochets. They had laid in a goodly supply of dry dead wood and had eaten a hearty breakfast and had a fresh pot of hot coffee ready to drink.

Sally suddenly giggled. Smoke looked at her. "You want to tell me what's so funny about this situation?"

"You remember me telling you about a man named Larry Tibbson?"

"The lawyer fellow from New York who tried to spark you when you both were in college?"

"That's him."

"What about him?"

She brought him up to date.

Smoke chuckled, the humor touching his eyes. "He's got nerve, I'll give him that. Does he have any idea what might have happened to him had I been home?"

"I think he does now."

Louis poured them all coffee in tin cups and passed them

around. The air was cold early in the morning; the hot coffee and the small fire felt good to them as they waited.

The firing stopped.

"They'll be moving soon," Louis said. His eyes touched the eyes of Smoke. The gambler minutely nodded his head. While Sally had slept, Smoke and Louis had talked. Smoke and Sally's children could get along without a father, but they needed a mother. If bad turned to worse, Louis was to take Sally and make a run for it, even if he had to punch her unconscious to do it. The dynamite was in place, and if Smoke was trapped on this side of the narrow pass, so be it.

"They're moving," Sally said. "They'll be able to get within range of us."

"Yes. Then we'll start picking them off," Louis said. "We have all the advantage. Our position is like a fort. We're shooting downhill, and that is easier to compensate for than shooting uphill. We have food and water and warmth. Know this now, Sally: come the night, they'd overrun us. At dusk, we're going to start the avalance and make a run for it. I . . ."

"I heard you both talking last night," she said softly. "You won't have to knock me out to make me go." She opened her pack and took out a smaller package wrapped in canvas. "These are medicines and bandages, Smoke. Potions to help relieve pain and to fight infection. I did not include any laudanum. I knew even if you were badly hurt, you wouldn't take it."

He kissed her gently while Louis discreetly looked away, a smile on his lips. She clung to him for a moment, then pulled back and squared her shoulders and took several deep breaths, getting her emotions under control and blinking away the tears that had gathered. "You come back to me now, you hear me, Smoke Jensen?"

"Yes, ma'am." Smoke smiled at her. "I'm going to take some lead, honey," he told her. "I'd have to be the luckiest man alive not to. But I'll make it out of this. And that's a promise."

A slug thudded into the logs they had placed against the rock wall behind them.

"They're in range," Louis said.

Smoke and Sally moved into position. Sally had laid aside her short-barreled carbine and had taken a longer-barreled, more accurate lever action from the saddle boot of a dead outlaw. She lined up the sights on part of a leg that was sticking out from behind a large rock and squeezed off a round.

The man started screaming hideously.

"You busted his knee, baby," Smoke told her.

"That's too bad," she said with a wicked grin. "I was aiming a little higher than that."

19

"Cease and desist," Mills shouted to a group of riders. "I'm a United States Marshal."

The riders all jerked iron and began pouring lead at the marshals and Larry. They dove for cover, leading their horses into timber.

"I'm a deputy sheriff of this county!" Larry shouted. "I order you in the name of the law to stop this immediately."

A slug howled past his nose and slammed into a tree, spraying him with bits of bark and bloodying his chin.

"Cretinous son of a bitch!" Larry mumbled, from his suddenly attained position flat on his belly on the ground. "No respect for law and order."

"You're learning," Mills said. "I had to."

The riders dismounted and took cover, continuing their firing at the marshals and Larry.

"Did you recognize any of them?" Winston asked.

"No. I think they're bounty hunters. But that doesn't make any difference now." Mills eared back the hammer on his Winchester.

"What do you mean?" Larry asked.

"They were warned as to who we are; they ignored that and fired at lawmen. That makes them criminals." Mills sighted in on one of the manhunters who had taken cover behind a tree that was just a tiny bit too small. He shot the man and knocked him sprawling. "Fire, damnit!" he ordered his men.

Two of the outlaws, or bounty hunters—the trio on the mountain didn't know and didn't care which—tried to carry the man with the busted knee down the slope. Smoke and Louis dropped them. The wounded man began his long rolling slide down the slope, screaming in pain as he hit rocks and scrub bushes. When he reached a flat, he lay still, either dead or unconscious.

"Riders coming," Sally announced, handing Smoke the field glasses.

Smoke studied the men. "Luttie Charles and his bunch. I count . . . ten, no, eleven of them."

"Getting crowded down there," Louis remarked, biting the end off an expensive imported cigar he'd taken from a silver holder and lighting up. When the ash was to his liking he laid the stogie aside and punched two more rounds into his rifle and jacked back the hammer, sighting in on an exposed forearm.

"That's a good hundred and fifty yards," Smoke said. "Five dollars says you can't make the shot."

"You just lost five dollars," the millionaire industrialist/ adventurer/gambler said, and squeezed the trigger.

The man yelled as the slug rendered his arm useless. He rolled to one side and exposed a boot. Smoke shot him in the foot, and the outlaw began the slow slide down the slope, hollering and screaming as he rolled and slid downward.

One man jumped out from cover to stop his buddy and Smoke, Sally, and Louis dusted the ground all around him. It was too far for accurate shooting, but after doing a little dancing, the outlaw jumped back into cover, unhit but with a new respect for those three on the mountain.

The arm- and foot-shot outlaw rolled off a plateau and fell screaming for several hundred feet. His screaming stopped when he impacted with solid rock. It sounded like a big watermelon dropped from a rooftop to a brick street.

"Fall back! Fall back!" the shout drifted to the trio. "This ain't no good. We'll take them come the night."

"Nap time," Louis said, and promptly stretched out, his hat over his face, and went to sleep.

The bounty hunters—those left alive—called out their surrender to Mills. They had suffered two dead and four wounded. Mills ordered the dead buried. When that was done, he lined up the living.

"I just don't have the time to arrest you properly and transport you into Rio for trial and incarceration," he told them. "But I have your names—whether they are your real names is a mystery that might never be solved—and your weapons. Ride out of here and don't come back. If I ever see any of you again, I shall place you under arrest and guarantee you all long prison terms. Now, move!"

The manhunters gone, the marshals and Larry exchanged glances. They were all a little shaky from the firefight, but all knew they had grown a bit in the experience field.

"I would say we conducted ourselves rather well," Larry said, trying to stuff and light his pipe with trembling fingers. He finally gave it up and put the pipe into a pocket.

"You did well," Mills said, putting a hand on Larry's shoulder. "I believe we all proved our mettle. I'm proud to ride with you, Larry."

"The shooting appears to have stopped," Moss said, looking toward the high peaks where they believed Smoke to be holed up.

"That's still a good day's ride from here," Mills said. "Let's get cracking."

The day dragged slowly on without another shot being exchanged. The outlaws and bounty hunters built fires for cooking and for warmth and waited for the night.

Smoke was silent for a time, deep in thought. Finally he made up his mind. He looked at his wife. "I want you gone from here, Sally, while there is good light to travel. I don't see the point in waiting for the night. It's a pretty good bet that nearly all of the manhunters and outlaws are right down there below us. You should have an easy ride back to Rio. Louis, take her out of here."

"All right," the gambler said. "I agree with you. But first let's load you up full and get you all the advantage we can give you."

They had taken all the rifles from the saddle boots of the dead outlaws and bounty hunters, as well as a dozen pistols. They were all loaded up full and placed within Smoke's reach. It would give him a tremendous amount of firepower before having to stop and reload.

Louis slipped out behind the rock wall to saddle up the horses and give Smoke and Sally a few moments alone.

"I'll make one last plea and then say no more about it," Sally said. "Come with us."

Smoke shook his head. "They'd just follow us, and we'd have to deal with it some other place. They'd probably even follow us back to the Sugarloaf or into town and that would get innocent people hurt or killed. So I might as well get it over with here and now."

He leaned over and kissed her. "See you in Rio, honey."

"You better get there," she told him with a forced grin. 'Cause if you don't, I'm going to be awfully angry."

"Let's go," Louis called from behind the rock wall. "We've got some clouds moving in."

Smoke shook hands with the gambler, and then they were gone, the rock wall concealing their departure from the many blood-hungry eyes below them.

Smoke put a fresh pot of coffee on to boil and gave the long fuses leading from his position to the dynamite a visual once-over. Everything seemed in order. He ate slowly, savoring each bite, and then rolled a cigarette and drank several cups of coffee. He knew it was going to be a very long and boring afternoon. But he was going to have to stay alert for any kind of sneak attack the outlaws might decide to launch at him.

Twice he went back to check on his horse. The animal seemed well rested and ready to go. The last time, with about an hour of daylight left, Smoke saddled him up and secured his gear.

As the shadows began to lengthen over the land, Smoke checked all his weapons. He could see the men moving toward him. A lot of men. He checked both flanks; men were moving in and out of the sparse timber and coming toward him. Still out of range, but not for long.

Smoke emptied the coffeepot and kicked out the fire, leaving only a few smoldering sticks. He drank his coffee and pulled his . 44-40 to his shoulder, sighting a man in and gently squeezing the trigger. The rifle fired, and the man fell to his knees, tried to get up, and then pitched forward on his face. Smoke shifted positions and emptied one rifle into the thin timber on his left flank. A scream came from the shadowy scrub. He emptied another rifle into that area and several men ran out, one limping badly, all of them heading down as fast as they dared, getting out of range.

Lead began howling off the rocks in front of him while

others slammed into the logs behind him. Men began rushing from cover to cover, panting heavily in the thin mountain air. This high up, the heart must work harder. Smoke fired and one man did not have to worry about breathing any longer. The .44-40 slug hit him in the face and tore off most of his jaw. He rolled and bounced his way down the mountain, leaving smears of blood along the way.

Rock splinters bloodied Smoke's face. He wiped the blood away and shifted to the other side, firing as he went, so the others would not know he was alone on the mountain.

On the right side of his little fort, Smoke noted with some alarm how close the manhunters were getting. He looked straight down the mountain. Men were moving in on him, working their way from sparse cover to sparse cover . . . but still coming. He ended the journey for two of them, head and neck shots. Smoke grabbed up a .44 carbine and began spraying the lead below him as fast as he could work the lever. That one empty, he grabbed up another and ran to the other side. The manhunters were getting closer. Too damn close. A slug ripped through the outside upper part of his left arm, bringing a grunt of pain.

Time to go!

He ignored the pain and ripped his shirt to see how bad it was. Not too bad. He tied a bandanna around the wound, then picked up a smoldering stick and lit the fuses. Smoke ran behind the rock wall and grabbed the horse's reins, running and leading the horse toward the narrow pass. He did not want to be in the saddle when the explosives went off. It was going to make a hell of a lot of noise, and the horse would be spooked.

"I think we got him, boys!" a man yelled. "Let's go, let's go."

The outlaws and manhunters came screaming and yelling triumphantly up the mountain. When no shots greeted them, they began cheering and slapping each other on the back.

The explosives blew, each charge five to ten seconds behind the other. One of Lee's co-leaders, Horton, about seventy-five yards from the small fort, looked up in horror at the tons of rock cascading toward them. He put a hand in front of his face as if that alone would stop the deadly thunder. A watermelon-sized rock, hurtling through the air, took his hand and drove it into his head.

His buddy, Max, seemed to be rooted to the mountainside, numbed with fear. He would forever be a part of the mountain as tons of rock buried him.

Pecos and his gang of young punks had not advanced nearly so far as the others. Screaming in terror, they ran into the timber and were safe from the deadly cascade.

McKay's legs were crushed, and Ray was pinned under a boulder. Both lay screaming, watching their blood stain the ground and life slowly ebb from them.

Lee Slater and his group, Al Martine and his pack of no-goods, and part of another team watched from below as the carnage continued high above them.

Al lifted field glasses and grimaced as he watched through the thick dust as Sonny tried to outrun the rampaging tons of rock. He could see the man's face was tight and white from mind-numbing fear. Sonny was swallowed by the rocks. All but one arm. It stuck out of the huge pile, the fingers working, opening and closing for a moment, a silent scream for help. The fingers suddenly stiffened into a human claw and stayed that way. As soon as the buzzards spotted it they would rip, tear, and eat it to the bone.

Jere and Summers almost made it. They had lost their weapons and were running and falling and stumbling down the mountain. Their mouths were working in soundless screams, the pale lips vivid in their frightened faces. Several huge boulders hit a stalled rock pile and came over, seeming to gain speed as they traveled through the air.

"Split up!" Al yelled. But his warning came too late and

could not be heard over the now-gradually dying roar of the avalanche.

The boulders landed square on the running men, squashing them against the rock surface of the mountain.

Al Martine crossed himself and cursed the day he ever agreed to leave California.

A bounty hunter known only as Chris turned to look behind him and tripped, falling hard, knocking the wind from him. "No!" he screamed, just seconds before the tons of rock landed on him. One boot stuck out of the now-motionless pile of stone. The boot trembled for a moment, then was still.

Huge clouds of dust began drifting upward to join the night skies.

"I'd a' not believed no one man could have done all this," Whit said, his voice husky from near exhaustion. He sank to his knees and put his hands to his face, trying to block from his mind all that he'd just witnessed.

Mac came limping out of the dust, dragging one foot. Reed was behind him. He did not appear to be hurt.

Luttie Charles, accompanied by his men, walked slowly up the slope to stand by his brother.

"Incredible," Luttie said, his voice small.

They all cringed and jumped, some yelling and running away, as another dull thud cut the darkening day.

"Musta been a pass back yonder," Milt said. "And Jensen just blowed it."

Rod and Randy giggled.

"Loco!" Lopez muttered.

Luttie started counting. Thirty men left standing here out of nearly seventy. Maybe eight or ten bounty hunters still working the wilderness alone. He coughed as the dust from the avalanche drifted down the mountain. Luttie waved his people farther back.

"We'll make camp at the base down yonder," he said, pointing. "Eat and rest and tomorrow we can take him."

"How you figure that?" his brother asked.

"You're forgetting, I know this country." He turned to his foreman, and the man grinned.

"I'll take two of the boys and plug up the only hole out of that area," the man said. "The gambler and the woman probably done made it out, but Smoke won't try it at night—too dangerous. We got him now, boss. Pinned in like a hog for slaughter."

The lonely cry of a lobo wolf drifted to them, abruptly changing into the blood-chilling scream of a big puma.

"Look!" the punk Peco yelled, pointing.

At the crest of the mountain, the men could just make out the figure of a man, sitting his saddle. The scream of the puma came again.

"It brings chills to my arms," Pedro said. "He is calling like el gato. Daring us to come and get him."

Smoke screamed his panther scream again, the sound drifting and echoing around the mountains, touching all those who hunted him. A big puma answered the call, the scream fading off into the puma's peculiar coughing sound.

Martine and Pedro looked at each other, neither of them liking this at all.

Smoke threw back his head and howled like a big wolf. It was so real that somewhere in the timber a big wolf replied, others joining in, lifting their voices in respect to a brother wolf.

"I've had it," Reed said. "The rest of you do what you want to, but as for me, I'm gone."

"You're yeller! Jeff," one of Peco's punks sneered at Reed. Wrong thing to do.

Reed palmed his .45 and put a hole in Jeff's chest. The punk hit the rocky ground and died.

"Anybody else want to call me yeller?" Reed said, jacking back the hammer of his pistol.

No one did.

"I'll watch your back for you, Reed," Dumas said. "You got a right to leave if'n you want to."

"Let me tell you all something, boys," Reed said. "That man up yonder was born with the bark on. We've all hunted him, trapped him, cornered him, and he's tooken some lead. Bet on that . . ." He shivered as Smoke's wolf howl drifted to them; it was soon joined by others. "Jesus God, I can't stand no more of that. Makes my blood run cold. I think the man's got some animal in him. Injuns think so." He shook his head as if to clear it. "And he'll probably take some more lead afore this is all over. You might get a bunch of lead in him. But you'll all be dead, and he'll be standin' when it's all over. Bet on it. And I will be too. 'Cause I'm leavin'. Goodbye."

Smoke howled again.

The men looked toward the crest of the mountain.

Smoke was gone, but his call still wavered in the air.

"Where'd he go?" Crown asked, the question almost a cry of fear.

No one replied. No one knew.

Carbone lifted his hands and looked at them. They were trembling.

Lopez noticed the trembling hands. "Si," he spoke softly, in a voice that only Carbone could hear. "I understand. He is of the mountains, one with the animals, brother of the wolf."

"And us?" Carbone asked in a soft tone.

"I think, amigo, that if we pursue the last mountain man, we are dead."

20

Smoke had approached the pass leading out of the valley very cautiously. He took his field glasses and squinted at the pass in the dim light the moon provided. The pass looked innocent enough, but warning bells were ringing in his head. He picketed his horse and approached the narrow pass on foot. The closer he got the more certain he became that the pass was guarded. He heard the faint whinny of a horse and stopped cold, listening. Another horse answered. Smoke began backtracking.

He returned to his horse and removed the saddle. He took his small pack, two rifles, and his saddlebags, then turned the animal loose. There was plenty of water and good graze in the valley. If the horse never found its way out, it would live a good and uneventful life.

Smoke returned to a spot near the mouth of the pass and rolled up in his blankets after eating a can of beans and the last of his now very stale bread. He slept soundly, awakening while the stars were still diamond-sparkling high above the mountains. He lay for half an hour, mentally preparing for the battle ahead.

They had him trapped, but he had been trapped before. Smoke was outnumbered and outgunned. He'd been there before, too. He lay in his blankets and purged his mind of all things that did not pertain to survival. He'd had lots of practice at that. He became a huge, dangerous, predatory animal. He became one with the mountains, the trees, the animals, the rocks, and the eagles and hawks that would soon be soaring above him, looking for food.

He came out of his blankets silently. He rolled his blankets in the groundsheet and left them. If the fight lasted more than one day, and he was forced to spend another night in the mountains, well, he'd been cold before. More than once in his life he had lain down on a blanket of leaves with only fresh-cut boughs covering him. He slung one rifle and picked up the other.

He did not think of Sally or his children. He had no thoughts of friends or family. He forced everything except survival from his mind. He had told Louis where he had cached supplies and his horses. If he died in this valley, Louis would see to his stock.

Just as dawn was streaking the sky with lances of silver and gold, Smoke Jensen, the last mountain man, threw back his head and screamed like an enraged panther.

The chirping of awakening birds and chattering of playing squirrels ceased as the terrible scream cut through the forest and echoed around the mountains.

Smoke was telling his enemies to come on; he was ready to meet them.

"My God!" Mills said, standing at the base of the mountain where so many men had died of gunshots and the avalanche. The sunlight was bright on the side of the slope, the rays reflecting off dark splotches of dried blood.

"The rumbling we heard yesterday," Larry said.

"Yes," Moss replied, looking at the hands and arms and legs sticking out from under tons of rock. His eyes touched upon what was left of two men who'd been crushed under huge boulders, the boulders rolling on after doing their damage.

"I can say in all honesty, I have never seen anything like this," Winston said.

"Do you suppose the fight is over?" Sharp asked.

"No," Albert called, squatting down off the rock face. "A group of men rode out of here. Heading that way." He pointed.

Mills consulted a map he'd purchased at the assayer's office. "If Smoke is still behind this death mountain, he's probably trapped. According to this, there is only one way in and one way out of that little valley. And you can bet the outlaws and bounty hunters know it and have sealed off the entrance."

"How far are we from the mouth of that pass?" Larry asked.

"I'm not sure, but—"

The sound of a shot echoed to them.

"It's started," Hugh said.

Smoke opened the dance. His .44-40 barked, the slug taking Dumas in the throat. The outlaw gasped and gurgled horribly and died as he watched his life's blood gush from the gaping wound.

Smoke lay about seventy-five yards from the mouth of the pass and watched and waited with all the patience of a great puma sunning itself.

"We got ourselves an em-pass-ee goin' here," Tom Post said.

"A what?" Lee asked.

"We can't go in, and he can't come out."

Rod and Randy giggled.

One-Eye looked at Morris Pattin and shook his head in disgust. Morris nodded his head in complete agreement.

"We got to go in," Luttie said. "We got to get him. It's a matter of honor now. We're finished in this country. No matter what, we're done here."

Ed and Curt exchanged glances and began crawling toward the mouth of the pass. They passed the bloody body of Dumas and tried not to look at it. Slowly, one by one, the others followed them, staying low on their bellies, offering Smoke no target. They knew that some of them were going to die breaching the mouth of that narrow pass. They also knew that once inside, they could track Smoke Jensen down and kill him. The money was unimportant now. Not even a secondary thought. Their honor was at stake. One man, Smoke Jensen, with a little help, had nearly destroyed a huge gang. He had to pay. That was their code.

They understood it, and Smoke Jensen understood it.

Bobby Jackson jumped up and ran toward the rocky mouth of the pass, firing as fast as he could work the lever of his rifle. Smoke put a slug into his belly, and the man folded up on the ground, his rifle clattering on the rocks.

But four outlaws had worked a dozen yards closer to the entrance.

A bounty hunter called Booker ran into the clearing and jumped for cover. He almost made it through unscathed. Smoke's .44-40 barked, and the slug hit Booker in the hip, turning him in the air. He hit the ground hollering in pain. But he was inside the valley and still holding on to his rifle.

"Come on!" Booker shouted, and began laying down a withering fire, forcing Smoke to keep his head down.

Tom Post, Martine, and Mac made it inside the valley and fanned out. Smoke saw them and backed up, crawling on his belly into a thick stand of timber. The other manhunters poured into the valley, sensing victory. That was very premature thinking on their part.

A rifle slug grazed the side of Smoke's head, knocking him to one side and addling him for several moments. He felt the warm stickiness of blood oozing down his cheek. He forced himself to ignore it as he shifted positions.

Smoke found better cover and sighted in on a man. Mac took the slug just below his belt buckle and hit the ground howling, unable to move his legs. The bullet had angled up and exited out his back, tearing his spinal cord. Keno dragged the screaming man back toward the entrance to the valley.

"I cain't move my legs!" Mac hollered. "I'm crippled. Finish me, Keno."

"All right," the outlaw said, and shot the man between the eyes.

Outside the valley, reporters and the curious had gathered nearby, but not so close as to risk getting shot. After Louis and Sally had told their stories, the town of Rio emptied in a rush. Saloon keepers had set up shop and were doing a brisk business in the wilderness. They kept people busy racing back and forth to town for more whiskey.

Sally was bathing in Louis' quarters. She had no intention of returning to the wilderness. She would be waiting here for her man—when he returned. Not if. When.

Louis had posted one of his men at the front and at the back of his quarters, with orders to shoot to kill any man who tried to breach Sally's privacy.

Louis was sitting by Charlie Starr's side, in a chair by the bed. Charlie was pale and hurting, but getting stronger.

"I know that valley," Charlie said. "Found it with Kit back in '48. Peaceful, pretty little place."

"It isn't peaceful now," Louis told him.

"How many you guess are in there after him?"

"Twenty to thirty."

"He'll take lead."

"He knows it. And so does Sally. But this last round is his. He told me so."

"It's got to be that way, Louis. It's the code of the mountain man. Preacher taught him that. You and me, we just shortened the odds some." He sighed. "I've known that boy for a long time. Me and Preacher went way back together. Them gunnies in that valley now, they don't really know what they're up agin. It's been playtime so far. Now Smoke's gonna get nasty. He laid in his blankets this mornin' and put ever'thing out of his mind except stayin' alive. He Injuned and made his peace with the gods. Asked the wind and the rain and the lightning and the animals and the trees and the mountains to help him. He's not quite human now, Louis. And as bad hurt as he might get, when this is over, he might stay up there for several hours or several days, fixin' his mind so's he can once more be fit to associate with normal human bein's. Depends on how bad it gets in his head."

Louis stirred in his chair. "I never saw him the way you just described him."

"Be thankful. It's a fearsome sight."

Lilly came in and shooed Louis out. She took a bottle of sleeping medicine from the bureau and poured a tablespoon full. Charlie took it without grumbling. He smiled at the madam.

"When I get my strength back, I'm gonna repay you, Lilly." He winked.

She returned the wink. "The saddle'll be ready for you to ride, Charlie. Now go to sleep." She drew the curtains to the small quarters in the big wagon. As she stepped down to the ground, her eyes flicked to the mountains. She'd been knowing Smoke Jensen ever since he was just a little tadpole roaming the country with that old reprobate Preacher. She'd heard Charlie telling Louis about how Smoke turned into some sort of unstoppable inhuman creature when he got all worked up. She knew it to be fact. She'd seen it one time. She hoped to God she never had to see it again. But she would, at least one more time. And soon.

It was a terrible, fearsome thing to witness.

Steve Bolt was crawling through the lushness of the little valley. He had dreams of being the man who killed Smoke Jensen. The money wasn't important—it was the reputation he sought.

"Lars?" he whispered. His partner was supposed to be a few yards away, to his right.

Lars didn't reply.

"Lars! Come on, man, where are you?"

Steve rose on his elbows, and his face froze with fear. Lars was standing up, sorta like a scarecrow, both arms wedged over low branches. His throat had been cut. Steve stood up to his knees, opening his mouth to scream.

A spear, about six feet long and sharpened on one end, caught him in the chest and drove all the way through him. Steve uttered a long, low moan as the pain registered in his brain. Both hands gripped the spear, and he tried to pull it out. He screamed in pain and gave that up.

"What's the matter, Steve?" another manhunter called in a low whisper.

Steve could only grunt in pain. His eyes were fixed on a tall, very muscular man who suddenly appeared about ten yards in front of him. He was hatless, his face bloody. His shirtfront was bloody. But it was his eyes that froze Steve's tongue. The brown eyes had a gold tint about them—they seemed to glow with rage. The man—it had to be Jensen—held several long spears in his left hand.

"Steve!" the call came again.

Steve found his voice and screamed like he had never

done before in his life. He cut his eyes. The tall bloody man had disappeared.

"Good God!" the third bounty hunter said, running over to Steve. His eyes touched the lifeless body of Lars, hanging from the branches. "No," he whispered.

That was the last thing he whispered. A long spear, hurled with strength that the average man only dreams about, struck the manhunter in the chest with such force it knocked him back against a tree. He died on his boots.

Keno was the first to find the three bounty hunters. He immediately dropped to his knees for cover and looked wildly around him. His mouth and throat and lips were suddenly very dry. And he realized that he was scared. Very badly scared. He'd been an outlaw since no more than a boy; he'd done some terrible, awful things and seen even worse. But he had never before faced such a man as Smoke Jensen. There were no rules. Jensen was a savage, through and through. Worser than any damn Injun that ever lived.

"Martine?" Keno called as softly as he could and still have a chance to be heard.

" 'Bout twenty yards behind you, Keno. What you got?"

"Steve, Lars, and that other fellow. All dead. Lars' throat is cut ear to ear. Steve and his buddy was kilt with spears."

Martine cursed softly in Spanish.

"Que haces?" Lopez questioned.

Mason Wright came running up, both hands filled with Colts. His eyes became wild with rage when he saw the three dead bounty hunters. "Jensen!" he screamed. "Goddamn you, Jensen. Me and Lars was compadres. You'll pay for this, you cowardly bastard. Step out here, face me."

A rifle cracked and a blue-black hole appeared in Mason's forehead. The gunfighter slumped to the ground, stayed on his knees for a moment, then fell over on his face. Both Colts went off when he hit the ground, and Keno screamed in pain as a slug tore through his shin and exited out the back of his calf. He rolled on the ground, yelling.

"Oh, Jesus!" Keno squalled. "You shot me, you stupid idiot! Oh, God, it hurts."

Luttie ran up, looked around, and hit the ground. "Fill the woods with lead," he yelled. "Everybody start shooting."

Lead started flying from all directions in all directions. "Don't shoot at me, you fools!" Luttie screamed. "Form a skirmish line, left and right of me. Jesus Christ, men, think!"

The outlaws and bounty hunters formed up and began filling the timber ahead of them with lead. But Smoke was gone. He knew if he was to survive, he had to think twice as fast as the outlaws and be two steps ahead of them at all times.

He chanced a return to the pass entrance, hoping against hope. But after scanning the entrance, he knew it had been posted with men. Safely behind and to the north of the outlaws, Smoke paused for a short rest while he looked around him at the high peaks surrounding the valley. Was this valley really a box? He knew a lot of cowboys called any canyon or valley they could not ride a horse out of a box. Maybe it was—maybe it wasn't. He was going to find out. Only problem was, he had no blankets to combat the intense cold of the high lonesome should he be trapped up there and have to spend the night.

A bullet slammed into a tree, just missing his head. Smoke jumped for cover.

"Here he is!" came the shout. "Come on, boys. Now we got him."

"Where, Malone?"

"Work your way north towards me. I'll keep him pinned down. That'll put him 'twixt you and me."

Smoke put a .44-40 'twixt Malone's ribs, right in the center of the V of the rib cage.

"Oh, God!" Malone yelled. "He plugged me."

Smoke ran to Malone and kicked the man's rifle away from him, smiling as he saw the rolled-up groundsheet and blanket tied across the man's back. He tore it from him and took his pistols.

"Help me," Malone moaned.

Smoke pointed his rifle at Malone and jacked back the hammer.

"Oh, Jesus!" the outlaw squalled. "Not thataway!"

"Then shut up and die quietly." Smoke was gone, running into the timber north of the gut-shot outlaw and at the base of a formidable-looking peak.

"He's run towards the mountains, boys!" Smoke heard Malone's yell, and knew he had to stand and fight for a time.

He bellied down behind a rotting log and punched rounds into his Winchester. One outlaw ran across the small clearing, running to help Malone. Smoke dropped him. The man threw his rifle high into the air and hit the ground. He did not move.

"You a devil, Jensen!" Malone yelled. "He was a-comin' to help me."

"Stay along the timberline," Luttie told his men. "Don't expose yourselves."

"What about Malone?" Jake asked.

"You want to go help him?"

Jake did not reply. The men stayed in cover until Malone's screaming ceased. They did not know if he had passed out or if he was dead. Most didn't care one way or the other.

"He's tooken Malone's bedroll," Whit said. "See yonder. It's gone."

"He's going to try for the peaks," Lee said. "But you said this was a box."

"It is." But that nagged at Luttie. He knew there were only two ways that a man could ride a horse in or out. Jensen had blown one of them closed. But was it possible for a man to climb out? He didn't know. He'd never tried it, and didn't know of anyone who ever had.

Luttie silently cursed. But if any man could climb out, it would be that damn Smoke Jensen.

"Fan out," Luttie ordered. "We can't let him get into the high-up. Remember what he done last time."

The outlaws and manhunters started cautiously fanning out. Some of them were rapidly losing their taste for the hunt and would leave if they got a chance. Honor be damned.

Smoke silently melted into the timber and the brush, climbing higher. He would pause now and then to scan the peaks with field glasses. A cup of coffee would taste good right now, but he didn't have any and could not dare risk a fire even if he did.

He found a small pool of clear, cold water and bathed his wounds carefully, treating them with the medicines Sally had packed for him. The wounds were not serious, and he knew that high altitudes slowed infections.

Smoke took the time to rig some deadfalls and other more lethal traps. That done, he hiked up another hundred yards and found a good location. To hell with it! He was tired and was going to rest.

"Come on, boys," he muttered. "You want me, here I am!"

21

They almost got him.

It was one of those freak shots that had nothing at all to do with skill. The slug howled off a rock, hit a tree a glancing blow, and struck Smoke in the side. Had it not lost much of its force, it probably would have killed him.

Smoke looked at the hole in his side. The bullet had hit the fleshy part of his back and exited out the front. It looked awful, hurt like hell, but was not a serious wound. It was, however, going to impede any attempts at climbing.

Smoke shifted positions, working his way out of the rocks and getting into a natural depression that offered less chance of a ricochet. He checked the sun. About ten o'clock, he figured. It was going to be a very long day.

Smoke sighted in what appeared to be a man's arm and fired. He missed his shot, but the outlaw yelled and scrambled back down the hill, finding a more protected spot.

Smoke kept his head down while the lead hammered and howled all around him. He knew they were advancing toward him during the fusillade, but it couldn't be helped.

While the outlaws frantically punched fresh rounds into their rifles, Smoke sighted in on a man running hard for cover . . . and alarmingly near Smoke's position. The .44-40 slug busted him, turning him around like a top. Smoke's second shot ended the spin.

"He got Tap!" a man yelled, jumping up in anger and excitement.

Smoke got him, too. He couldn't tell if it was a killing shot, but the man went down limp and didn't move.

"Damn!" he heard a man say. "Whit's had it."

"I've had it too," another man said. "I'm gone. Done. Finished."

Two more agreed with him, and Smoke let them leave, even though he had a clear shot at one of them and a maybe shot at another.

Smoke pulled back. He was so muddy and bloody he blended in with the earth and the foliage. He ached all over and longed for a hot tub of water with a big bar of soap. What he got was dirt and rocks and twigs kicked into his face by a bullet. He wiped his vision clear and slipped into cover, his face bleeding.

He watched through a sturdy mountain bush as a man limped from one tree to another. Smoke ended his limping with a single shot.

"Damnit!" a man said. "I told Keno to head back out of the valley."

"He shore ain't goin' nowheres now," another man said. 'Ceptin' the grave, if he's lucky."

"I want his boots," a man yelled. "I was with him when he stole 'em. Them's brand-new. Mine's wore slap out."

Keep talking, Smoke thought, shifting around to face the direction of the closest voice and earing back the hammer on his Winchester.

He waited and saw what he felt was the tip of a boot. The boot moved just a bit, exposing several more inches of leather. He laid a bead and squeezed the trigger. A howl of pain erupted from behind the cluster of low rocks.

"My foot's ruint!" a man yelled. "Oh, God, it hurts! He blowed my toes off."

"Now you shore need some boots," a man told him, ending with a dirty laugh.

Smoke put three fast rounds into the bushes where he felt the smart-mouth was hiding. He watched as a man rose slowly to his feet. He looked down at his bullet-perforated and bloody shirtfront. "You bastard," the outlaw said, then toppled over on his face.

"It ain't workin', Luttie." The sound came to Smoke. "He's pickin' us off one by one."

"Then leave, you yeller-belly!" Luttie said. "You're paid up. Haul your ashes."

"I believe I'll just do that little thing. I'm pullin' out, Jensen. You hear me?"

"I hear you."

"Don't shoot. I'm gone."

Smoke let him go while the remaining outlaws poured lead into Smoke's position. Smoke stayed low, hating it, knowing they were inching closer, but unable to prevent it.

He heard panting coming from only a few feet away and knew if he didn't move, they would have him cold.

"Goddamnit, he must have moved!" The voice was only inches away.

"He's got to be in there. Are you stone blind, Crown?" Lee yelled.

No. Crown was just stone dead. Smoke shot him in the belly at point-blank range, pulled out the man's twin Remingtons, and emptied them downhill. He lunged out of the hole and ran into the bushes, lead whining and howling and clipping branches and thudding into trees all around him.

"Somebody kill him, damn it!" Luttie screamed. "Cain't nobody shoot straight no more?"

Smoke climbed higher, pausing often to rest. His wounds were taking a toll on him, gradually sapping his strength. Although still bull-strong, he couldn't last another day; he knew that. He had to bring this fight to an end.

Something slammed into his head and knocked him spinning. The last thing he remembered was falling into darkness.

"They claim they killed him," Mills said, after speaking to several people in the huge crowd around the mouth of the valley entrance.

"I don't believe it," Winston said.

Mills shrugged his shoulders. "Smoke is a mortal man, Winston. A big tough bear of a man, but still mortal. Look, I don't want to believe it either, but face facts. He's been fighting terrible odds for days."

"Where's the body?" Larry asked, a sick feeling in the pit of his stomach.

"They said he fell down into a ravine. No way to retrieve the body. But they have his rifle."

"Oh, my God!" Hugh shook his head. "It must be true."

"We'll arrest the outlaws as they come out," Mills ordered. "If they offer just the slightest hint of resistance, kill them on the spot."

"You don't mean that, Mills!" Sharp said.

"The hell I don't!"

Sally looked up into the face of Lilly LaFevere. Johnny North, Cotton, Earl, and Louis were with her. All their faces were grim.

"Give it to me straight," Sally said.

"Word is they killed your man, honey."

"Where's the body?"

"A bounty hunter told a reporter that it can't be recovered. Smoke supposedly fell off into a ravine after being shot in the head," Louis said grimly. "We're riding to the valley. Sheriff Silva and a posse are here now, to keep order. Stay with her, Lilly."

"I'll do that."

Cold.

Smoke opened his eyes and for one panicky moment felt he was blind. But it was dried blood that had caked his eyes shut. He dug the blood away with as little movement as possible, not wanting to draw attention. His entire left side hurt, and the right side of his head throbbed with pain. But not his left side. Curious. He wondered how that could be.

When his vision cleared, he realized just how bad his position was.

He was lying on a ledge that jutted out a few yards from the face of the ravine. It was about a five-hundred-foot drop to the bottom. Smoke looked up and guessed that he'd fallen no more than fifteen or twenty feet. When he hit, the bedroll had protected his head. That was why only the bullet-creased side ached. When he hit, he had rolled against the face of the cliff, protected from eyes above by a little outcropping of rock. He was stiff and sore and bruised all over . . . but he was alive.

He lay still for a moment, going over his problems, and they were many. He rolled over on his stomach and had to stifle a groan of pain as his torn and bruised body protested.

The ledge snaked around a bend. He had no idea what lay around that bend. He had no rope to aid in his climbing out. He had no idea how badly hurt he might be. He had no idea how far the ledge ran. If he stayed where he was, he would die. It was that simple. If he tried to climb out, the odds of his making it were slim to none.

But he damn sure was going to try.

Food. He had to eat. He fumbled around in his saddlebag and found some hard crackers. He ate them, drank a swallow of water left in his busted canteen, and felt better. If I felt any worse, he thought with dark humor, I'd be dead.

Smoke wriggled around on the ledge, being very careful not to get too close to the edge, for the rock looked very flaky and unstable there. On his belly, he checked his guns, which had stayed in leather thanks to the hammer thongs. The guns were dirty, and he carefully cleaned them, working the action and reloading. He checked the knife on his belt and the shorter-bladed knife in his leggings. Both were still in place and both still sharp enough to shave with.

Smoke was tired, so very, very tired. He would have liked to just lay his head on his arm and go to sleep. Maybe just rest for a few moments. He shook himself like a big shaggy dog. No time for rest. He felt for his pocketwatch and was not surprised to see it busted, the hands stopping at eleven thirty-five. He judged the time to be close to four, maybe four-thirty. He didn't have all that much daylight left him.

Taking a deep breath, he crawled forward. Wouldn't it be interesting, he thought, to come face-to-face with a mountain lion on this narrow trail with a five-hundred-foot drop below?

He decided it would not be interesting. Just deadly for one of them.

He crawled on, smiling at what faced him a few yards around the curve in the trail. The mountain pass ended, but it did not end sheer; it ended in an upside-down V. Now if there were just sufficient handholds or jutting rocks that were stable, he could climb out. It was only about twenty feet to the top, and he could hear no sounds above him except the sighing of the mountain winds. He reached the end of the narrow ledge and rested for a time. God, he was worn out.

Smoke crawled to his knees and put one foot on the other side of the narrow gorge. He willed himself not to look down. The slight protruding of rock felt secure under his foot, and he leaned forward, gripping two outcroppings, one in each hand. He lifted his left foot to a toehold about two feet off the trail, and now he was committed to the mountain.

It took him twenty minutes to climb about twenty feet, and using brute strength while dangling over a five-hundred-foot drop was not something he wished to repeat. Ever.

When he crawled over the top he was exhausted. If he had not been wearing leather gloves, he probably would not have made it; the rocks would have cut his hands to bloody ribbons. He belly-crawled into a copse of timber and rolled up in his blankets. He had to rest.

"Can you believe this?" Mills almost shouted the words, as he waved a court order that was hand-delivered to him that afternoon.

"Yeah, I can believe it," Johnny said. The marshals and the deputies had returned to town after the court order had been delivered.

Judge Richards had obviously pre-signed pardons for all the outlaws in the Lee Slater gang. The order had just been found and delivered.

"I turned all the jailed outlaws loose," Earl said. "I thought Sheriff Silva was going to have a heart attack."

It was midnight in Rio, and the town was sleeping. The outlaws were due to ride in the next day, as soon as the reward money was stagecoached in on the afternoon stage, to collect their blood money. And outlaws being what they are, they were also going to collect the reward money that had been on the heads of their now departed friends.

"The end of an era," Larry said, soaking his feet in a bucket of lukewarm water. "I would have liked to meet Mr. Smoke Jensen, to shake his hand and tell him how wrong I was about him."

"Don't sell Smoke short," Louis said. "I'll not believe he's dead until I see the body."

"But he fell off a mountain!" Mills said. "Or rather down into a deep chasm."

"Yes," the gambler said. "And chasms and ravines have outcroppings that are not always visible from above. I don't believe he's dead."

"Neither do I," Johnny said. "Hurt, yes. Dead?" He shook his head. "No."

"Sally?" Earl asked.

"I don't think she believes it either."

"I aim to be in the street when them outlaws ride in tomorrow," Johnny said.

"Me too," Cotton said.

"I'll be with you boys." Earl made three.

"I shall certainly be there," Louis said, standing up.

"Count me in." Larry surprised them all. "I owe this much to his memory. I certainly maligned the man while he was alive."

Six U.S. Marshals' badges hit the desk. "And we shall be standing with you," Mills said.

"Gonna be a hell of a party." Cotton summed it up with a wicked grin.

Smoke awakened at midnight. He was aching and sore, but feeling a lot better. His clothes were stiff with dried blood and mud and sweat, but his hands opened and closed easily. He rolled his blankets and started walking. Less than an hour later, he found a riderless horse, still saddled and bridled. Probably had belonged to one of the dead outlaws or bounty hunters. He stripped saddle and bridle from the animal and let it graze and roll while he went through the saddlebags and poke-sack and found food, coffee, frying pan, and coffeepot.

He checked out the rifle in the boot; it was loaded full with .44s. He led the horse back behind some boulders and picketed the animal. Then he built a fire and fried bacon and potatoes and made a pot of coffee. Being a coffee-loving man, he drank the coffee right out of the pot while his food was cooking; then he settled down and ate leisurely and drank more coffee out of a cup.

An hour later, he had carefully put out the fire and was in the saddle, riding for the pass. The pass was deserted when he rode through it. On the other side of the pass, however, he could see where it looked like hundreds of people had held a wild party. Empty beer kegs and empty whiskey bottles lay all over the place.

"I wonder if they were celebrating the news of my death?" he muttered, then rode on.

He came upon what appeared to be a dead man lying by the side of the road that led to Rio. He dismounted and knelt down beside him, rolling him over. Not dead, just dead drunk. Smoke slapped him awake.

The man opened his eyes and started to scream when he recognized the man standing over him. Smoke put a hand on the man's mouth, shushing him.

"Don't yell," he told him. "You understand?"

"But you're dead!" the man said, after Smoke removed his hand.

"I'm a long way from being dead." Smoke corrected him. "Do I look dead to you?"

"No. But you shore look some terrible tore up."

"Tell me what went on back by the pass."

The man brought Smoke up to date, still convinced he was conversing with a ghost.

"I see," Smoke said, when the man had finished. "You're going to freeze to death if you lie out here the rest of the night."

"It don't seem to have bothered you none! 'Sides, I got

me a claim about a mile from here. I can make it, providin' I don't run into no more ghosts."

Chuckling, Smoke left the man and rode on. Just about ten miles outside of town, Smoke found a good place to camp and bedded down for the rest of the night. He slept deeply and awakened well after dawn, feeling at least part of his enormous strength once more returning to him. He did a few exercises, copied after a great cat's stretchings, to get the kinks out of his muscles, then cooked the last of the dead outlaws' food and boiled the last of the coffee.

He pulled out his makin's sack and rolled a cigarette, enjoying that with the last cup of coffee. He found a spare six-gun in the saddlebags and dug out the two extra he had in his pack. He checked them all out and loaded them up full, then checked the rifle again.

He talked to the horse for a moment before saddling up, and the horse seemed eager to ride. He wondered if Louis had gone back and gotten his horses. He would soon know.

He had traveled about three miles, he reckoned, when the sounds of galloping horses reached him, coming up fast behind him. He pulled off into timber and waited.

The Lee Slater gang, Luttie with them, along with One-Eyed Jake and his bounty hunters. Smoke wanted them to get into town and have one good drink of whiskey before he threw down the challenge.

He stopped to water his horse, and as he knelt down to drink, he was shocked at the reflection staring back at him. His face was bloody and cut and swollen. His hair was matted with dried blood from where the slug had grazed him— on both sides. He looked like something out of Hell.

Which was fine with him. The gun hands better get used to Hell, 'cause that's where Smoke intended to send them.

22

Smoke reined up and dismounted at the edge of town. He looked up at the sun. Directly overhead. High noon. He pulled saddle and bridle off the horse and turned it loose to water and roll and graze.

Smoke loosened his guns in leather, then stuck the extra .44s behind his gun belt, the fifth .44 jammed down into his legging, right side. He waved a burly, bearded man over to him.

"Yeah?" the man asked, walking over to him. He took a long second look, his mouth dropping open. "Holy Christ!" the man whispered.

"Clear the streets," Smoke told him.

"Yes, sir, Mr. Smoke. Ever'body said you was dead!"

"Well, I'm not. I just look it. Move."

The miner ran toward the marshal's office and threw open the door, and almost got himself shot for that rash act. "Whoa!" he cried, as Johnny, Louis, Earl, and Cotton jerked iron. "I ain't even carryin' no sidearm. Smoke Jensen just rode into town. He's up yonder." He pointed. "He looks like death warmed over. But he said to clear the streets. He's all muddy and bloody and mean clear through. Got guns a-hangin' all over him."

"Hot damn!" Earl said.

"I'll run tell Charlie!" Mills said. "Sharp, take the men and clear the streets of people and horses."

Louis pointed a finger at Cotton. "Go to Sally. Tell her the news."

"I'm gone!" Cotton ran from the office.

"This is Smoke's fight," Louis said. "But we can keep an eye out for ambushers and back-shooters."

The men took down sawed-off shotguns, stuffed their pockets with shells, and stepped out of the office. The main street was already deserted.

Luttie was lifting his second glass of rye to his lips when the wild scream of an enraged panther cut the still, hot air. He spilled half his drink down his shirtfront.

"Jesus Christ!" Tom said.

"It can't be!" Pecos shouted, frantically brushing at his crotch where he'd dropped his cigarette. "He fell off a damn mountain."

Rod and Randy giggled.

Dan Diamond looked at One-Eyed Jake, disbelief in his eyes.

Frankie Deevers loaded up his guns full.

Martine's fingers were trembling as the cry of a panther changed to the howling of a lobo wolf. He crossed himself and stood up.

Charlie Starr chuckled in his bed and propped a couple of pillows behind him, then lifted the canvas and tied it back. He pulled out his long-barreled six-guns and checked them.

Sally smiled and put on a pot of coffee. Smoke would want a good strong cup of coffee when this was over. She knew her man well.

Larry Tibbson loaded up a sawed-off express gun and took a position near the center of the boomtown.

The stage rolled in, the driver and guard taking a quick look at the deserted street. "Oh, my God!" the driver said, his eyes touching on the tall bloody man standing at the end of the long street. He threw the strongbox and mail pouch to the ground and yelled at his horses to get gone.

Mills tore open the mail pouch and jerked out a letter, quickly scanning it. With a yell of excitement, he jumped up and said, "Here it is! The warrants against Smoke Jensen have been dropped. It's signed by the President of the United States!"

"Damn that President Arthur!" Luttie said.

Morris Pattin stepped out of the barbershop where he'd just had a haircut and a bath. He brushed back his new coat, freeing his guns, and walked up the street toward Smoke Jensen. He was shocked at the man's appearance. Jensen looked like something out of hell.

"I'll take you now, Jensen," he called.

"You'll kiss the devil's behind before you do," Smoke told him, then lifted his rifle in his left hand and drilled the bounty hunter from a hundred yards out.

The slug hit the manhunter in the center of his chest, and Morris was down and dying without ever having a chance to pull iron—not that it would have done him a bit of good at that distance.

Sally moved the coffeepot off the griddle and decided she would wait a few minutes before dumping in the coffee. She wanted Smoke to have a good hot fresh cup of coffee.

Charlie caught movement by the edge of a building and jacked back the hammer on his old six-gun. It would be a good shot for him, but he figured he could do it. He smiled as he recognized the gunfighter from down Yuma way. Couldn't think of his name. Didn't make no difference; the grave digger could just carve "Yuma" on the marker.

Yuma lifted his rifle and sighted Smoke in. Charlie took him out with a neck shot at seventy-five yards.

"Damn good shootin'," Charlie complimented himself, as Yuma slumped to the dirt. "I'd a' not done 'er with one of them now short-barreled things."

Photographers had quickly set up their boxy equipment, filled the flash-trays, and were ready to record it all for posterity.

Smoke stepped out of the street and ducked into an alley.

Tom Post looked up and down and all around. "Where'd he go?" he asked Lopez. The men were in the general store, pricing new suits of clothes they planned to buy with the reward money. Or steal them, now that the shopkeeper and his woman had locked themselves in the storeroom.

"Right behind you," Smoke said calmly.

Tom and Lopez turned, jerking iron.

They were far too slow.

Smoke had leaned the rifle up against a counter and stood with both hands filled with Colts, the Colts spitting lead and belching fire and gun smoke.

Lopez took two rounds in the chest, dropped his guns, staggered backward, and fell out one of the big storefront windows. He crashed to the boardwalk and lay amid the broken glass, kicking and cursing his life away.

Tom was doubled over with two slugs in his belly. He fell to the floor and lay moaning. Smoke kicked the man's gun away and reloaded his own. He took a sawed-off shotgun from the rack and broke it open, shoving in shells and filling his pockets from the open box.

"You a no-good sorry son!" Post groaned.

"Don't lose any sleep over it," Smoke told him, then stepped out to the back of the store.

The young punk Bull, from Pecos' gang, was running up the alley, wild-eyed, cussing, and both hands full of guns. Smoke let him have both barrels of the sawed-off twelve-gauge. The buckshot lifted the punk off his boots and sent him crashing into an open-doored outhouse. The punk died sitting on the hole, crapping into his pants.

Smoke punched fresh rounds into the Greener and walked on, pausing when he heard the sounds of someone running.

Curt Holt rounded a corner, running as hard as he could, his hands full of six-guns. He slid to a halt and lifted them. Smoke blew what was left of him—after the man took two rounds of buckshot at point blank range in the guts—through a window of someone's living quarters behind a saddle shop.

"Good Jesus Christ!" he heard someone shout from inside. "What a mess."

"I believe Mr. Jensen is very upset," Larry muttered to Sharp, who had joined him.

"I wholeheartedly agree," the U.S. Marshal said.

In the saloon, Rod and Randy giggled insanely, Rod saying, "Come, brother. We'll put an end to this nonsense."

Johnny North was waiting on the boardwalk. As soon as the brothers stepped through the batwings, Johnny started shooting, cocking and firing in one long continuous roar of thunder and smoke. The Karl brothers did a macabre dance of the dying on the boardwalk as they soaked up lead. Randy fell into a horse trough and died with both arms hanging over the sides. Rod lay draped over a hitch rail. He giggled as he died.

Dewey and Gooden, freshly released from jail, stepped out into the street and yelled at Johnny, knowing his guns were probably empty.

Louis stepped out of his gambling hall, his eyes hard. He emptied his guns into the pair. They lay in the dust, their outlawing days over.

Reporters were scribbling and photographers' flash pans were puffing as they recorded it all for their readers back East.

The foreman of the Seven Slash stepped into the alley and faced Smoke, both hands hovering over the butts of his guns. "You ain't got the balls to drop that Greener and drag iron with me, Jensen."

"Courage has nothing to do with it," Smoke told him. "But time is of the essence."

He pulled the triggers on the express gun, and the foreman's earthly cares and woes were a thing of the past.

Smoke walked up the alley to stand in the cool shadows, looking out into the street.

In the saloon, Luttie looked at Lee. "It's been a good, long run, Lee. Now it's over."

Lee swore. "It may be over for you, but it ain't over for me. I'm gonna kill that damn Jensen oncest and forever."

"I wish you luck," his brother said, lifting a shot glass in salute.

Lee walked out the back of the saloon.

"You're a fool, brother. But then, I've always known that." Luttie drank his whiskey and turned around, his back to the bar, facing the batwings.

Smoke heard the hammer cocking behind him and dropped to his knees in the alley just as the slug hammered the pine boards above his head. Smoke leveled the shotgun, and gave Curly a gutful of buckshot. Curly's boots flew out from under him, and he smashed down to earth, lying on his back; the charge had nearly cut him in two.

Smoke was out of shotgun shells. He laid the Greener down and pulled his Colts, jacking the hammers back. He scanned the street for trouble. He couldn't see it, but knew it was there, waiting for him.

Smoke eased back down the alley, .44s in both hands. He was facing south, the sun just beginning its dip toward the west. A thin shadow fell across the end of the alleyway. Smoke paused, pressing against the outside wall of the building.

"You see him, Milt?" someone called in a hoarse, softly accented whisper.

"Naw," the voice came from just around the corner, back of the building, belonging to the shadow that was still evident on the weedy ground.

Milt stepped out and Smoke drilled him, the slug snapping his head back as it hit him in the forehead.

Smoke hit the ground and rolled under the building.

Pedro jumped out, a puzzled look on his face. Smoke shot him twice in the belly, and the puzzled look was replaced by one of intense pain. The outlaw fell to his knees, both .45s going off, blowing up dirt and dust and rocks. He cursed for a moment, then fell over, still alive, but for how long was something that only God could answer.

Dan Diamond and One-Eye were walking boldly down the boardwalk, toward the sounds of shooting when Cotton stepped out of a doorway and faced them.

"I told you it'd be someday, One-Eye," Cotton said. "Why not now?" He jerked iron and shot the manhunter in the belly.

Dan fired just as Cotton stepped to one side, the slug knocking a chunk out of the building. He missed but Cotton didn't. Dan folded and sat down heavily on the boardwalk for a moment. He looked up at Cotton.

"Is Pickens really your last name?"

"That it is."

"Cotton Pickens," Dan said, then died with a smile on his lips.

Smoke was standing in the alley when the manhunters Davy and Val rode out. He nodded at them and they nodded at him and then were gone. Smoke let them go. They just came after the wrong man, that's all.

Smoke stepped out and walked up the steps to the boardwalk. The town was eerily quiet. Most of the citizens were either inside looking out of windows, or had locked themselves behind doors. The reporters and photographers were the only ones other than the combatants on the street, crouching behind horse troughs and peeking out of open alleyways. Smoke had always figured that reporters didn't have a lick of sense.

A man stepped out of the shadows. Lee Slater. His hands were wrapped around the butts of Colts, as were Smoke's hands. "I'm gonna kill you, Jensen!" he screamed.

A rifle barked, the slug striking Lee in the middle of his back and exiting out the front. The outlaw gang leader lay dead on the hot dusty street.

Sally Jensen stepped back into Louis' gambling hall and jacked another round into her carbine.

Smoke smiled at her and walked on down the boardwalk.

"Looking for me, amigo?" Al Martine spoke from the shadows of a doorway. His guns were in leather.

"Not really. Ride on, Al."

"Why would you make such an offer to me? I am an outlaw, a killer. I hunted you in the mountains."

"You have a family, Al?"

"Si. A father and mother, brothers and sister, all down in Mexico."

"Why don't you go pay them a visit? Hang up your guns for a time."

The Mexican smiled and finished rolling a cigarette. He lit it and held it to Smoke's lips.

"Thanks, Al."

"Thank you, Smoke. I shall be in Chihuahua. If you ever need me, send word, everybody knows where to find me. I will come very quickly."

"I might do that."

"Adios, compadre." Al stepped off the boardwalk and was gone.

Smoke finished the cigarette, grateful for the lift the tobacco gave him. His eyes never stopped moving, scanning the buildings, the alleyways, the street.

He caught movement on the second floor of the saloon, the hotel part. Sunlight off a rifle barrel. He lifted a .44 and triggered off two fast rounds. The rifle dropped to the awning, a man following it out. Zack fell through the awning and crashed to the boardwalk. He did not move.

Rich Coleman and Frankie stepped out of the saloon, throwing lead, and Smoke dived for the protection of a water trough.

"I got him!" Frankie yelled.

Smoke rose to one knee and changed Frankie's whole outlook on life—what remained of it.

Rich turned to run back into the saloon, and Smoke fired, the slug hitting him in the shoulder and knocking him through the batwings. He got to his boots and staggered back out, lifting a .45 and drilling a hole in the water trough as he screamed curses at Smoke.

Smoke finished it with one shot. Rich staggered forward, grabbing anything he could for support. He died with his arms around an awning post.

The thunder of hooves cut the afternoon air. Sheriff Silva and a huge posse rode up in a cloud of dust.

"That's it, Smoke," the sheriff announced. "It's over. You're a free man, and all these other yahoos are gonna be behind bars."

"Suits me," Smoke said, and holstered his guns.

Luttie Charles stepped out of the saloon, a gun in each hand, and shot the sheriff out of the saddle. The possemen filled Luttie so full of lead the undertaker had to hire another man to help tote the casket.

"Damnit!" Sheriff Silva said, getting to his boots. "I been shot twice in my life and both times in the same damn arm!"

"No, it ain't over!" the scream came from up the street.

Everybody looked. Pecos stood there, his hands over the butts of his fancy engraved .45s.

"Oh, crap!" Smoke said.

"Don't do it, kid!" Carbone called from the boardwalk. "It's over. He'll kill you, boy."

"Hell with you, you greasy son of a bitch!" Pecos yelled.

Carbone stiffened. Cut his eyes to Smoke.

"Man sure shouldn't have to take a cut like that, Carbone," Smoke told him.

Carbone stepped out into the street, his big silver spurs jingling. "Kid, you can insult me all day. But you cannot insult my mother."

Pecos laughed and told him what he thought about Carbone's sister, too.

Carbone shot him before the kid could even clear leather. The Pecos Kid died in the dusty street of a town that would be gone in ten years. He was buried in an unmarked grave.

"If you hurry, Carbone," Smoke called, "I think you could catch up with Martine. Me and him smoked a cigarette together a few minutes ago, and he told me he was going back to Chihuahua to visit his folks."

Carbone grinned and saluted Smoke. A minute later he was riding out of town, heading south.

23

Smoke soaked in a hot tub of water for an hour before he would let the doctor tend to his wounds.

"You're a lucky man," the doctor told him, after shaking his head in amazement at the old bullet scars that dotted Smoke's body. "That side wound could have killed you."

"What happened to John Seale and the others?" Smoke asked the sheriff, who was lying on the other table in the makeshift operating room.

"I gave them an option: a ride or a rope. They chose to take a ride. What are you going to do about all those reporters gathered outside like a gaggle of geese?"

"What I've always done. Ignore them."

"You plan on staying around here for any length of time?"

"Two days and I'm gone."

"Good. Maybe then this county will settle down."

"You can't ride in two days!" the doctor protested.

"Watch me," Smoke told him.

* * *

Two days later, Smoke and Sally rode out with Johnny North. Smoke on Buck, Sally on the blue steel stallion.

Charlie Starr stood with Lilly and Earl and Louis on the boardwalk and watched them leave. Cotton and Mills and Larry stood with them.

"That's a hell of a man there," Larry said, looking at Smoke Jensen.

Louis smiled. "The last mountain man."